SNOOPY™

TO THE RESCUE

A PEANUTS™ Collection

CHARLES M. SCHULZ

Andrews McMeel Publishing®

a division of Andrews McMeel Universal

Other *Peanuts* AMP! Comics for Kids Books

Snoopy: Cowabunga

Charlie Brown and Friends

Charlie Brown: Pow!

Woodstock: Master of Disguise

Snoopy: Contact!

Snoopy: Party Animal

Charlie Brown: Here We Go Again

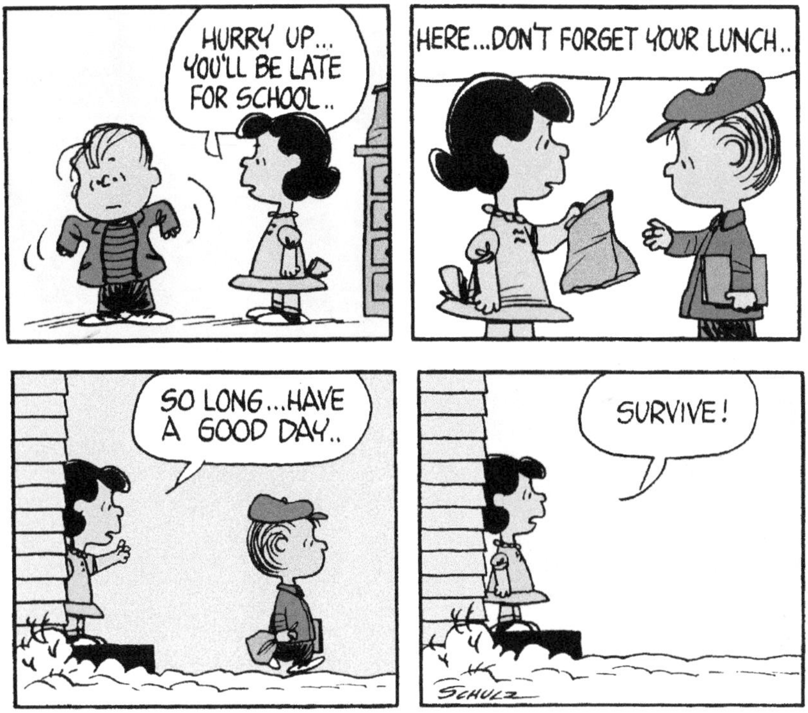
HURRY UP... YOU'LL BE LATE FOR SCHOOL..
HERE...DON'T FORGET YOUR LUNCH..
SO LONG...HAVE A GOOD DAY..
SURVIVE!
SCHULZ

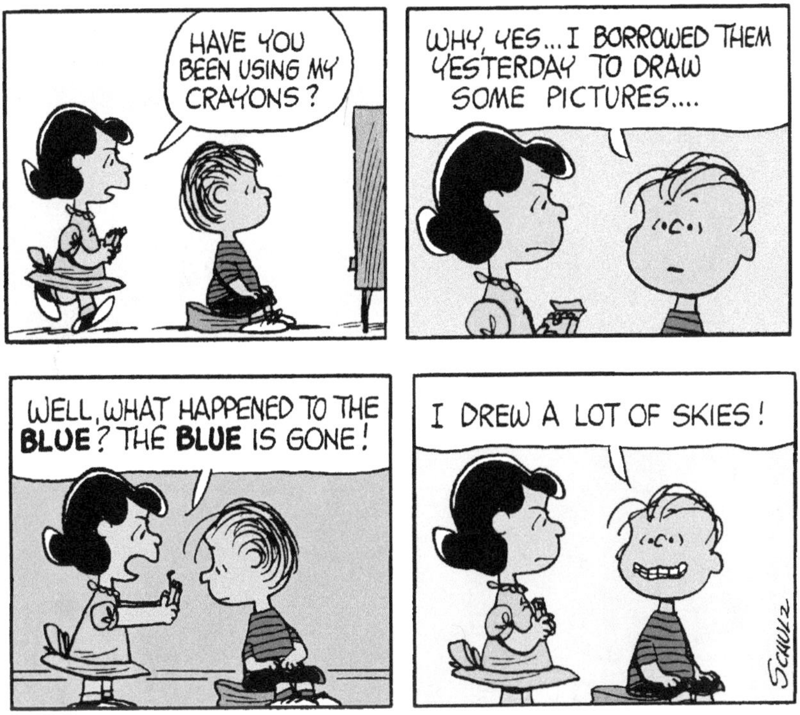
HAVE YOU BEEN USING MY CRAYONS?
WHY, YES...I BORROWED THEM YESTERDAY TO DRAW SOME PICTURES....
WELL, WHAT HAPPENED TO THE **BLUE**? THE **BLUE** IS GONE!
I DREW A LOT OF SKIES!
SCHULZ

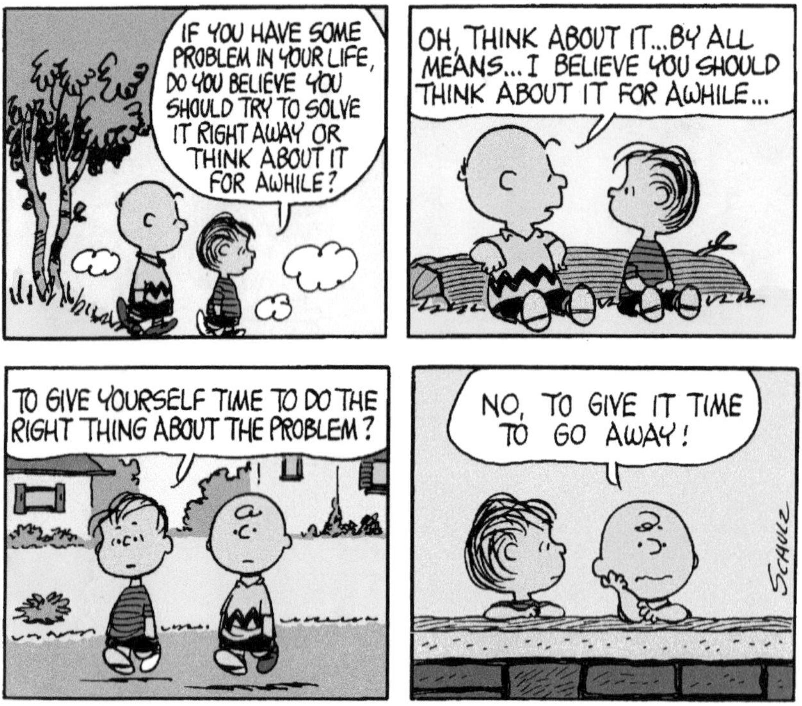
IF YOU HAVE SOME PROBLEM IN YOUR LIFE, DO YOU BELIEVE YOU SHOULD TRY TO SOLVE IT RIGHT AWAY OR THINK ABOUT IT FOR AWHILE?
OH, THINK ABOUT IT...BY ALL MEANS...I BELIEVE YOU SHOULD THINK ABOUT IT FOR AWHILE...
TO GIVE YOURSELF TIME TO DO THE RIGHT THING ABOUT THE PROBLEM?
NO, TO GIVE IT TIME TO GO AWAY!
SCHULZ

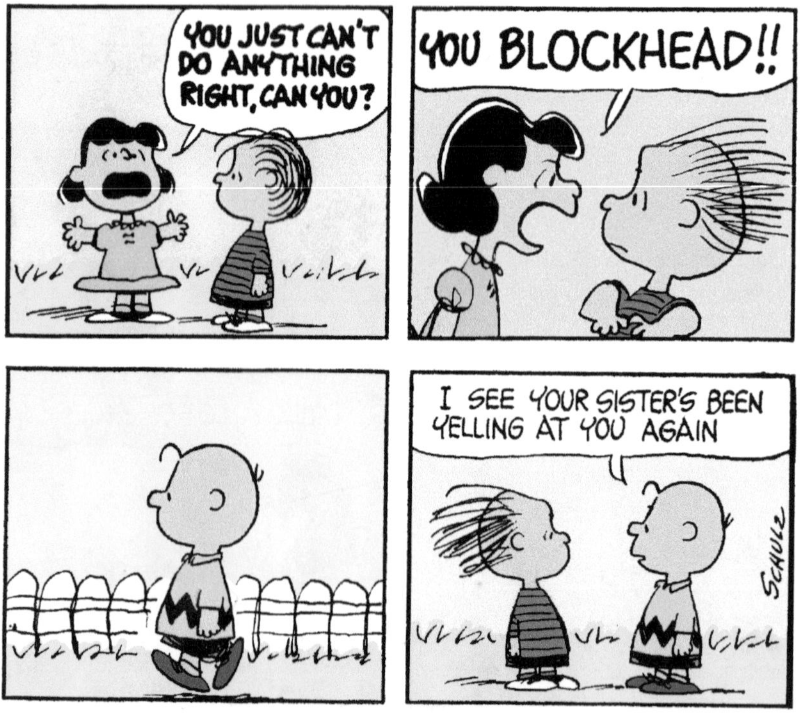
YOU JUST CAN'T DO ANYTHING RIGHT, CAN YOU?
YOU BLOCKHEAD!!
I SEE YOUR SISTER'S BEEN YELLING AT YOU AGAIN
SCHULZ

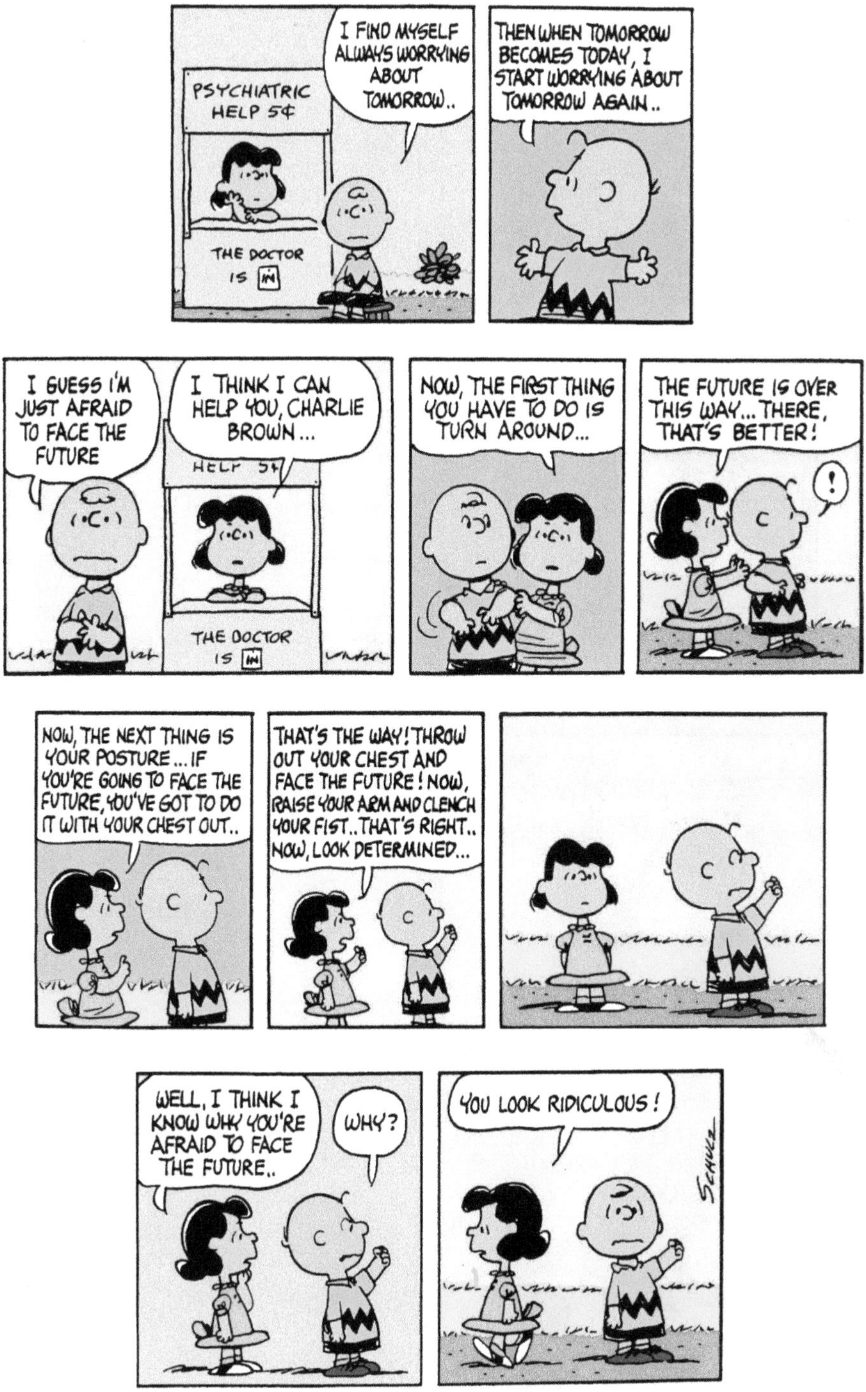

PSYCHIATRIC HELP 5¢
THE DOCTOR IS IN
I FIND MYSELF ALWAYS WORRYING ABOUT TOMORROW..
THEN WHEN TOMORROW BECOMES TODAY, I START WORRYING ABOUT TOMORROW AGAIN..
I GUESS I'M JUST AFRAID TO FACE THE FUTURE
I THINK I CAN HELP YOU, CHARLIE BROWN...
THE DOCTOR IS IN
NOW, THE FIRST THING YOU HAVE TO DO IS TURN AROUND...
THE FUTURE IS OVER THIS WAY... THERE, THAT'S BETTER!
!
NOW, THE NEXT THING IS YOUR POSTURE... IF YOU'RE GOING TO FACE THE FUTURE, YOU'VE GOT TO DO IT WITH YOUR CHEST OUT..
THAT'S THE WAY! THROW OUT YOUR CHEST AND FACE THE FUTURE! NOW, RAISE YOUR ARM AND CLENCH YOUR FIST.. THAT'S RIGHT.. NOW, LOOK DETERMINED...
WELL, I THINK I KNOW WHY YOU'RE AFRAID TO FACE THE FUTURE..
WHY?
YOU LOOK RIDICULOUS!
SCHULZ

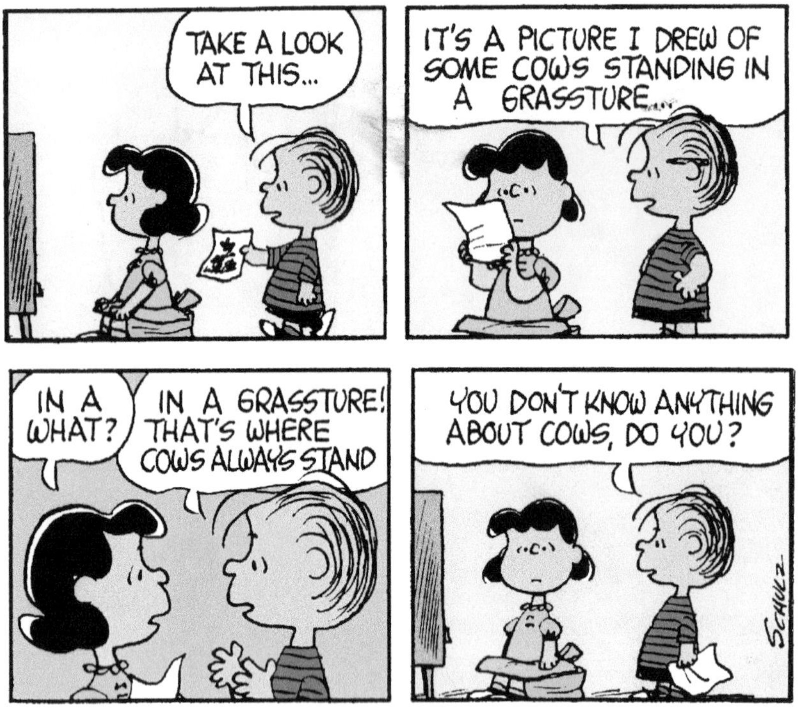
TAKE A LOOK AT THIS...
IT'S A PICTURE I DREW OF SOME COWS STANDING IN A GRASSTURE...
IN A WHAT?
IN A GRASSTURE! THAT'S WHERE COWS ALWAYS STAND
YOU DON'T KNOW ANYTHING ABOUT COWS, DO YOU?
SCHULZ

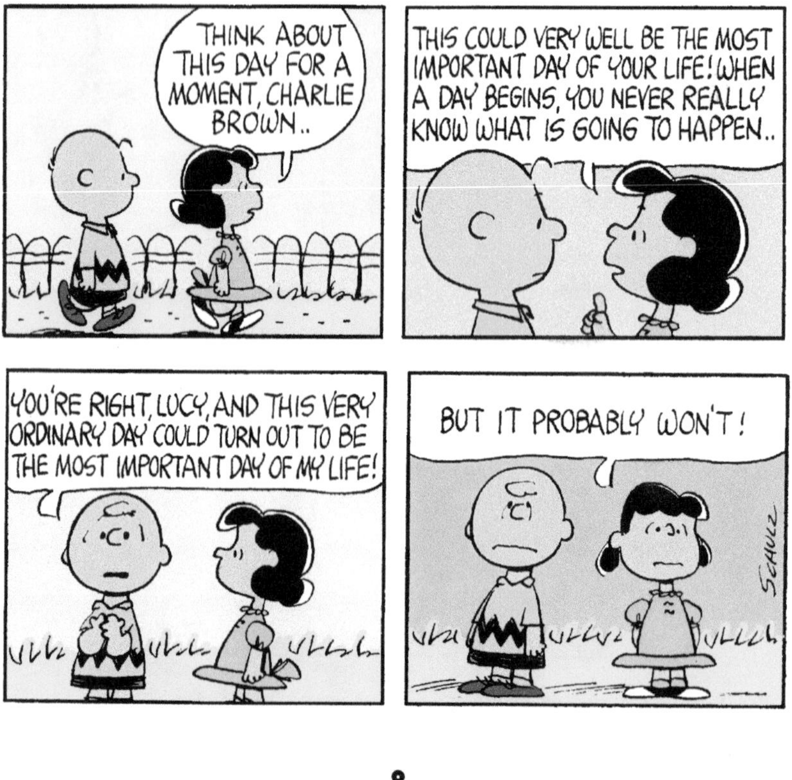
THINK ABOUT THIS DAY FOR A MOMENT, CHARLIE BROWN..
THIS COULD VERY WELL BE THE MOST IMPORTANT DAY OF YOUR LIFE! WHEN A DAY BEGINS, YOU NEVER REALLY KNOW WHAT IS GOING TO HAPPEN..
YOU'RE RIGHT, LUCY, AND THIS VERY ORDINARY DAY COULD TURN OUT TO BE THE MOST IMPORTANT DAY OF MY LIFE!
BUT IT PROBABLY WON'T!
SCHULZ

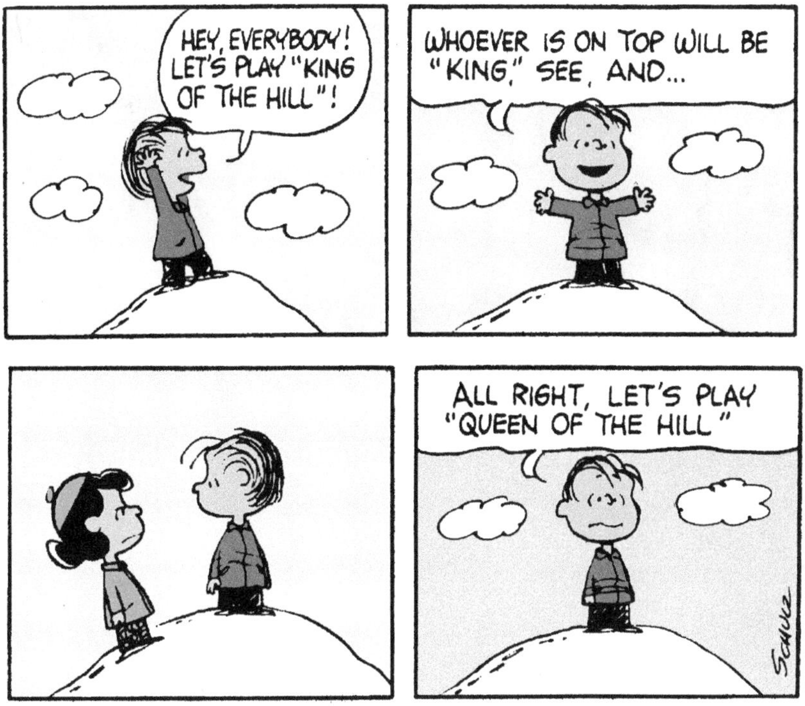
HEY, EVERYBODY! LET'S PLAY "KING OF THE HILL"!
WHOEVER IS ON TOP WILL BE "KING," SEE, AND...
ALL RIGHT, LET'S PLAY "QUEEN OF THE HILL"
SCHULZ

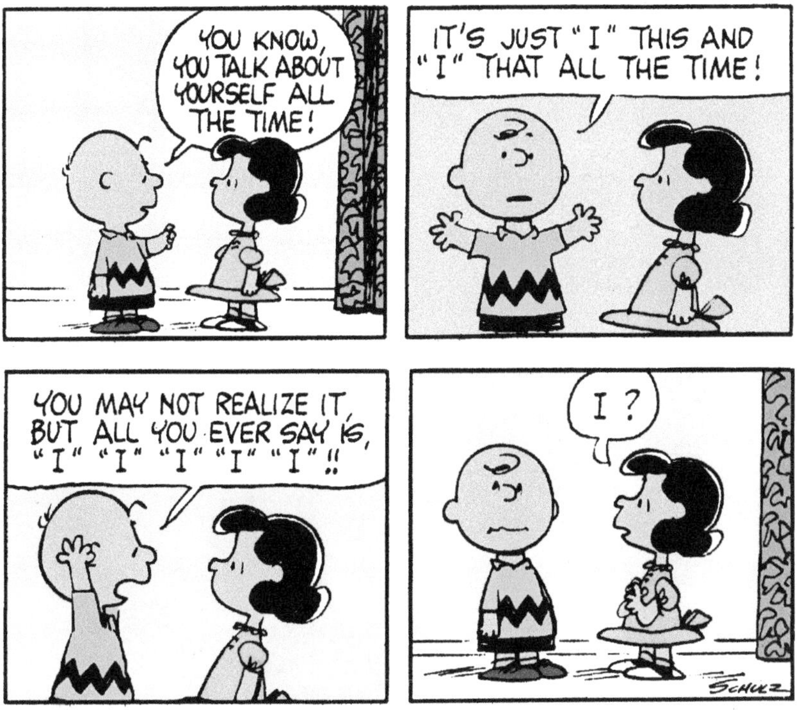
YOU KNOW, YOU TALK ABOUT YOURSELF ALL THE TIME!
IT'S JUST "I" THIS AND "I" THAT ALL THE TIME!
YOU MAY NOT REALIZE IT, BUT ALL YOU EVER SAY IS, "I" "I" "I" "I" "I"!!
I ?
SCHULZ

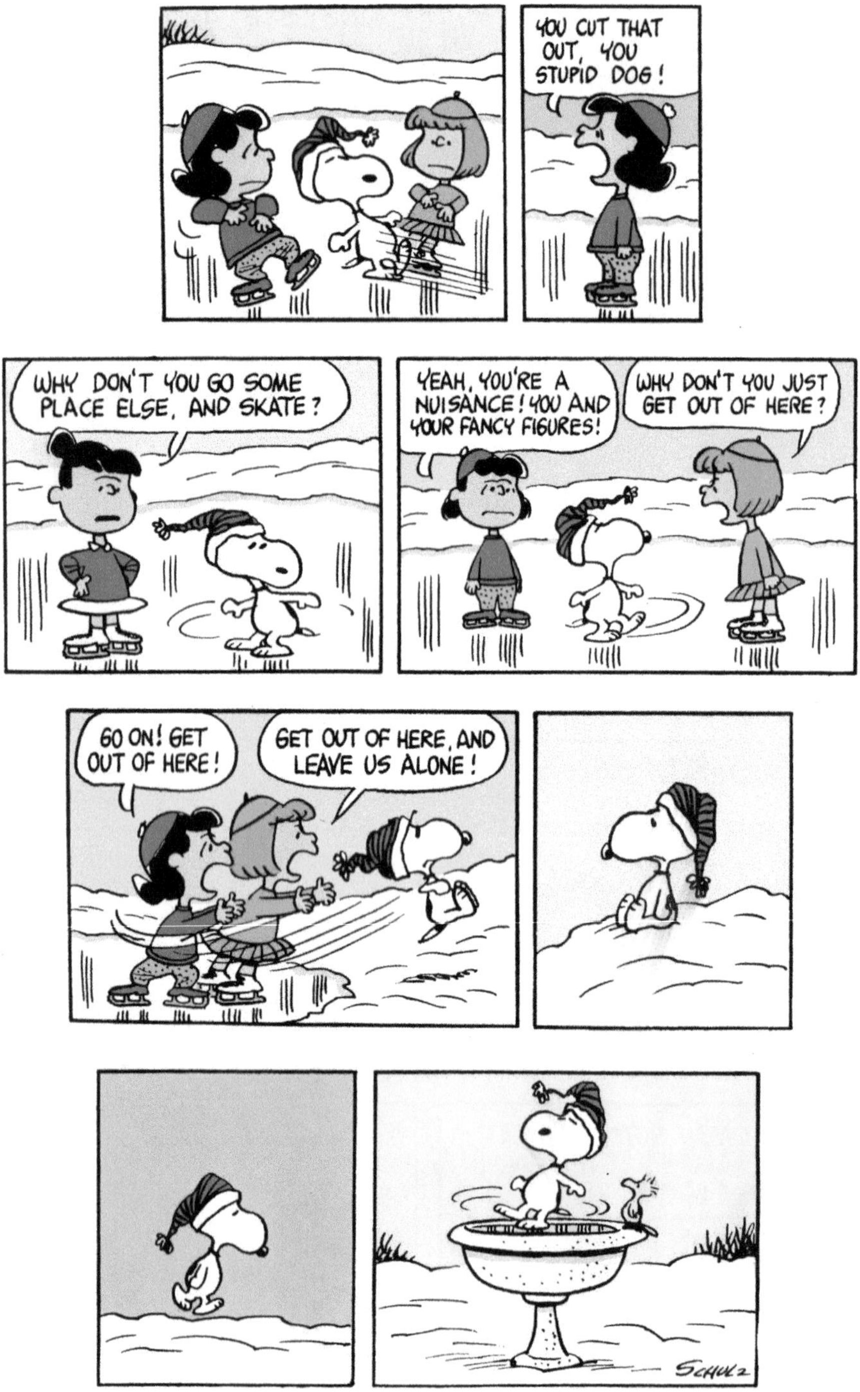
YOU CUT THAT OUT, YOU STUPID DOG!
WHY DON'T YOU GO SOME PLACE ELSE, AND SKATE?
YEAH, YOU'RE A NUISANCE! YOU AND YOUR FANCY FIGURES!
WHY DON'T YOU JUST GET OUT OF HERE?
GO ON! GET OUT OF HERE!
GET OUT OF HERE, AND LEAVE US ALONE!
SCHULZ

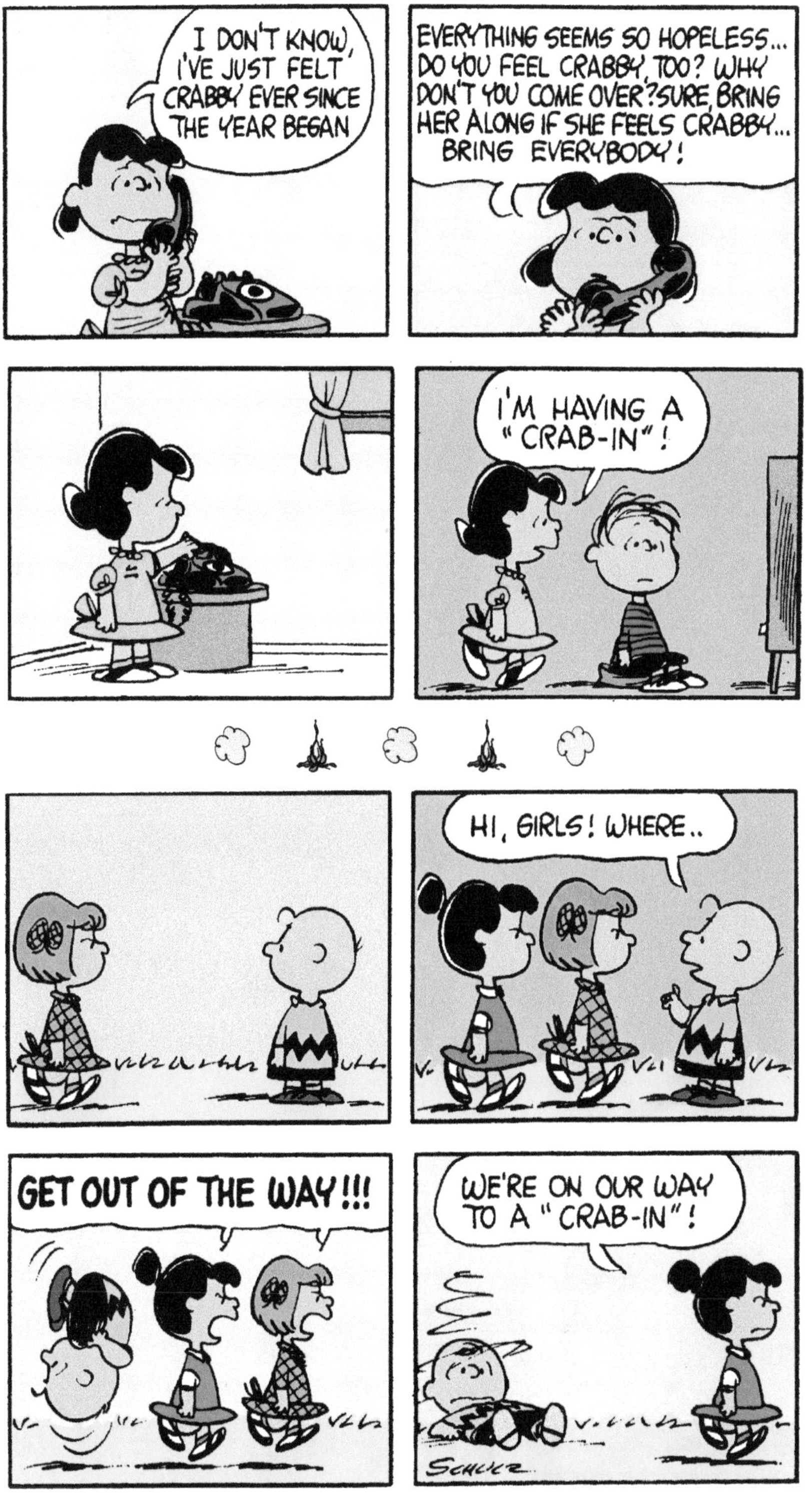
I DON'T KNOW, I'VE JUST FELT CRABBY EVER SINCE THE YEAR BEGAN
EVERYTHING SEEMS SO HOPELESS... DO YOU FEEL CRABBY, TOO? WHY DON'T YOU COME OVER? SURE, BRING HER ALONG IF SHE FEELS CRABBY... BRING EVERYBODY!
I'M HAVING A "CRAB-IN"!
HI, GIRLS! WHERE..
GET OUT OF THE WAY!!!
WE'RE ON OUR WAY TO A "CRAB-IN"!
SCHULZ

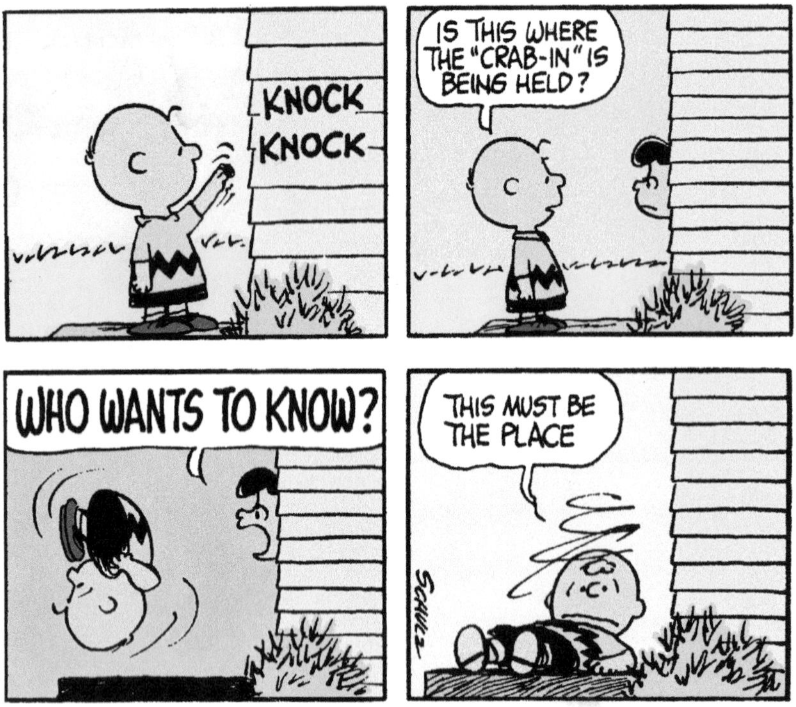
KNOCK
KNOCK
IS THIS WHERE THE "CRAB-IN" IS BEING HELD?
WHO WANTS TO KNOW?
THIS MUST BE THE PLACE
SCHULZ

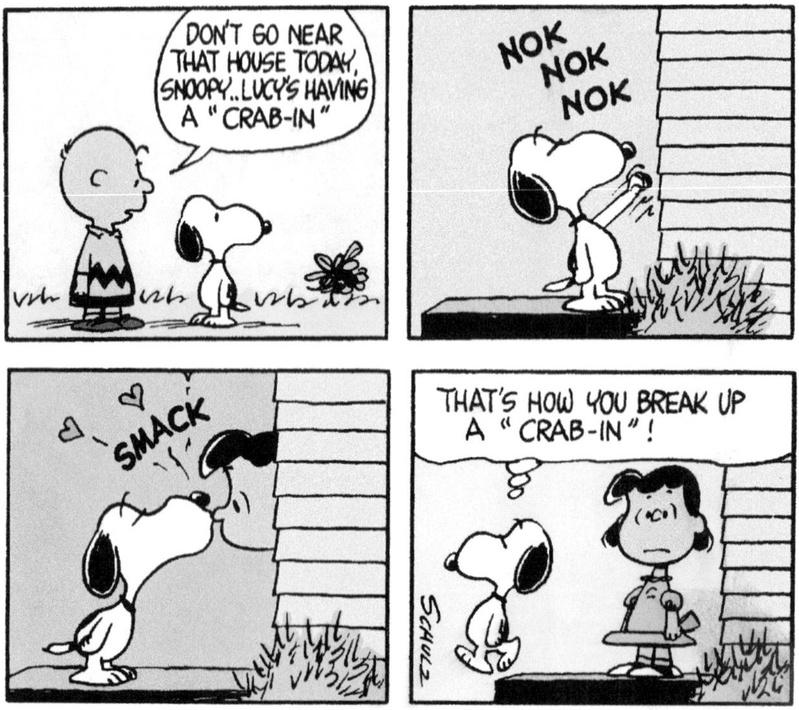
DON'T GO NEAR THAT HOUSE TODAY, SNOOPY..LUCY'S HAVING A "CRAB-IN"
NOK
NOK
NOK
SMACK
THAT'S HOW YOU BREAK UP A "CRAB-IN"!
SCHULZ

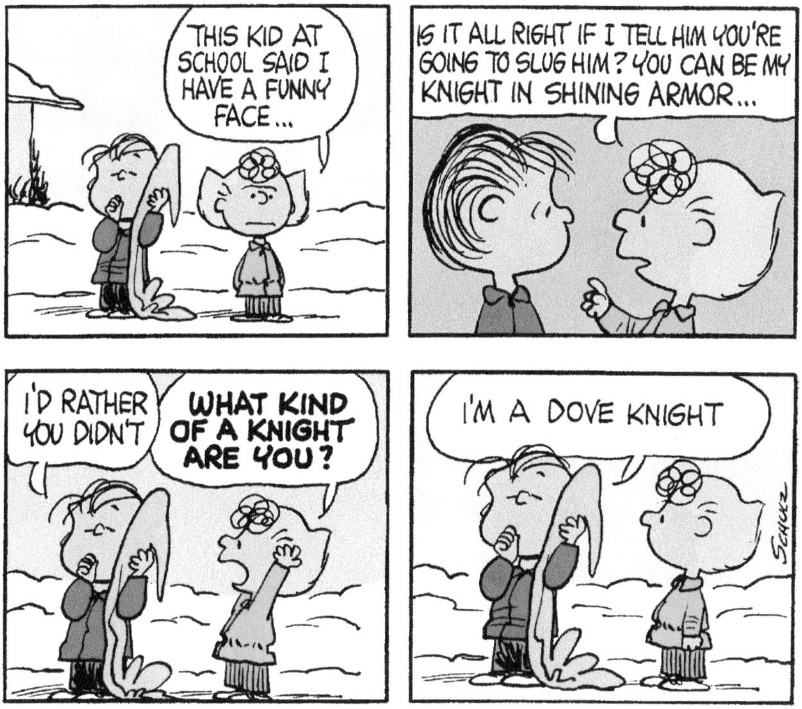
THIS KID AT SCHOOL SAID I HAVE A FUNNY FACE...
IS IT ALL RIGHT IF I TELL HIM YOU'RE GOING TO SLUG HIM? YOU CAN BE MY KNIGHT IN SHINING ARMOR...
I'D RATHER YOU DIDN'T
WHAT KIND OF A KNIGHT ARE YOU?
I'M A DOVE KNIGHT
SCHULZ

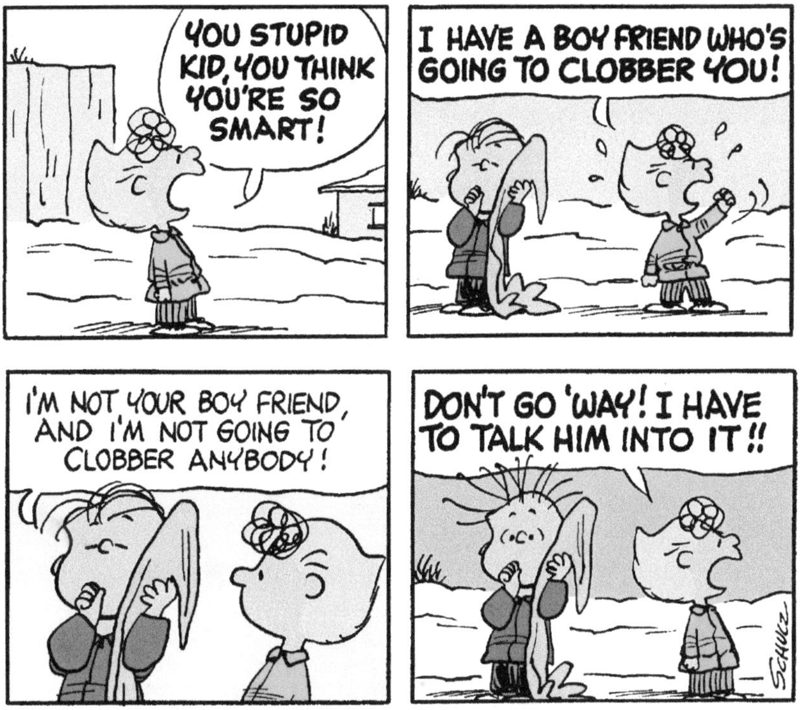
YOU STUPID KID, YOU THINK YOU'RE SO SMART!
I HAVE A BOY FRIEND WHO'S GOING TO CLOBBER YOU!
I'M NOT YOUR BOY FRIEND, AND I'M NOT GOING TO CLOBBER ANYBODY!
DON'T GO 'WAY! I HAVE TO TALK HIM INTO IT!!
SCHULZ

ONE, PLEASE
ONE, PLEASE
ONE, PLEASE

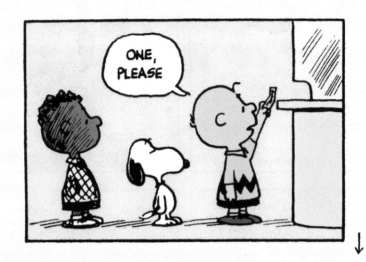

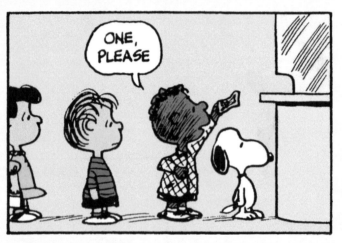

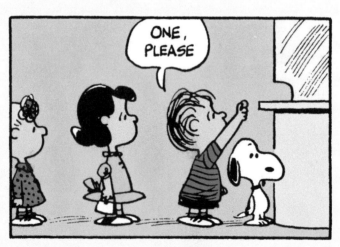

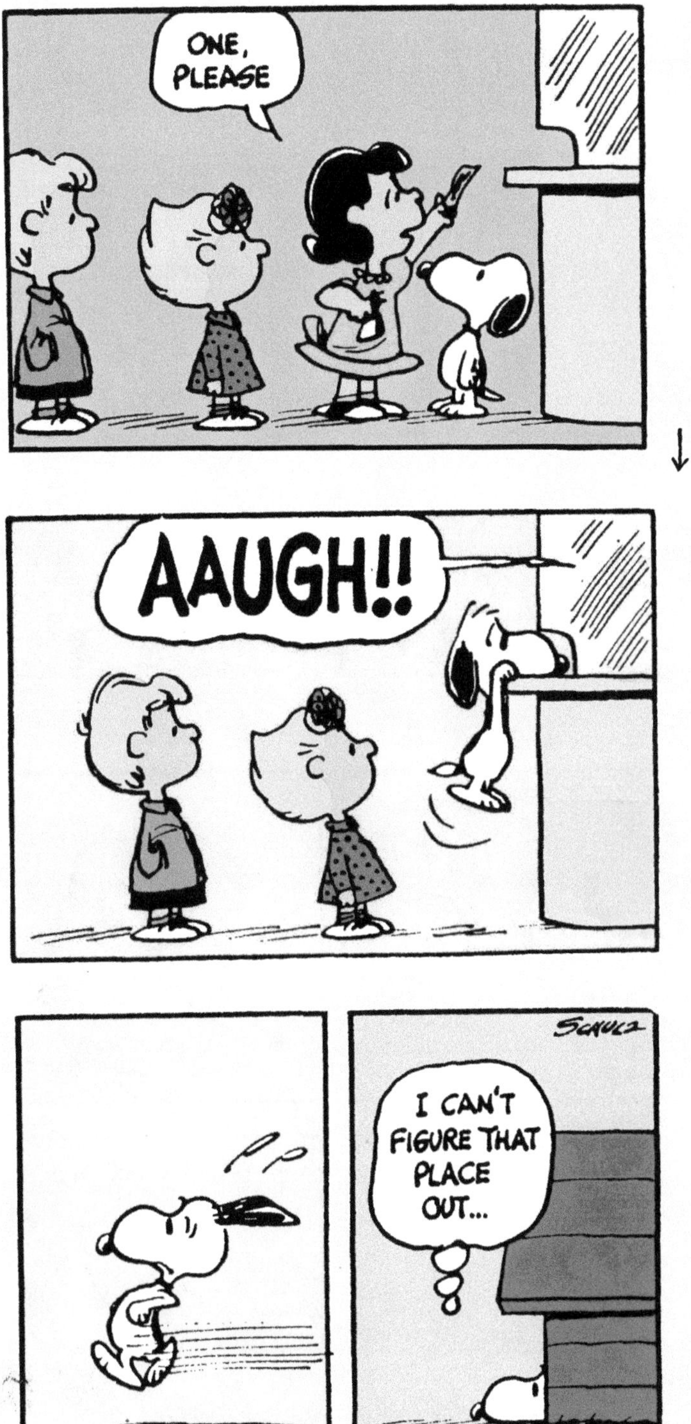
ONE, PLEASE
AAUGH!!
I CAN'T FIGURE THAT PLACE OUT...
SCHULZ

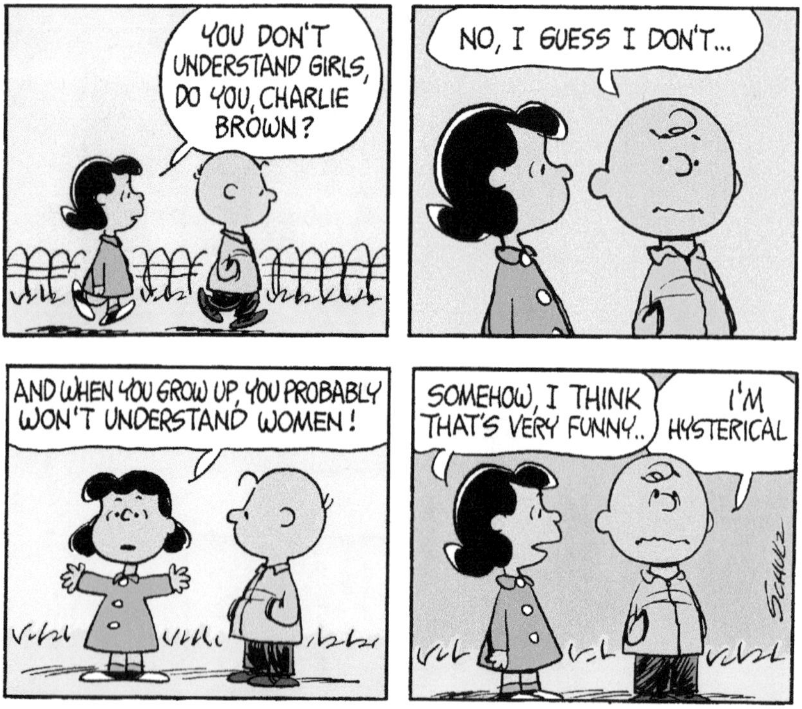
YOU DON'T UNDERSTAND GIRLS, DO YOU, CHARLIE BROWN?
NO, I GUESS I DON'T...
AND WHEN YOU GROW UP, YOU PROBABLY WON'T UNDERSTAND WOMEN!
SOMEHOW, I THINK THAT'S VERY FUNNY..
I'M HYSTERICAL
SCHULZ

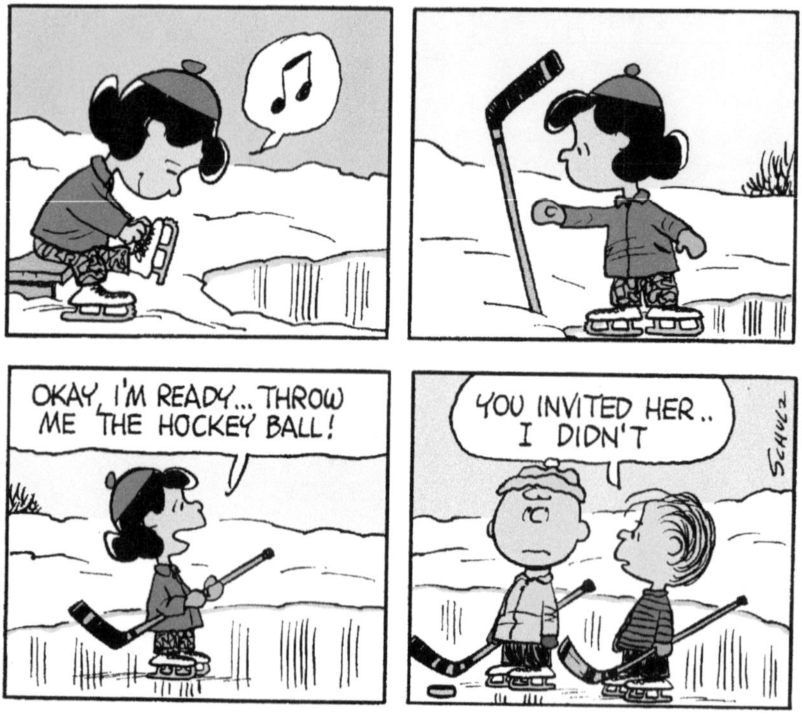
OKAY, I'M READY... THROW ME THE HOCKEY BALL!
YOU INVITED HER.. I DIDN'T
SCHULZ

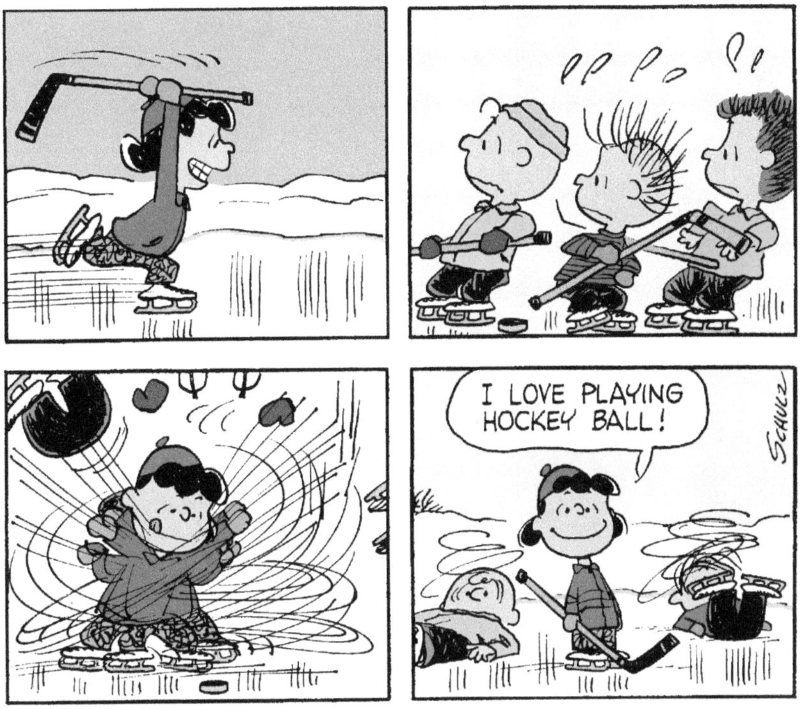
I LOVE PLAYING HOCKEY BALL!

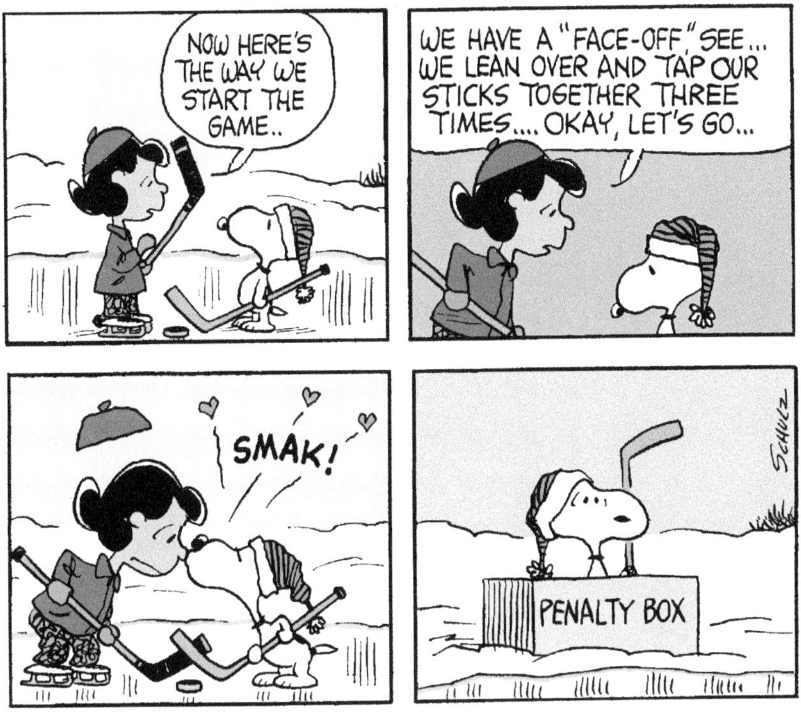
NOW HERE'S THE WAY WE START THE GAME..
WE HAVE A "FACE-OFF," SEE... WE LEAN OVER AND TAP OUR STICKS TOGETHER THREE TIMES.... OKAY, LET'S GO...
SMAK!
PENALTY BOX

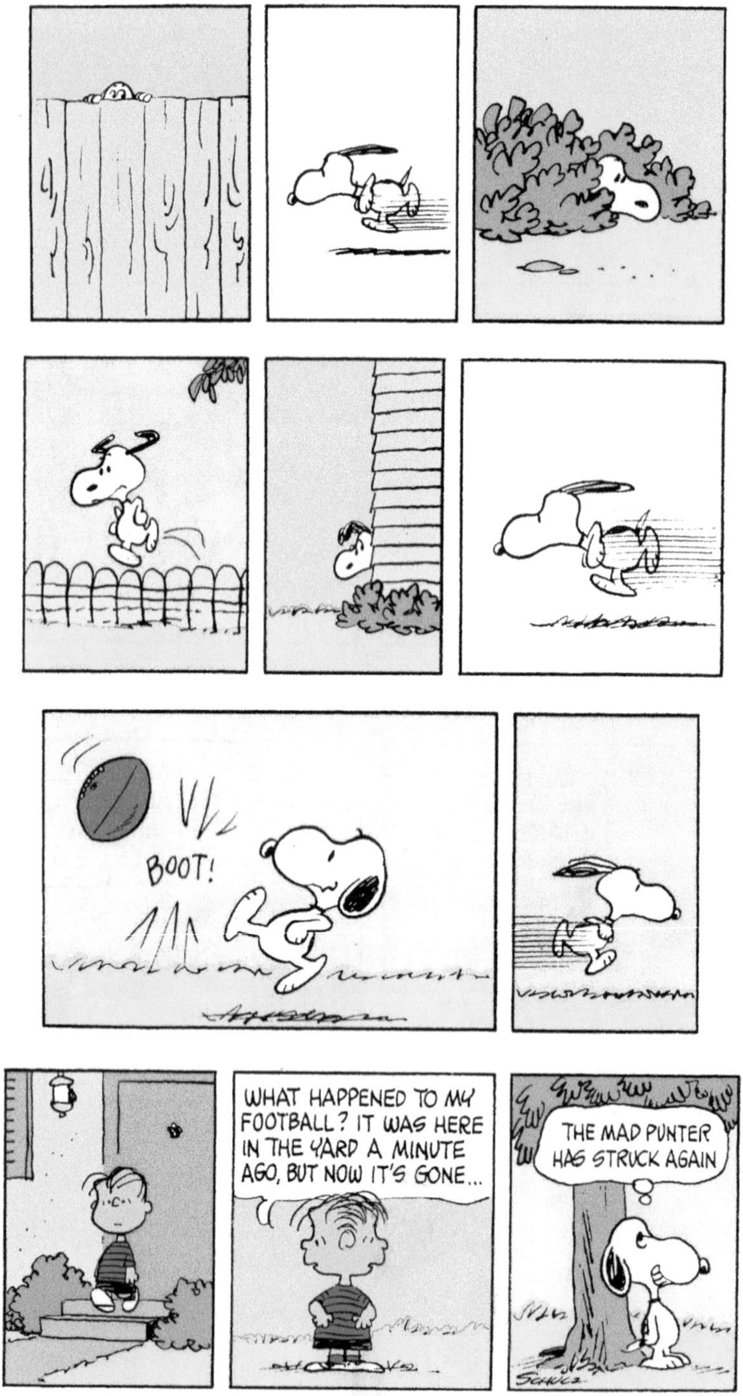
BOOT!
WHAT HAPPENED TO MY FOOTBALL? IT WAS HERE IN THE YARD A MINUTE AGO, BUT NOW IT'S GONE...
THE MAD PUNTER HAS STRUCK AGAIN
SCHULZ

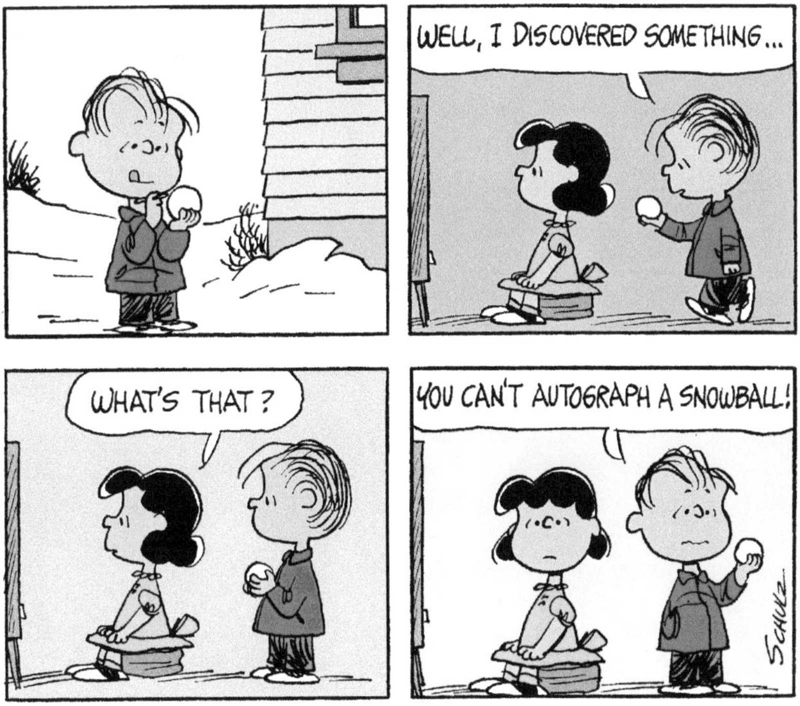
WELL, I DISCOVERED SOMETHING...
WHAT'S THAT ?
YOU CAN'T AUTOGRAPH A SNOWBALL!

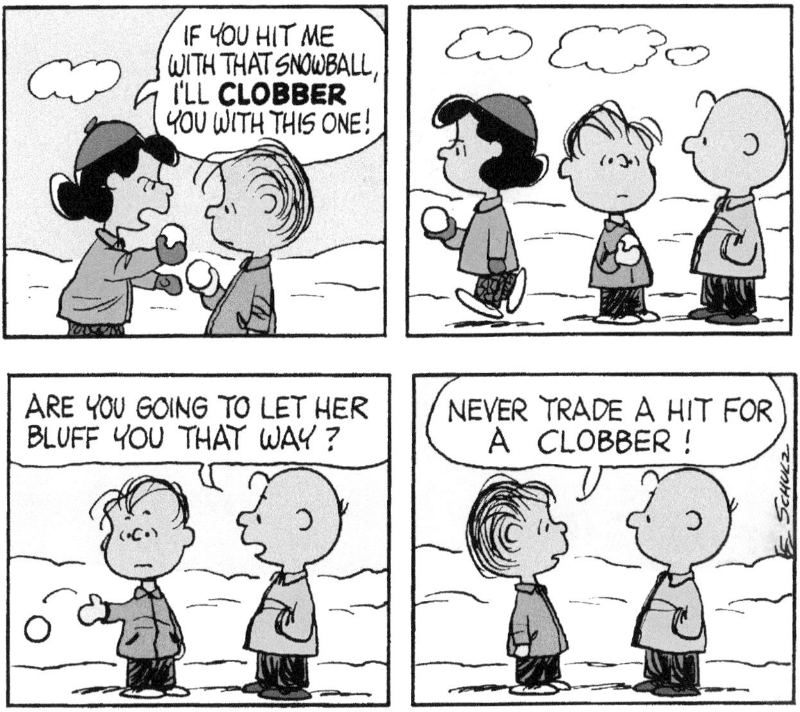
IF YOU HIT ME WITH THAT SNOWBALL, I'LL **CLOBBER** YOU WITH THIS ONE!
ARE YOU GOING TO LET HER BLUFF YOU THAT WAY ?
NEVER TRADE A HIT FOR A CLOBBER !

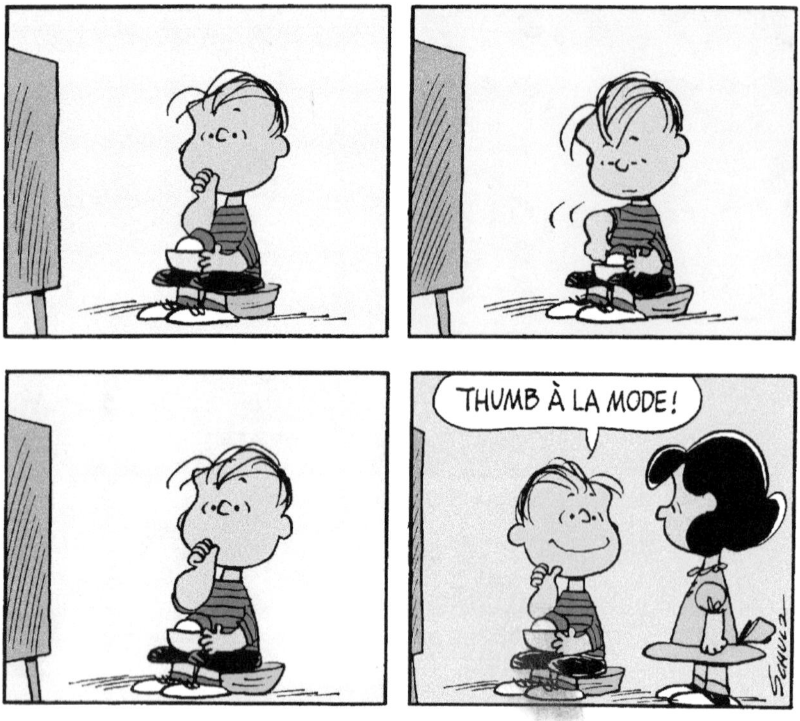
THUMB À LA MODE!
SCHULZ

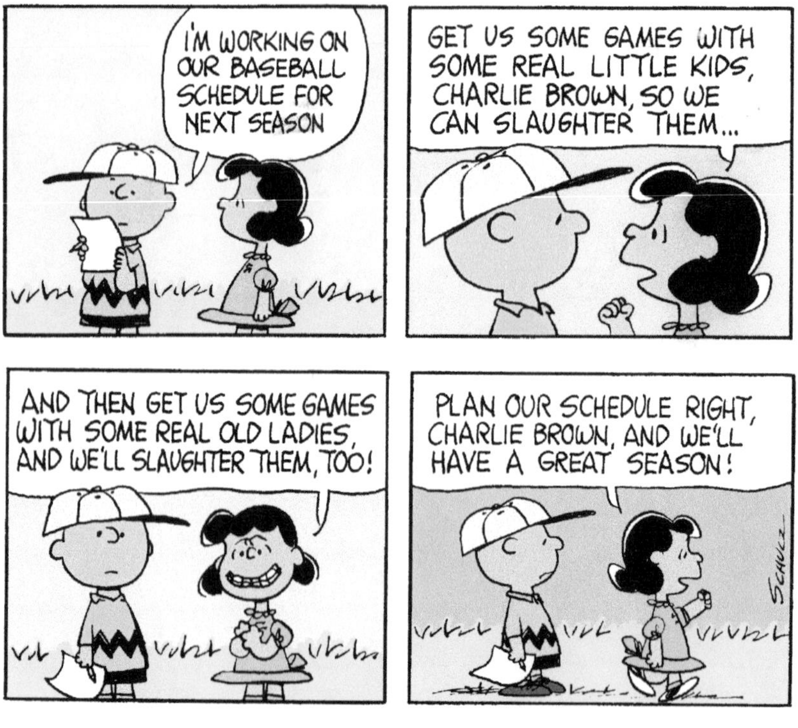
I'M WORKING ON OUR BASEBALL SCHEDULE FOR NEXT SEASON
GET US SOME GAMES WITH SOME REAL LITTLE KIDS, CHARLIE BROWN, SO WE CAN SLAUGHTER THEM...
AND THEN GET US SOME GAMES WITH SOME REAL OLD LADIES, AND WE'LL SLAUGHTER THEM, TOO!
PLAN OUR SCHEDULE RIGHT, CHARLIE BROWN, AND WE'LL HAVE A GREAT SEASON!

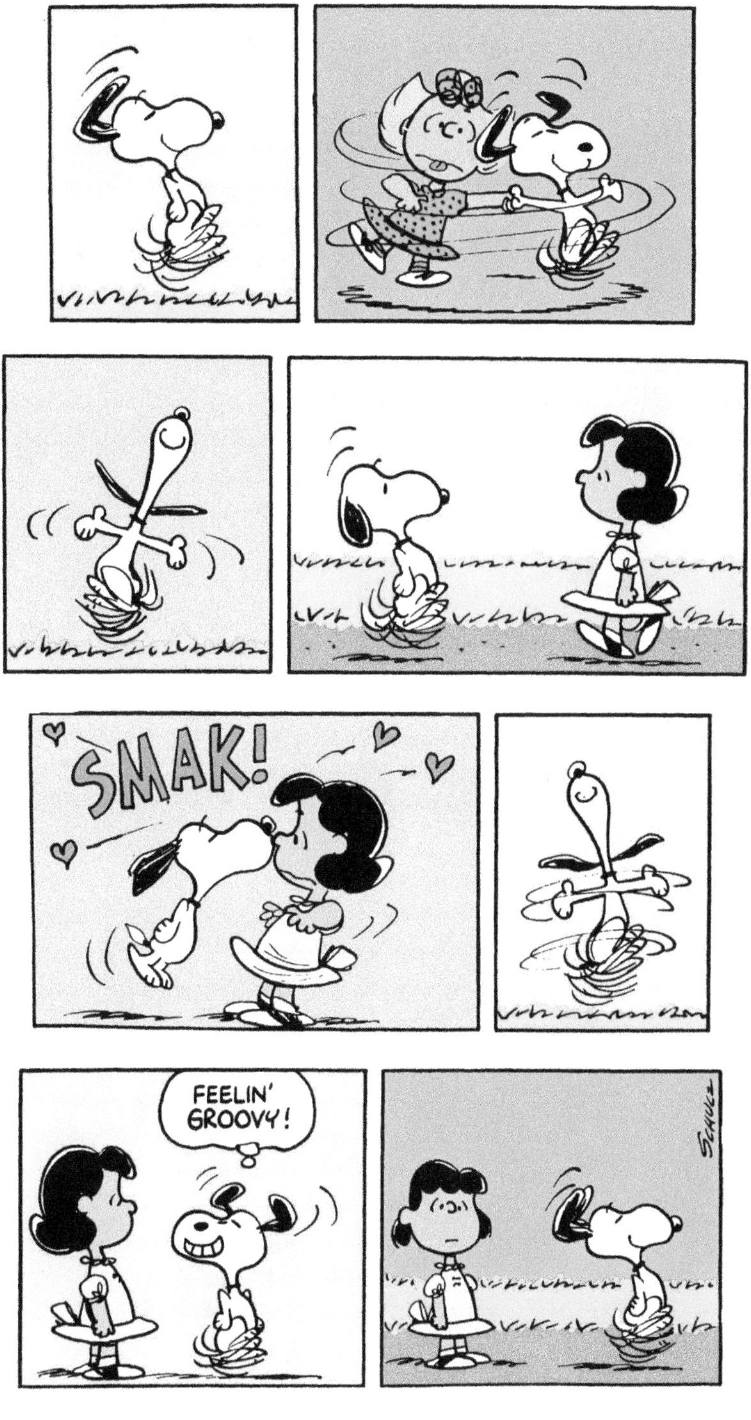
SMAK!
FEELIN' GROOVY!
SCHULZ

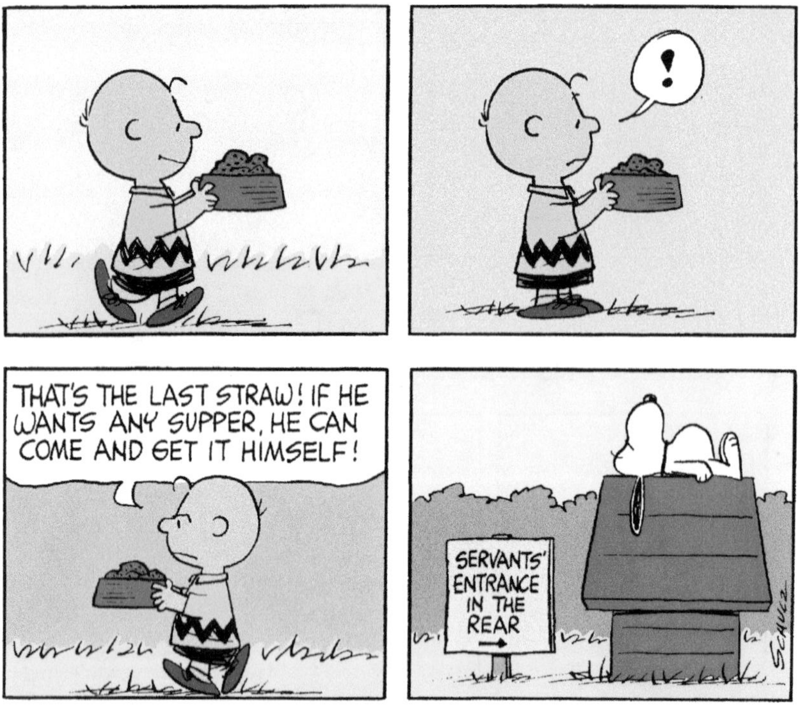
!
THAT'S THE LAST STRAW! IF HE WANTS ANY SUPPER, HE CAN COME AND GET IT HIMSELF!
SERVANTS' ENTRANCE IN THE REAR
SCHULZ

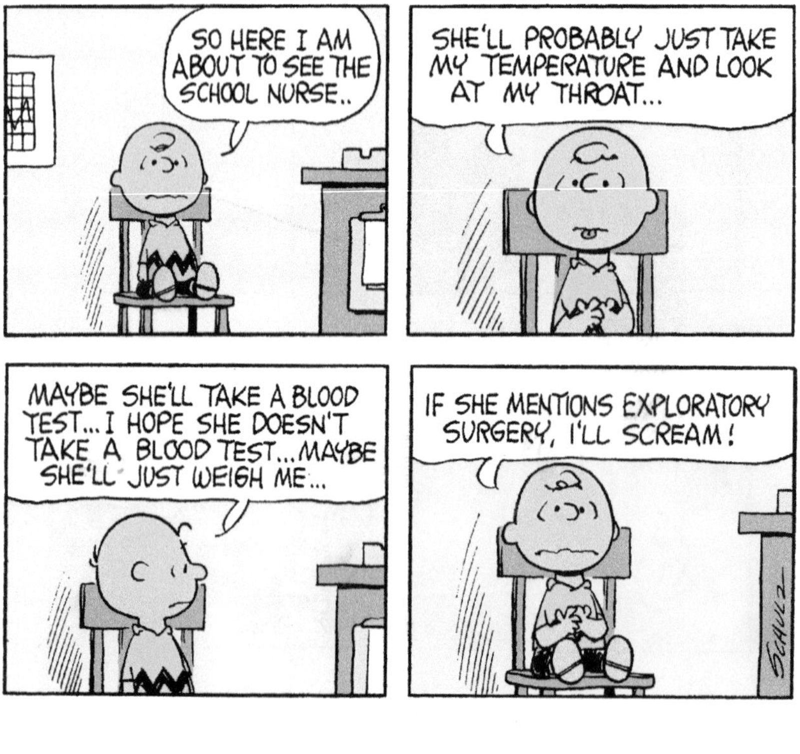
SO HERE I AM ABOUT TO SEE THE SCHOOL NURSE..
SHE'LL PROBABLY JUST TAKE MY TEMPERATURE AND LOOK AT MY THROAT...
MAYBE SHE'LL TAKE A BLOOD TEST...I HOPE SHE DOESN'T TAKE A BLOOD TEST...MAYBE SHE'LL JUST WEIGH ME...
IF SHE MENTIONS EXPLORATORY SURGERY, I'LL SCREAM!
SCHULZ

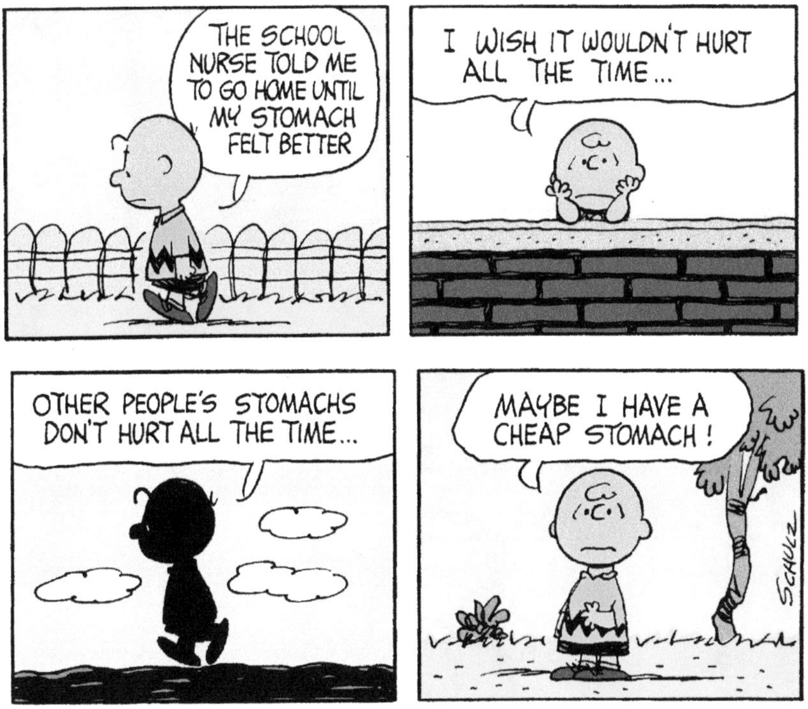
THE SCHOOL NURSE TOLD ME TO GO HOME UNTIL MY STOMACH FELT BETTER
I WISH IT WOULDN'T HURT ALL THE TIME...
OTHER PEOPLE'S STOMACHS DON'T HURT ALL THE TIME...
MAYBE I HAVE A CHEAP STOMACH!
SCHULZ

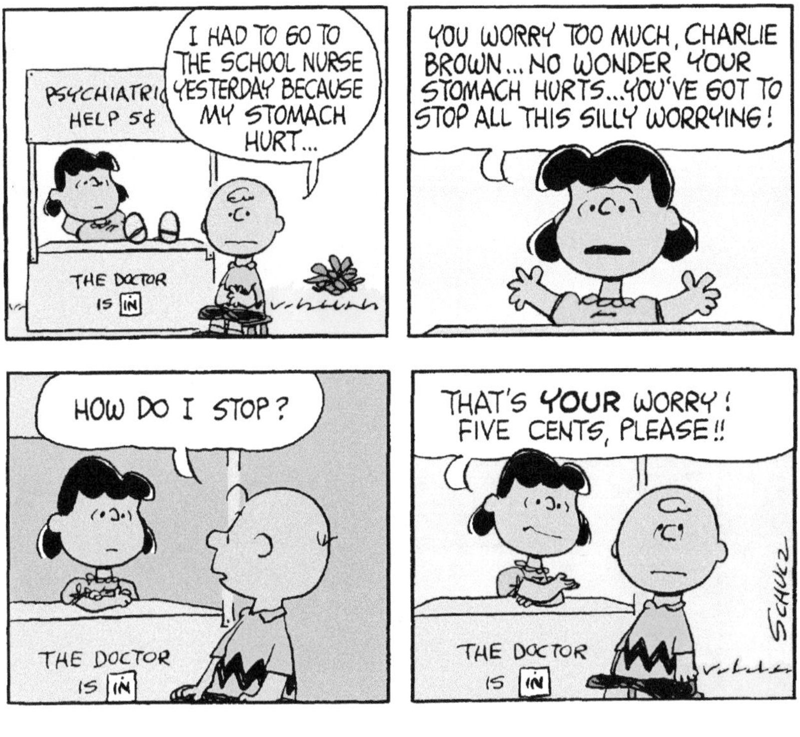
PSYCHIATRIC HELP 5¢
THE DOCTOR IS IN
I HAD TO GO TO THE SCHOOL NURSE YESTERDAY BECAUSE MY STOMACH HURT...
YOU WORRY TOO MUCH, CHARLIE BROWN... NO WONDER YOUR STOMACH HURTS... YOU'VE GOT TO STOP ALL THIS SILLY WORRYING!
HOW DO I STOP?
THE DOCTOR IS IN
THAT'S **YOUR** WORRY! FIVE CENTS, PLEASE!!
THE DOCTOR IS IN
SCHULZ

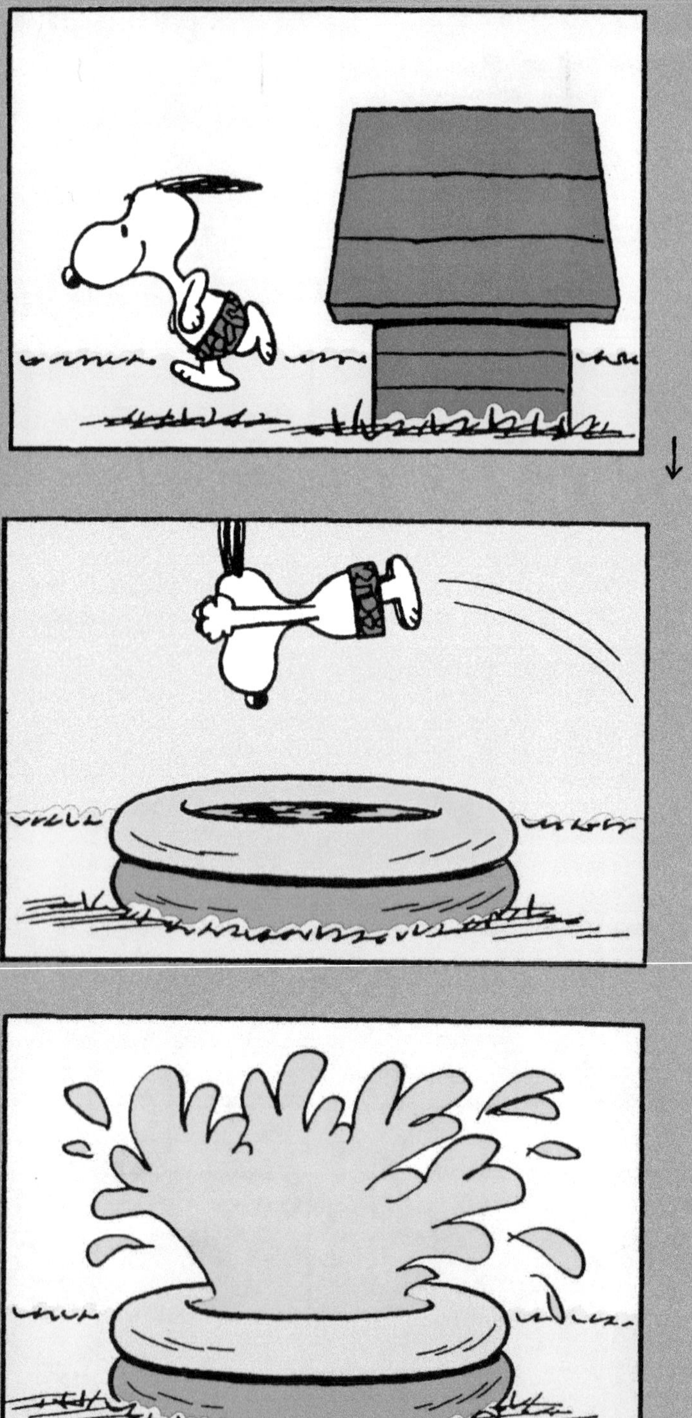

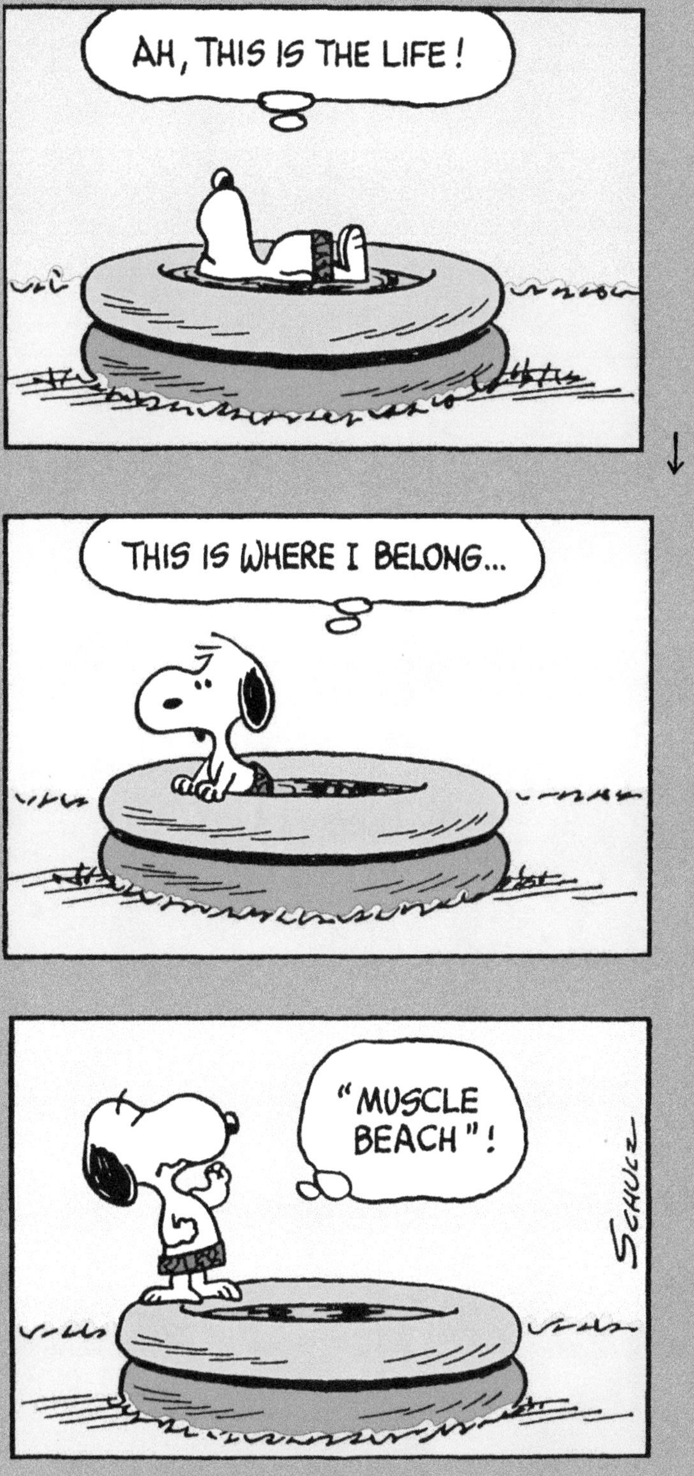
AH, THIS IS THE LIFE!
THIS IS WHERE I BELONG...
"MUSCLE BEACH"!
SCHULZ

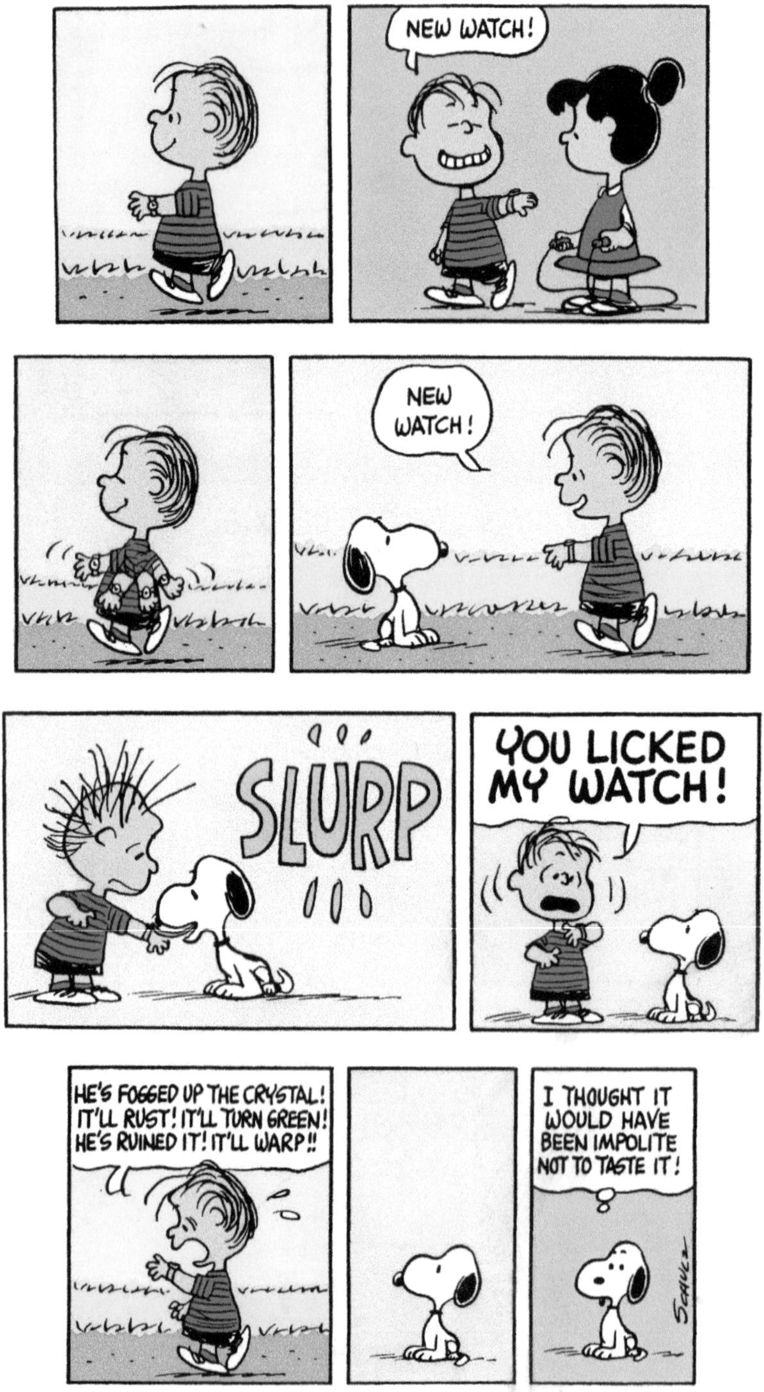
NEW WATCH!
NEW WATCH!
SLURP
YOU LICKED MY WATCH!
HE'S FOGGED UP THE CRYSTAL! IT'LL RUST! IT'LL TURN GREEN! HE'S RUINED IT! IT'LL WARP!!
I THOUGHT IT WOULD HAVE BEEN IMPOLITE NOT TO TASTE IT!
SCHULZ

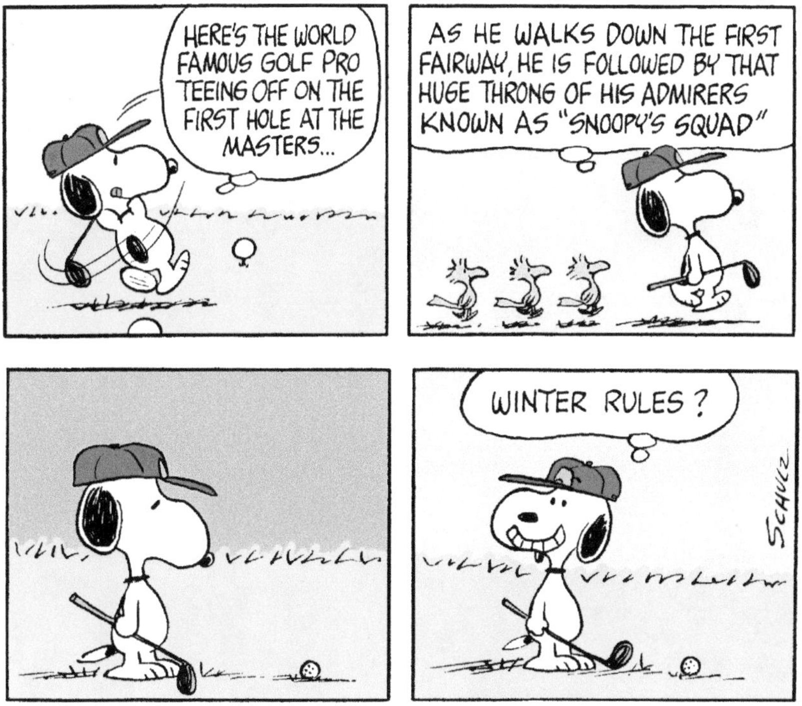
HERE'S THE WORLD FAMOUS GOLF PRO TEEING OFF ON THE FIRST HOLE AT THE MASTERS...
AS HE WALKS DOWN THE FIRST FAIRWAY, HE IS FOLLOWED BY THAT HUGE THRONG OF HIS ADMIRERS KNOWN AS "SNOOPY'S SQUAD"
WINTER RULES ?

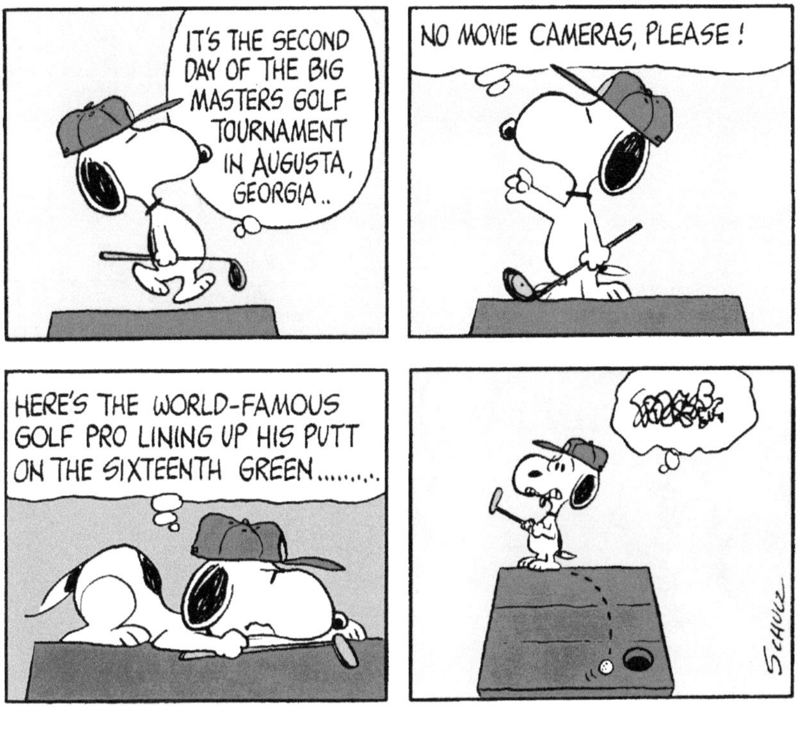
IT'S THE SECOND DAY OF THE BIG MASTERS GOLF TOURNAMENT IN AUGUSTA, GEORGIA..
NO MOVIE CAMERAS, PLEASE !
HERE'S THE WORLD-FAMOUS GOLF PRO LINING UP HIS PUTT ON THE SIXTEENTH GREEN.........

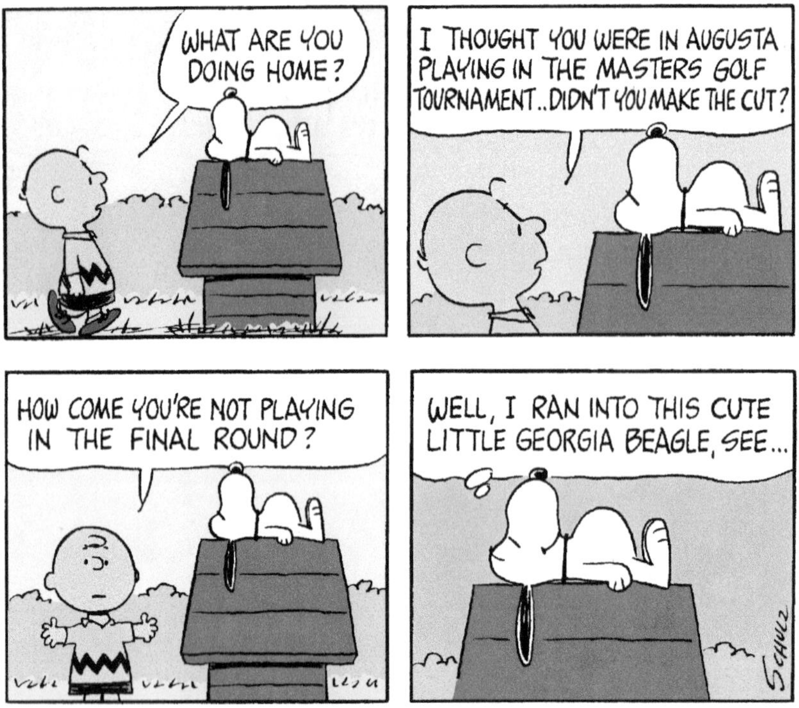
WHAT ARE YOU DOING HOME?
I THOUGHT YOU WERE IN AUGUSTA PLAYING IN THE MASTERS GOLF TOURNAMENT..DIDN'T YOU MAKE THE CUT?
HOW COME YOU'RE NOT PLAYING IN THE FINAL ROUND?
WELL, I RAN INTO THIS CUTE LITTLE GEORGIA BEAGLE, SEE...
SCHULZ

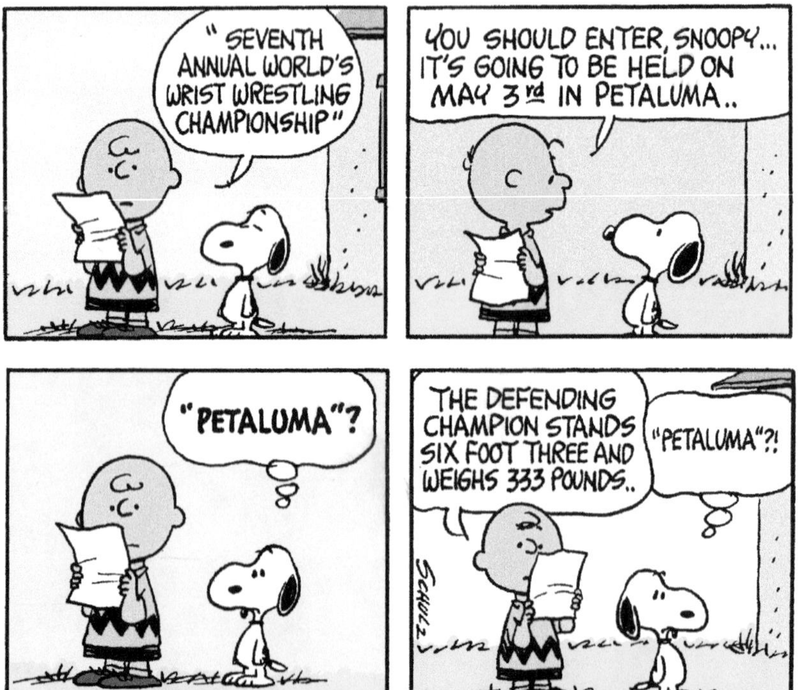
" SEVENTH ANNUAL WORLD'S WRIST WRESTLING CHAMPIONSHIP"
YOU SHOULD ENTER, SNOOPY... IT'S GOING TO BE HELD ON MAY 3rd IN PETALUMA..
"PETALUMA"?
THE DEFENDING CHAMPION STANDS SIX FOOT THREE AND WEIGHS 333 POUNDS..
"PETALUMA"?!
SCHULZ

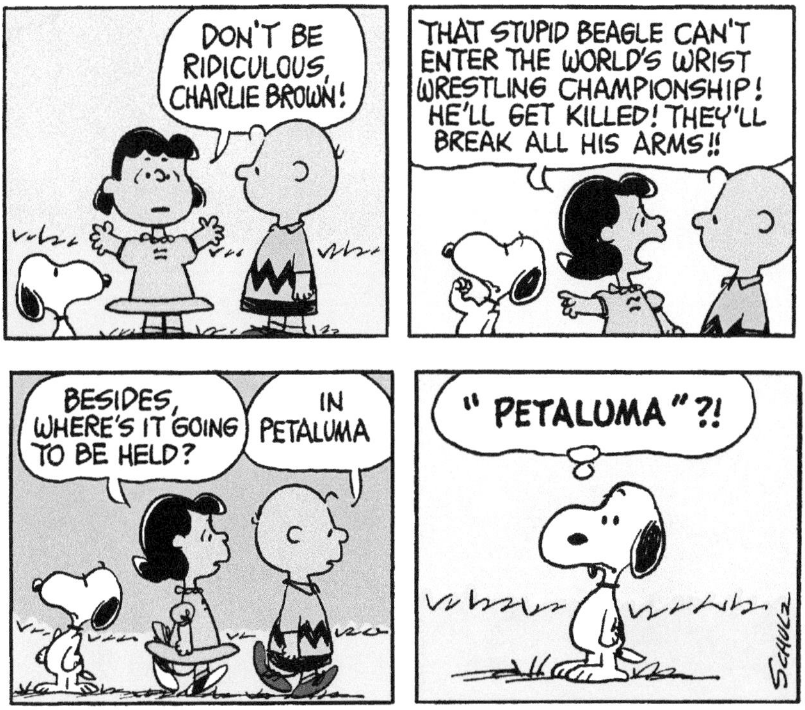
DON'T BE RIDICULOUS, CHARLIE BROWN!
THAT STUPID BEAGLE CAN'T ENTER THE WORLD'S WRIST WRESTLING CHAMPIONSHIP! HE'LL GET KILLED! THEY'LL BREAK ALL HIS ARMS!!
BESIDES, WHERE'S IT GOING TO BE HELD?
IN PETALUMA
"PETALUMA"?!
SCHULZ

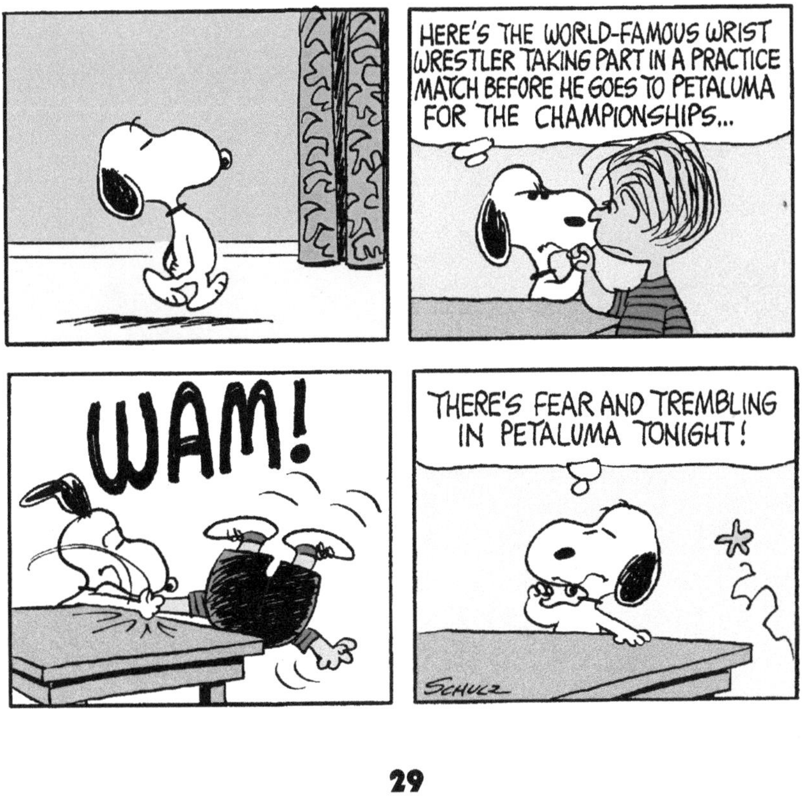
HERE'S THE WORLD-FAMOUS WRIST WRESTLER TAKING PART IN A PRACTICE MATCH BEFORE HE GOES TO PETALUMA FOR THE CHAMPIONSHIPS...
WAM!
THERE'S FEAR AND TREMBLING IN PETALUMA TONIGHT!
SCHULZ

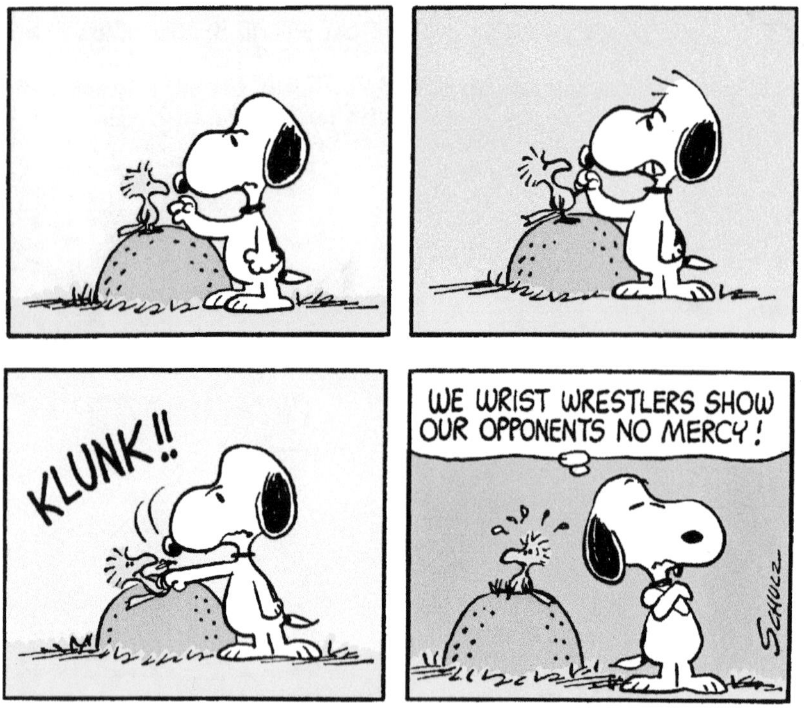
KLUNK!!
WE WRIST WRESTLERS SHOW OUR OPPONENTS NO MERCY!
SCHULZ

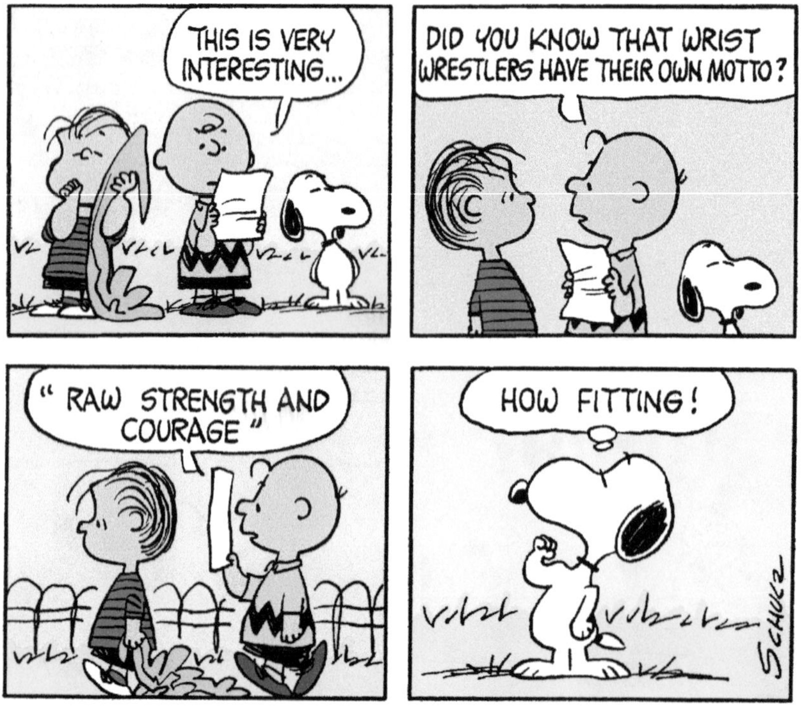
THIS IS VERY INTERESTING...
DID YOU KNOW THAT WRIST WRESTLERS HAVE THEIR OWN MOTTO?
" RAW STRENGTH AND COURAGE "
HOW FITTING!
SCHULZ

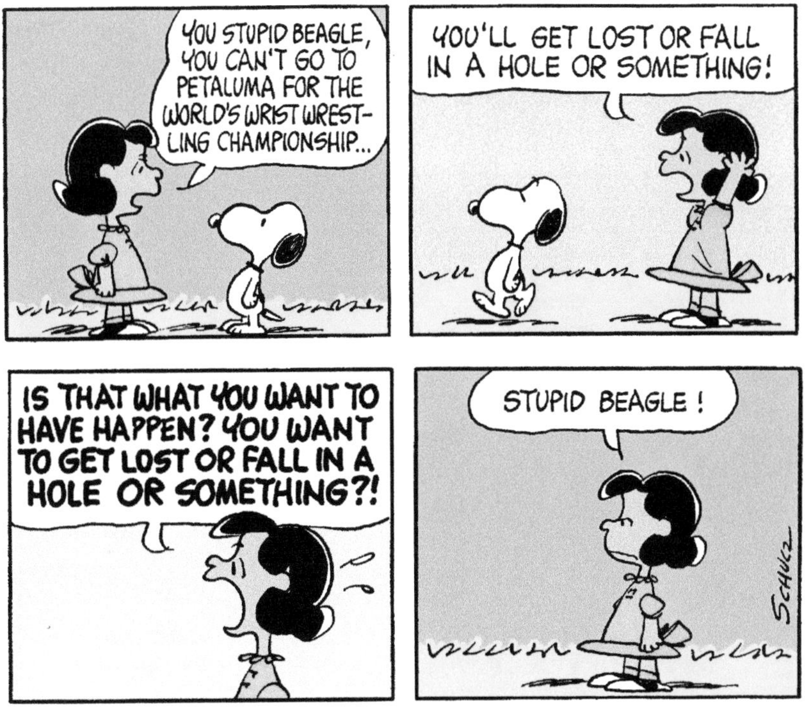
YOU STUPID BEAGLE, YOU CAN'T GO TO PETALUMA FOR THE WORLD'S WRIST WRESTLING CHAMPIONSHIP...
YOU'LL GET LOST OR FALL IN A HOLE OR SOMETHING!
IS THAT WHAT YOU WANT TO HAVE HAPPEN? YOU WANT TO GET LOST OR FALL IN A HOLE OR SOMETHING?!
STUPID BEAGLE!
SCHULZ

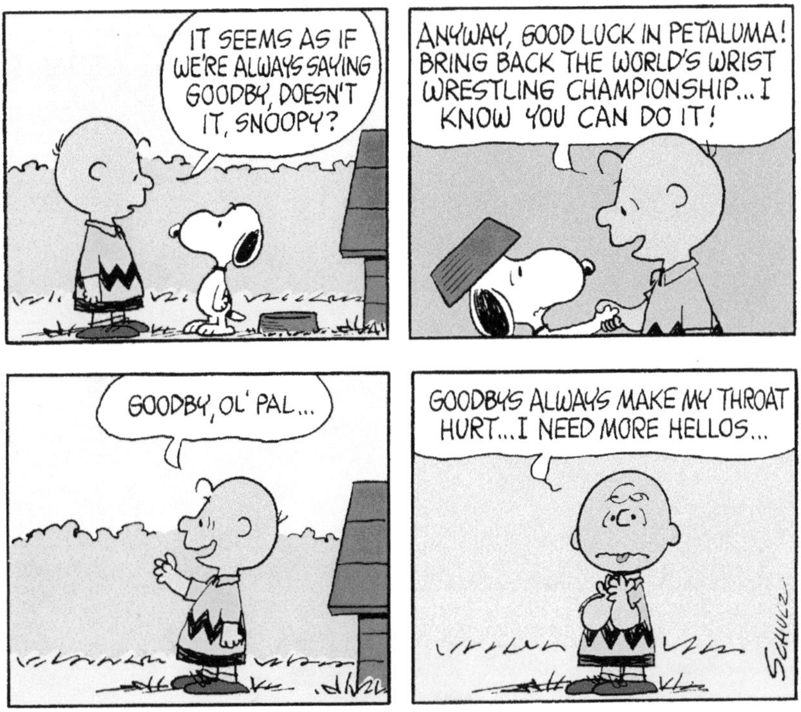
IT SEEMS AS IF WE'RE ALWAYS SAYING GOODBY, DOESN'T IT, SNOOPY?
ANYWAY, GOOD LUCK IN PETALUMA! BRING BACK THE WORLD'S WRIST WRESTLING CHAMPIONSHIP... I KNOW YOU CAN DO IT!
GOODBY, OL' PAL...
GOODBYS ALWAYS MAKE MY THROAT HURT... I NEED MORE HELLOS...
SCHULZ

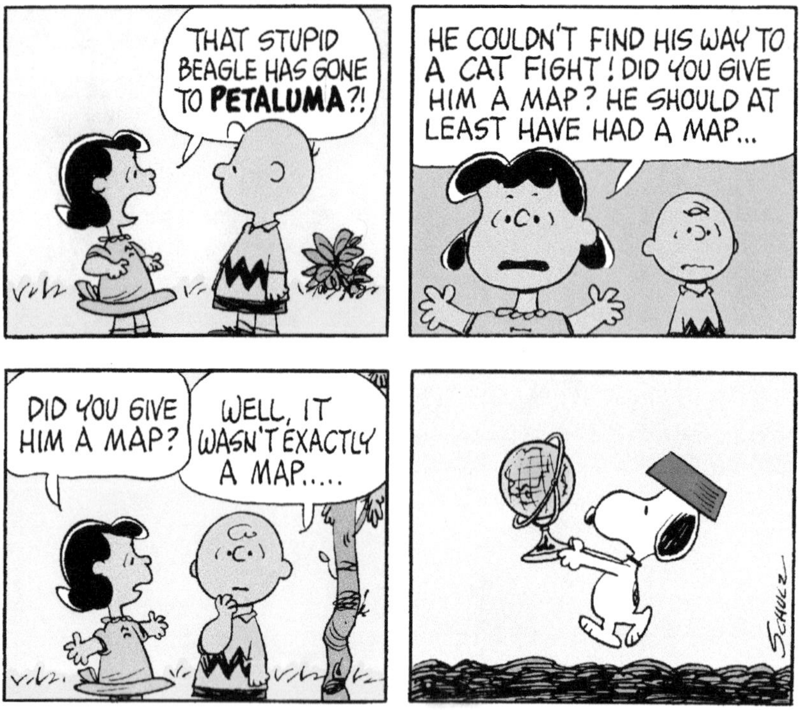
THAT STUPID BEAGLE HAS GONE TO **PETALUMA**?!
HE COULDN'T FIND HIS WAY TO A CAT FIGHT! DID YOU GIVE HIM A MAP? HE SHOULD AT LEAST HAVE HAD A MAP...
DID YOU GIVE HIM A MAP?
WELL, IT WASN'T EXACTLY A MAP.....
SCHULZ

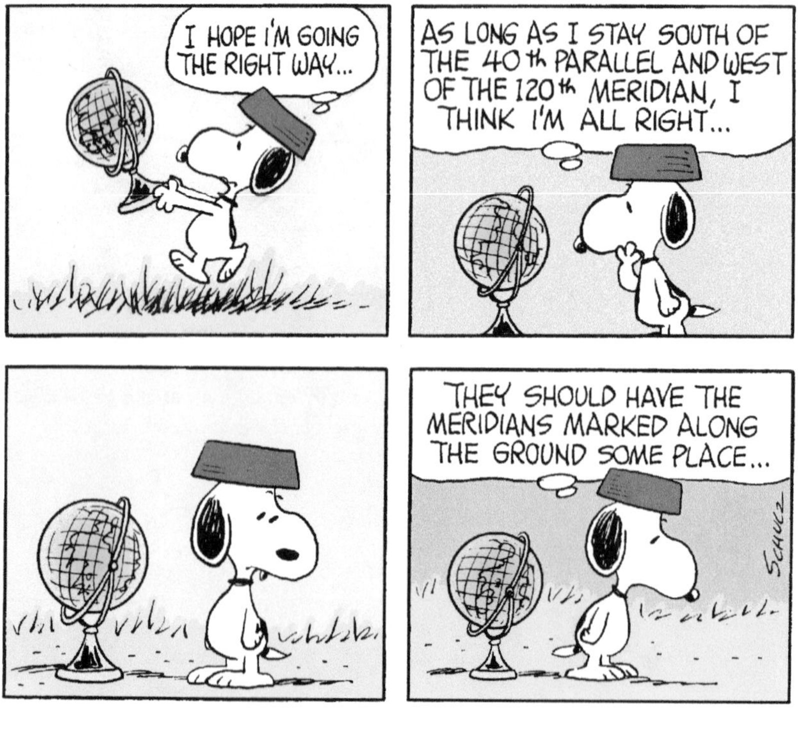
I HOPE I'M GOING THE RIGHT WAY...
AS LONG AS I STAY SOUTH OF THE 40th PARALLEL AND WEST OF THE 120th MERIDIAN, I THINK I'M ALL RIGHT...
THEY SHOULD HAVE THE MERIDIANS MARKED ALONG THE GROUND SOME PLACE...
SCHULZ

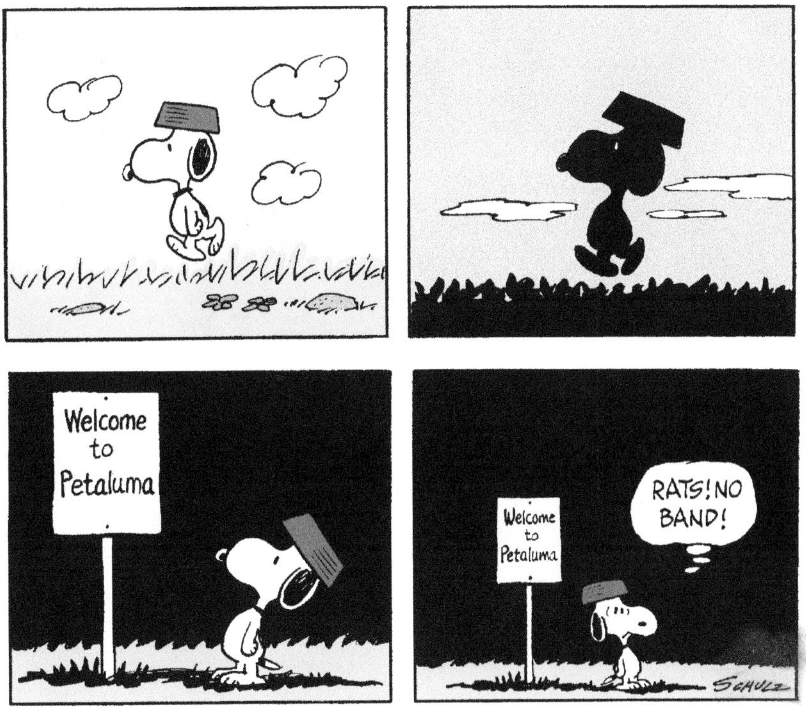
Welcome to Petaluma
Welcome to Petaluma
RATS! NO BAND!
SCHULZ

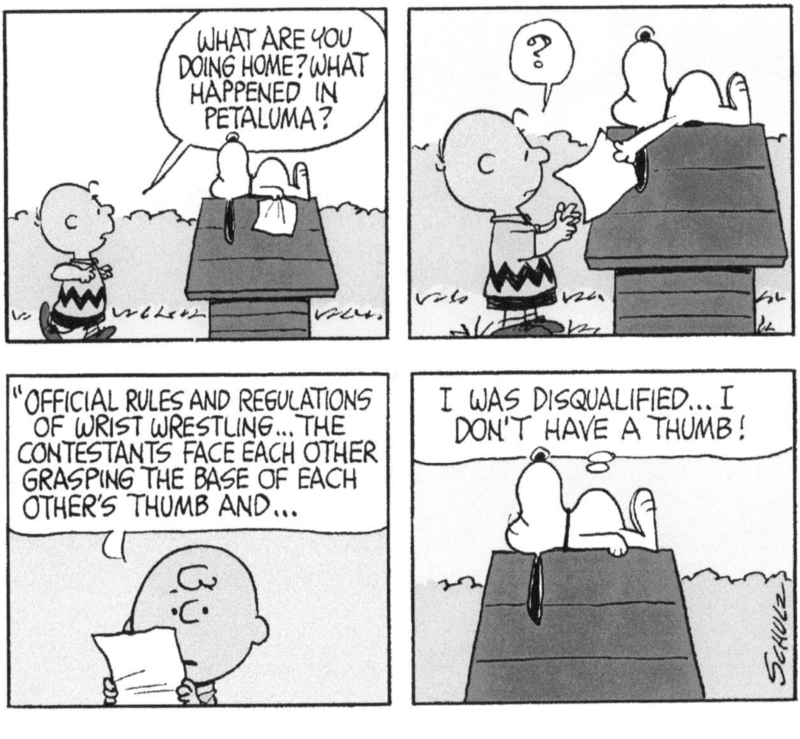
WHAT ARE YOU DOING HOME? WHAT HAPPENED IN PETALUMA?
?
"OFFICIAL RULES AND REGULATIONS OF WRIST WRESTLING... THE CONTESTANTS FACE EACH OTHER GRASPING THE BASE OF EACH OTHER'S THUMB AND...
I WAS DISQUALIFIED... I DON'T HAVE A THUMB!
SCHULZ

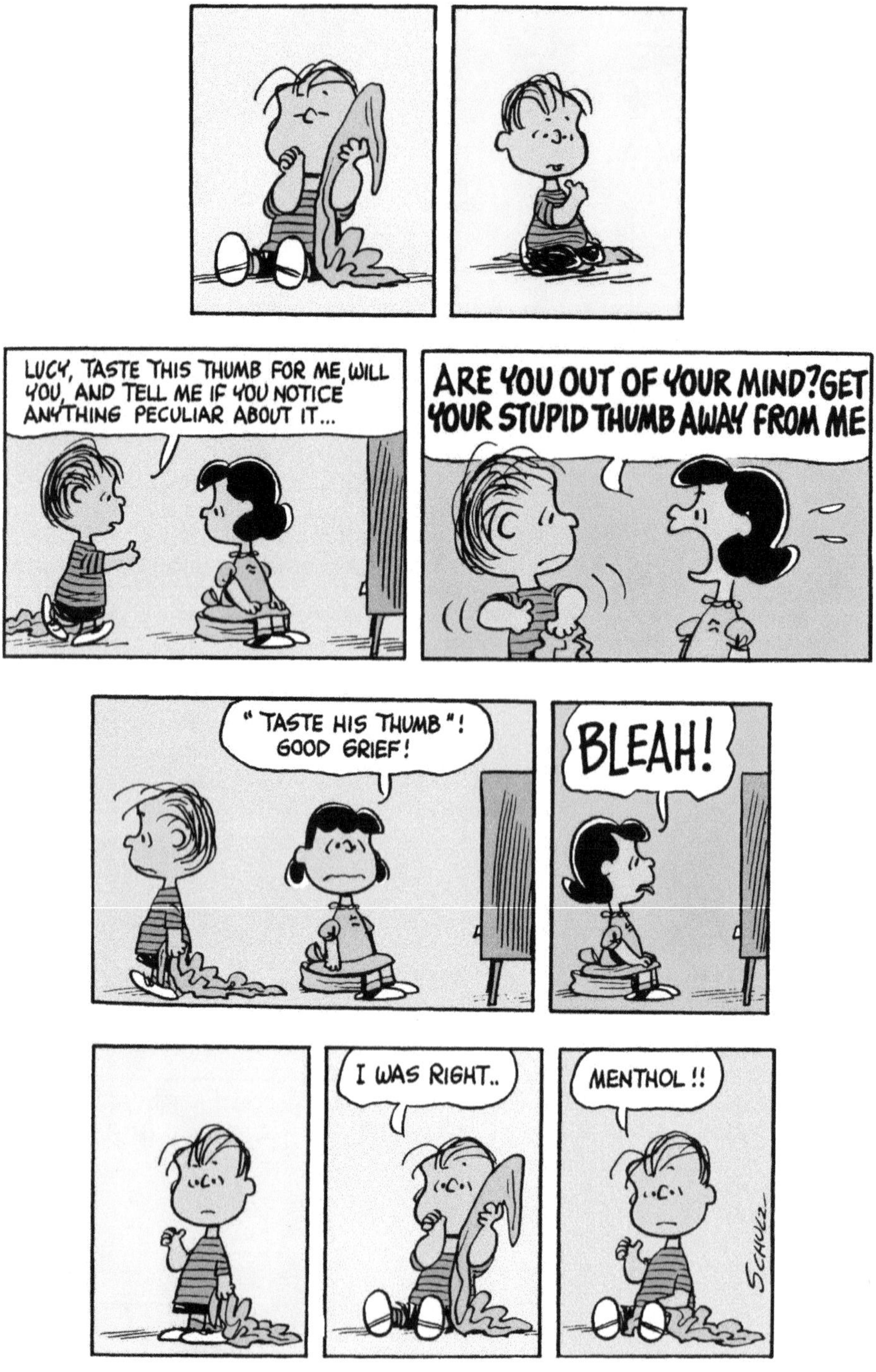
LUCY, TASTE THIS THUMB FOR ME, WILL YOU, AND TELL ME IF YOU NOTICE ANYTHING PECULIAR ABOUT IT...
ARE YOU OUT OF YOUR MIND? GET YOUR STUPID THUMB AWAY FROM ME
"TASTE HIS THUMB"! GOOD GRIEF!
BLEAH!
I WAS RIGHT..
MENTHOL !!
SCHULZ

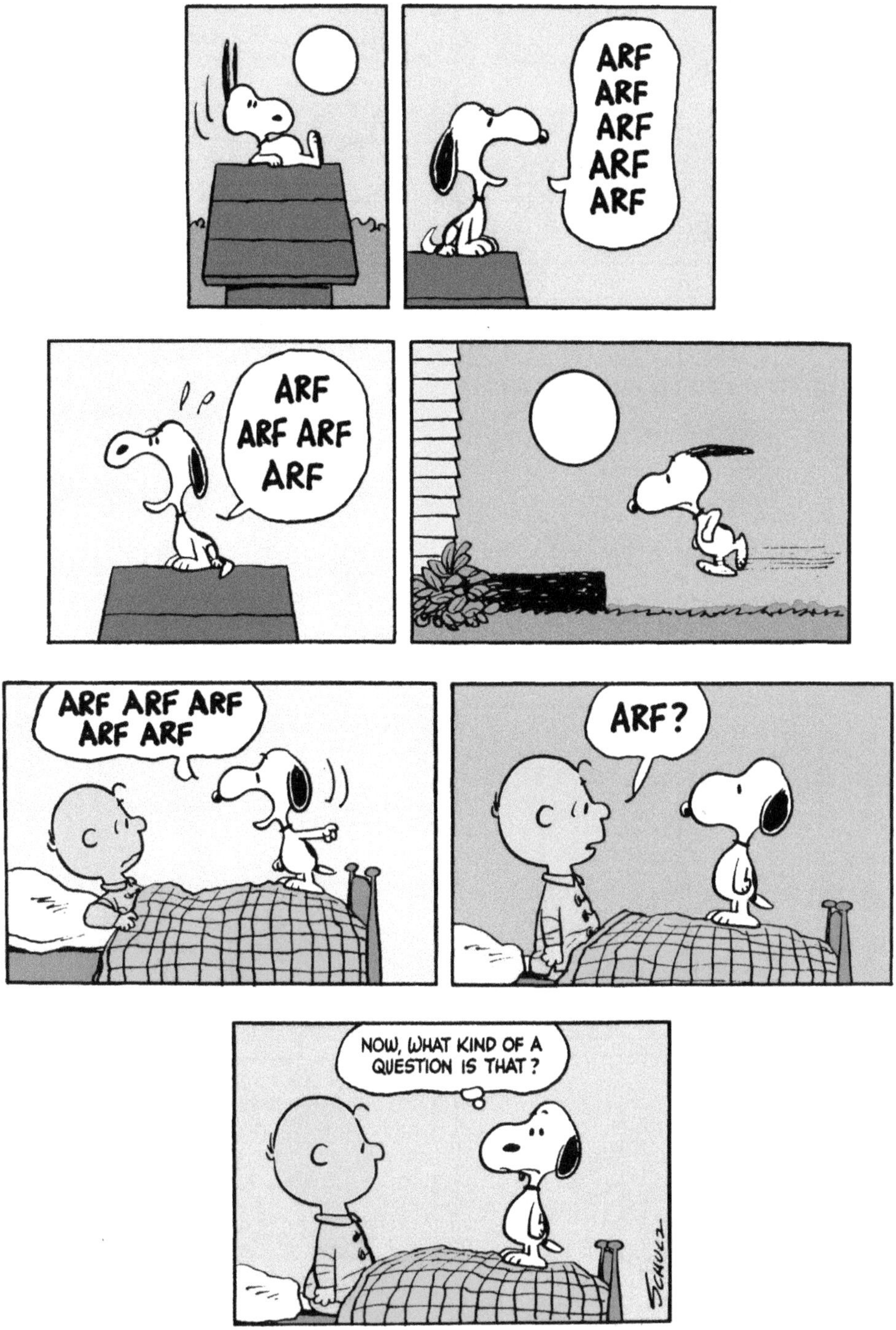
ARF ARF ARF ARF ARF
ARF ARF ARF ARF
ARF ARF ARF ARF ARF
ARF?
NOW, WHAT KIND OF A QUESTION IS THAT?
SCHULZ

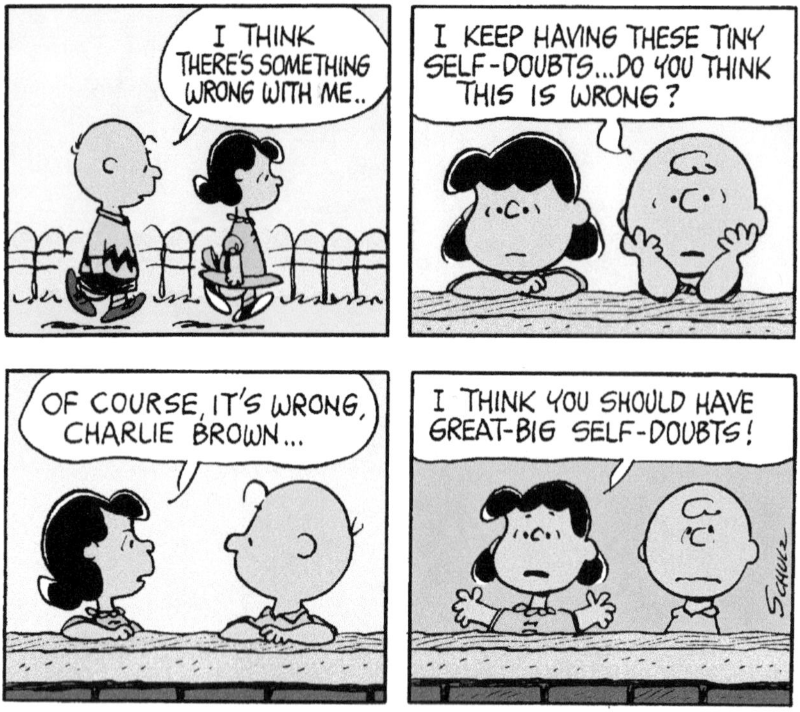
I THINK THERE'S SOMETHING WRONG WITH ME..
I KEEP HAVING THESE TINY SELF-DOUBTS...DO YOU THINK THIS IS WRONG?
OF COURSE, IT'S WRONG, CHARLIE BROWN...
I THINK YOU SHOULD HAVE GREAT-BIG SELF-DOUBTS!
SCHULZ

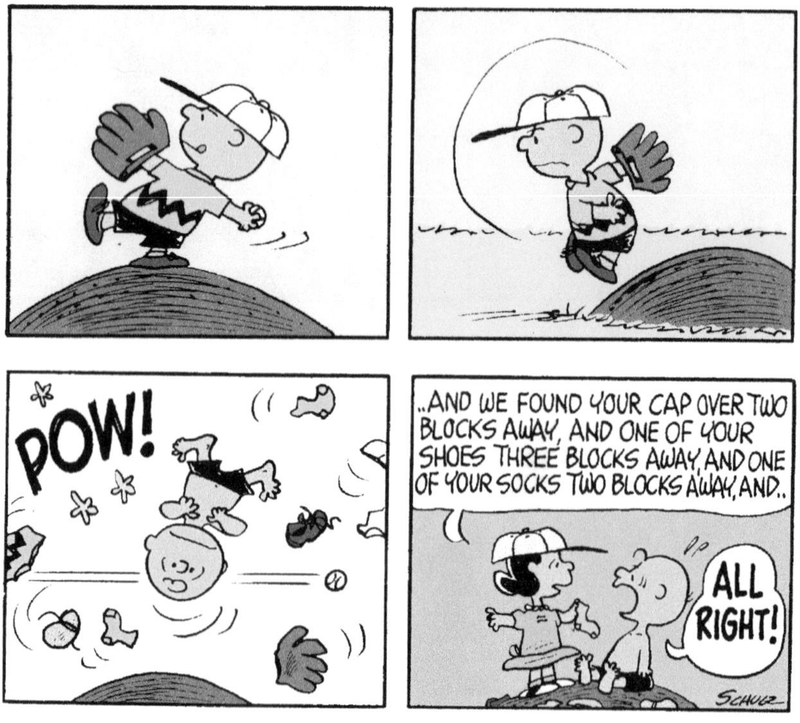
POW!
..AND WE FOUND YOUR CAP OVER TWO BLOCKS AWAY, AND ONE OF YOUR SHOES THREE BLOCKS AWAY, AND ONE OF YOUR SOCKS TWO BLOCKS AWAY, AND..
ALL RIGHT!
SCHULZ

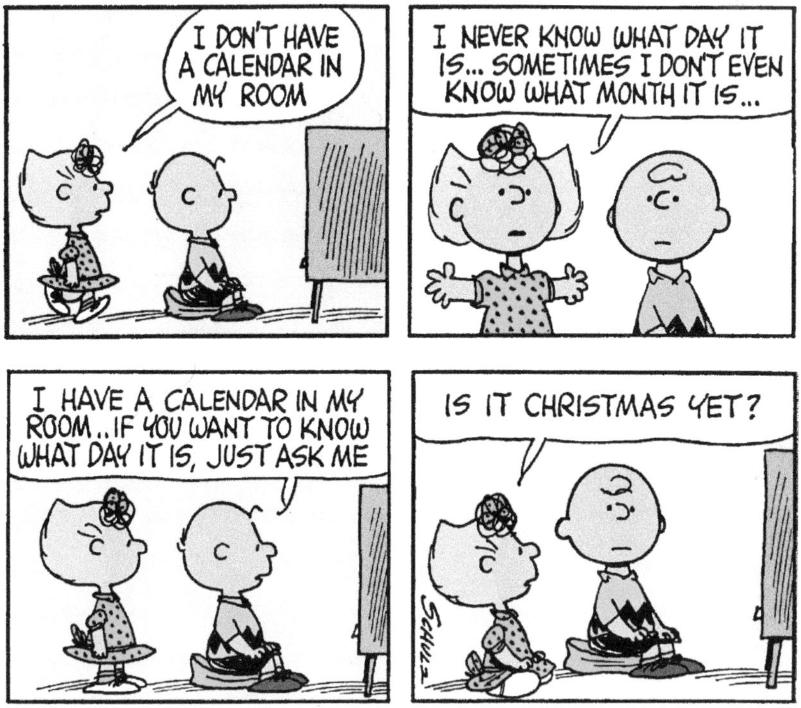
I DON'T HAVE A CALENDAR IN MY ROOM
I NEVER KNOW WHAT DAY IT IS... SOMETIMES I DON'T EVEN KNOW WHAT MONTH IT IS...
I HAVE A CALENDAR IN MY ROOM..IF YOU WANT TO KNOW WHAT DAY IT IS, JUST ASK ME
IS IT CHRISTMAS YET?

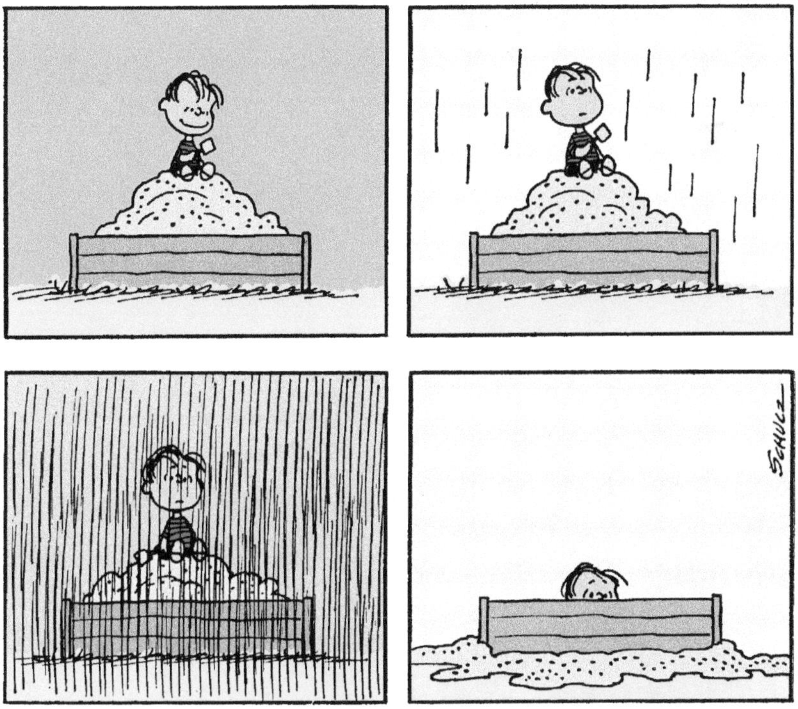

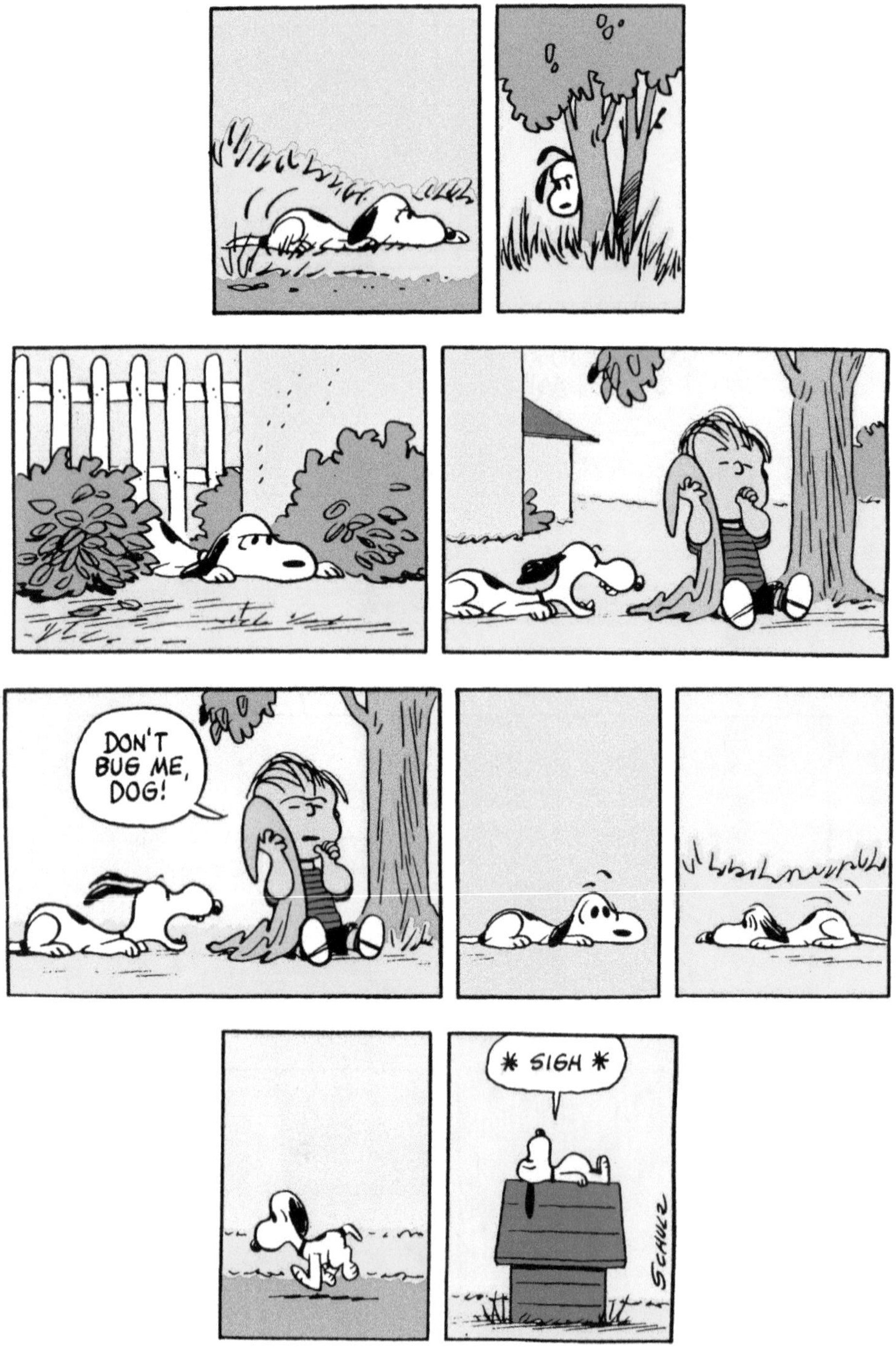
DON'T BUG ME, DOG!
* SIGH *
SCHULZ

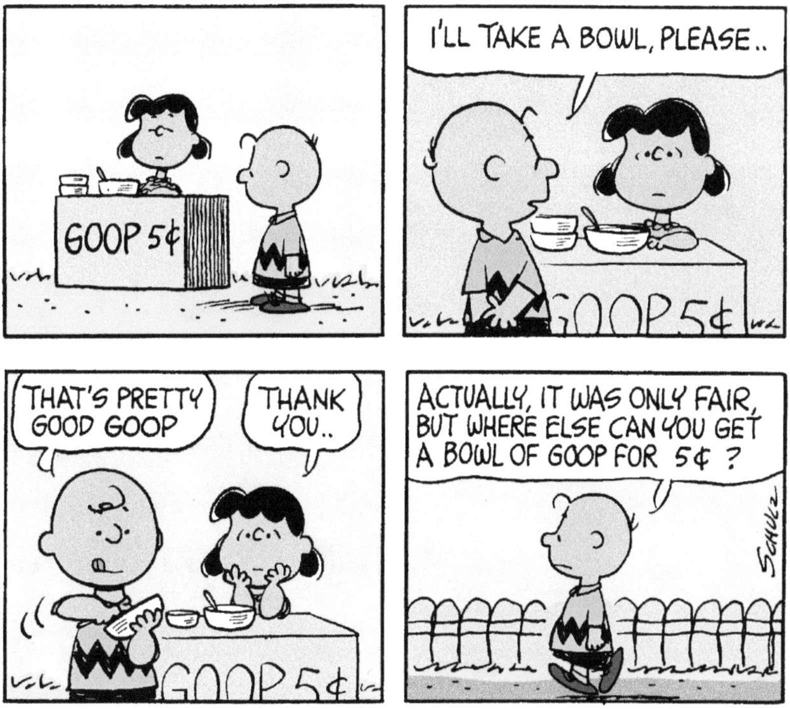
GOOP 5¢
I'LL TAKE A BOWL, PLEASE..
THAT'S PRETTY GOOD GOOP
THANK YOU..
ACTUALLY, IT WAS ONLY FAIR, BUT WHERE ELSE CAN YOU GET A BOWL OF GOOP FOR 5¢ ?
SCHULZ

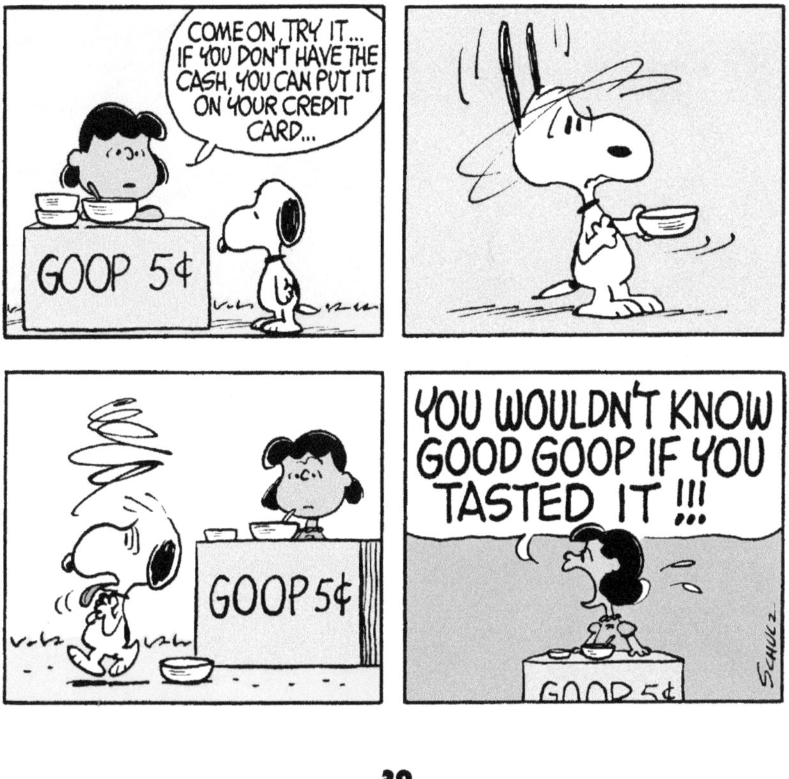
COME ON, TRY IT... IF YOU DON'T HAVE THE CASH, YOU CAN PUT IT ON YOUR CREDIT CARD...
GOOP 5¢
GOOP 5¢
YOU WOULDN'T KNOW GOOD GOOP IF YOU TASTED IT !!!
SCHULZ

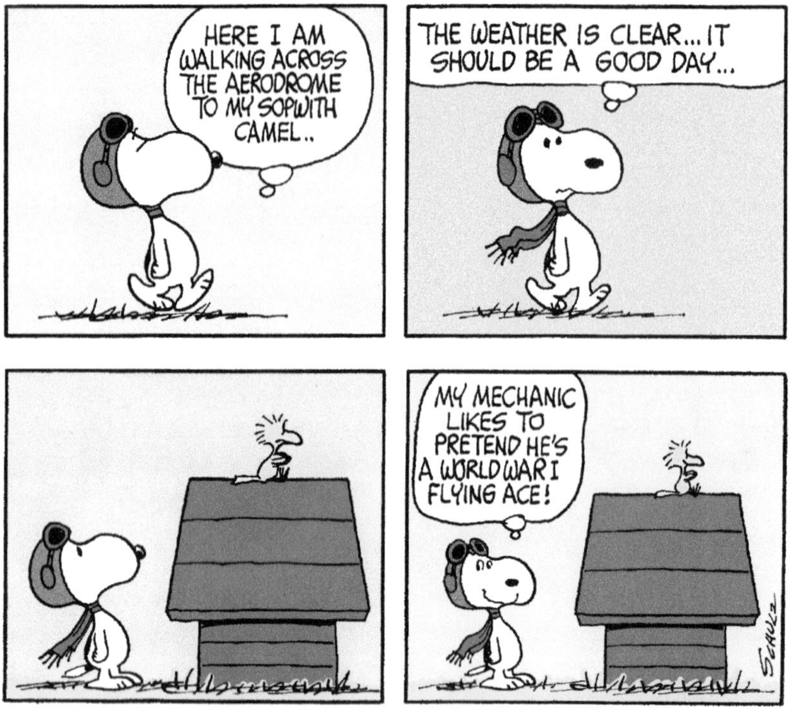
HERE I AM WALKING ACROSS THE AERODROME TO MY SOPWITH CAMEL..
THE WEATHER IS CLEAR... IT SHOULD BE A GOOD DAY...
MY MECHANIC LIKES TO PRETEND HE'S A WORLD WAR I FLYING ACE!
SCHULZ

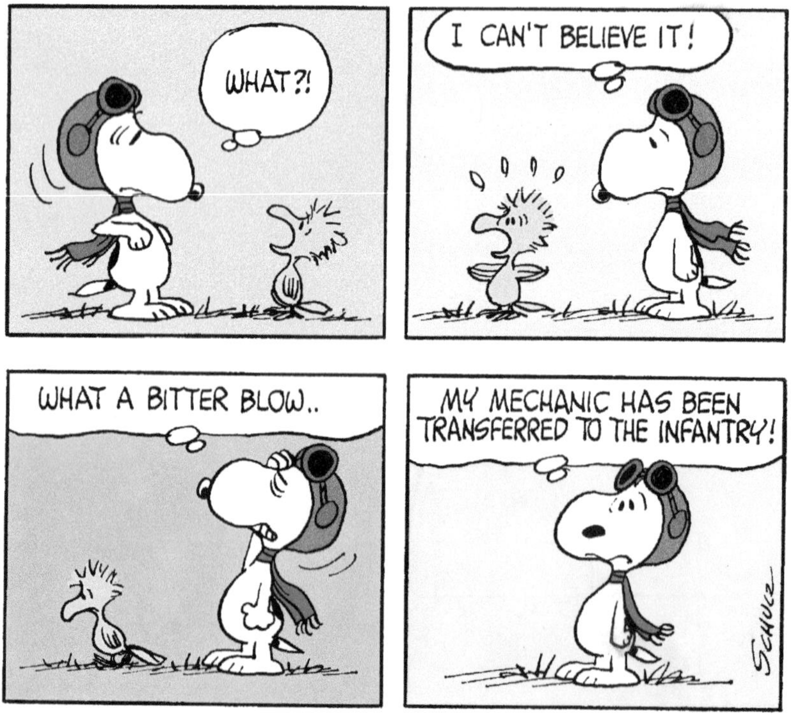
WHAT?!
I CAN'T BELIEVE IT!
WHAT A BITTER BLOW..
MY MECHANIC HAS BEEN TRANSFERRED TO THE INFANTRY!
SCHULZ

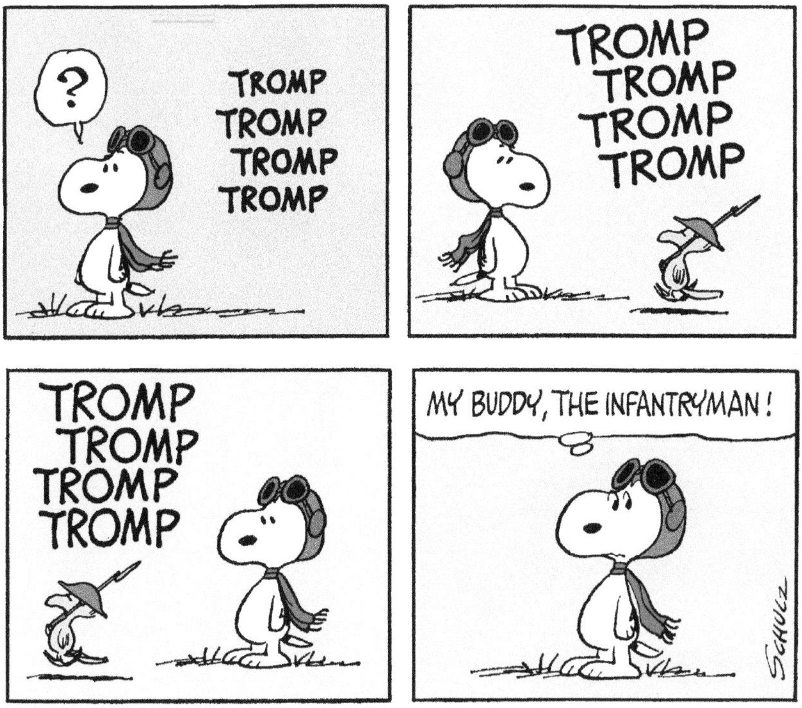
?
TROMP
TROMP
TROMP
TROMP
TROMP
TROMP
TROMP
TROMP
TROMP
TROMP
TROMP
TROMP
MY BUDDY, THE INFANTRYMAN!
SCHULZ

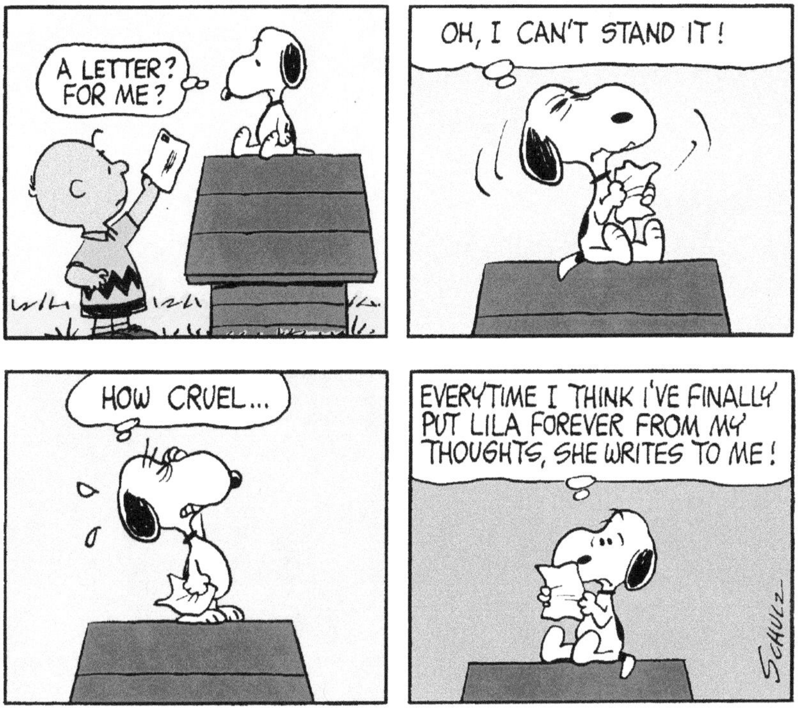
A LETTER? FOR ME?
OH, I CAN'T STAND IT!
HOW CRUEL...
EVERYTIME I THINK I'VE FINALLY PUT LILA FOREVER FROM MY THOUGHTS, SHE WRITES TO ME!
SCHULZ

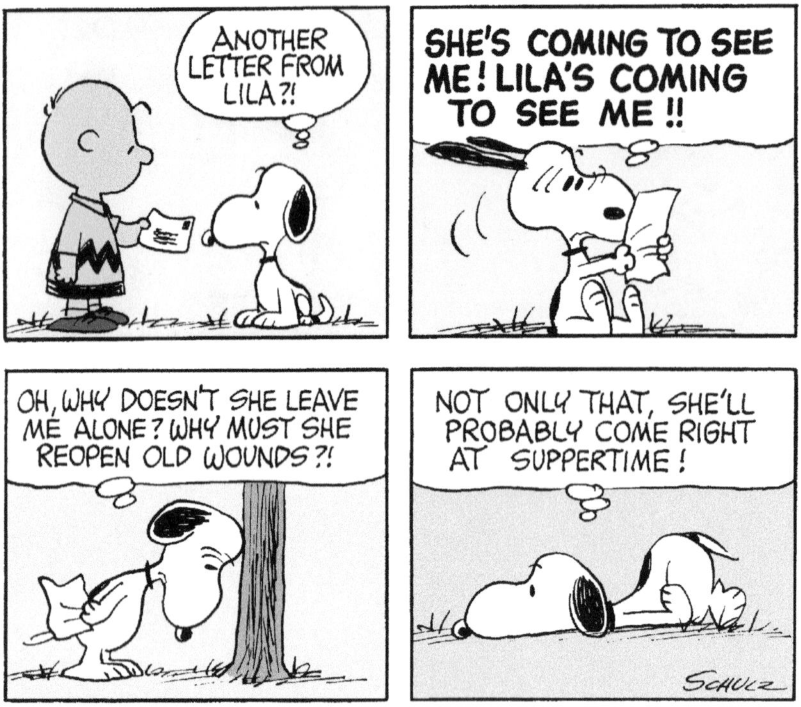
ANOTHER LETTER FROM LILA?!
SHE'S COMING TO SEE ME! LILA'S COMING TO SEE ME!!
OH, WHY DOESN'T SHE LEAVE ME ALONE? WHY MUST SHE REOPEN OLD WOUNDS?!
NOT ONLY THAT, SHE'LL PROBABLY COME RIGHT AT SUPPERTIME!
SCHULZ

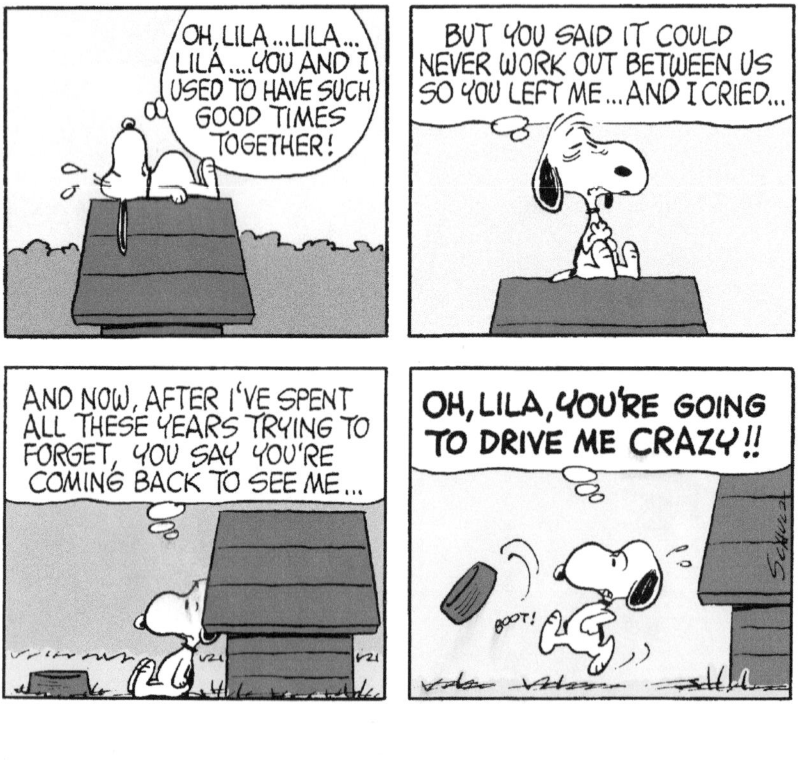
OH, LILA...LILA... LILA....YOU AND I USED TO HAVE SUCH GOOD TIMES TOGETHER!
BUT YOU SAID IT COULD NEVER WORK OUT BETWEEN US SO YOU LEFT ME...AND I CRIED...
AND NOW, AFTER I'VE SPENT ALL THESE YEARS TRYING TO FORGET, YOU SAY YOU'RE COMING BACK TO SEE ME...
OH, LILA, YOU'RE GOING TO DRIVE ME CRAZY!!
BOOT!

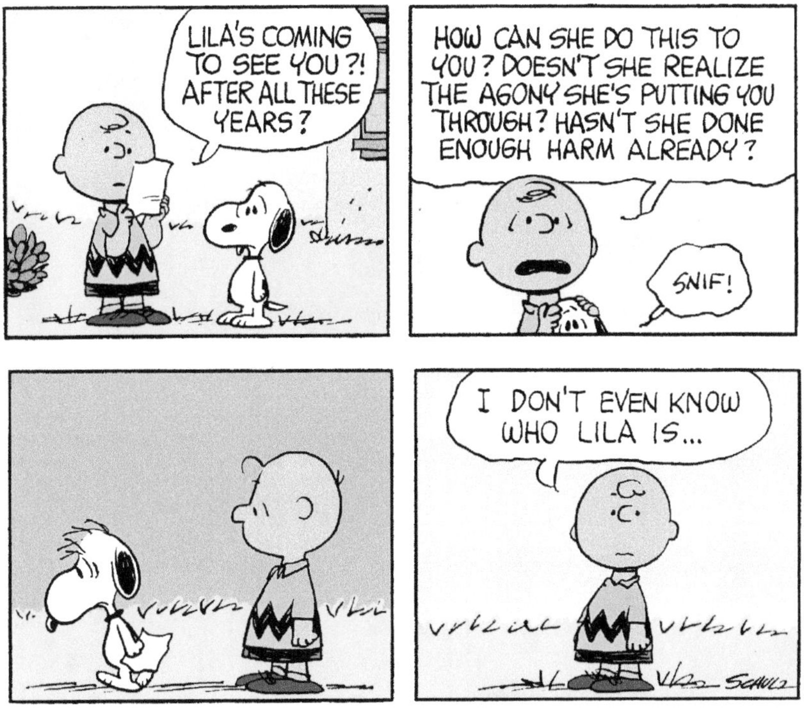
LILA'S COMING TO SEE YOU?! AFTER ALL THESE YEARS?
HOW CAN SHE DO THIS TO YOU? DOESN'T SHE REALIZE THE AGONY SHE'S PUTTING YOU THROUGH? HASN'T SHE DONE ENOUGH HARM ALREADY?
SNIF!
I DON'T EVEN KNOW WHO LILA IS...
SCHULZ

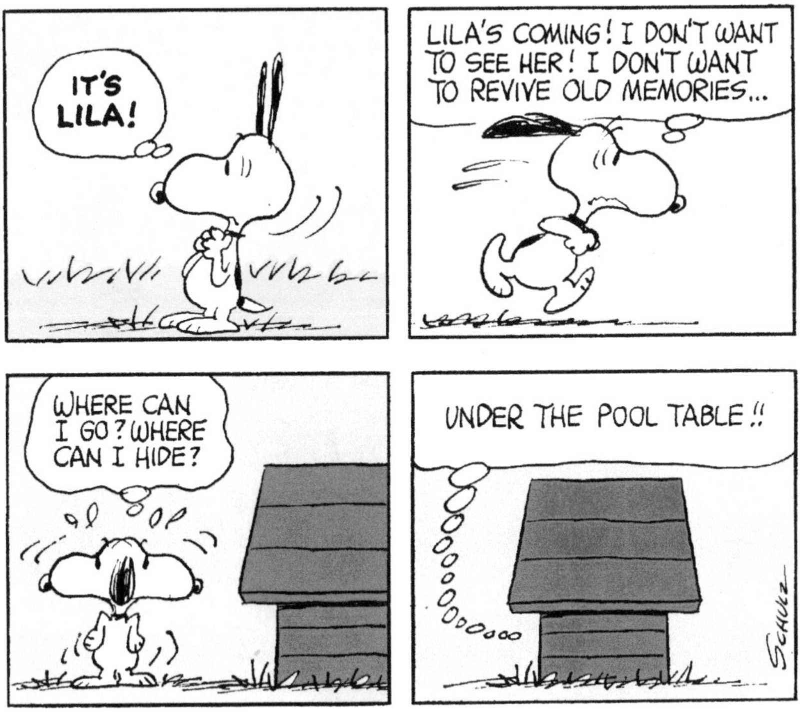
IT'S LILA!
LILA'S COMING! I DON'T WANT TO SEE HER! I DON'T WANT TO REVIVE OLD MEMORIES...
WHERE CAN I GO? WHERE CAN I HIDE?
UNDER THE POOL TABLE!!
SCHULZ

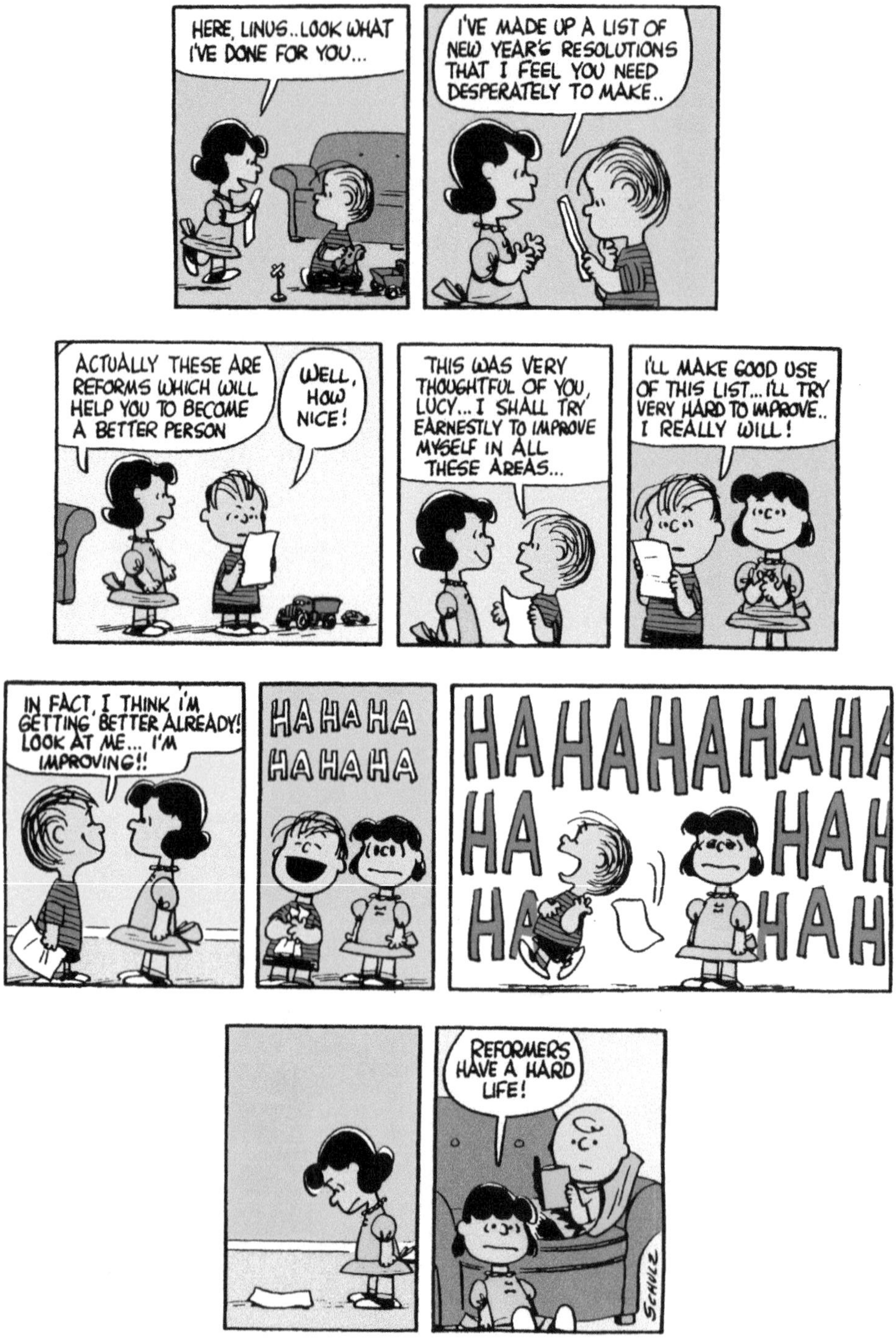
HERE, LINUS..LOOK WHAT I'VE DONE FOR YOU...
I'VE MADE UP A LIST OF NEW YEAR'S RESOLUTIONS THAT I FEEL YOU NEED DESPERATELY TO MAKE..
ACTUALLY THESE ARE REFORMS WHICH WILL HELP YOU TO BECOME A BETTER PERSON
WELL, HOW NICE!
THIS WAS VERY THOUGHTFUL OF YOU, LUCY...I SHALL TRY EARNESTLY TO IMPROVE MYSELF IN ALL THESE AREAS...
I'LL MAKE GOOD USE OF THIS LIST...I'LL TRY VERY HARD TO IMPROVE.. I REALLY WILL!
IN FACT, I THINK I'M GETTING BETTER ALREADY! LOOK AT ME... I'M IMPROVING!!
HA HA HA
HA HA HA
HAHAHAHAHAHA
HA HAH
HA HAH
REFORMERS HAVE A HARD LIFE!
SCHULZ

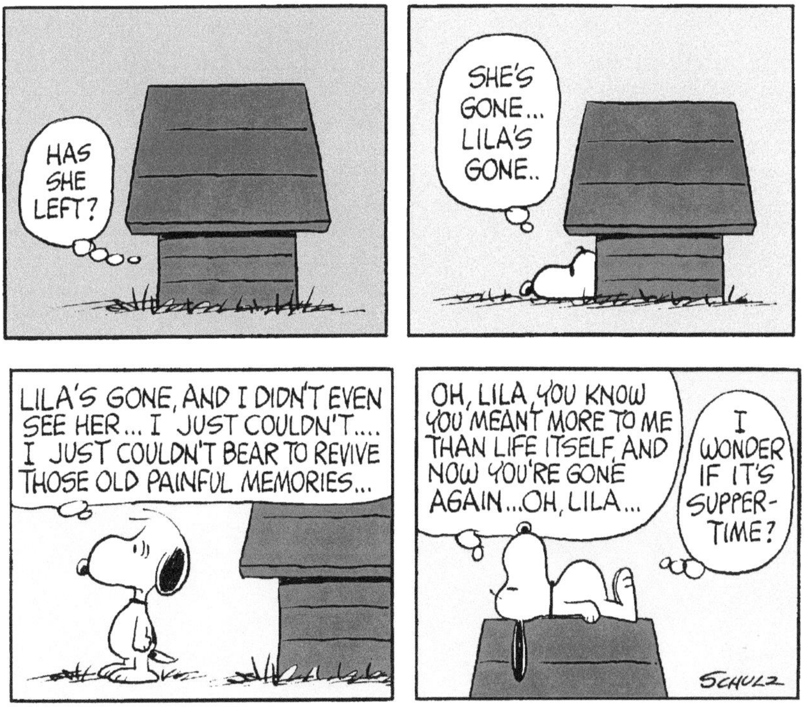
HAS SHE LEFT?
SHE'S GONE... LILA'S GONE..
LILA'S GONE, AND I DIDN'T EVEN SEE HER... I JUST COULDN'T.... I JUST COULDN'T BEAR TO REVIVE THOSE OLD PAINFUL MEMORIES...
OH, LILA, YOU KNOW YOU MEANT MORE TO ME THAN LIFE ITSELF, AND NOW YOU'RE GONE AGAIN...OH, LILA...
I WONDER IF IT'S SUPPER-TIME?
SCHULZ

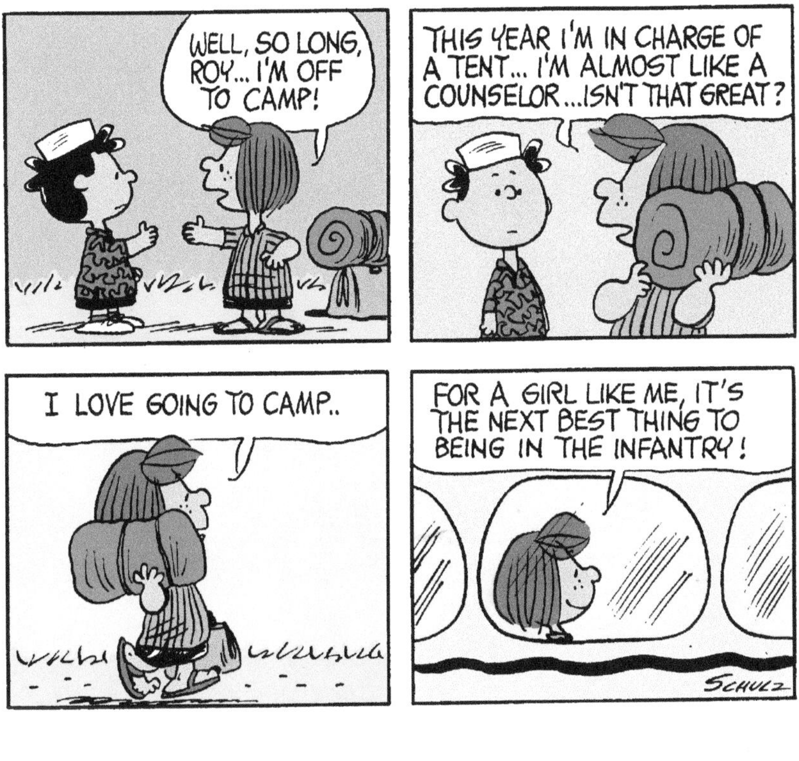
WELL, SO LONG, ROY... I'M OFF TO CAMP!
THIS YEAR I'M IN CHARGE OF A TENT... I'M ALMOST LIKE A COUNSELOR...ISN'T THAT GREAT?
I LOVE GOING TO CAMP..
FOR A GIRL LIKE ME, IT'S THE NEXT BEST THING TO BEING IN THE INFANTRY!
SCHULZ

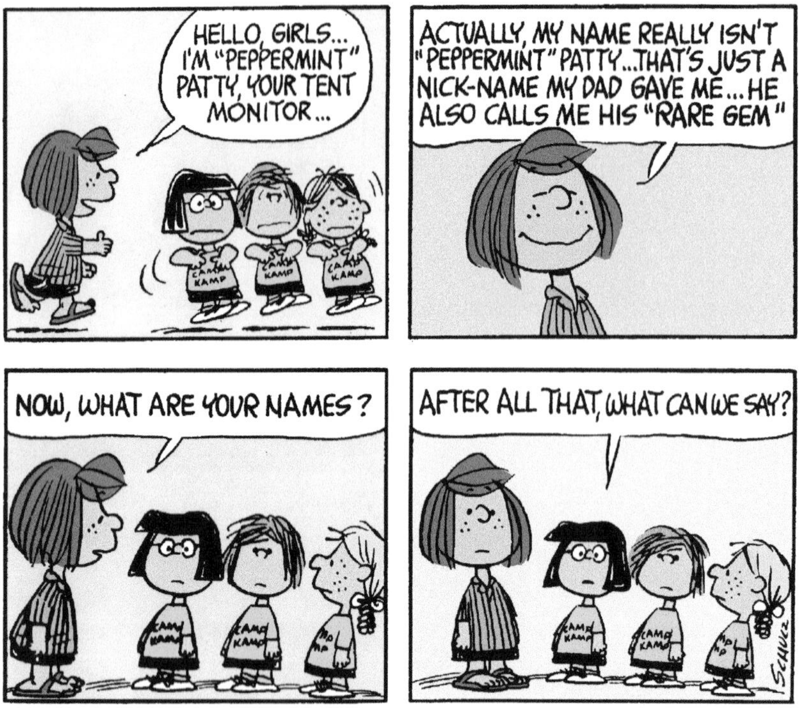
HELLO, GIRLS... I'M "PEPPERMINT" PATTY, YOUR TENT MONITOR...
ACTUALLY, MY NAME REALLY ISN'T "PEPPERMINT" PATTY...THAT'S JUST A NICK-NAME MY DAD GAVE ME...HE ALSO CALLS ME HIS "RARE GEM"
NOW, WHAT ARE YOUR NAMES?
AFTER ALL THAT, WHAT CAN WE SAY?

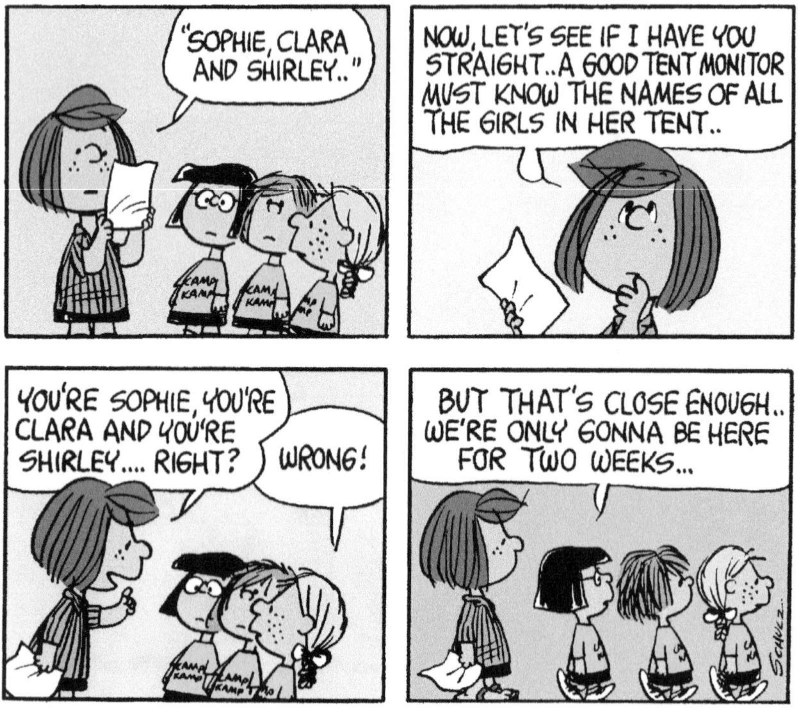
"SOPHIE, CLARA AND SHIRLEY.."
NOW, LET'S SEE IF I HAVE YOU STRAIGHT..A GOOD TENT MONITOR MUST KNOW THE NAMES OF ALL THE GIRLS IN HER TENT..
YOU'RE SOPHIE, YOU'RE CLARA AND YOU'RE SHIRLEY.... RIGHT?
WRONG!
BUT THAT'S CLOSE ENOUGH.. WE'RE ONLY GONNA BE HERE FOR TWO WEEKS...

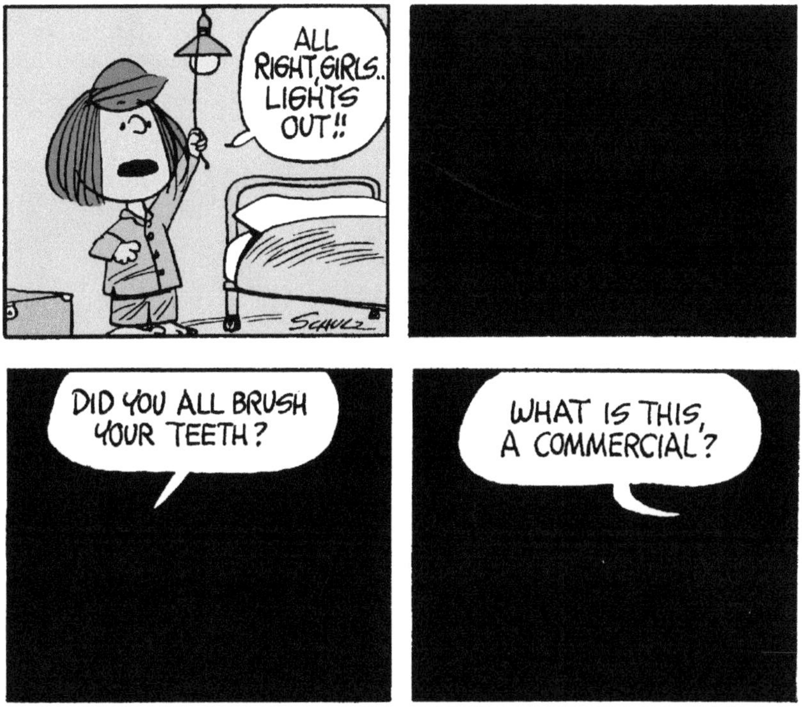
ALL RIGHT, GIRLS.. LIGHTS OUT!!
DID YOU ALL BRUSH YOUR TEETH?
WHAT IS THIS, A COMMERCIAL?

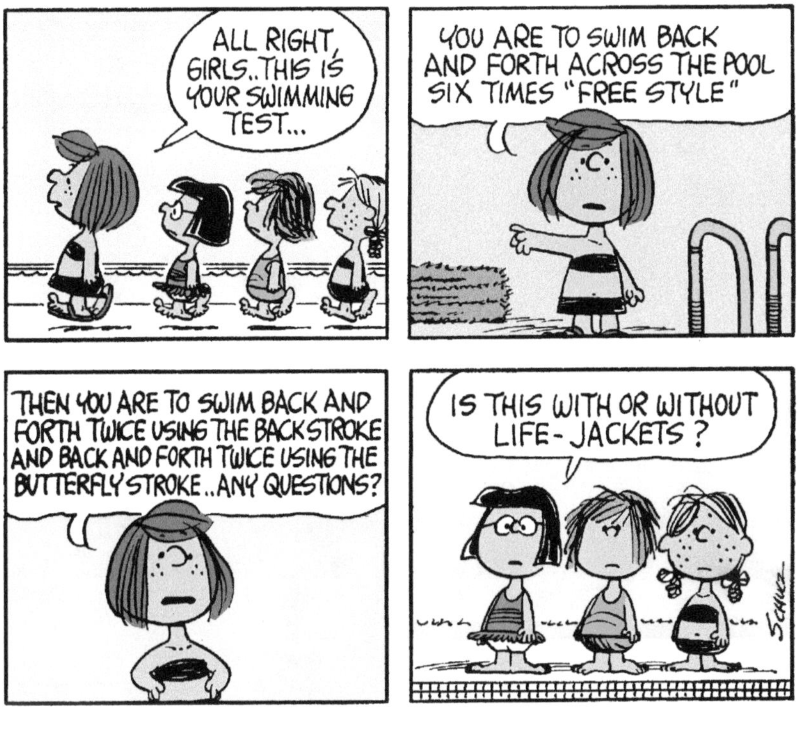
ALL RIGHT, GIRLS..THIS IS YOUR SWIMMING TEST...
YOU ARE TO SWIM BACK AND FORTH ACROSS THE POOL SIX TIMES "FREE STYLE"
THEN YOU ARE TO SWIM BACK AND FORTH TWICE USING THE BACKSTROKE AND BACK AND FORTH TWICE USING THE BUTTERFLY STROKE..ANY QUESTIONS?
IS THIS WITH OR WITHOUT LIFE-JACKETS?

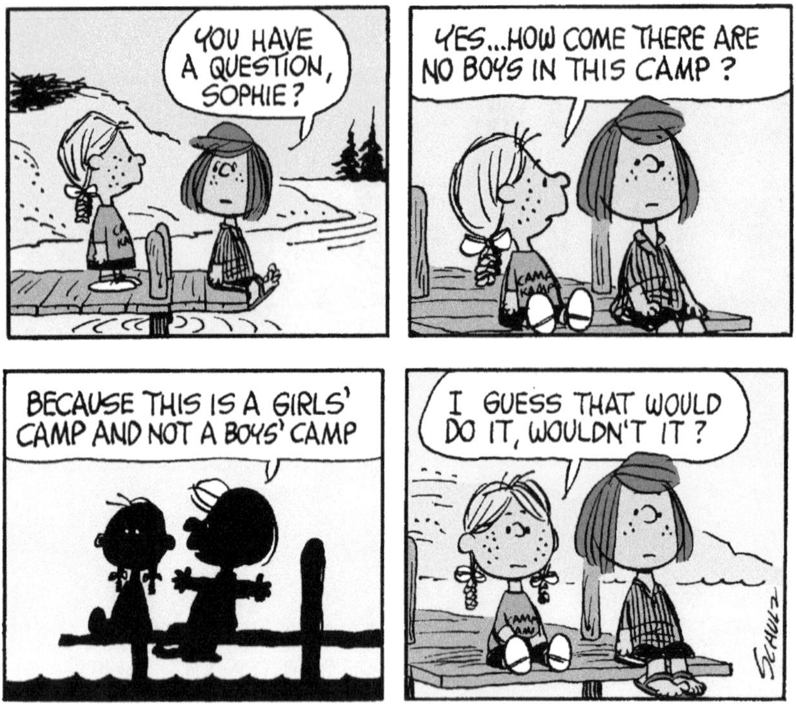
YOU HAVE A QUESTION, SOPHIE?
YES...HOW COME THERE ARE NO BOYS IN THIS CAMP ?
BECAUSE THIS IS A GIRLS' CAMP AND NOT A BOYS' CAMP
I GUESS THAT WOULD DO IT, WOULDN'T IT ?
SCHULZ

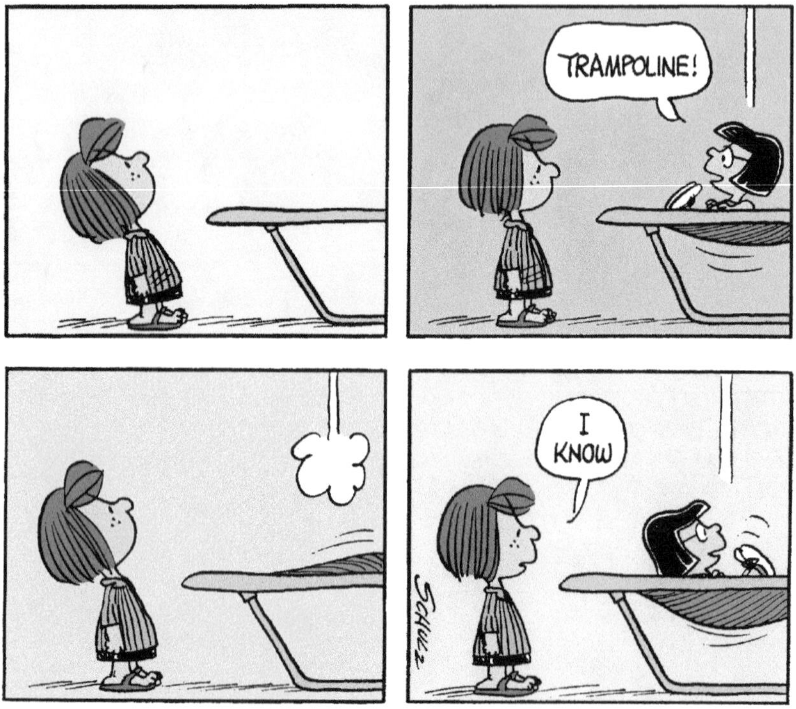
TRAMPOLINE!
I KNOW
SCHULZ

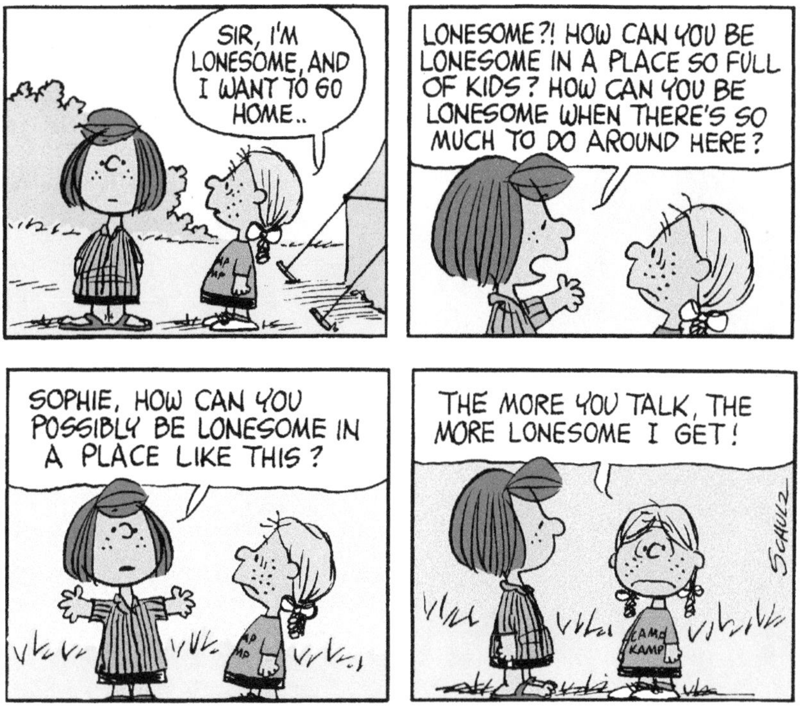
SIR, I'M LONESOME, AND I WANT TO GO HOME..
LONESOME?! HOW CAN YOU BE LONESOME IN A PLACE SO FULL OF KIDS? HOW CAN YOU BE LONESOME WHEN THERE'S SO MUCH TO DO AROUND HERE?
SOPHIE, HOW CAN YOU POSSIBLY BE LONESOME IN A PLACE LIKE THIS?
THE MORE YOU TALK, THE MORE LONESOME I GET!

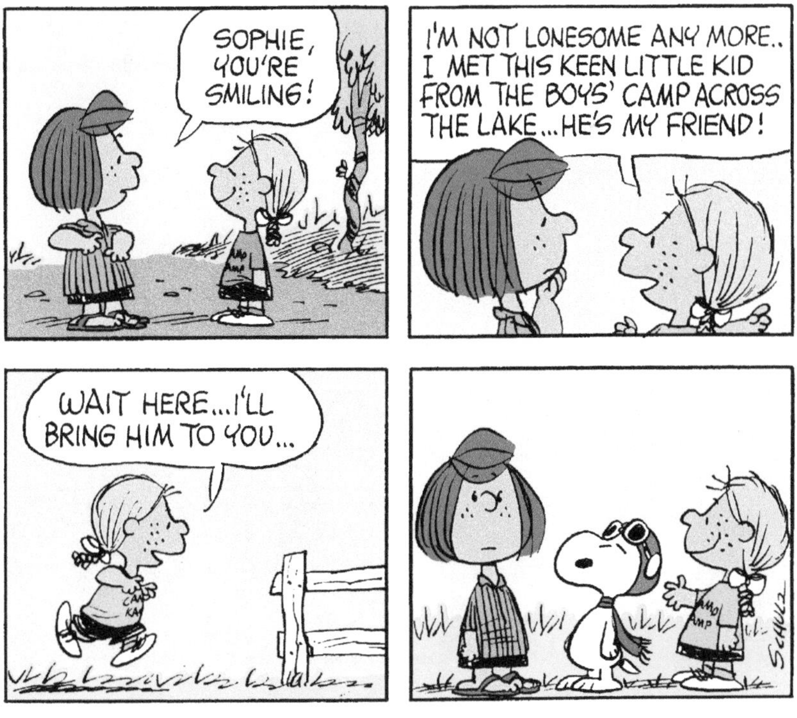
SOPHIE, YOU'RE SMILING!
I'M NOT LONESOME ANY MORE.. I MET THIS KEEN LITTLE KID FROM THE BOYS' CAMP ACROSS THE LAKE...HE'S MY FRIEND!
WAIT HERE...I'LL BRING HIM TO YOU...

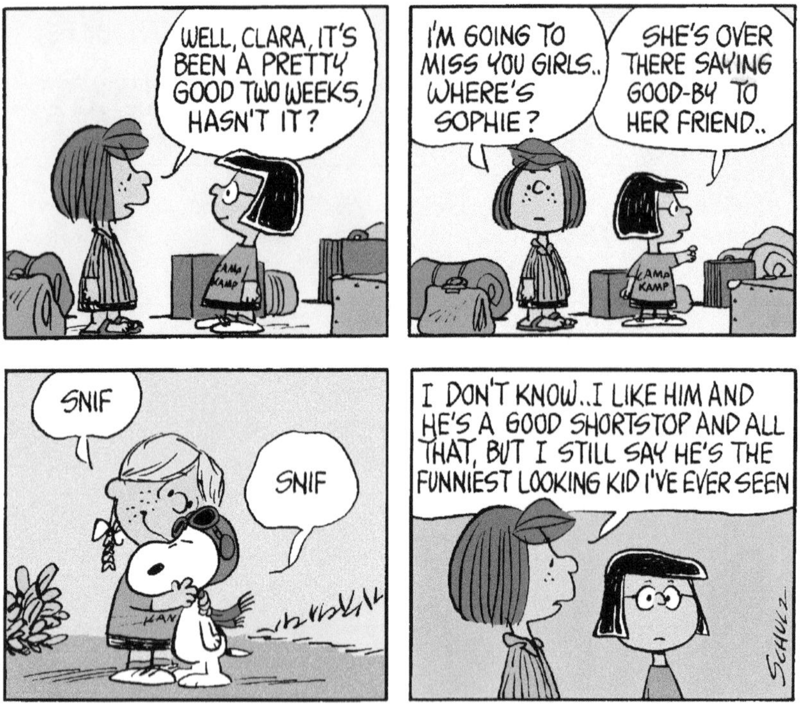
WELL, CLARA, IT'S BEEN A PRETTY GOOD TWO WEEKS, HASN'T IT?
I'M GOING TO MISS YOU GIRLS.. WHERE'S SOPHIE?
SHE'S OVER THERE SAYING GOOD-BY TO HER FRIEND..
SNIF
SNIF
I DON'T KNOW..I LIKE HIM AND HE'S A GOOD SHORTSTOP AND ALL THAT, BUT I STILL SAY HE'S THE FUNNIEST LOOKING KID I'VE EVER SEEN
SCHULZ

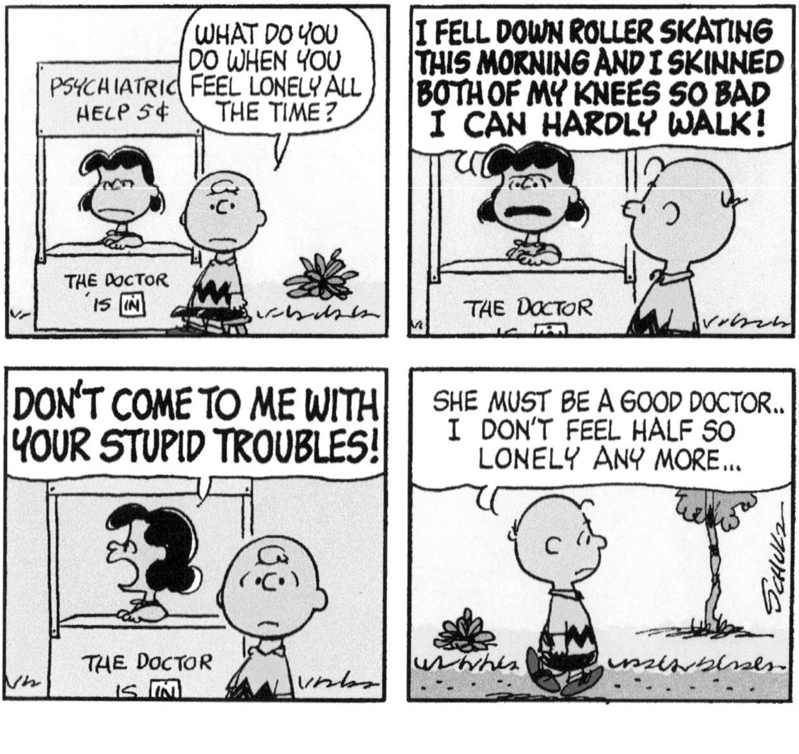
PSYCHIATRIC HELP 5¢
WHAT DO YOU DO WHEN YOU FEEL LONELY ALL THE TIME?
THE DOCTOR IS IN
I FELL DOWN ROLLER SKATING THIS MORNING AND I SKINNED BOTH OF MY KNEES SO BAD I CAN HARDLY WALK!
THE DOCTOR
DON'T COME TO ME WITH YOUR STUPID TROUBLES!
THE DOCTOR IS IN
SHE MUST BE A GOOD DOCTOR.. I DON'T FEEL HALF SO LONELY ANY MORE...
SCHULZ

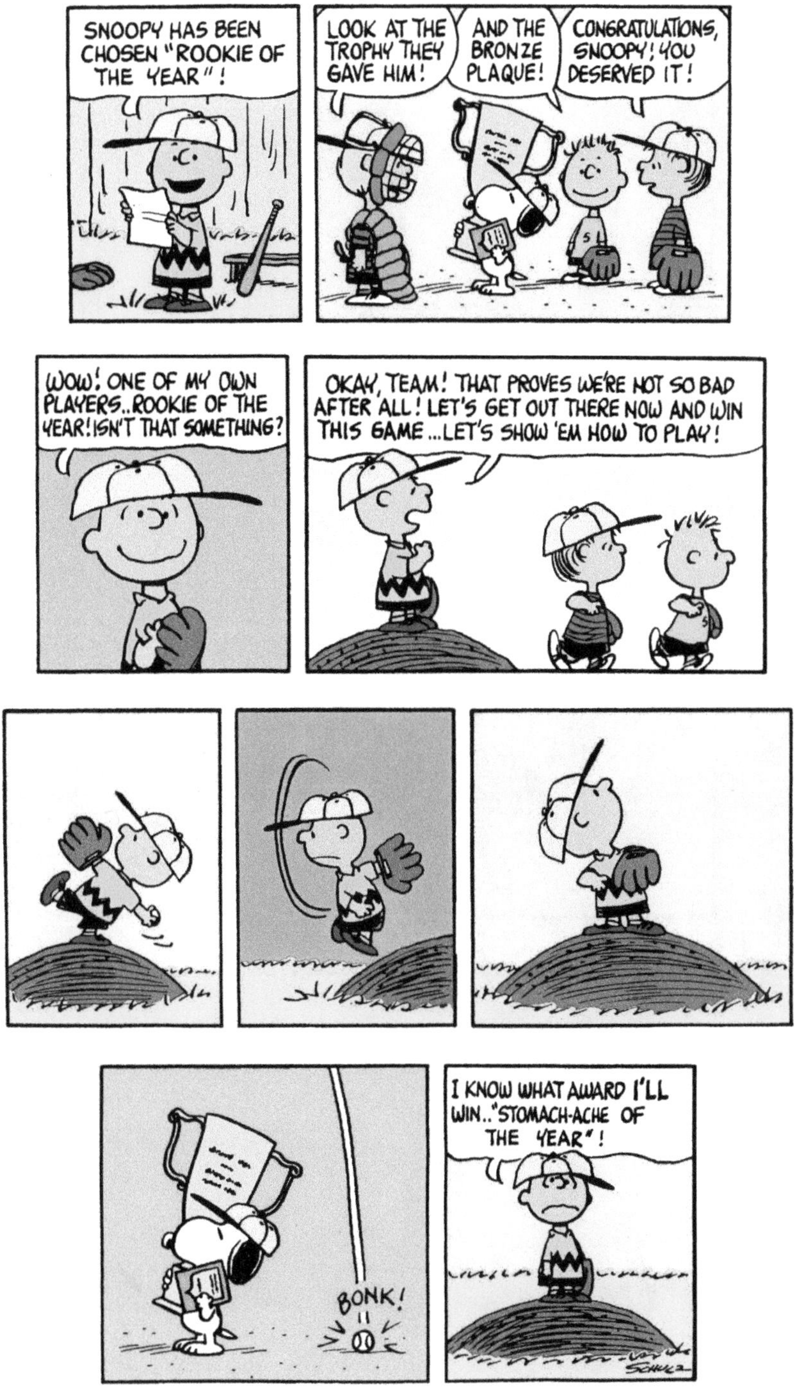
SNOOPY HAS BEEN CHOSEN "ROOKIE OF THE YEAR"!
LOOK AT THE TROPHY THEY GAVE HIM!
AND THE BRONZE PLAQUE!
CONGRATULATIONS, SNOOPY! YOU DESERVED IT!
WOW! ONE OF MY OWN PLAYERS..ROOKIE OF THE YEAR! ISN'T THAT SOMETHING?
OKAY, TEAM! THAT PROVES WE'RE NOT SO BAD AFTER ALL! LET'S GET OUT THERE NOW AND WIN THIS GAME...LET'S SHOW 'EM HOW TO PLAY!
BONK!
I KNOW WHAT AWARD I'LL WIN.."STOMACH-ACHE OF THE YEAR"!
SCHULZ

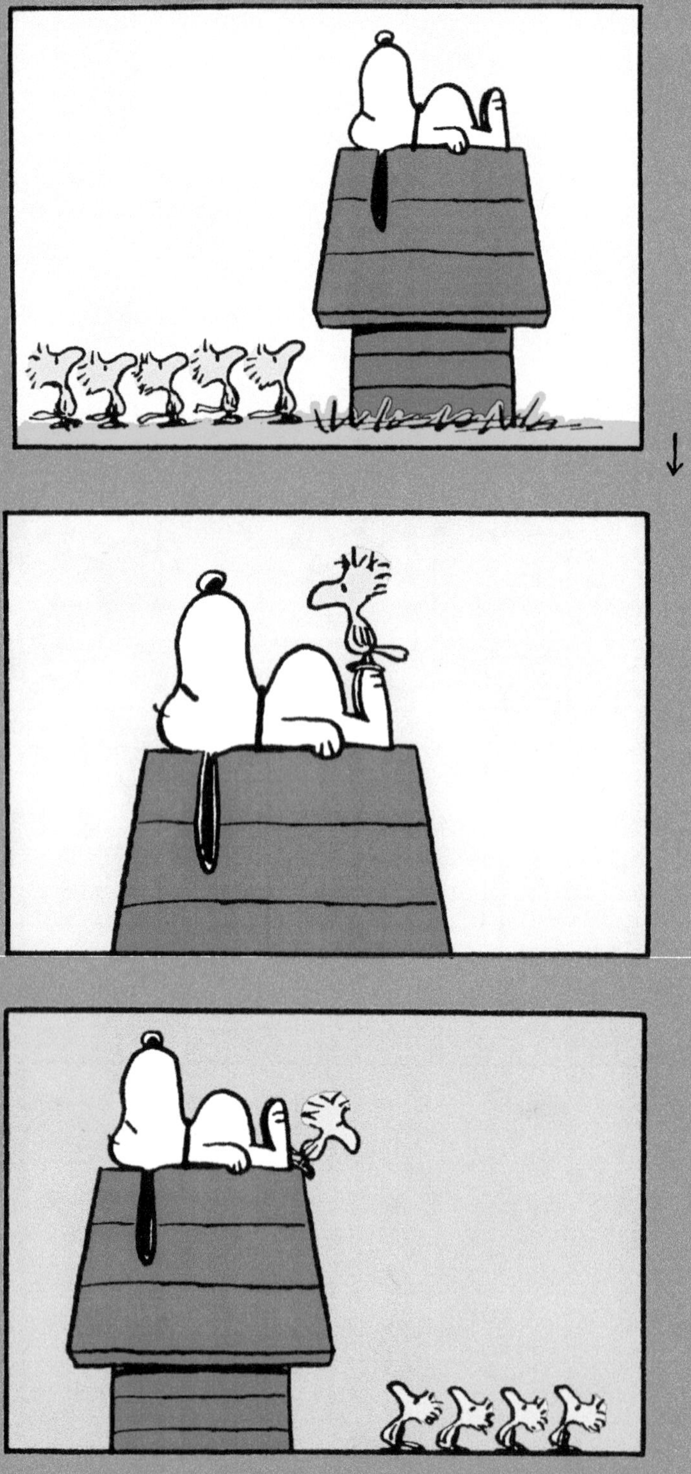

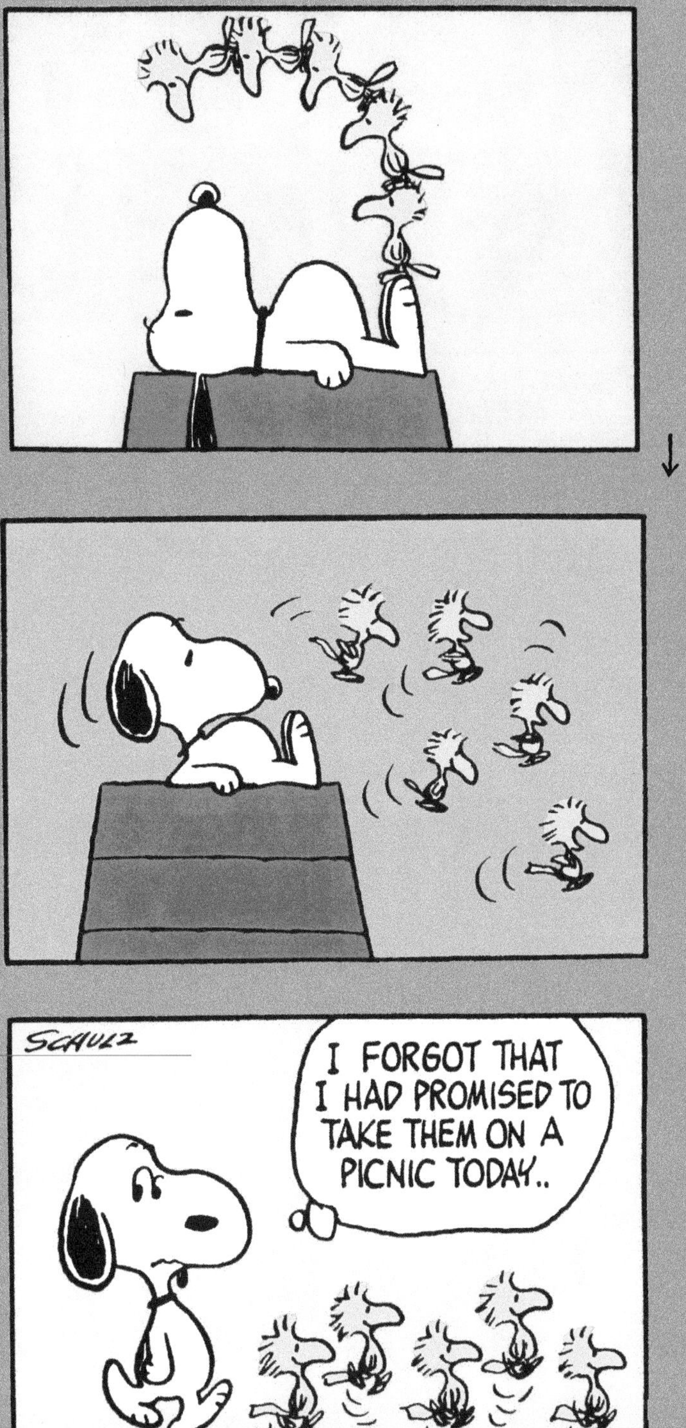
SCHULZ
I FORGOT THAT I HAD PROMISED TO TAKE THEM ON A PICNIC TODAY..

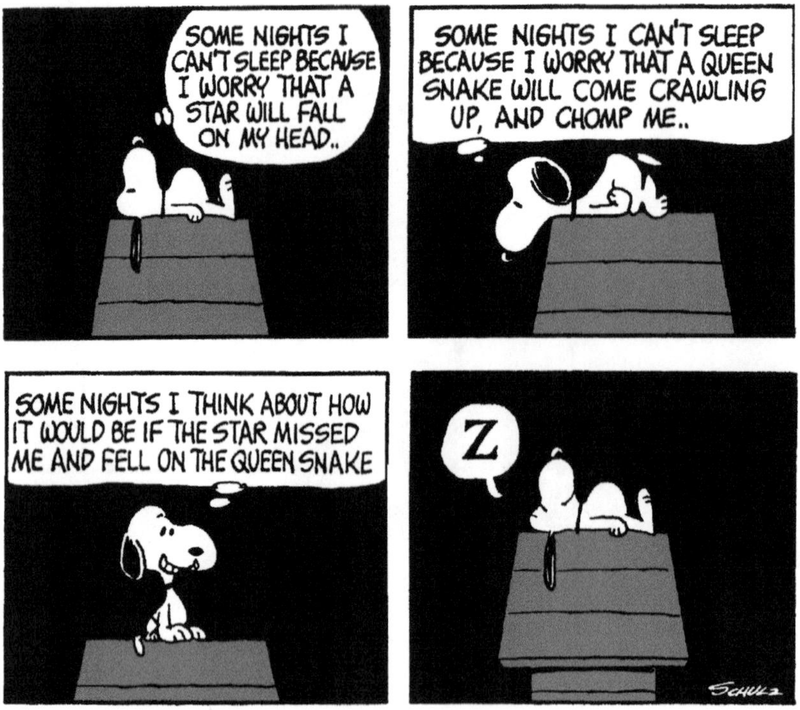
SOME NIGHTS I CAN'T SLEEP BECAUSE I WORRY THAT A STAR WILL FALL ON MY HEAD..
SOME NIGHTS I CAN'T SLEEP BECAUSE I WORRY THAT A QUEEN SNAKE WILL COME CRAWLING UP, AND CHOMP ME..
SOME NIGHTS I THINK ABOUT HOW IT WOULD BE IF THE STAR MISSED ME AND FELL ON THE QUEEN SNAKE
Z

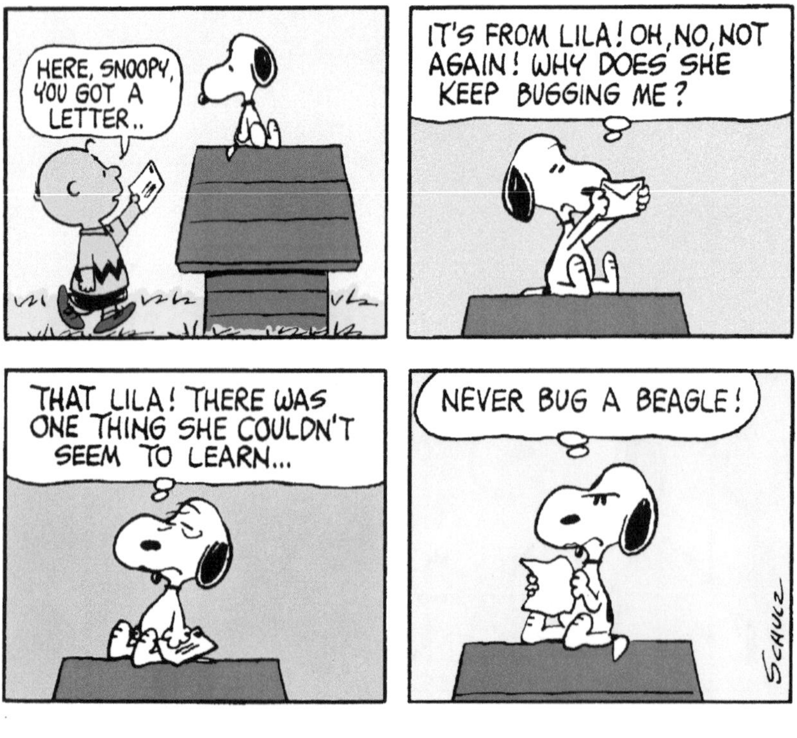
HERE, SNOOPY, YOU GOT A LETTER..
IT'S FROM LILA! OH, NO, NOT AGAIN! WHY DOES SHE KEEP BUGGING ME?
THAT LILA! THERE WAS ONE THING SHE COULDN'T SEEM TO LEARN...
NEVER BUG A BEAGLE!

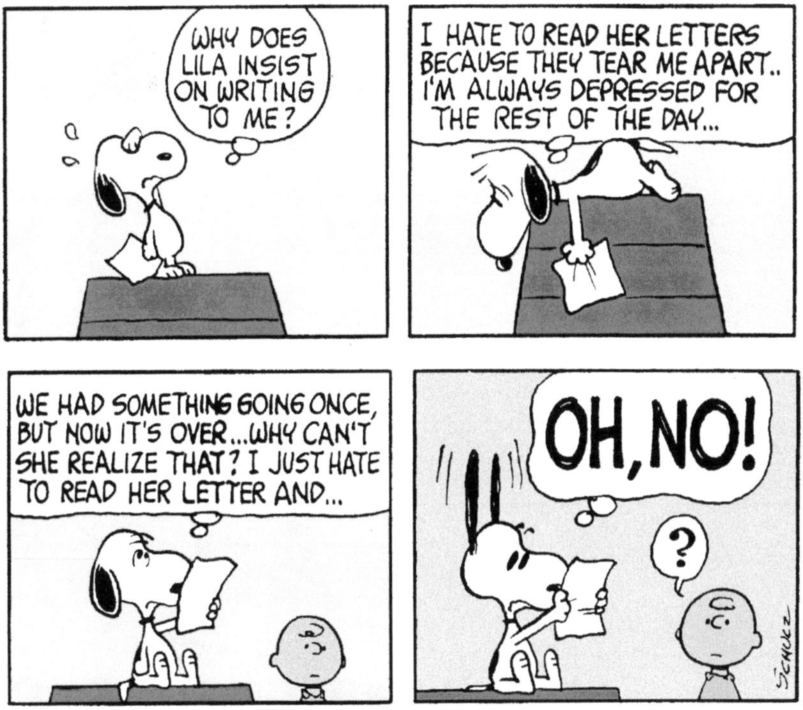
WHY DOES LILA INSIST ON WRITING TO ME?
I HATE TO READ HER LETTERS BECAUSE THEY TEAR ME APART.. I'M ALWAYS DEPRESSED FOR THE REST OF THE DAY...
WE HAD SOMETHING GOING ONCE, BUT NOW IT'S OVER...WHY CAN'T SHE REALIZE THAT? I JUST HATE TO READ HER LETTER AND...
OH, NO!
?
SCHULZ

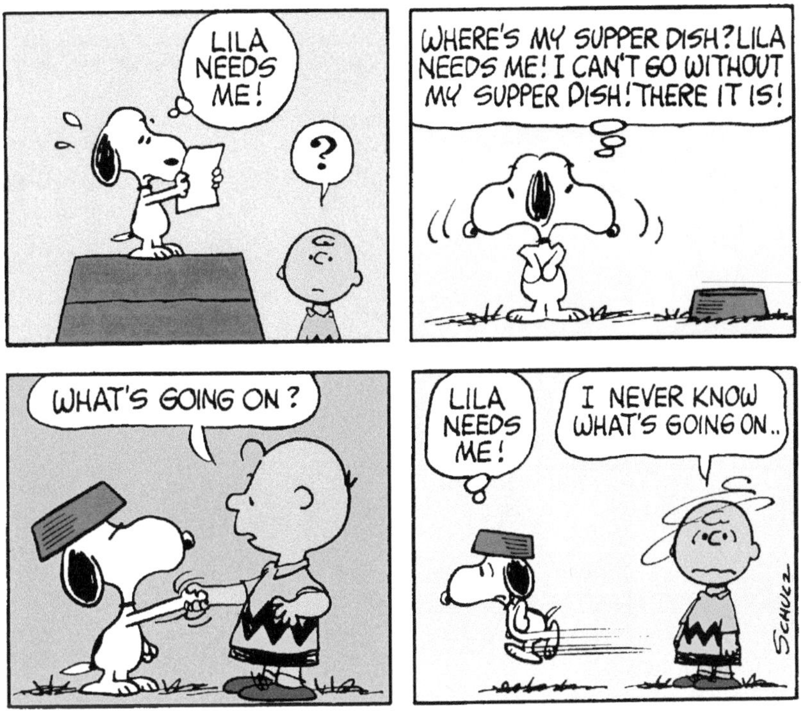
LILA NEEDS ME!
?
WHERE'S MY SUPPER DISH? LILA NEEDS ME! I CAN'T GO WITHOUT MY SUPPER DISH! THERE IT IS!
WHAT'S GOING ON?
LILA NEEDS ME!
I NEVER KNOW WHAT'S GOING ON..
SCHULZ

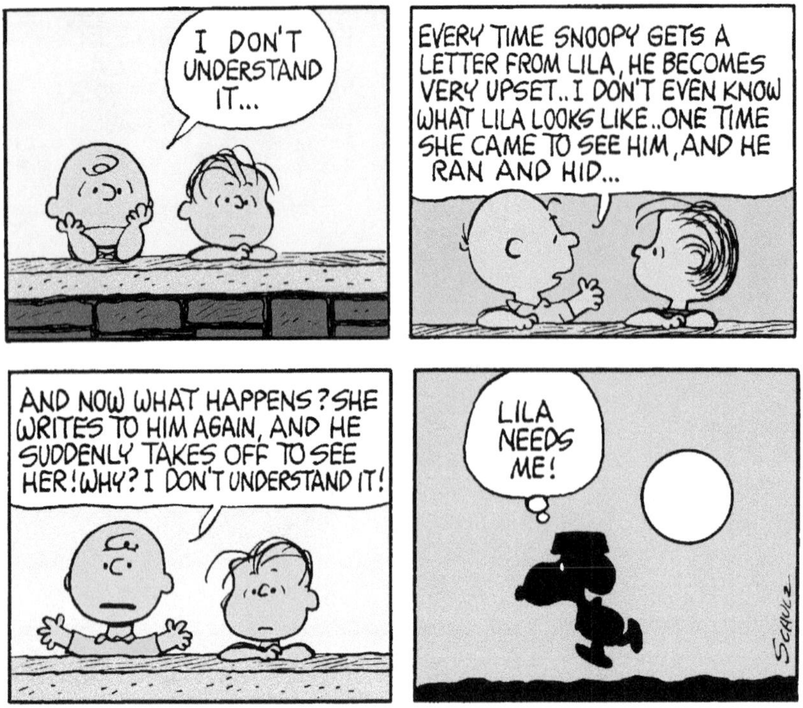
I DON'T UNDERSTAND IT...
EVERY TIME SNOOPY GETS A LETTER FROM LILA, HE BECOMES VERY UPSET.. I DON'T EVEN KNOW WHAT LILA LOOKS LIKE..ONE TIME SHE CAME TO SEE HIM, AND HE RAN AND HID...
AND NOW WHAT HAPPENS? SHE WRITES TO HIM AGAIN, AND HE SUDDENLY TAKES OFF TO SEE HER! WHY? I DON'T UNDERSTAND IT!
LILA NEEDS ME!
SCHULZ

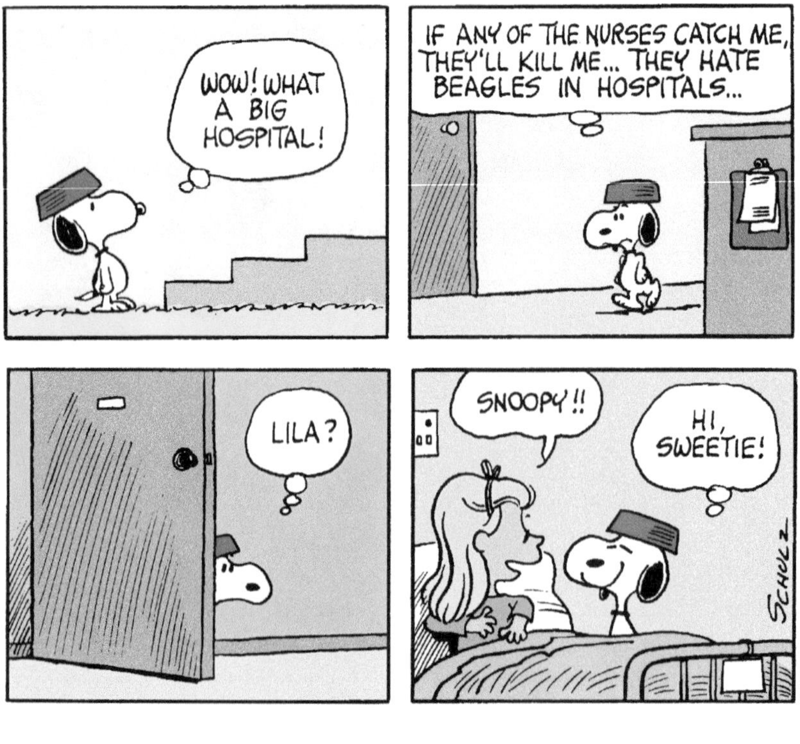
WOW! WHAT A BIG HOSPITAL!
IF ANY OF THE NURSES CATCH ME, THEY'LL KILL ME... THEY HATE BEAGLES IN HOSPITALS...
LILA?
SNOOPY!!
HI, SWEETIE!
SCHULZ

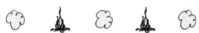

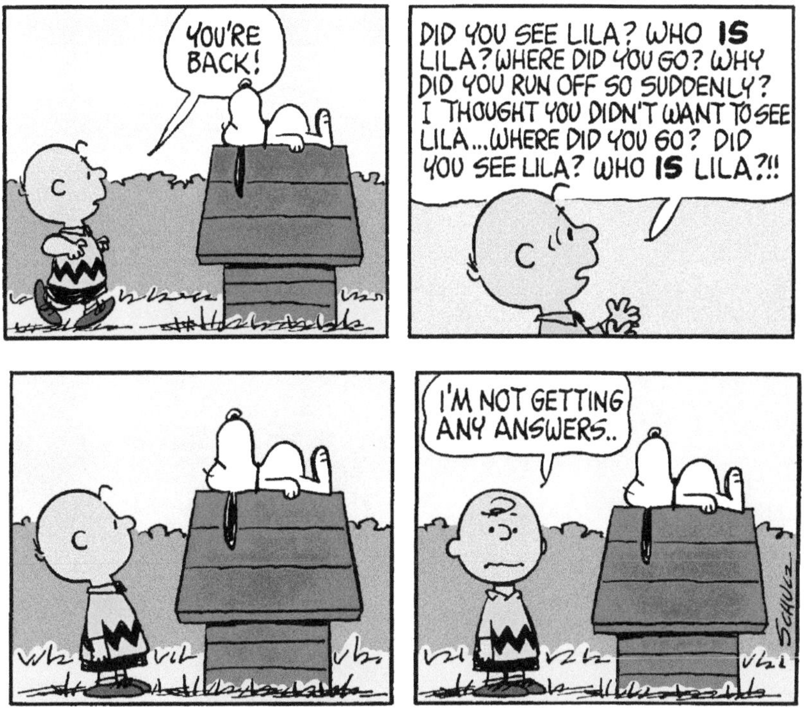
YOU'RE BACK!
DID YOU SEE LILA? WHO IS LILA? WHERE DID YOU GO? WHY DID YOU RUN OFF SO SUDDENLY? I THOUGHT YOU DIDN'T WANT TO SEE LILA...WHERE DID YOU GO? DID YOU SEE LILA? WHO IS LILA?!!
I'M NOT GETTING ANY ANSWERS..
SCHULZ

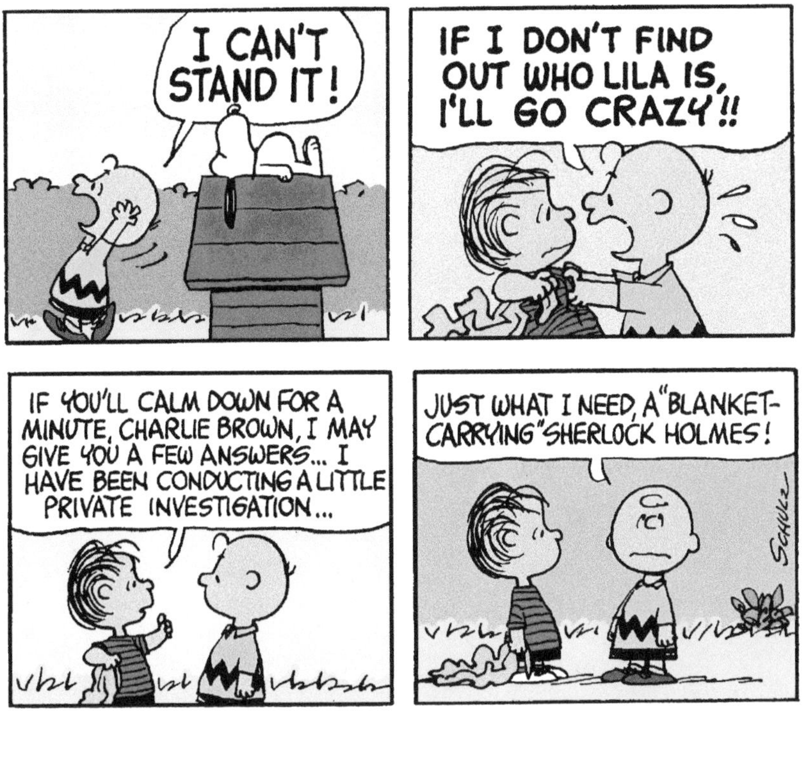
I CAN'T STAND IT!
IF I DON'T FIND OUT WHO LILA IS, I'LL GO CRAZY!!
IF YOU'LL CALM DOWN FOR A MINUTE, CHARLIE BROWN, I MAY GIVE YOU A FEW ANSWERS... I HAVE BEEN CONDUCTING A LITTLE PRIVATE INVESTIGATION...
JUST WHAT I NEED, A "BLANKET-CARRYING" SHERLOCK HOLMES!
SCHULZ

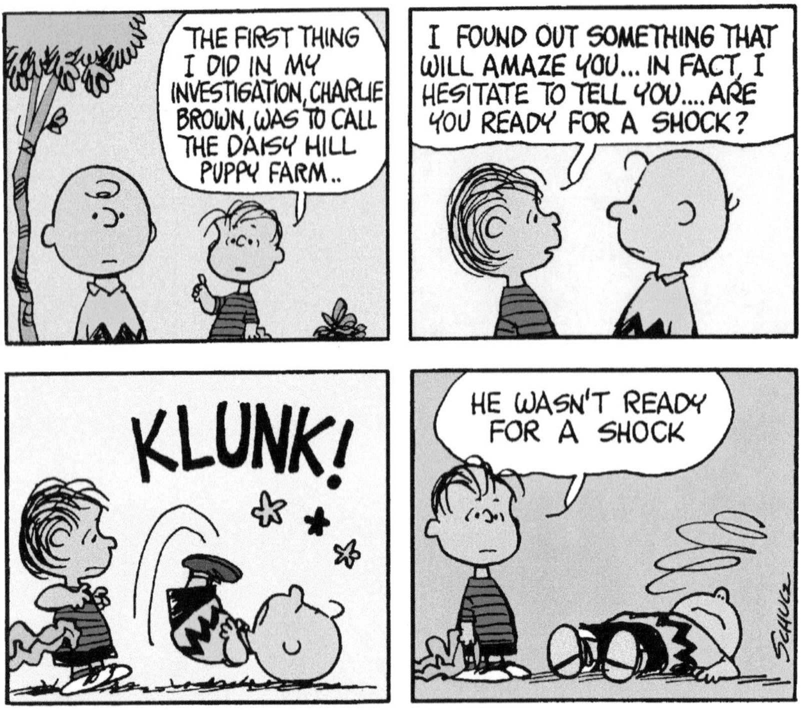
THE FIRST THING I DID IN MY INVESTIGATION, CHARLIE BROWN, WAS TO CALL THE DAISY HILL PUPPY FARM..
I FOUND OUT SOMETHING THAT WILL AMAZE YOU... IN FACT, I HESITATE TO TELL YOU.... ARE YOU READY FOR A SHOCK?
KLUNK!
HE WASN'T READY FOR A SHOCK
SCHULZ

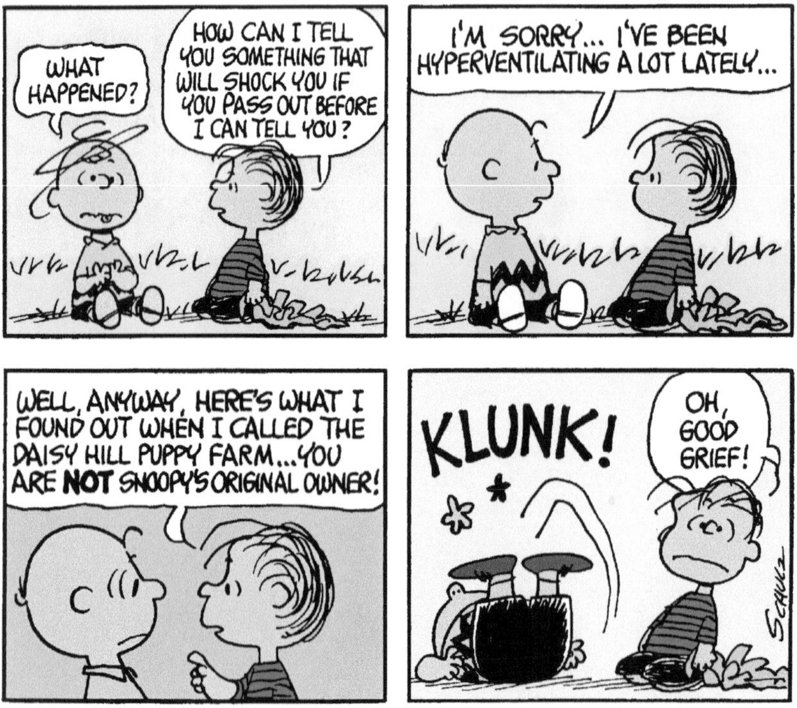
WHAT HAPPENED?
HOW CAN I TELL YOU SOMETHING THAT WILL SHOCK YOU IF YOU PASS OUT BEFORE I CAN TELL YOU?
I'M SORRY... I'VE BEEN HYPERVENTILATING A LOT LATELY...
WELL, ANYWAY, HERE'S WHAT I FOUND OUT WHEN I CALLED THE DAISY HILL PUPPY FARM...YOU ARE NOT SNOOPY'S ORIGINAL OWNER!
KLUNK!
OH, GOOD GRIEF!
SCHULZ

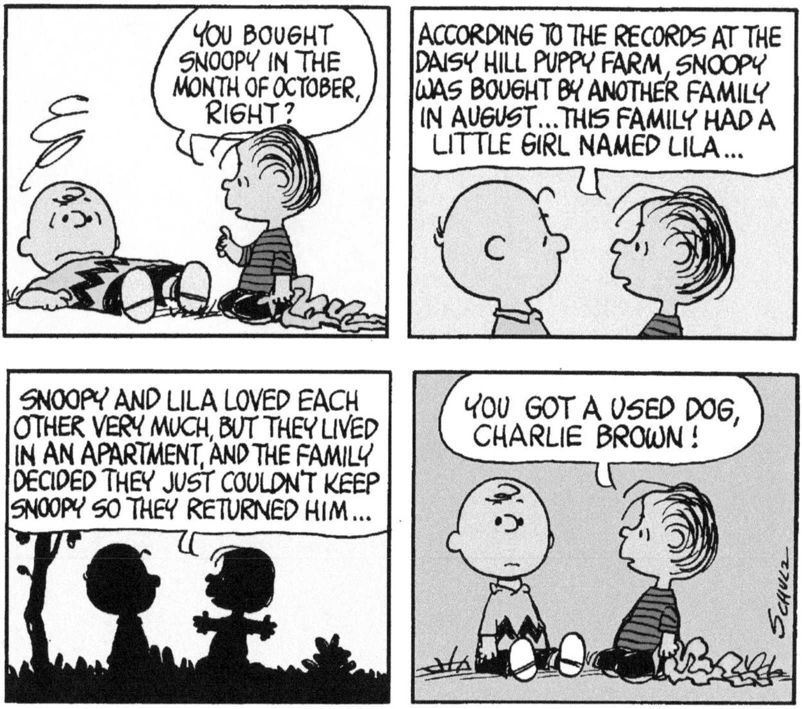
YOU BOUGHT SNOOPY IN THE MONTH OF OCTOBER, RIGHT?
ACCORDING TO THE RECORDS AT THE DAISY HILL PUPPY FARM, SNOOPY WAS BOUGHT BY ANOTHER FAMILY IN AUGUST...THIS FAMILY HAD A LITTLE GIRL NAMED LILA...
SNOOPY AND LILA LOVED EACH OTHER VERY MUCH, BUT THEY LIVED IN AN APARTMENT, AND THE FAMILY DECIDED THEY JUST COULDN'T KEEP SNOOPY SO THEY RETURNED HIM...
YOU GOT A USED DOG, CHARLIE BROWN!
SCHULZ

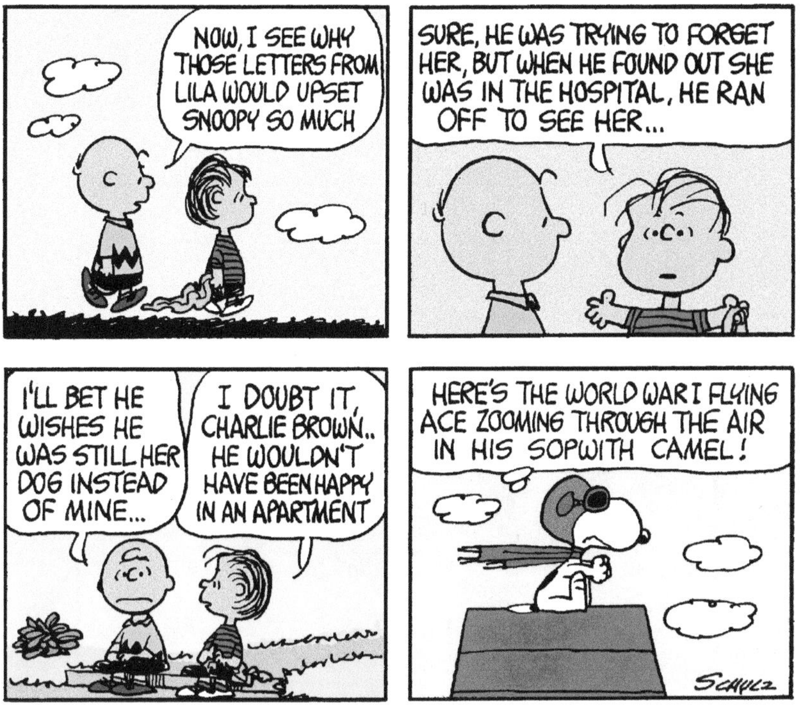
NOW, I SEE WHY THOSE LETTERS FROM LILA WOULD UPSET SNOOPY SO MUCH
SURE, HE WAS TRYING TO FORGET HER, BUT WHEN HE FOUND OUT SHE WAS IN THE HOSPITAL, HE RAN OFF TO SEE HER...
I'LL BET HE WISHES HE WAS STILL HER DOG INSTEAD OF MINE...
I DOUBT IT, CHARLIE BROWN.. HE WOULDN'T HAVE BEEN HAPPY IN AN APARTMENT
HERE'S THE WORLD WAR I FLYING ACE ZOOMING THROUGH THE AIR IN HIS SOPWITH CAMEL!
SCHULZ

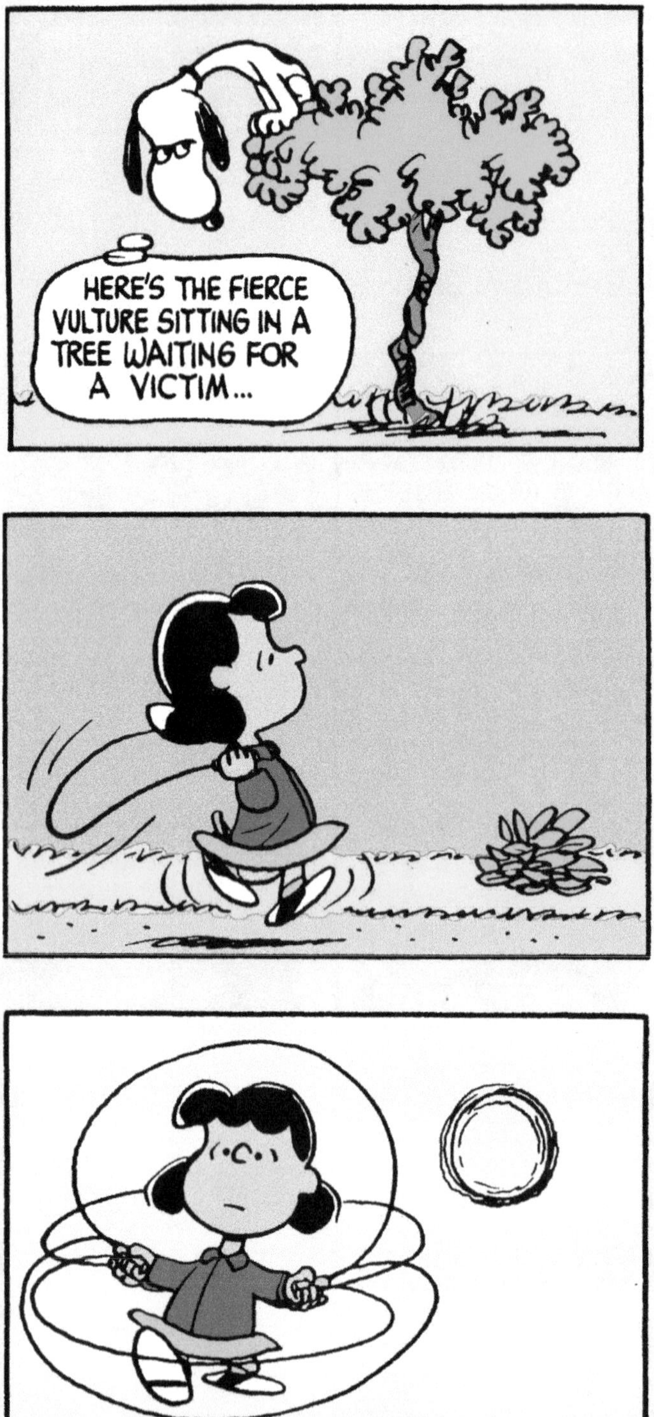
HERE'S THE FIERCE VULTURE SITTING IN A TREE WAITING FOR A VICTIM...

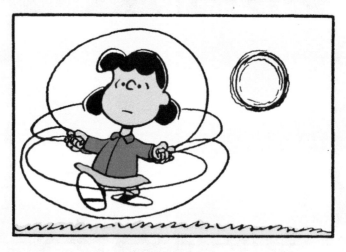

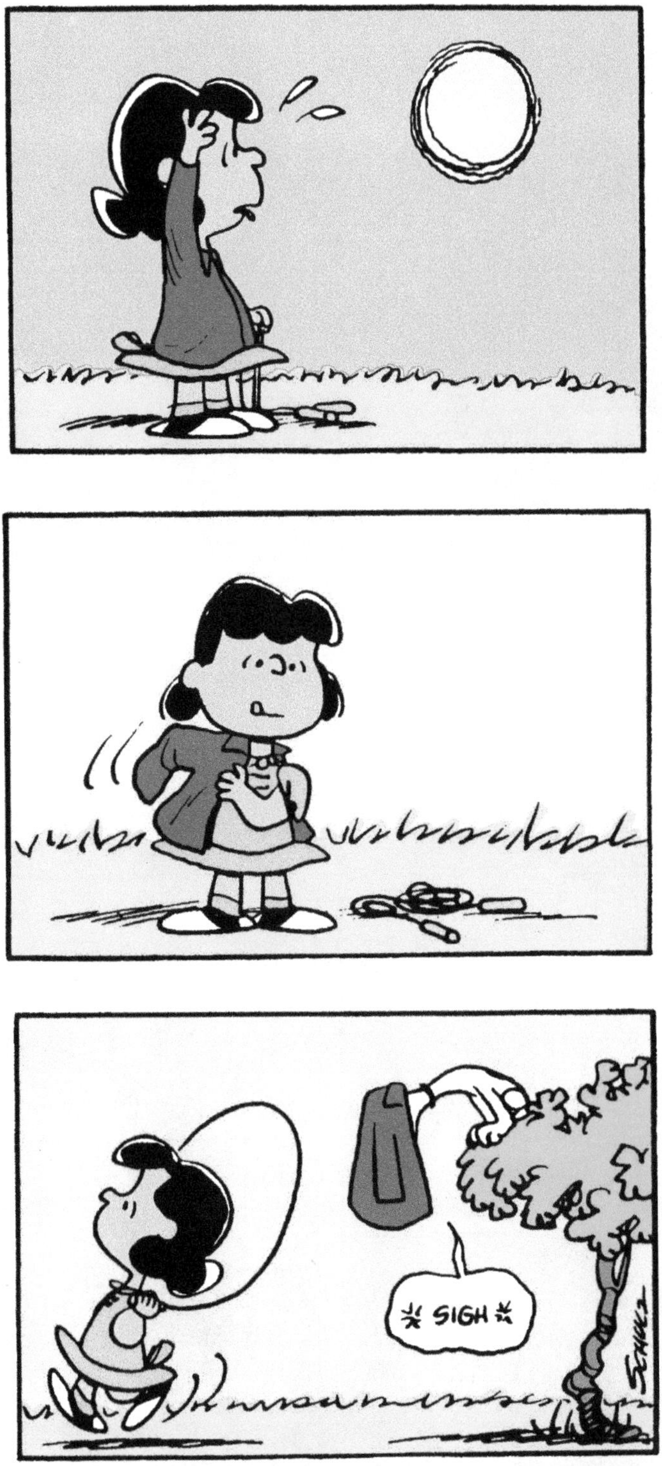
SIGH

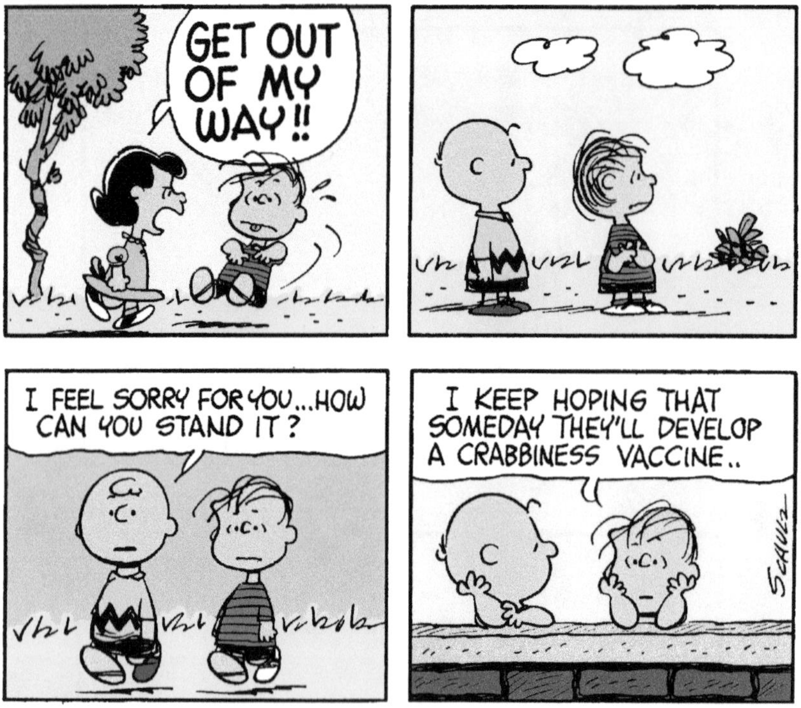
GET OUT OF MY WAY!!
I FEEL SORRY FOR YOU...HOW CAN YOU STAND IT?
I KEEP HOPING THAT SOMEDAY THEY'LL DEVELOP A CRABBINESS VACCINE..
SCHULZ

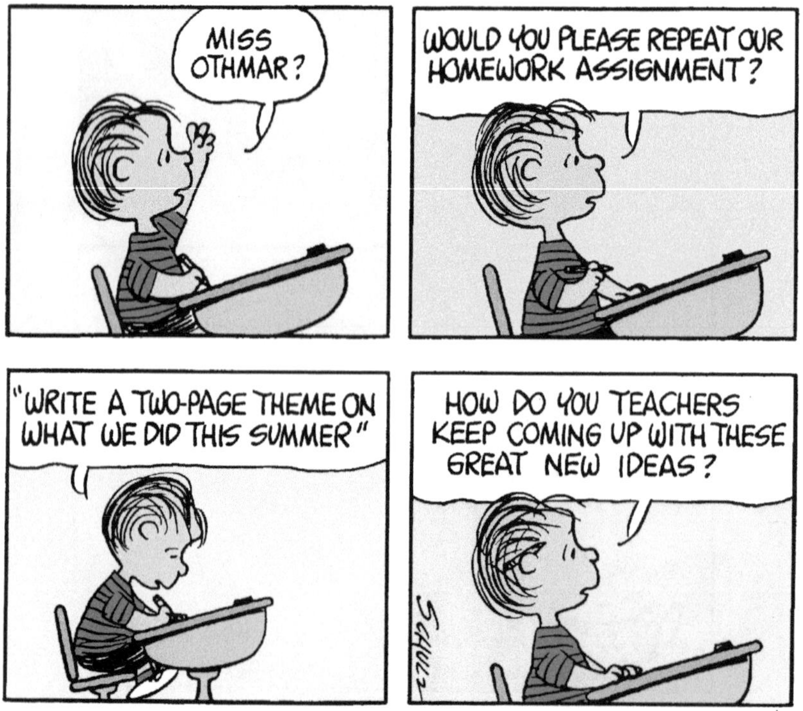
MISS OTHMAR?
WOULD YOU PLEASE REPEAT OUR HOMEWORK ASSIGNMENT?
"WRITE A TWO-PAGE THEME ON WHAT WE DID THIS SUMMER"
HOW DO YOU TEACHERS KEEP COMING UP WITH THESE GREAT NEW IDEAS?
SCHULZ

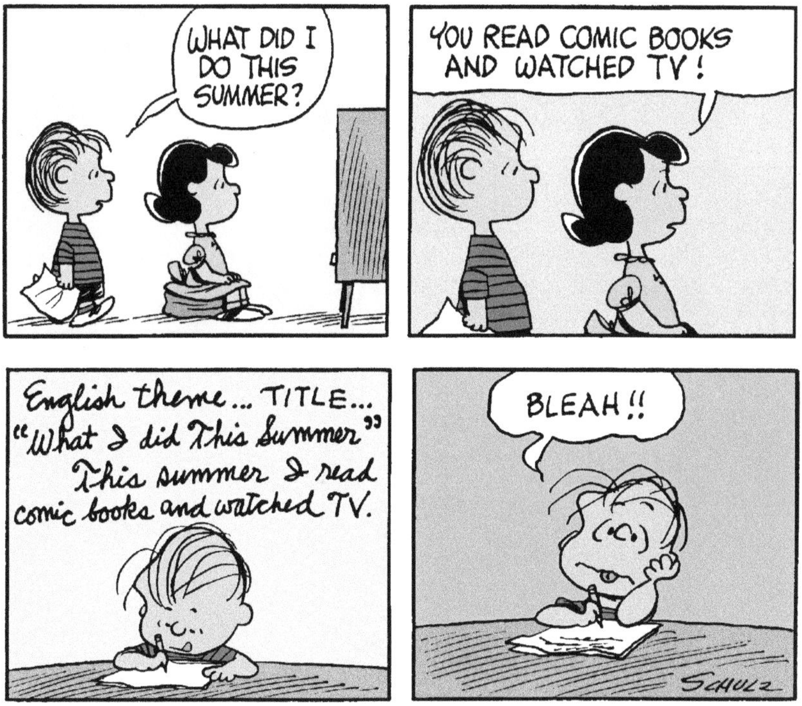
WHAT DID I DO THIS SUMMER?
YOU READ COMIC BOOKS AND WATCHED TV!
English theme... TITLE... "What I did This Summer" This summer I read comic books and watched TV.
BLEAH!!
SCHULZ

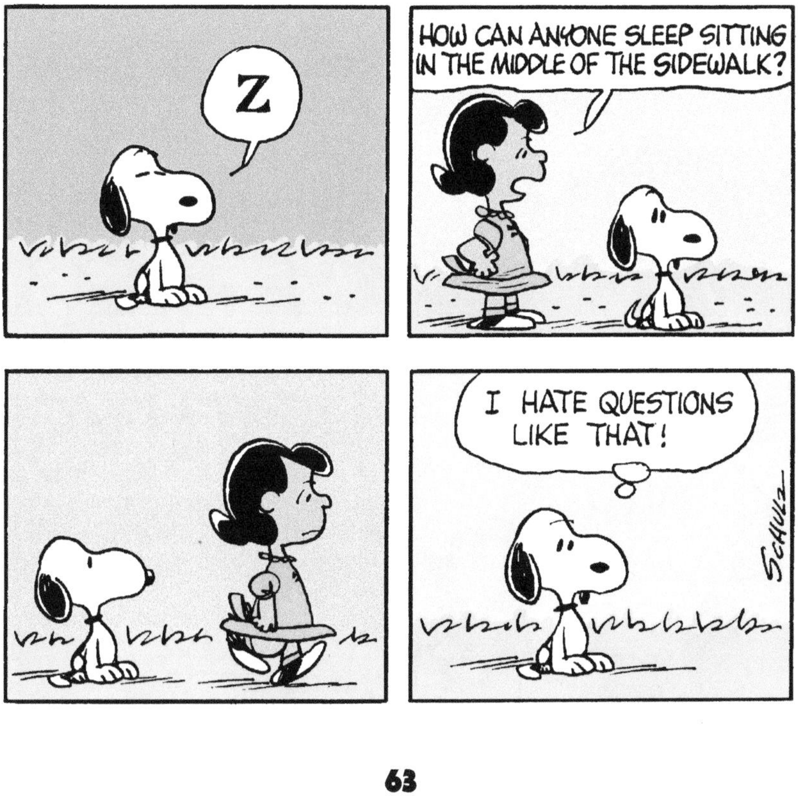
Z
HOW CAN ANYONE SLEEP SITTING IN THE MIDDLE OF THE SIDEWALK?
I HATE QUESTIONS LIKE THAT!
SCHULZ

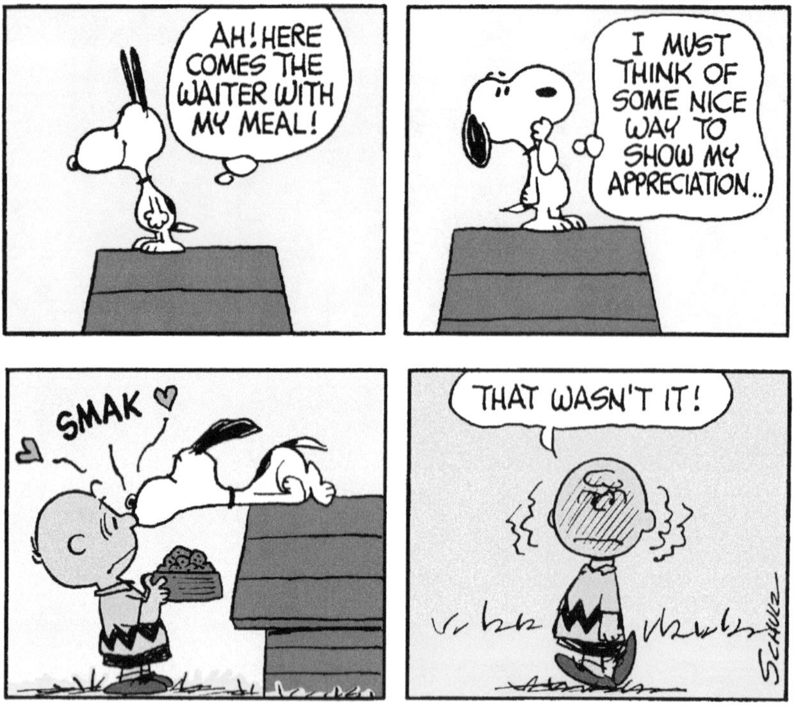
AH! HERE COMES THE WAITER WITH MY MEAL!
I MUST THINK OF SOME NICE WAY TO SHOW MY APPRECIATION..
SMAK
THAT WASN'T IT!
SCHULZ

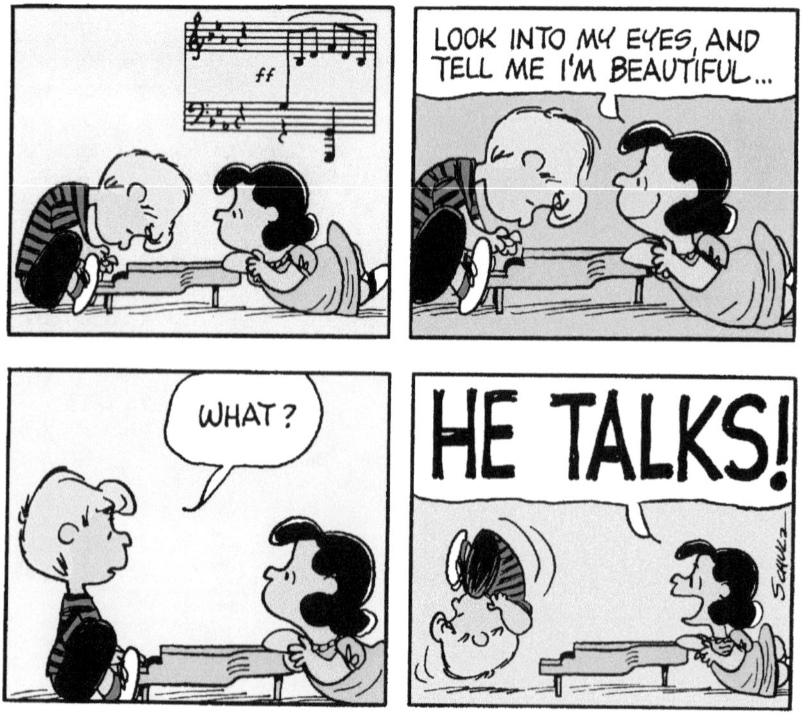
ff
LOOK INTO MY EYES, AND TELL ME I'M BEAUTIFUL...
WHAT?
HE TALKS!
SCHULZ

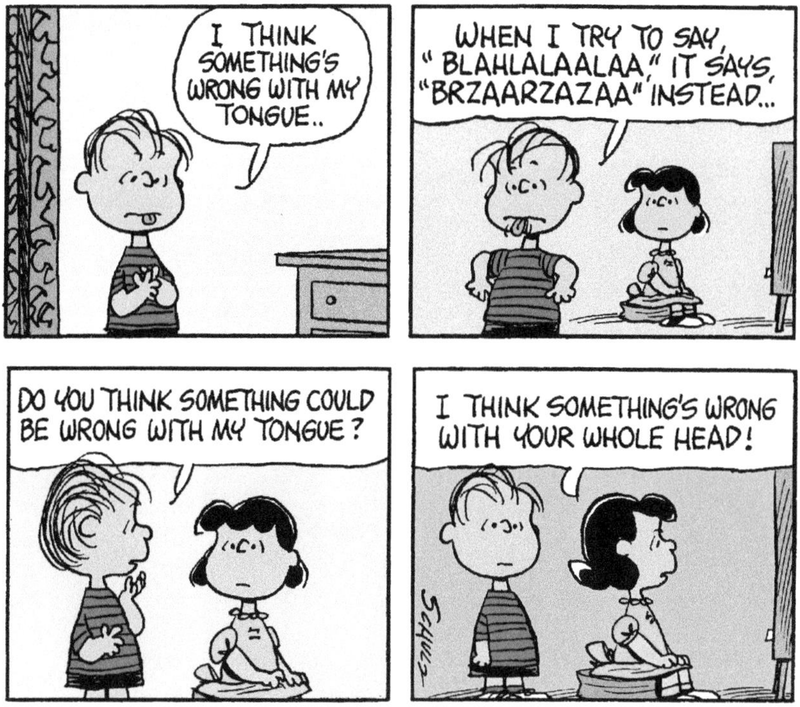
I THINK SOMETHING'S WRONG WITH MY TONGUE..
WHEN I TRY TO SAY, "BLAHLALAALAA," IT SAYS, "BRZAARZAZAA" INSTEAD...
DO YOU THINK SOMETHING COULD BE WRONG WITH MY TONGUE?
I THINK SOMETHING'S WRONG WITH YOUR WHOLE HEAD!

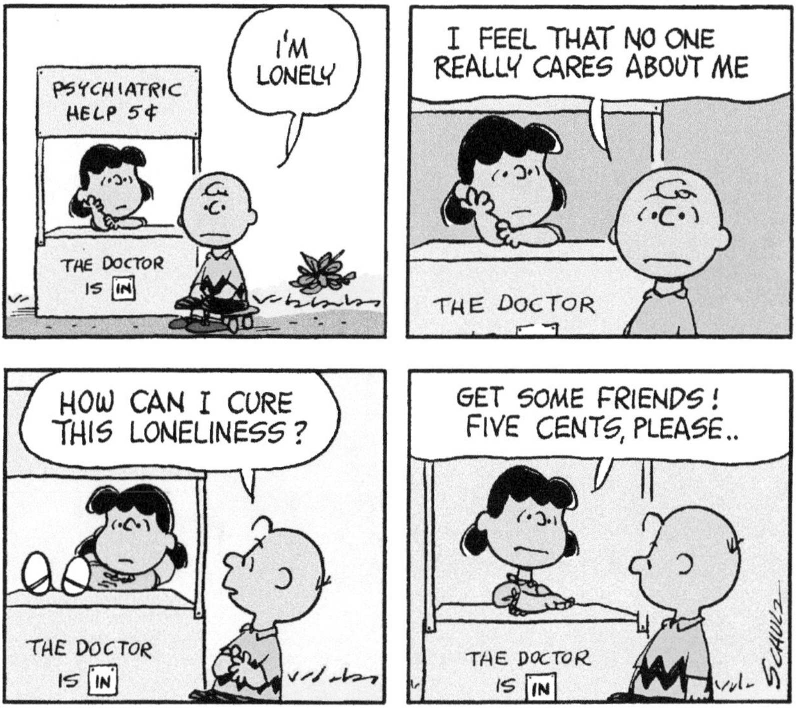
PSYCHIATRIC HELP 5¢
THE DOCTOR IS IN
I'M LONELY
I FEEL THAT NO ONE REALLY CARES ABOUT ME
THE DOCTOR
HOW CAN I CURE THIS LONELINESS?
THE DOCTOR IS IN
GET SOME FRIENDS! FIVE CENTS, PLEASE..
THE DOCTOR IS IN

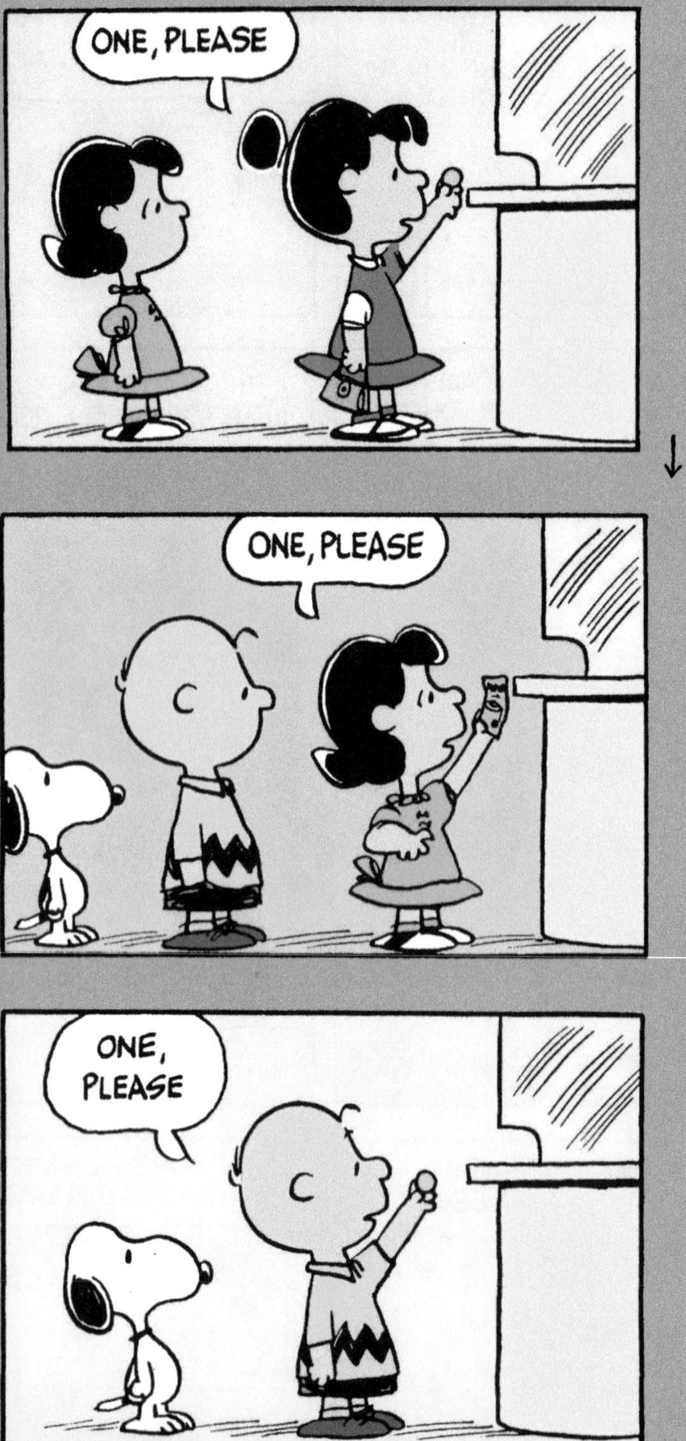
ONE, PLEASE
ONE, PLEASE
ONE, PLEASE

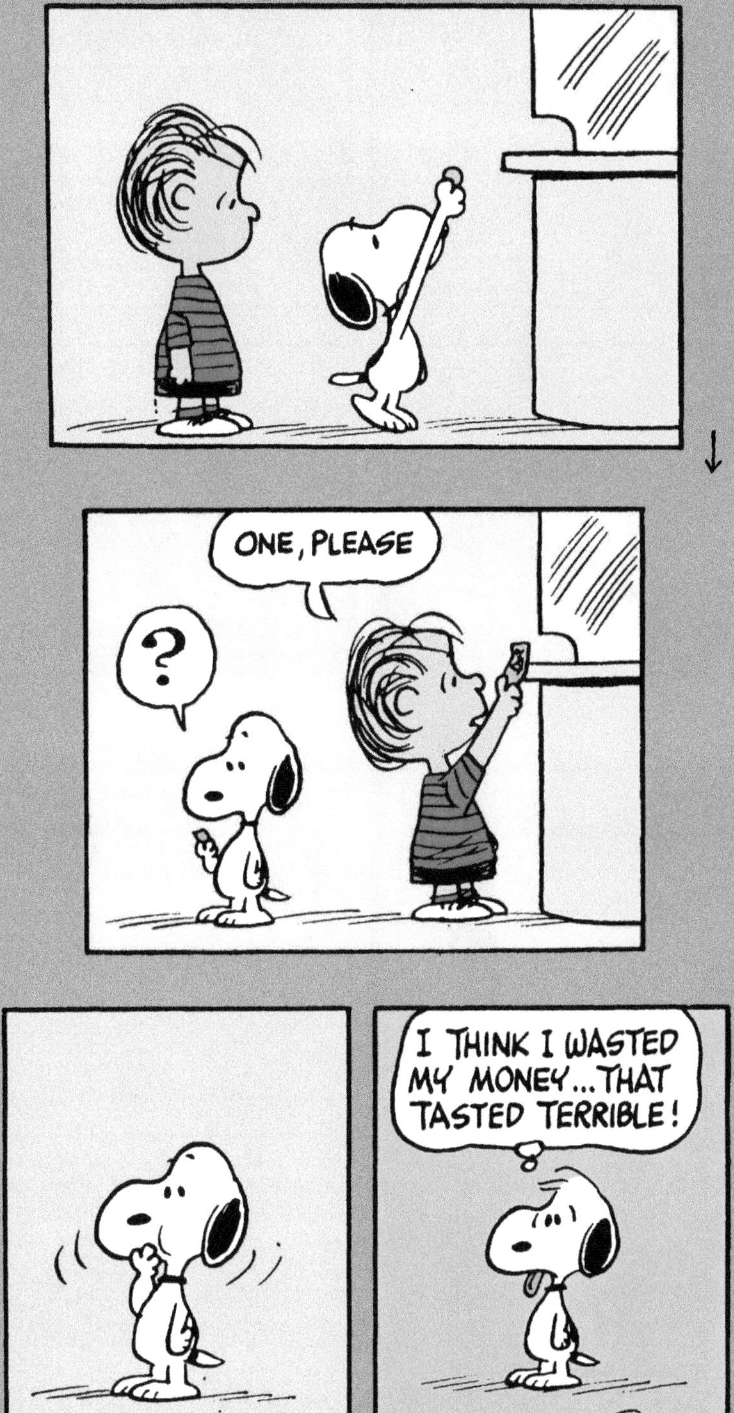
ONE, PLEASE
?
I THINK I WASTED MY MONEY...THAT TASTED TERRIBLE!
SCHULZ

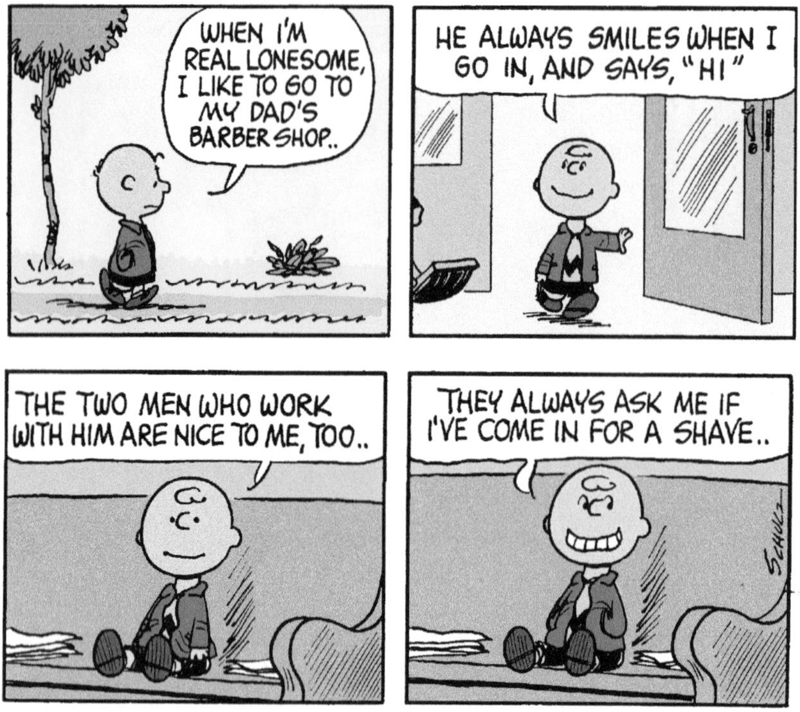
WHEN I'M REAL LONESOME, I LIKE TO GO TO MY DAD'S BARBER SHOP..
HE ALWAYS SMILES WHEN I GO IN, AND SAYS, "HI"
THE TWO MEN WHO WORK WITH HIM ARE NICE TO ME, TOO..
THEY ALWAYS ASK ME IF I'VE COME IN FOR A SHAVE..
SCHULZ

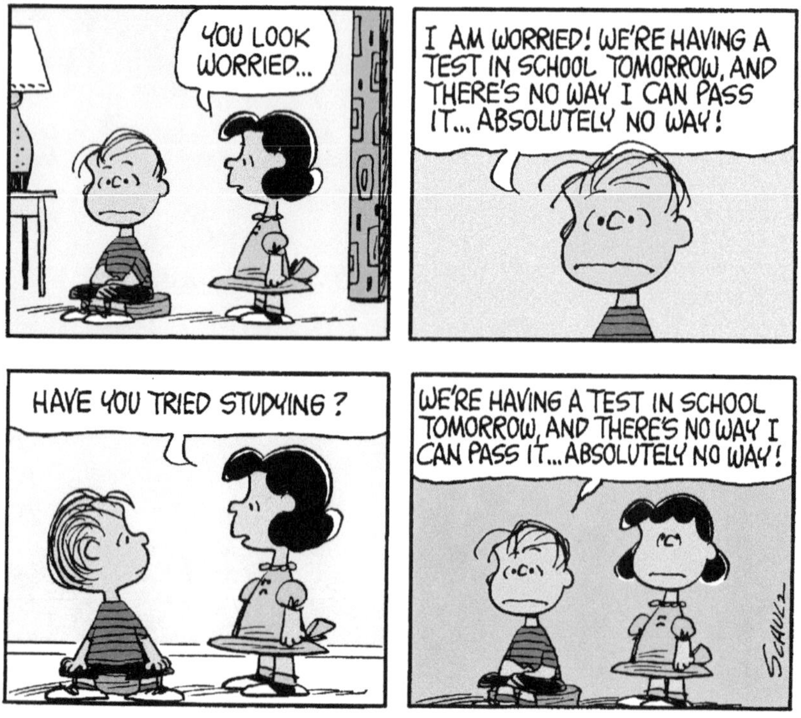
YOU LOOK WORRIED...
I AM WORRIED! WE'RE HAVING A TEST IN SCHOOL TOMORROW, AND THERE'S NO WAY I CAN PASS IT... ABSOLUTELY NO WAY!
HAVE YOU TRIED STUDYING?
WE'RE HAVING A TEST IN SCHOOL TOMORROW, AND THERE'S NO WAY I CAN PASS IT... ABSOLUTELY NO WAY!
SCHULZ

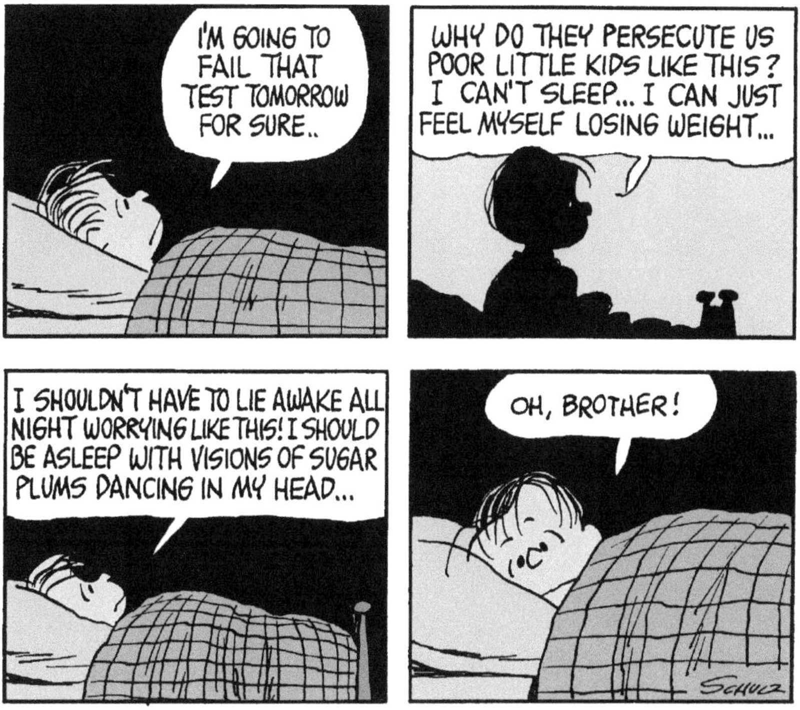
I'M GOING TO FAIL THAT TEST TOMORROW FOR SURE..
WHY DO THEY PERSECUTE US POOR LITTLE KIDS LIKE THIS? I CAN'T SLEEP... I CAN JUST FEEL MYSELF LOSING WEIGHT...
I SHOULDN'T HAVE TO LIE AWAKE ALL NIGHT WORRYING LIKE THIS! I SHOULD BE ASLEEP WITH VISIONS OF SUGAR PLUMS DANCING IN MY HEAD...
OH, BROTHER!
SCHULZ

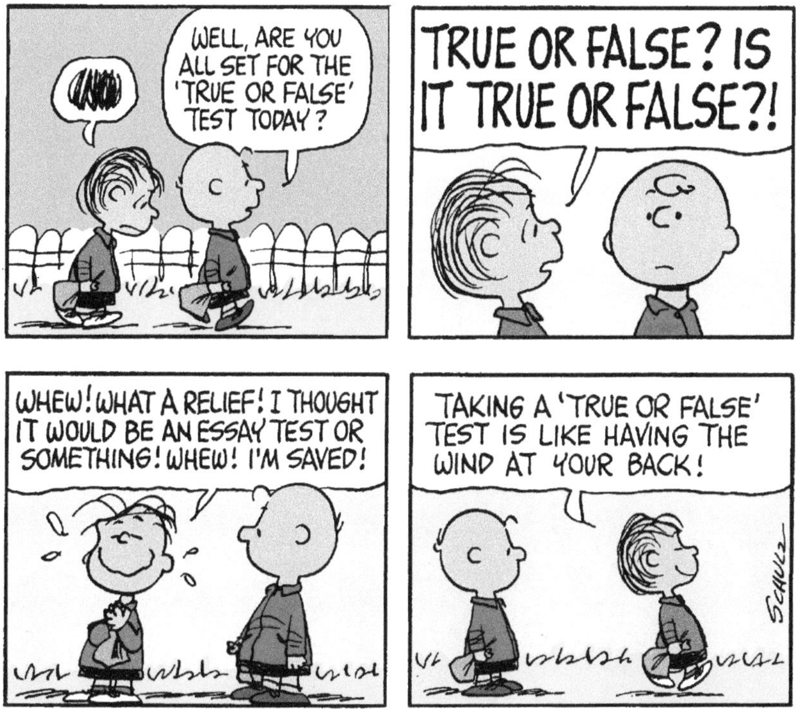
WELL, ARE YOU ALL SET FOR THE 'TRUE OR FALSE' TEST TODAY?
TRUE OR FALSE? IS IT TRUE OR FALSE?!
WHEW! WHAT A RELIEF! I THOUGHT IT WOULD BE AN ESSAY TEST OR SOMETHING! WHEW! I'M SAVED!
TAKING A 'TRUE OR FALSE' TEST IS LIKE HAVING THE WIND AT YOUR BACK!
SCHULZ

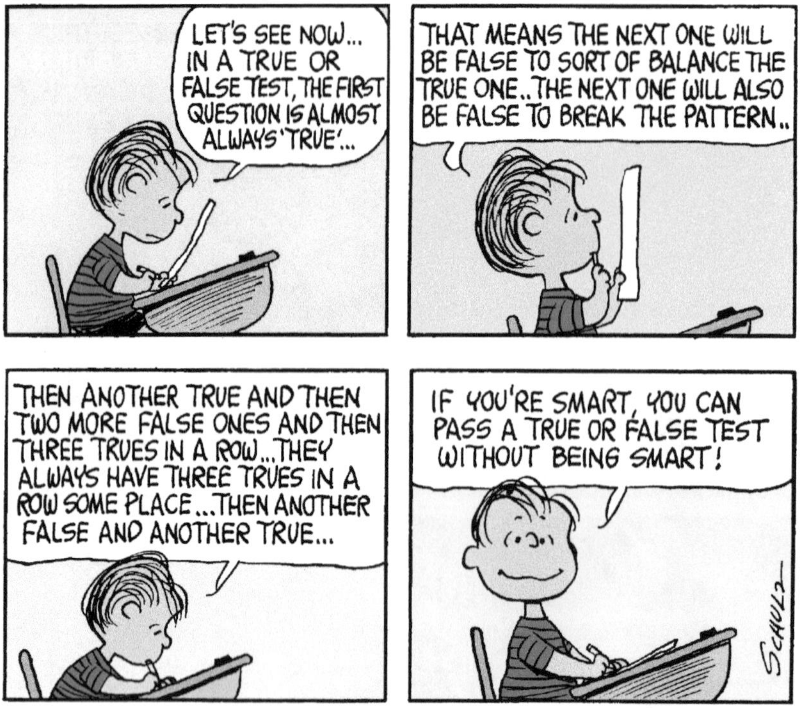
LET'S SEE NOW... IN A TRUE OR FALSE TEST, THE FIRST QUESTION IS ALMOST ALWAYS 'TRUE'...
THAT MEANS THE NEXT ONE WILL BE FALSE TO SORT OF BALANCE THE TRUE ONE.. THE NEXT ONE WILL ALSO BE FALSE TO BREAK THE PATTERN..
THEN ANOTHER TRUE AND THEN TWO MORE FALSE ONES AND THEN THREE TRUES IN A ROW... THEY ALWAYS HAVE THREE TRUES IN A ROW SOME PLACE... THEN ANOTHER FALSE AND ANOTHER TRUE...
IF YOU'RE SMART, YOU CAN PASS A TRUE OR FALSE TEST WITHOUT BEING SMART!
SCHULZ

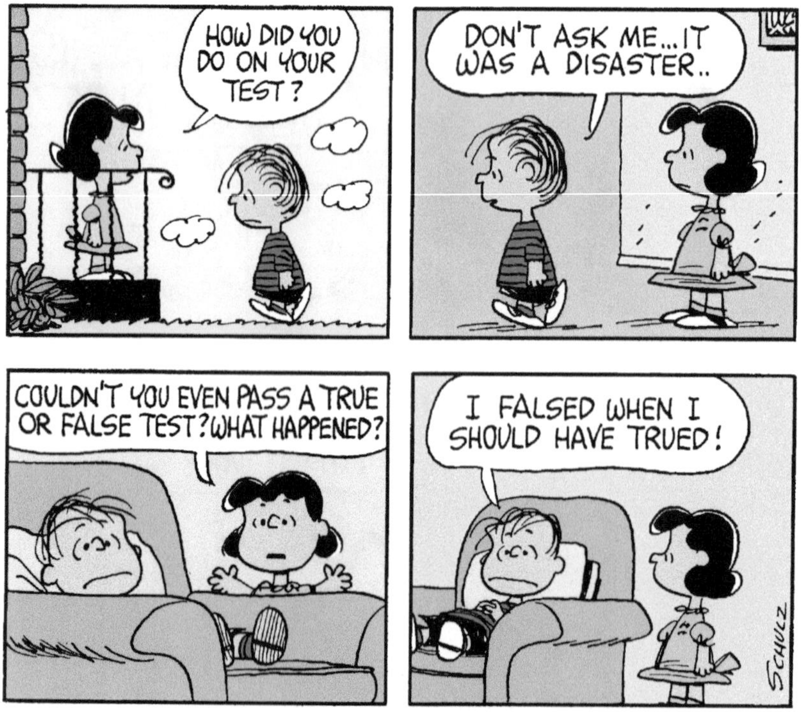
HOW DID YOU DO ON YOUR TEST?
DON'T ASK ME... IT WAS A DISASTER..
COULDN'T YOU EVEN PASS A TRUE OR FALSE TEST? WHAT HAPPENED?
I FALSED WHEN I SHOULD HAVE TRUED!
SCHULZ

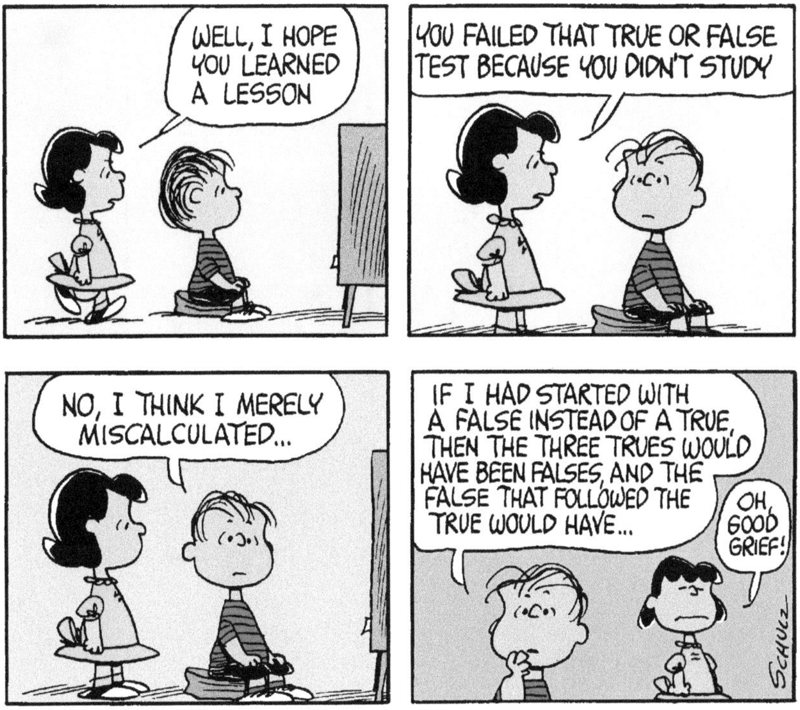
WELL, I HOPE YOU LEARNED A LESSON
YOU FAILED THAT TRUE OR FALSE TEST BECAUSE YOU DIDN'T STUDY
NO, I THINK I MERELY MISCALCULATED...
IF I HAD STARTED WITH A FALSE INSTEAD OF A TRUE, THEN THE THREE TRUES WOULD HAVE BEEN FALSES, AND THE FALSE THAT FOLLOWED THE TRUE WOULD HAVE...
OH, GOOD GRIEF!
SCHULZ

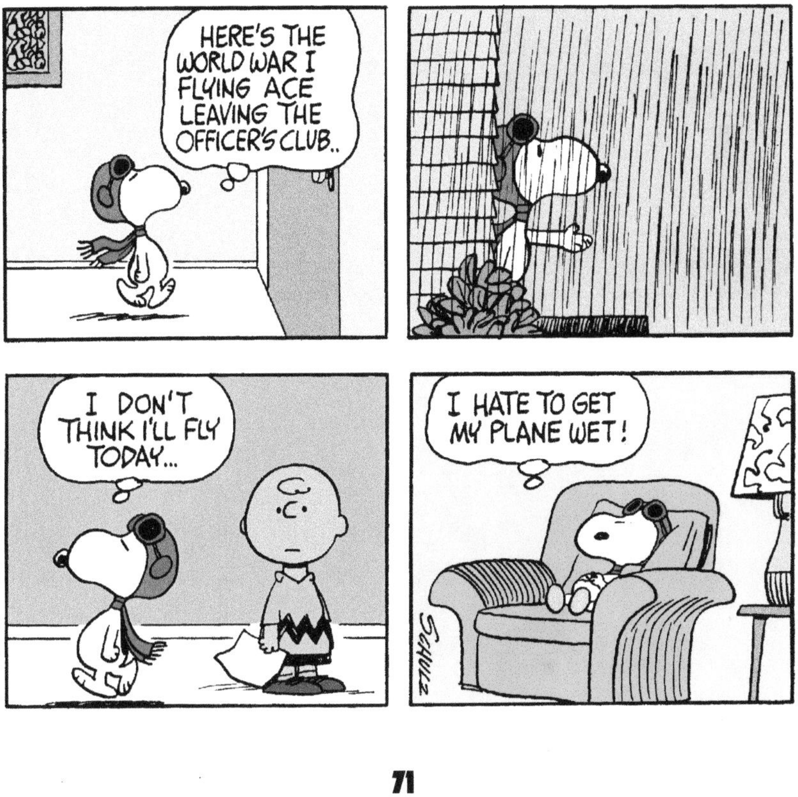
HERE'S THE WORLD WAR I FLYING ACE LEAVING THE OFFICER'S CLUB..
I DON'T THINK I'LL FLY TODAY...
I HATE TO GET MY PLANE WET!
SCHULZ

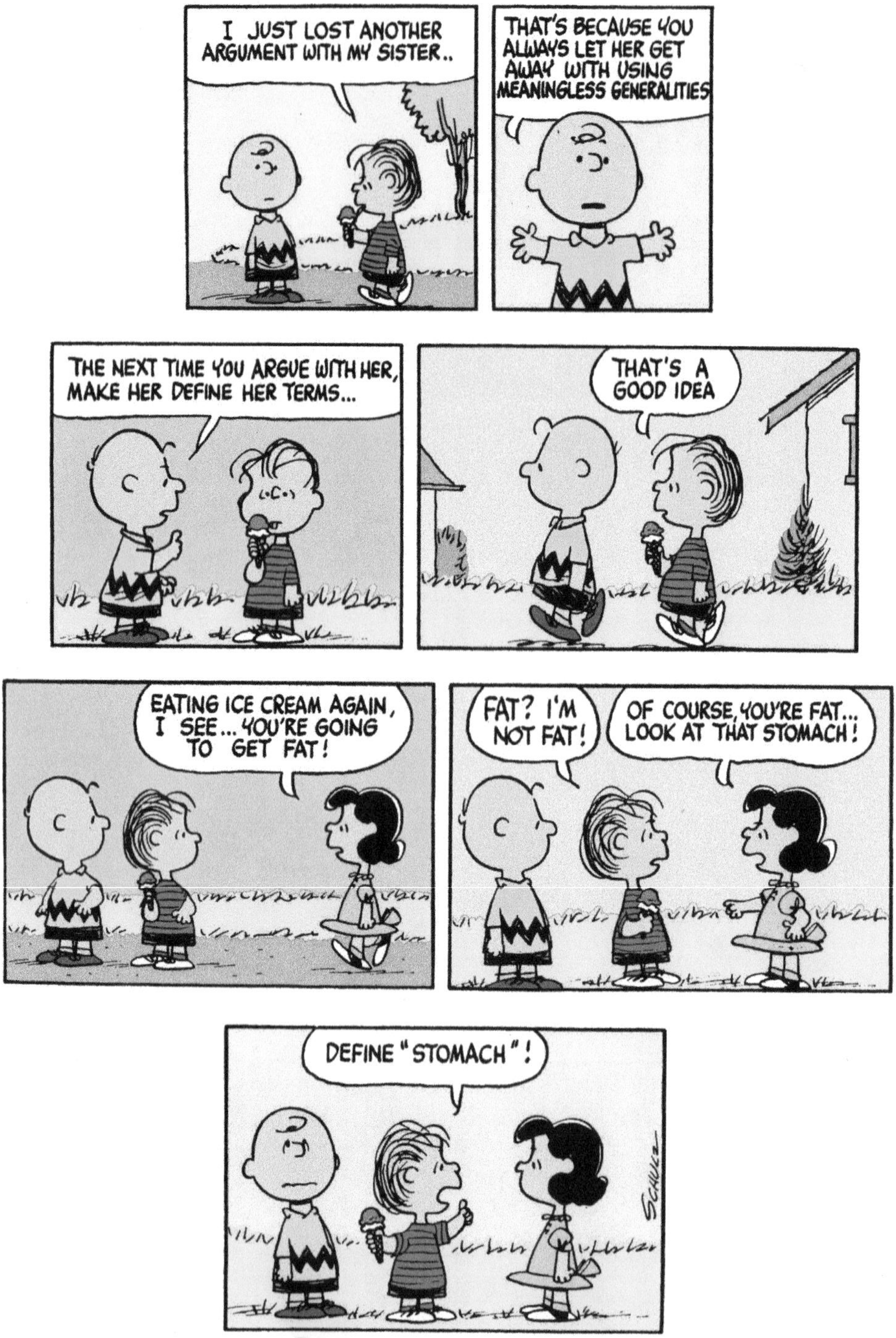
I JUST LOST ANOTHER ARGUMENT WITH MY SISTER..
THAT'S BECAUSE YOU ALWAYS LET HER GET AWAY WITH USING MEANINGLESS GENERALITIES
THE NEXT TIME YOU ARGUE WITH HER, MAKE HER DEFINE HER TERMS...
THAT'S A GOOD IDEA
EATING ICE CREAM AGAIN, I SEE... YOU'RE GOING TO GET FAT!
FAT? I'M NOT FAT!
OF COURSE, YOU'RE FAT... LOOK AT THAT STOMACH!
DEFINE "STOMACH"!
SCHULZ

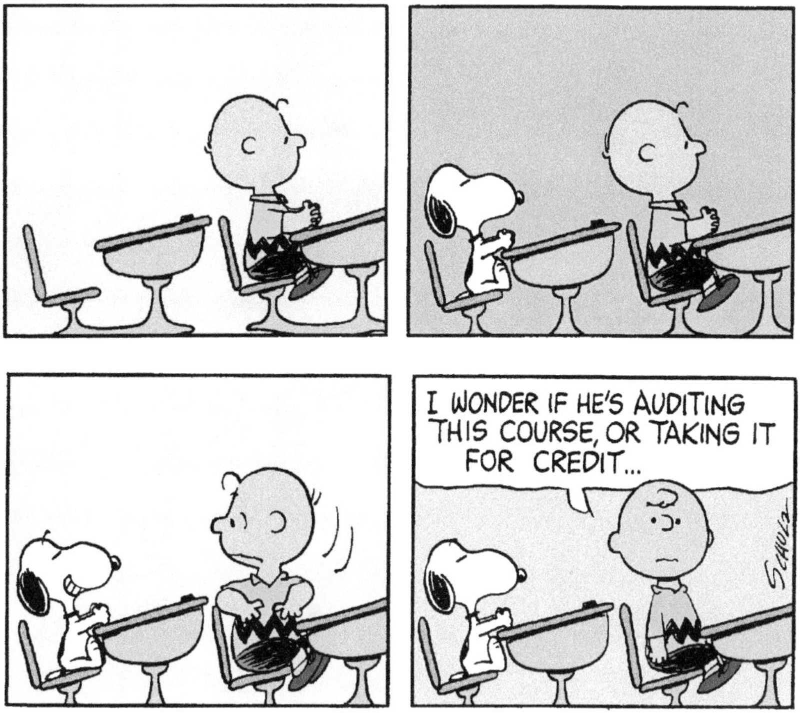
I WONDER IF HE'S AUDITING THIS COURSE, OR TAKING IT FOR CREDIT...
SCHULZ

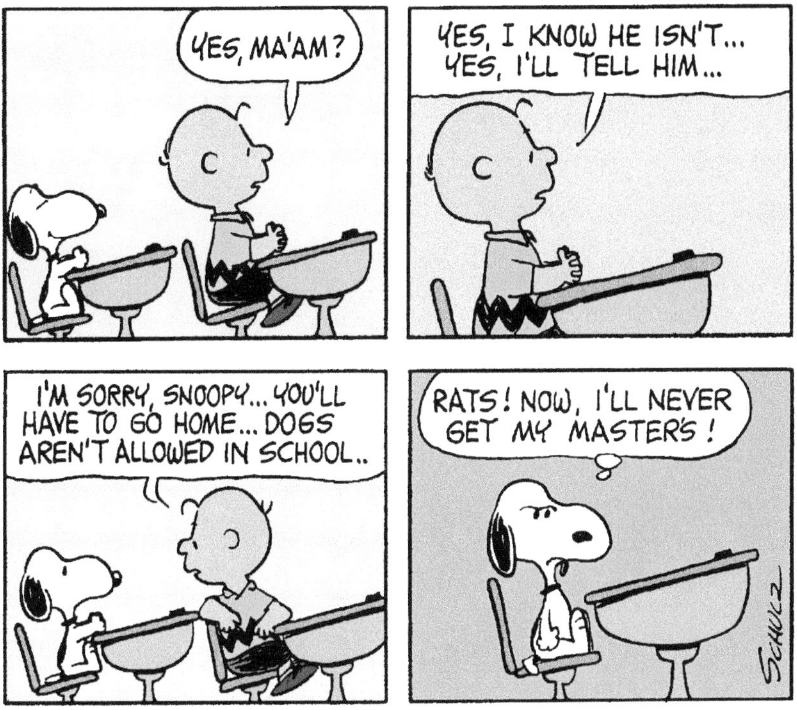
YES, MA'AM?
YES, I KNOW HE ISN'T... YES, I'LL TELL HIM...
I'M SORRY, SNOOPY... YOU'LL HAVE TO GO HOME... DOGS AREN'T ALLOWED IN SCHOOL..
RATS! NOW, I'LL NEVER GET MY MASTER'S!
SCHULZ

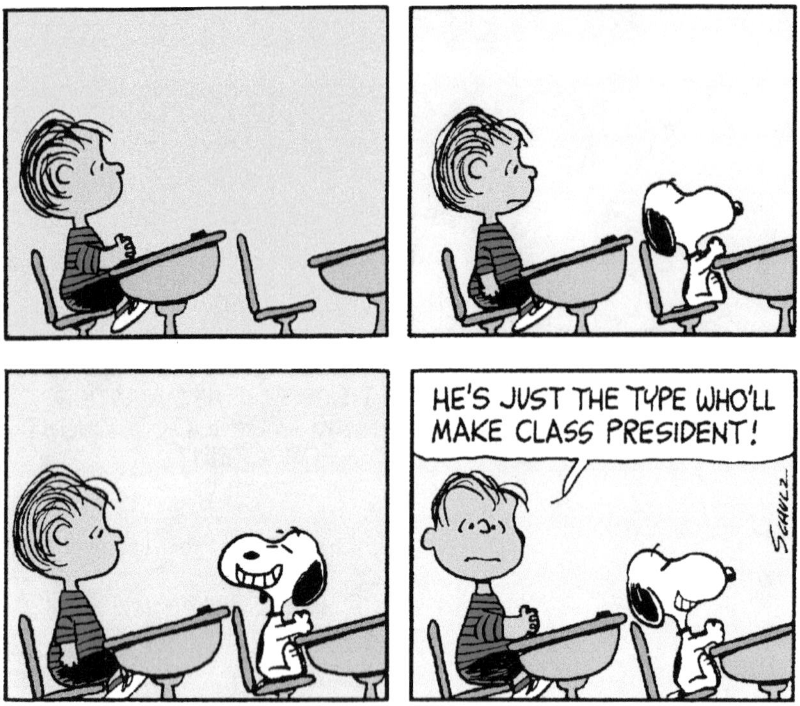
HE'S JUST THE TYPE WHO'LL MAKE CLASS PRESIDENT!

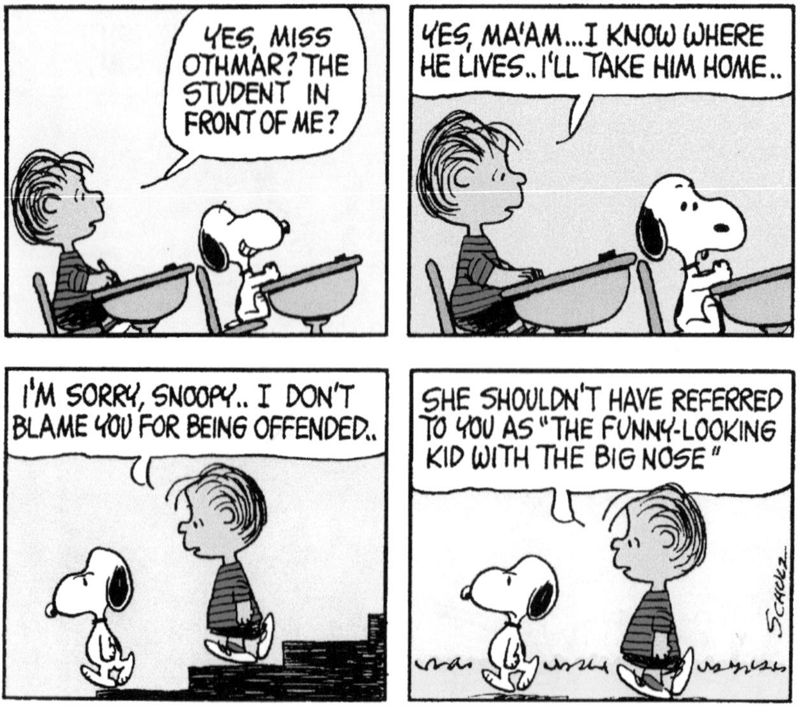
YES, MISS OTHMAR? THE STUDENT IN FRONT OF ME?
YES, MA'AM...I KNOW WHERE HE LIVES.. I'LL TAKE HIM HOME..
I'M SORRY, SNOOPY.. I DON'T BLAME YOU FOR BEING OFFENDED..
SHE SHOULDN'T HAVE REFERRED TO YOU AS "THE FUNNY-LOOKING KID WITH THE BIG NOSE"

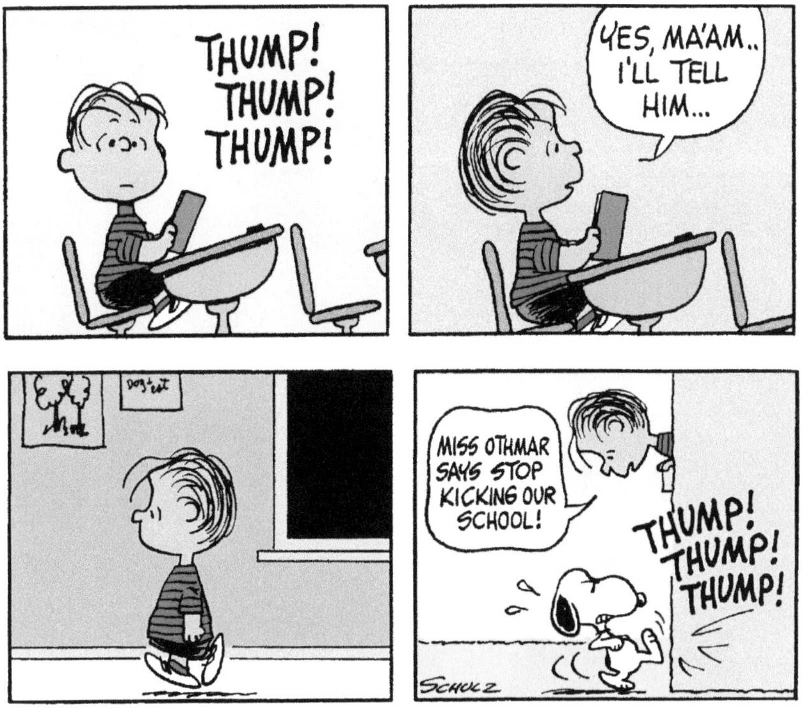
THUMP! THUMP! THUMP!
YES, MA'AM.. I'LL TELL HIM...
MISS OTHMAR SAYS STOP KICKING OUR SCHOOL!
THUMP! THUMP! THUMP!

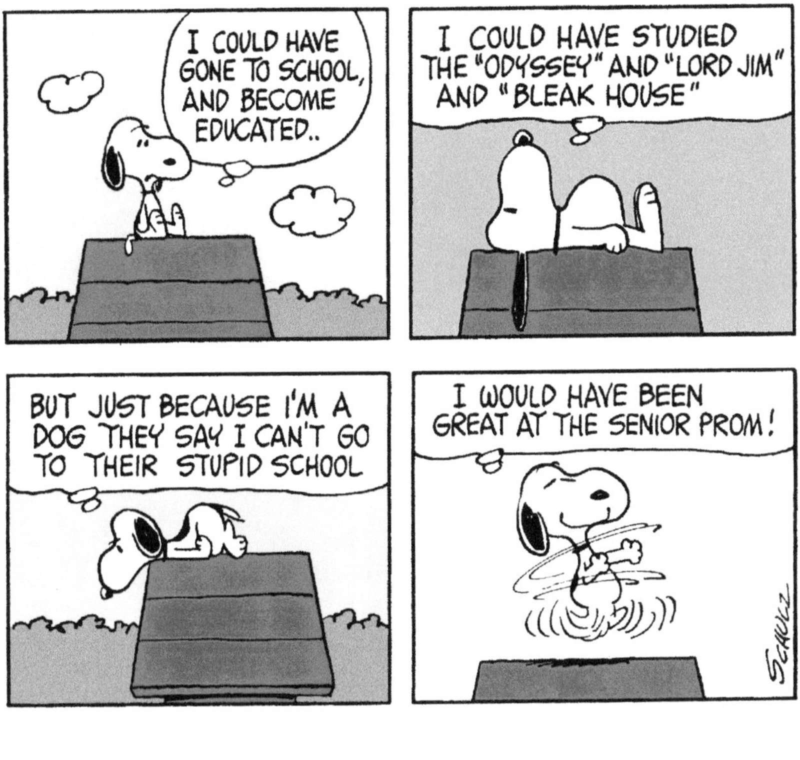
I COULD HAVE GONE TO SCHOOL, AND BECOME EDUCATED..
I COULD HAVE STUDIED THE "ODYSSEY" AND "LORD JIM" AND "BLEAK HOUSE"
BUT JUST BECAUSE I'M A DOG THEY SAY I CAN'T GO TO THEIR STUPID SCHOOL
I WOULD HAVE BEEN GREAT AT THE SENIOR PROM!

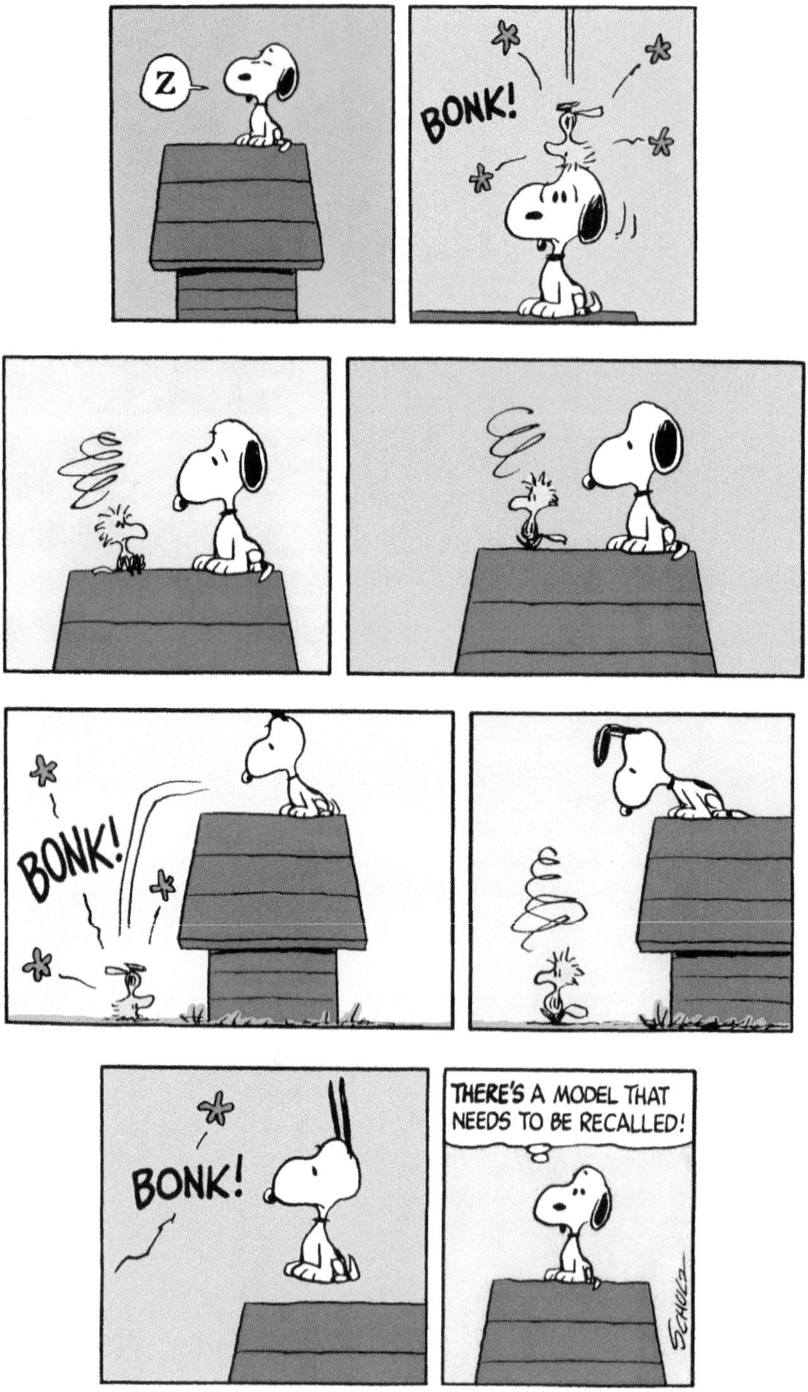
Z
BONK!
BONK!
BONK!
THERE'S A MODEL THAT NEEDS TO BE RECALLED!
SCHULZ

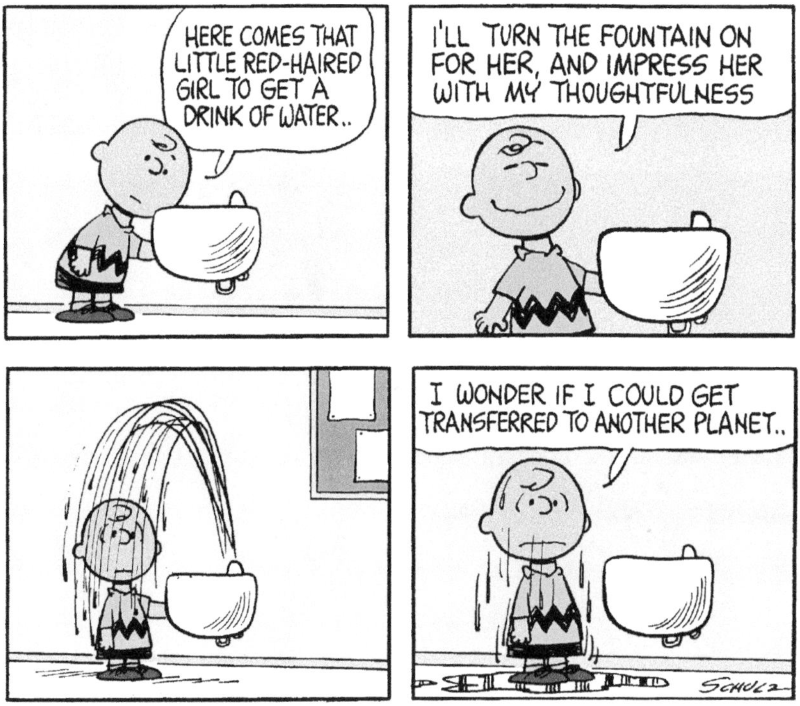
HERE COMES THAT LITTLE RED-HAIRED GIRL TO GET A DRINK OF WATER..
I'LL TURN THE FOUNTAIN ON FOR HER, AND IMPRESS HER WITH MY THOUGHTFULNESS
I WONDER IF I COULD GET TRANSFERRED TO ANOTHER PLANET..
SCHULZ

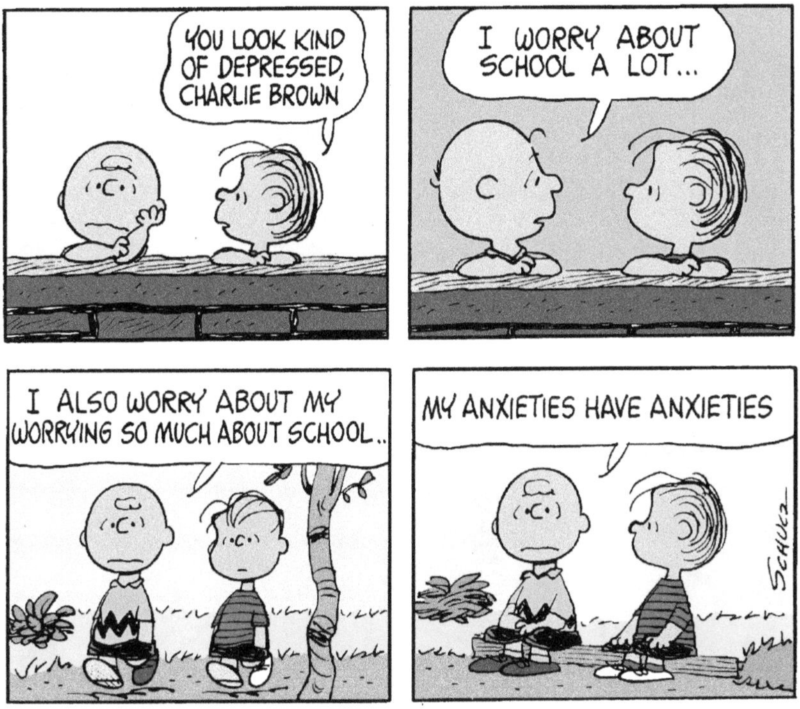
YOU LOOK KIND OF DEPRESSED, CHARLIE BROWN
I WORRY ABOUT SCHOOL A LOT...
I ALSO WORRY ABOUT MY WORRYING SO MUCH ABOUT SCHOOL..
MY ANXIETIES HAVE ANXIETIES
SCHULZ

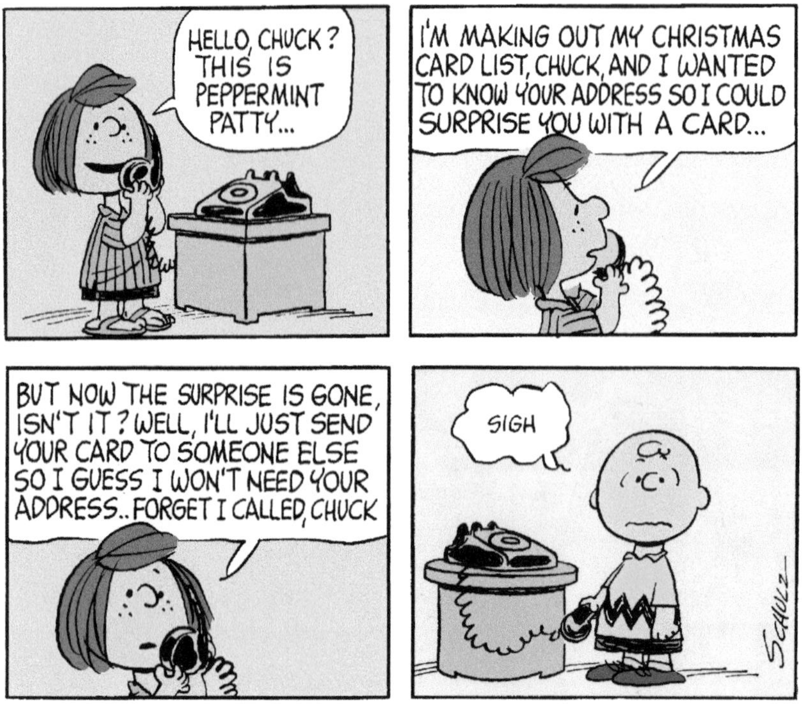
HELLO, CHUCK? THIS IS PEPPERMINT PATTY...
I'M MAKING OUT MY CHRISTMAS CARD LIST, CHUCK, AND I WANTED TO KNOW YOUR ADDRESS SO I COULD SURPRISE YOU WITH A CARD...
BUT NOW THE SURPRISE IS GONE, ISN'T IT? WELL, I'LL JUST SEND YOUR CARD TO SOMEONE ELSE SO I GUESS I WON'T NEED YOUR ADDRESS.. FORGET I CALLED, CHUCK
SIGH
SCHULZ

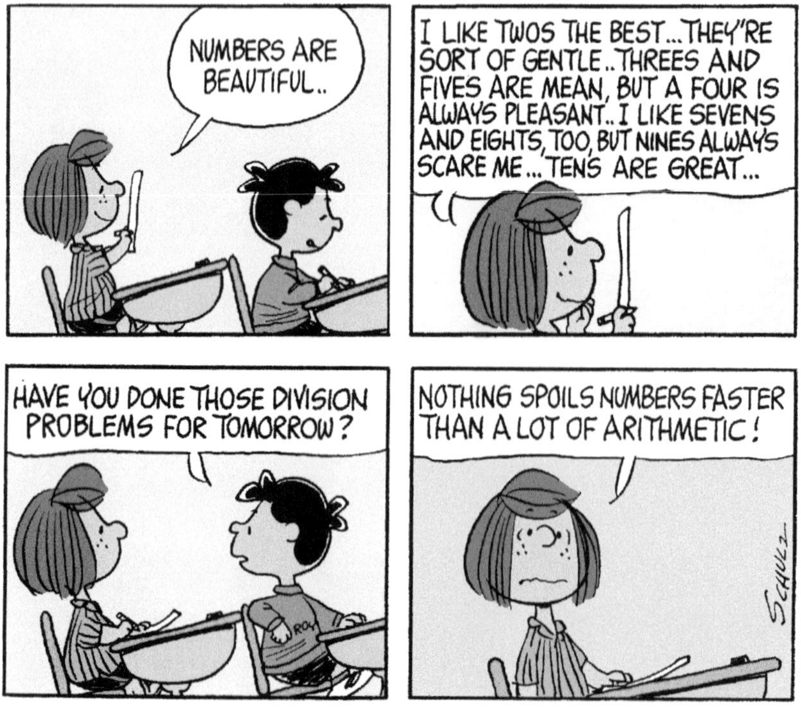
NUMBERS ARE BEAUTIFUL..
I LIKE TWOS THE BEST... THEY'RE SORT OF GENTLE.. THREES AND FIVES ARE MEAN, BUT A FOUR IS ALWAYS PLEASANT.. I LIKE SEVENS AND EIGHTS, TOO, BUT NINES ALWAYS SCARE ME... TENS ARE GREAT...
HAVE YOU DONE THOSE DIVISION PROBLEMS FOR TOMORROW?
NOTHING SPOILS NUMBERS FASTER THAN A LOT OF ARITHMETIC!
SCHULZ

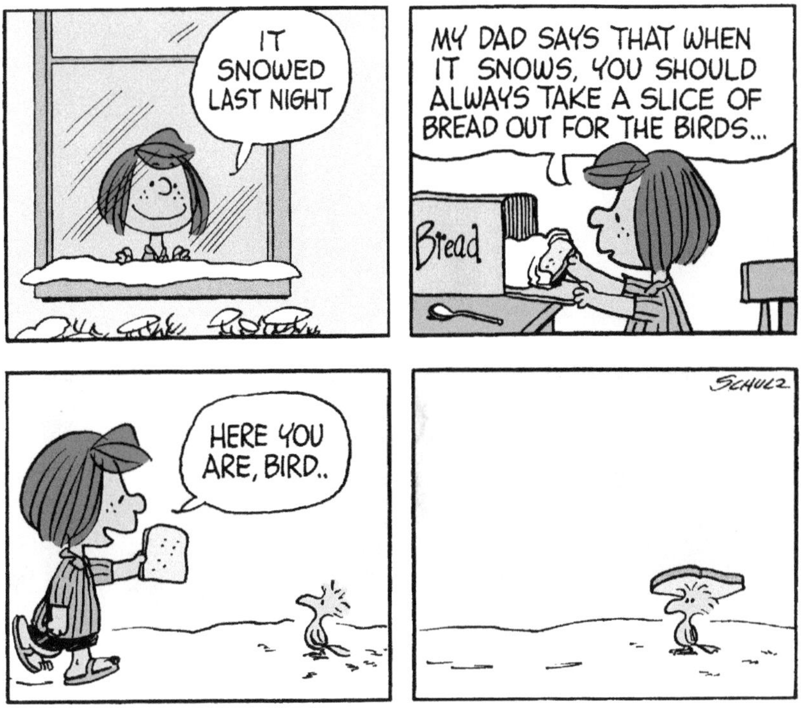
IT SNOWED LAST NIGHT
MY DAD SAYS THAT WHEN IT SNOWS, YOU SHOULD ALWAYS TAKE A SLICE OF BREAD OUT FOR THE BIRDS...
Bread
HERE YOU ARE, BIRD..
SCHULZ

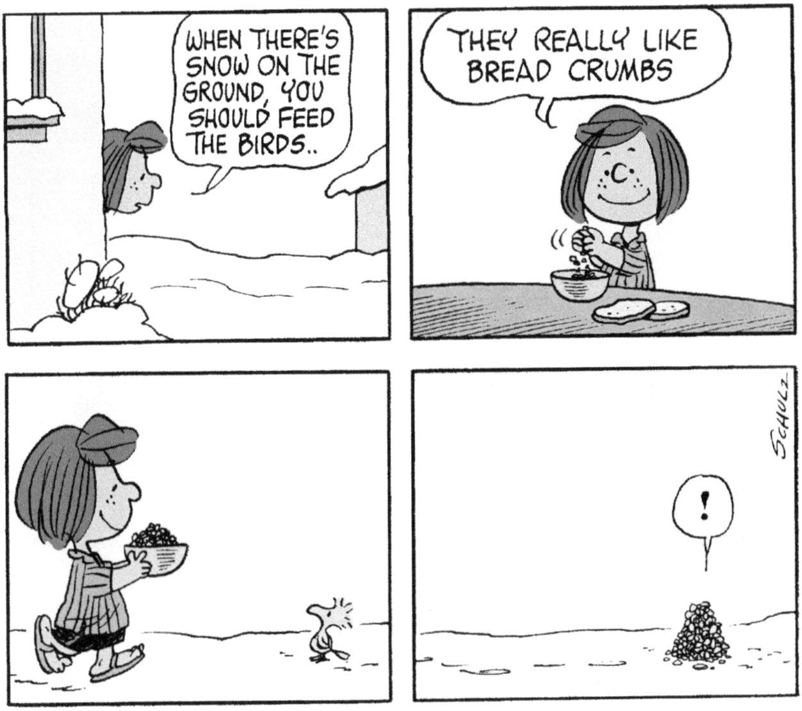
WHEN THERE'S SNOW ON THE GROUND, YOU SHOULD FEED THE BIRDS..
THEY REALLY LIKE BREAD CRUMBS
!
SCHULZ

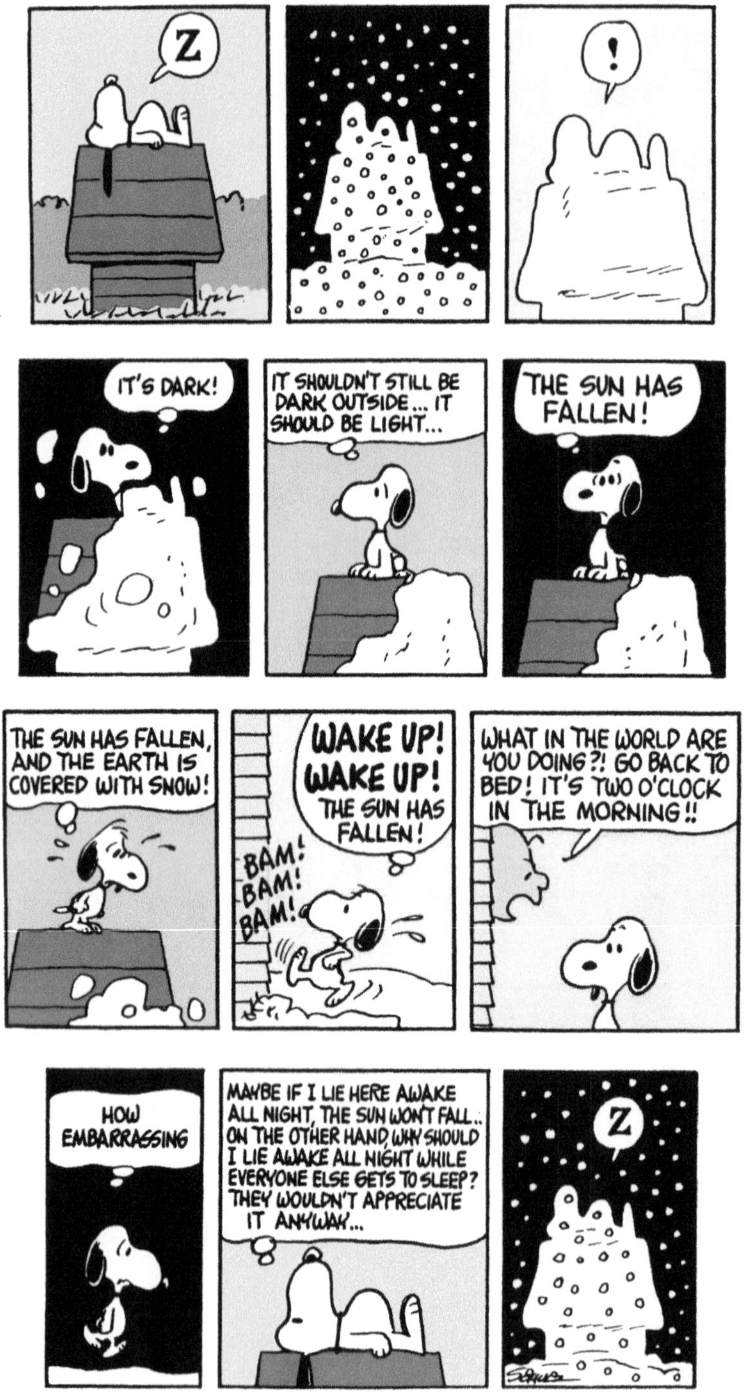
Z
!
IT'S DARK!
IT SHOULDN'T STILL BE DARK OUTSIDE... IT SHOULD BE LIGHT...
THE SUN HAS FALLEN!
THE SUN HAS FALLEN, AND THE EARTH IS COVERED WITH SNOW!
WAKE UP! WAKE UP! THE SUN HAS FALLEN!
BAM! BAM! BAM!
WHAT IN THE WORLD ARE YOU DOING?! GO BACK TO BED! IT'S TWO O'CLOCK IN THE MORNING!!
HOW EMBARRASSING
MAYBE IF I LIE HERE AWAKE ALL NIGHT, THE SUN WON'T FALL.. ON THE OTHER HAND, WHY SHOULD I LIE AWAKE ALL NIGHT WHILE EVERYONE ELSE GETS TO SLEEP? THEY WOULDN'T APPRECIATE IT ANYWAY...
Z

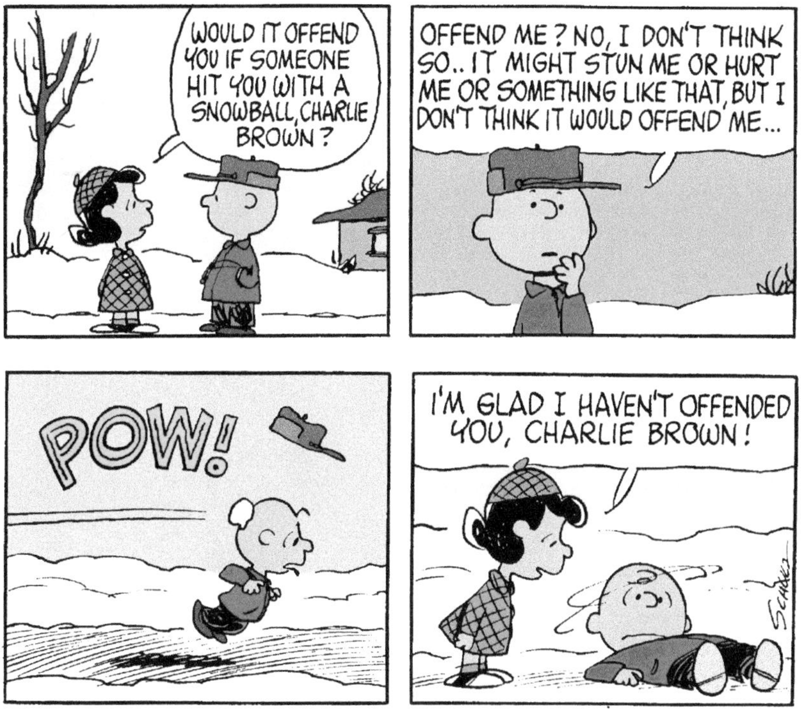
WOULD IT OFFEND YOU IF SOMEONE HIT YOU WITH A SNOWBALL, CHARLIE BROWN?
OFFEND ME? NO, I DON'T THINK SO.. IT MIGHT STUN ME OR HURT ME OR SOMETHING LIKE THAT, BUT I DON'T THINK IT WOULD OFFEND ME...
POW!
I'M GLAD I HAVEN'T OFFENDED YOU, CHARLIE BROWN!
SCHULZ

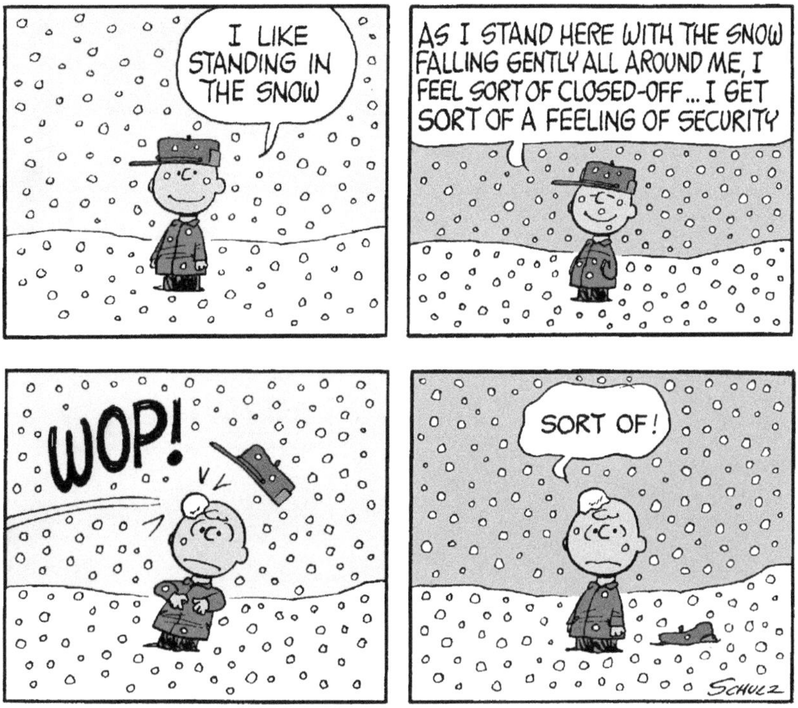
I LIKE STANDING IN THE SNOW
AS I STAND HERE WITH THE SNOW FALLING GENTLY ALL AROUND ME, I FEEL SORT OF CLOSED-OFF... I GET SORT OF A FEELING OF SECURITY
WOP!
SORT OF!
SCHULZ

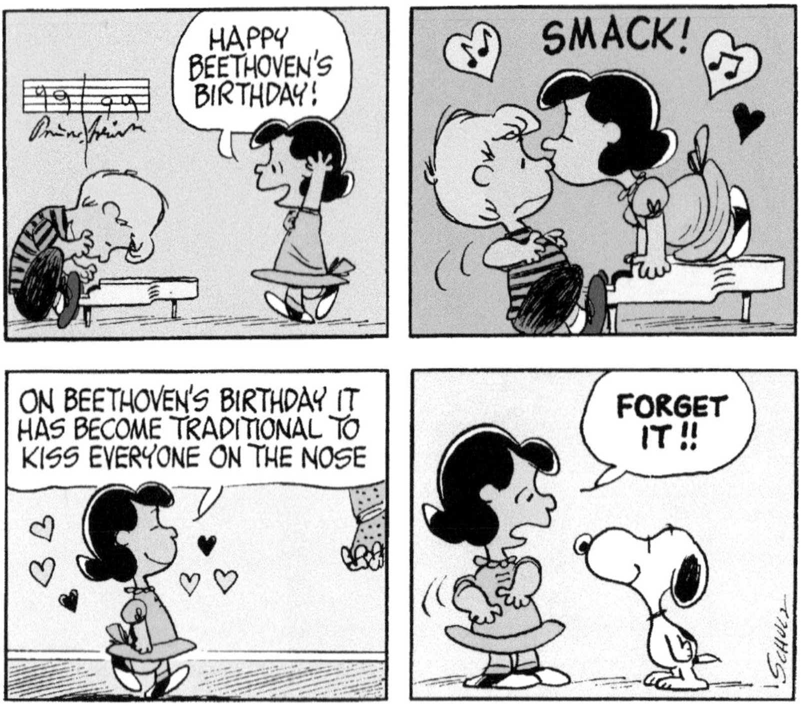
HAPPY BEETHOVEN'S BIRTHDAY!
SMACK!
ON BEETHOVEN'S BIRTHDAY IT HAS BECOME TRADITIONAL TO KISS EVERYONE ON THE NOSE
FORGET IT!!
SCHULZ

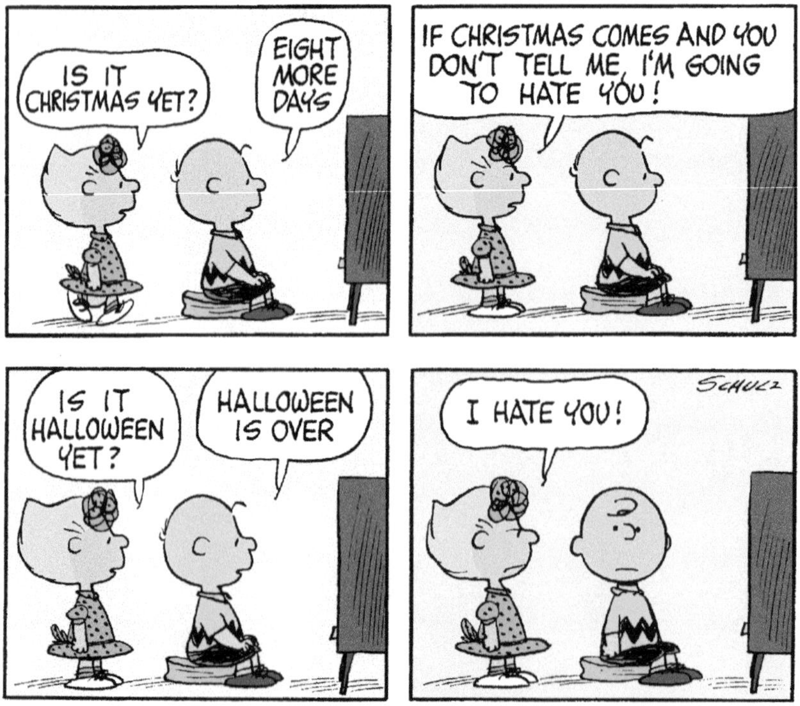
IS IT CHRISTMAS YET?
EIGHT MORE DAYS
IF CHRISTMAS COMES AND YOU DON'T TELL ME, I'M GOING TO HATE YOU!
IS IT HALLOWEEN YET?
HALLOWEEN IS OVER
SCHULZ
I HATE YOU!

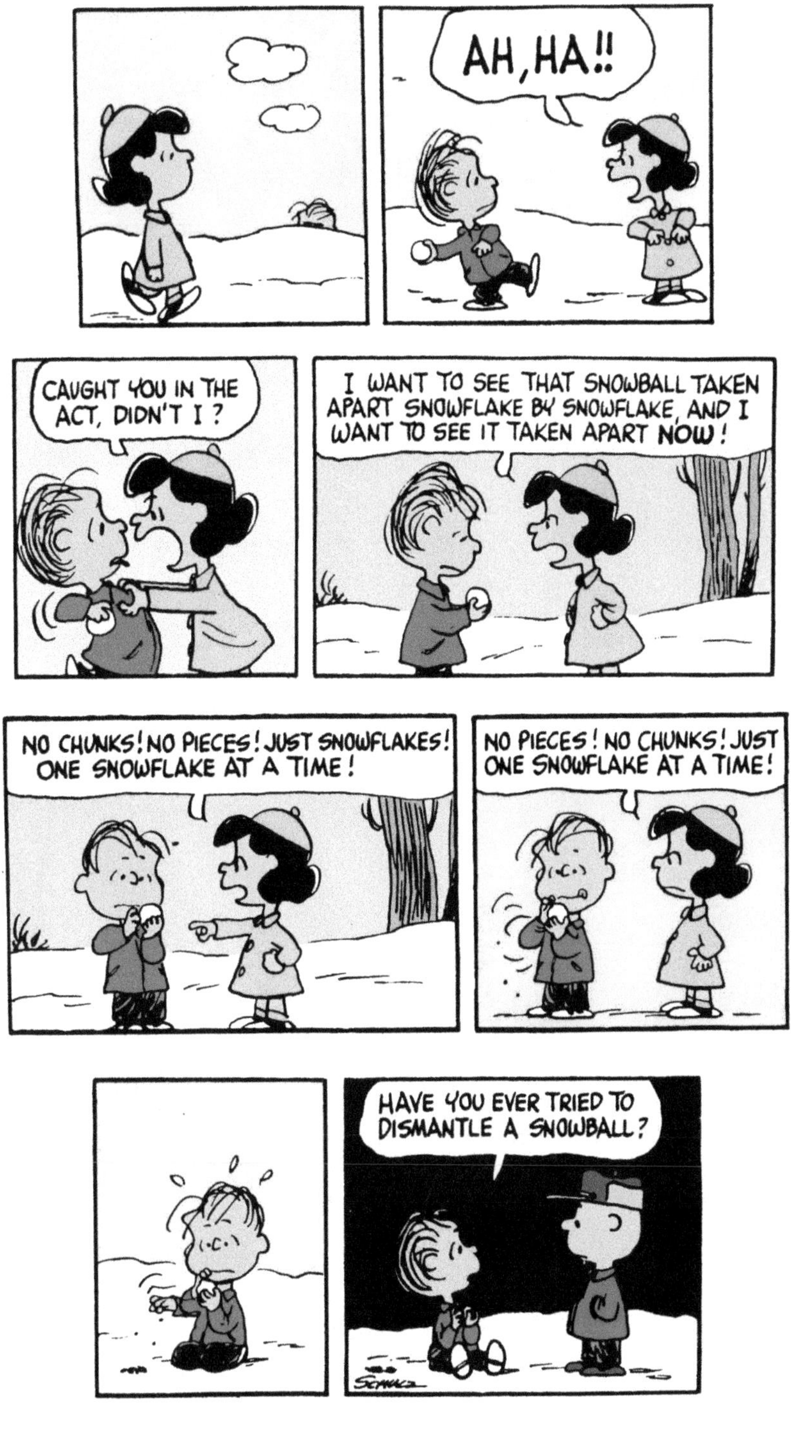

AH, HA!!
CAUGHT YOU IN THE ACT, DIDN'T I ?
I WANT TO SEE THAT SNOWBALL TAKEN APART SNOWFLAKE BY SNOWFLAKE, AND I WANT TO SEE IT TAKEN APART NOW !
NO CHUNKS! NO PIECES! JUST SNOWFLAKES! ONE SNOWFLAKE AT A TIME!
NO PIECES! NO CHUNKS! JUST ONE SNOWFLAKE AT A TIME!
HAVE YOU EVER TRIED TO DISMANTLE A SNOWBALL?
SCHULZ

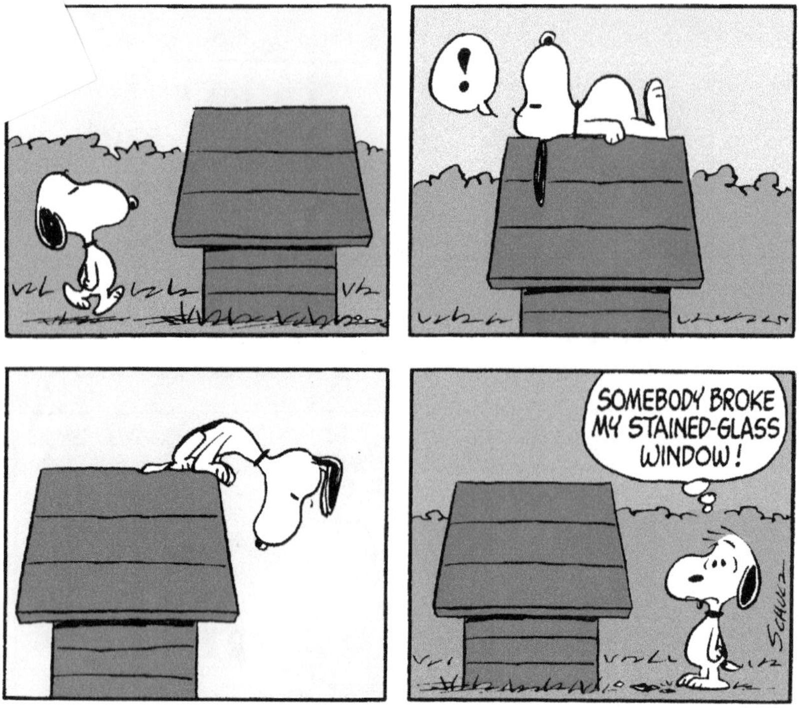
!
SOMEBODY BROKE MY STAINED-GLASS WINDOW!

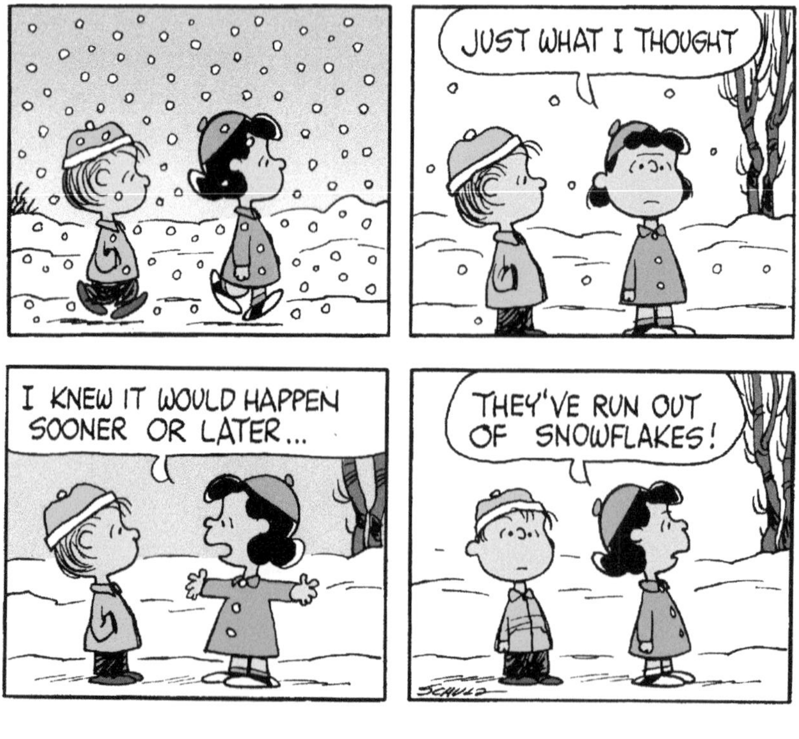
JUST WHAT I THOUGHT
I KNEW IT WOULD HAPPEN SOONER OR LATER...
THEY'VE RUN OUT OF SNOWFLAKES!

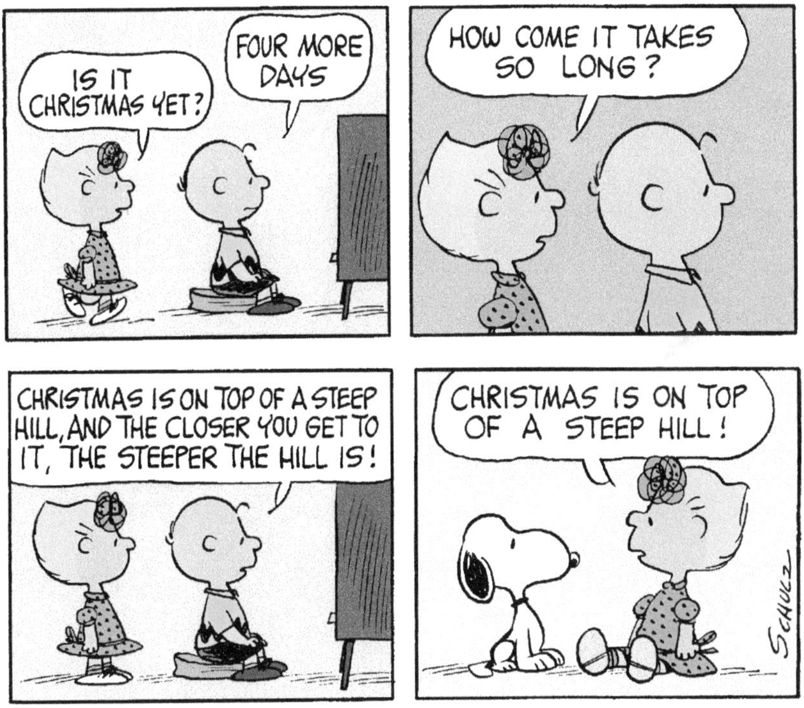
IS IT CHRISTMAS YET?
FOUR MORE DAYS
HOW COME IT TAKES SO LONG?
CHRISTMAS IS ON TOP OF A STEEP HILL, AND THE CLOSER YOU GET TO IT, THE STEEPER THE HILL IS!
CHRISTMAS IS ON TOP OF A STEEP HILL!
SCHULZ

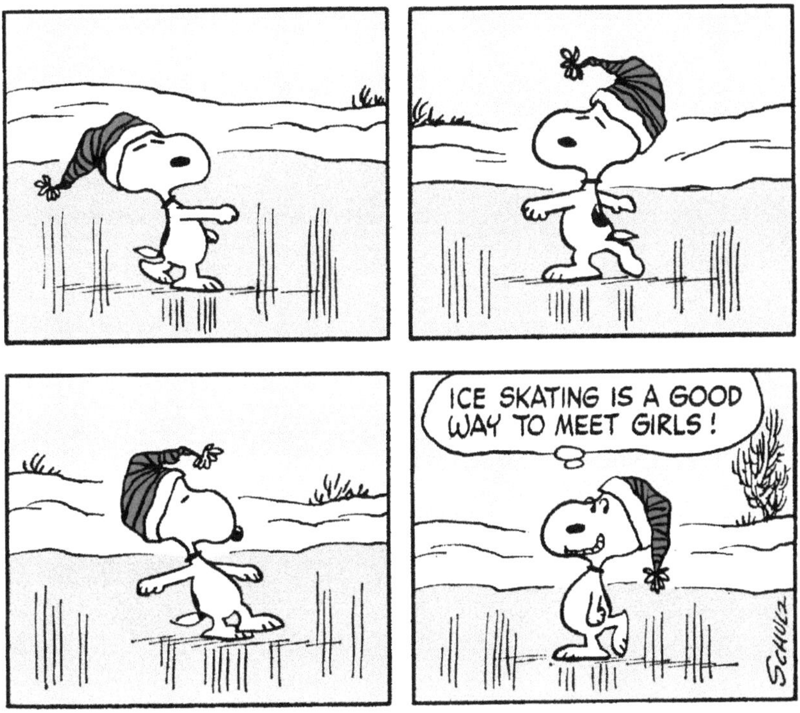
ICE SKATING IS A GOOD WAY TO MEET GIRLS!
SCHULZ

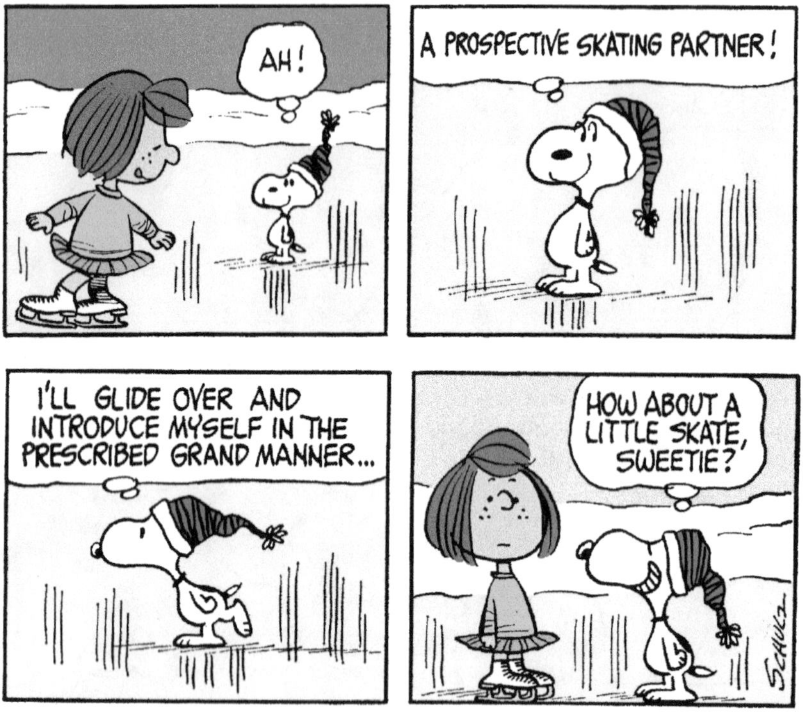
AH!
A PROSPECTIVE SKATING PARTNER!
I'LL GLIDE OVER AND INTRODUCE MYSELF IN THE PRESCRIBED GRAND MANNER...
HOW ABOUT A LITTLE SKATE, SWEETIE?
SCHULZ

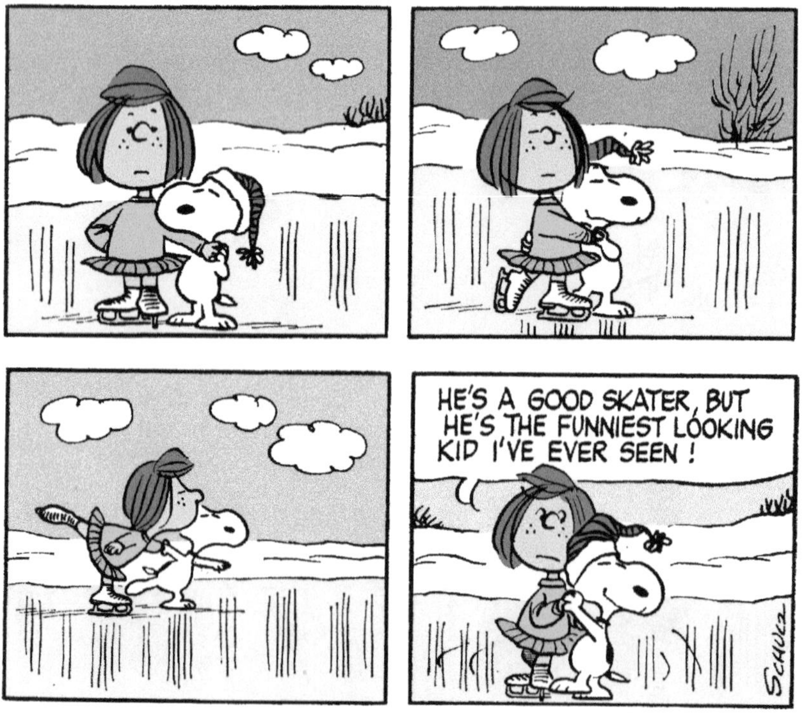
HE'S A GOOD SKATER, BUT HE'S THE FUNNIEST LOOKING KID I'VE EVER SEEN!
SCHULZ

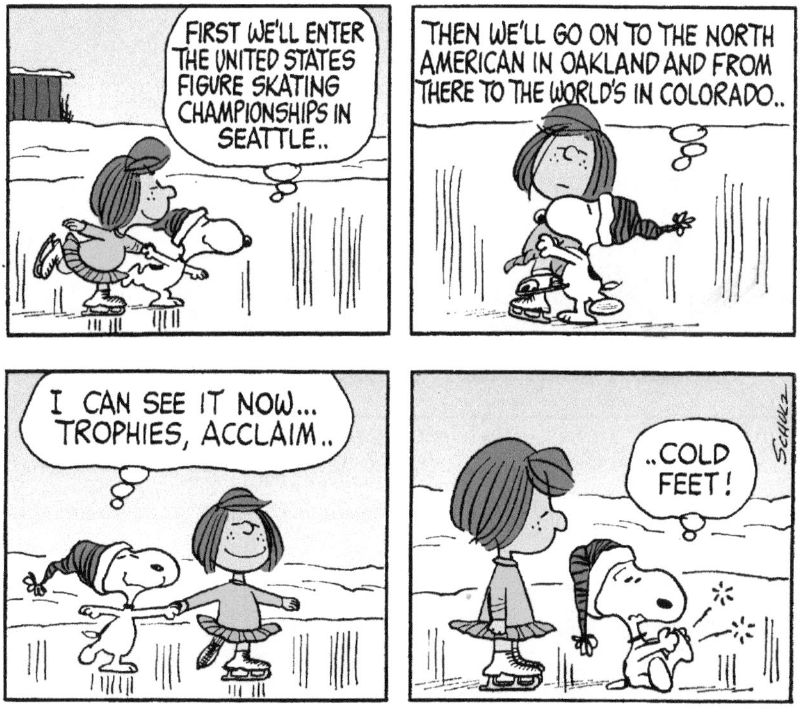
FIRST WE'LL ENTER THE UNITED STATES FIGURE SKATING CHAMPIONSHIPS IN SEATTLE..
THEN WE'LL GO ON TO THE NORTH AMERICAN IN OAKLAND AND FROM THERE TO THE WORLD'S IN COLORADO..
I CAN SEE IT NOW... TROPHIES, ACCLAIM..
..COLD FEET!
SCHULZ

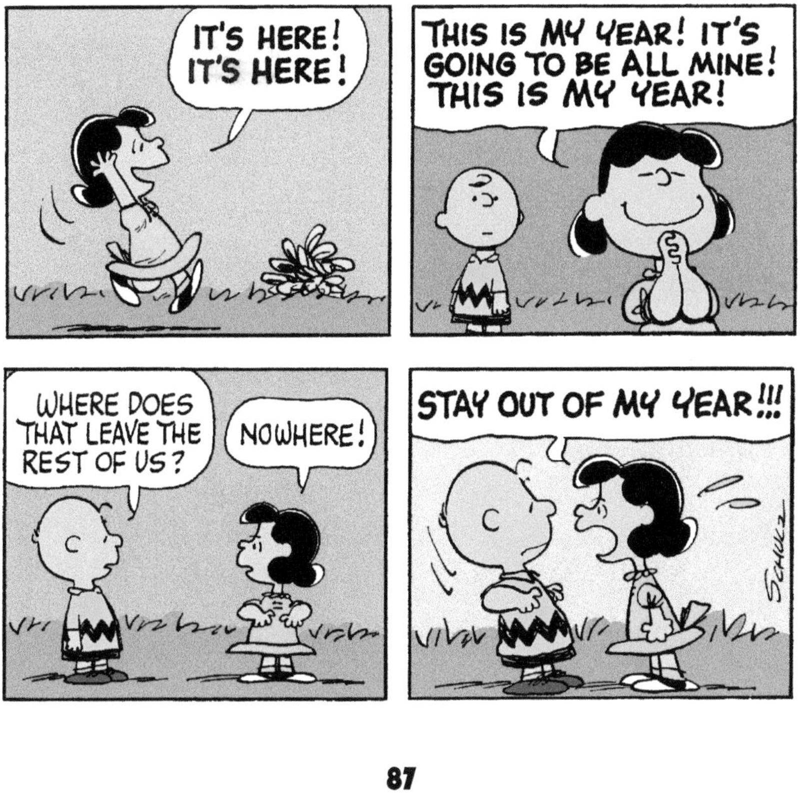
IT'S HERE! IT'S HERE!
THIS IS MY YEAR! IT'S GOING TO BE ALL MINE! THIS IS MY YEAR!
WHERE DOES THAT LEAVE THE REST OF US?
NOWHERE!
STAY OUT OF MY YEAR!!!
SCHULZ

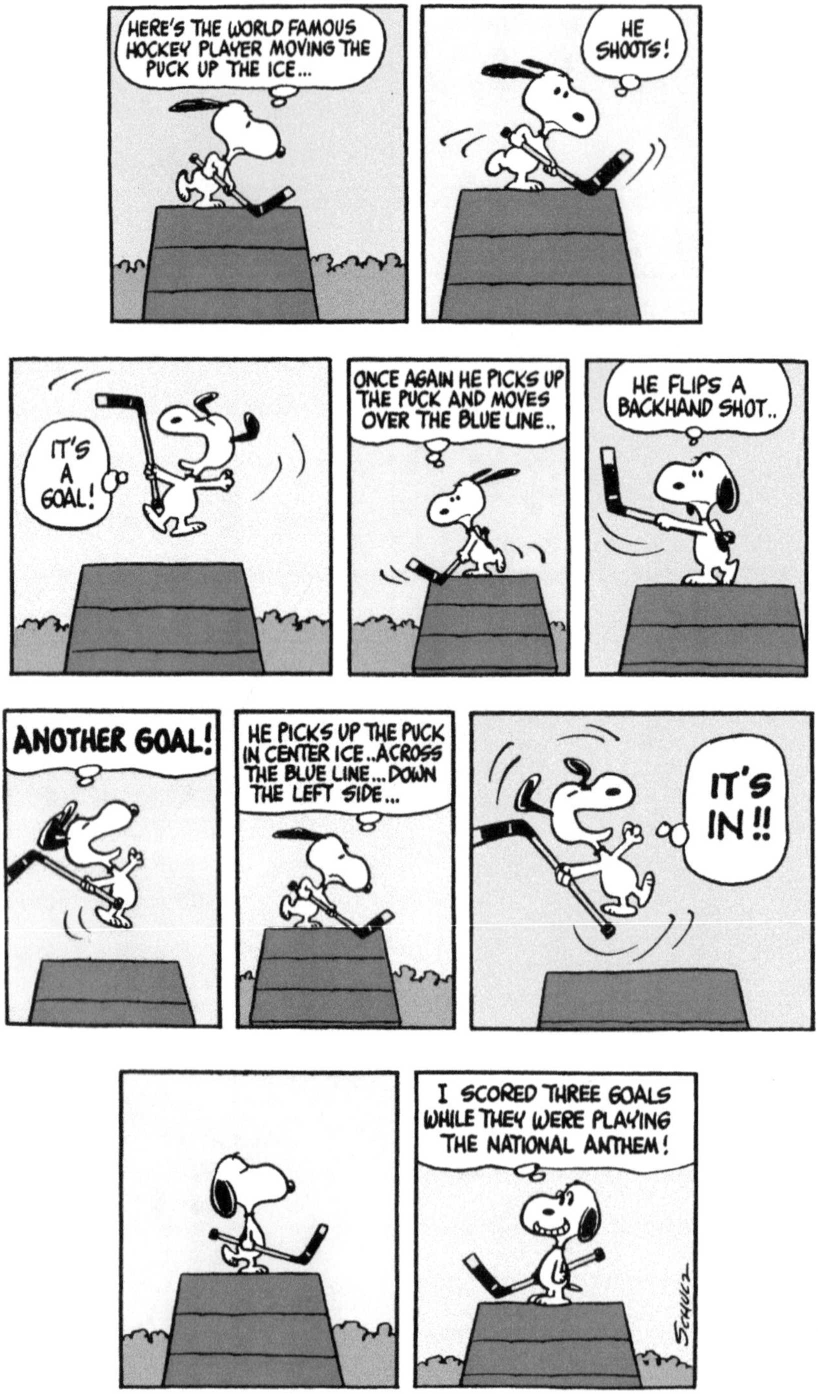
HERE'S THE WORLD FAMOUS HOCKEY PLAYER MOVING THE PUCK UP THE ICE...
HE SHOOTS!
IT'S A GOAL!
ONCE AGAIN HE PICKS UP THE PUCK AND MOVES OVER THE BLUE LINE..
HE FLIPS A BACKHAND SHOT..
ANOTHER GOAL!
HE PICKS UP THE PUCK IN CENTER ICE..ACROSS THE BLUE LINE...DOWN THE LEFT SIDE...
IT'S IN!!
I SCORED THREE GOALS WHILE THEY WERE PLAYING THE NATIONAL ANTHEM!
SCHULZ

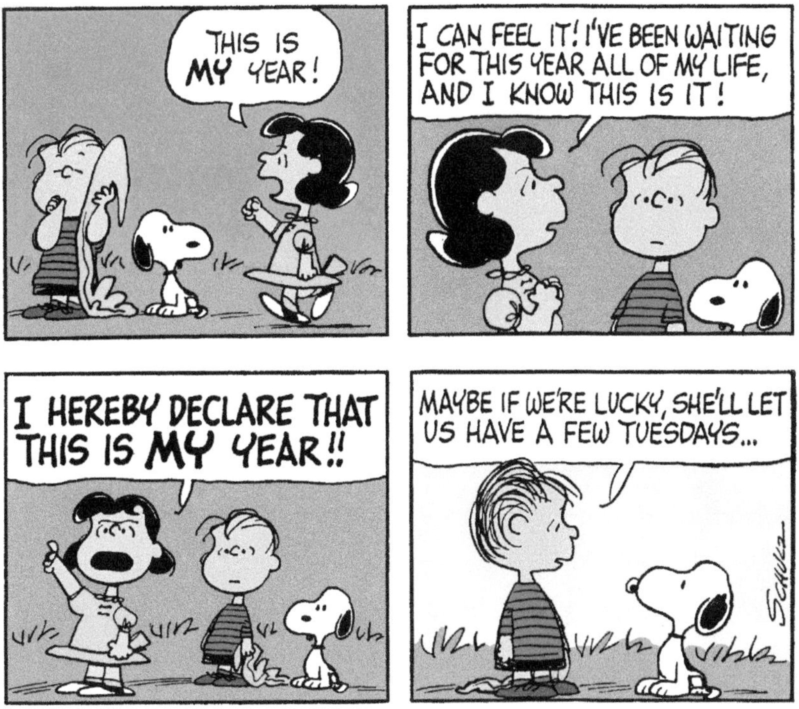
THIS IS MY YEAR!
I CAN FEEL IT! I'VE BEEN WAITING FOR THIS YEAR ALL OF MY LIFE, AND I KNOW THIS IS IT!
I HEREBY DECLARE THAT THIS IS MY YEAR!!
MAYBE IF WE'RE LUCKY, SHE'LL LET US HAVE A FEW TUESDAYS...
SCHULZ

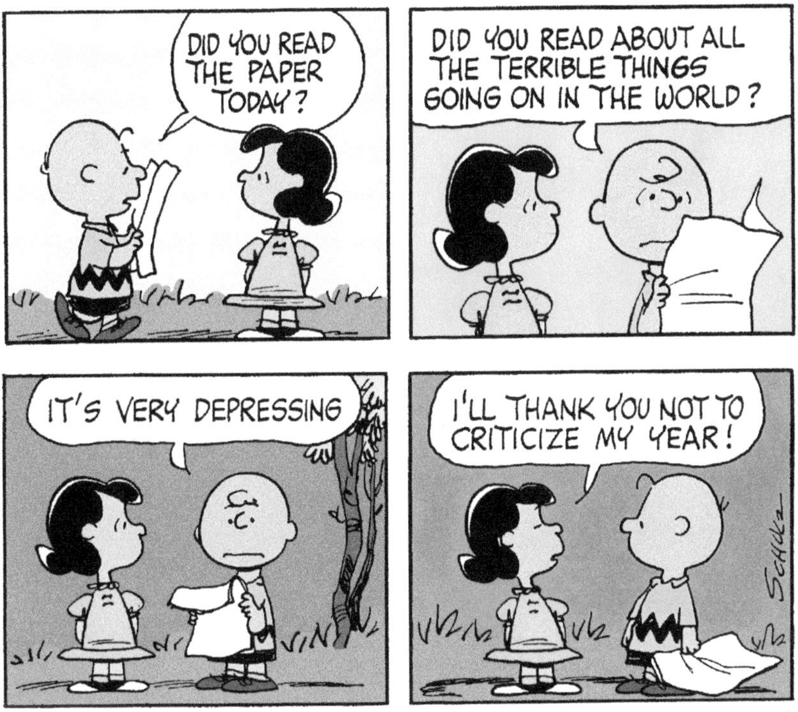
DID YOU READ THE PAPER TODAY?
DID YOU READ ABOUT ALL THE TERRIBLE THINGS GOING ON IN THE WORLD?
IT'S VERY DEPRESSING
I'LL THANK YOU NOT TO CRITICIZE MY YEAR!
SCHULZ

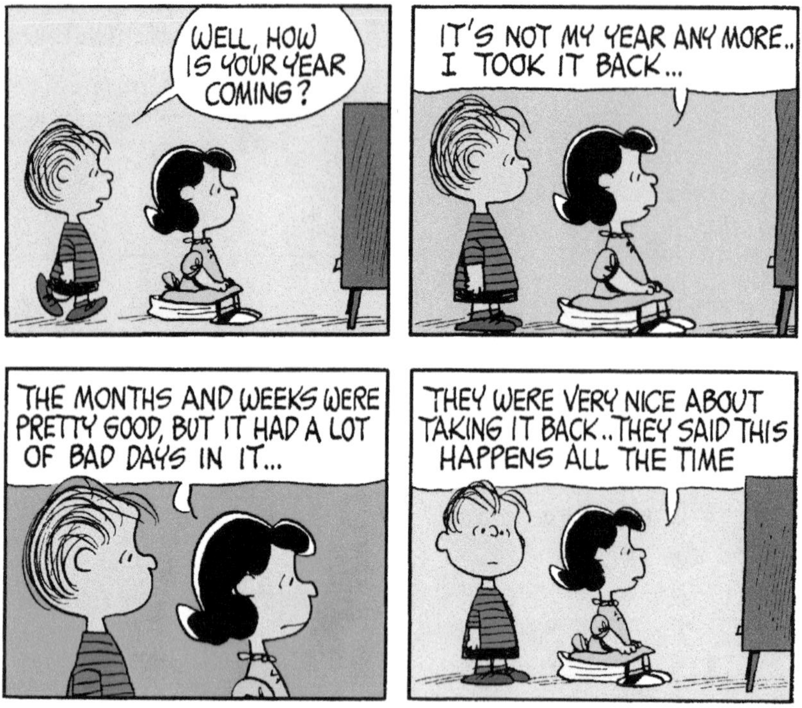
WELL, HOW IS YOUR YEAR COMING?
IT'S NOT MY YEAR ANY MORE.. I TOOK IT BACK...
THE MONTHS AND WEEKS WERE PRETTY GOOD, BUT IT HAD A LOT OF BAD DAYS IN IT...
THEY WERE VERY NICE ABOUT TAKING IT BACK..THEY SAID THIS HAPPENS ALL THE TIME

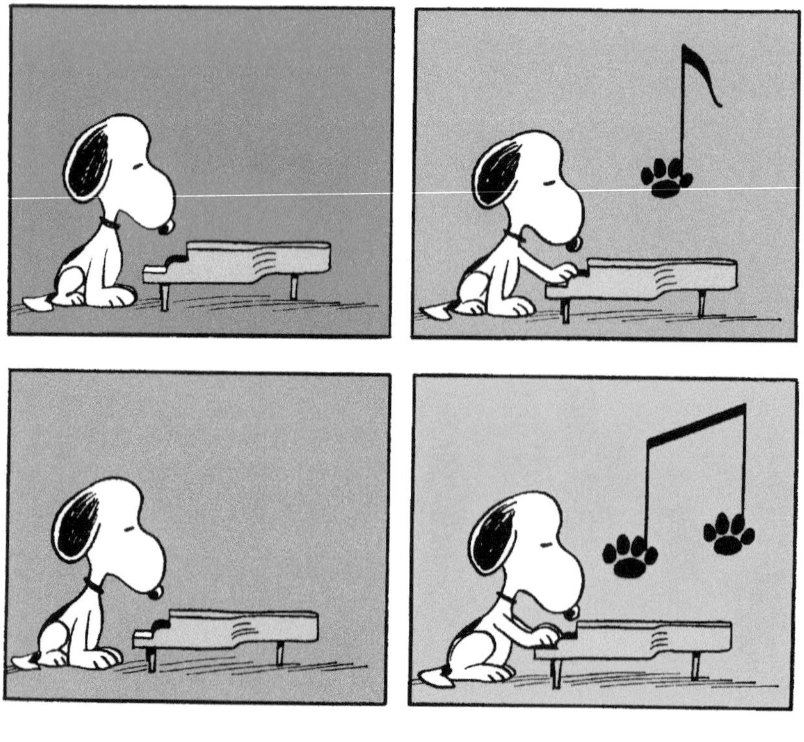

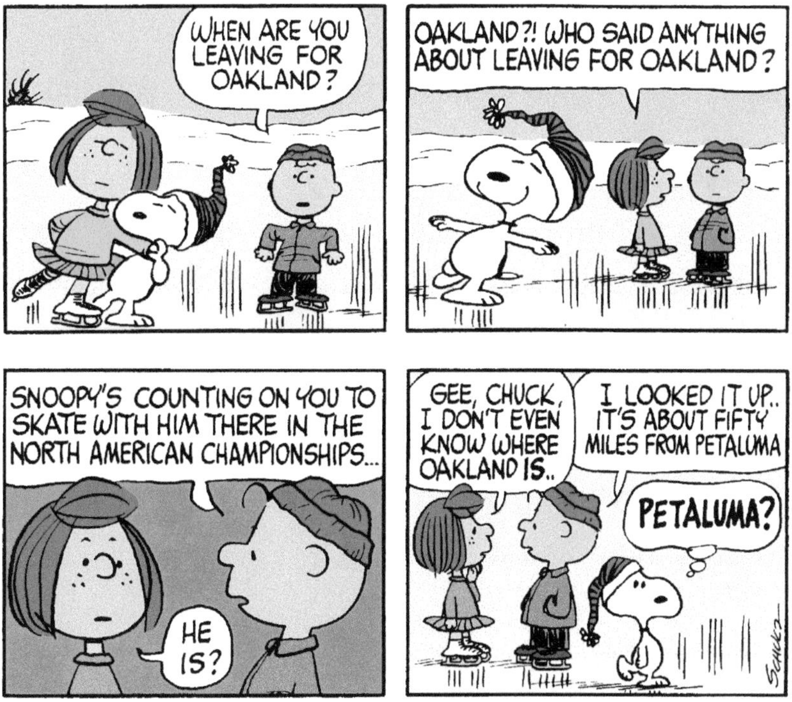
WHEN ARE YOU LEAVING FOR OAKLAND?
OAKLAND?! WHO SAID ANYTHING ABOUT LEAVING FOR OAKLAND?
SNOOPY'S COUNTING ON YOU TO SKATE WITH HIM THERE IN THE NORTH AMERICAN CHAMPIONSHIPS...
HE IS?
GEE, CHUCK, I DON'T EVEN KNOW WHERE OAKLAND IS..
I LOOKED IT UP.. IT'S ABOUT FIFTY MILES FROM PETALUMA
PETALUMA?

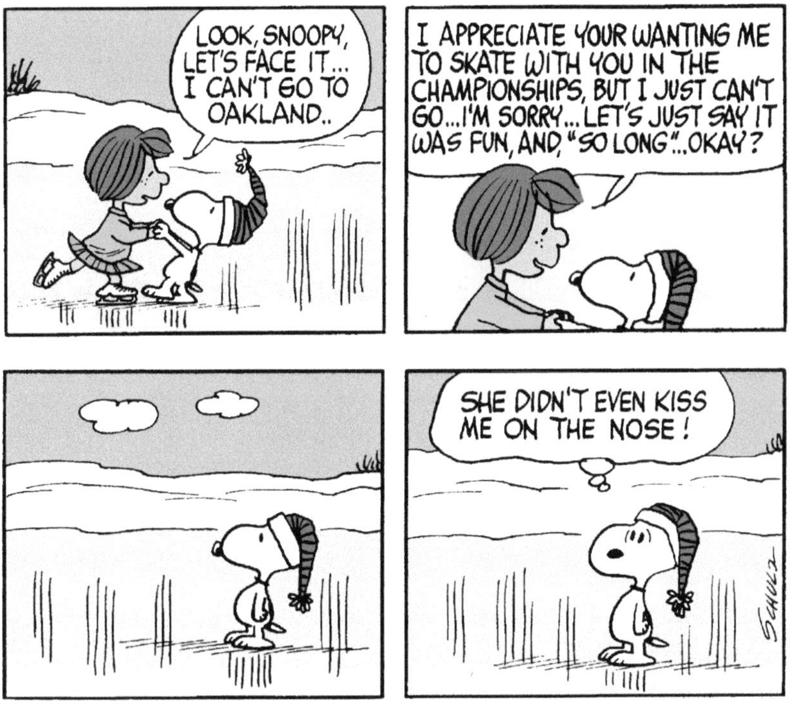
LOOK, SNOOPY, LET'S FACE IT... I CAN'T GO TO OAKLAND..
I APPRECIATE YOUR WANTING ME TO SKATE WITH YOU IN THE CHAMPIONSHIPS, BUT I JUST CAN'T GO...I'M SORRY... LET'S JUST SAY IT WAS FUN, AND "SO LONG"...OKAY?
SHE DIDN'T EVEN KISS ME ON THE NOSE!

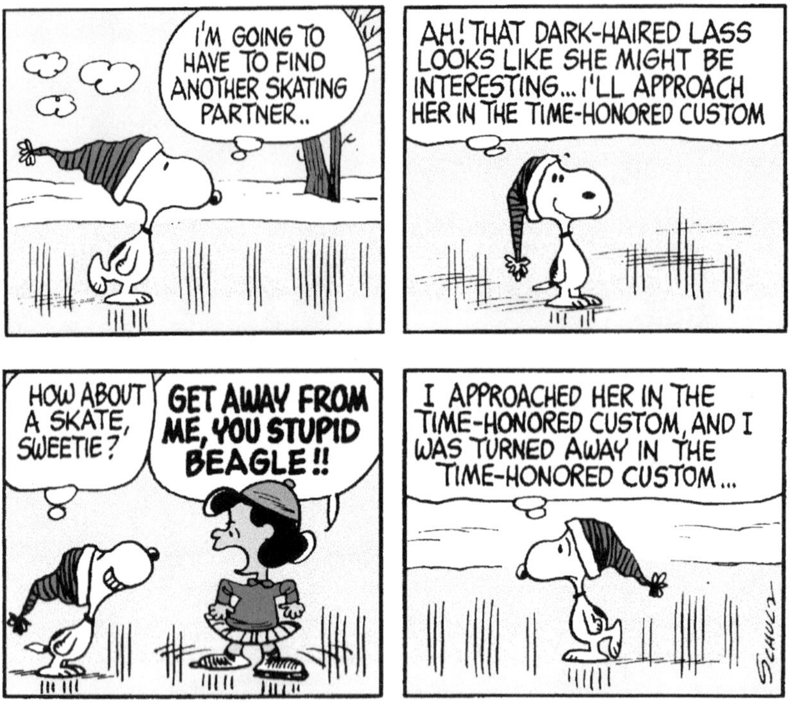
I'M GOING TO HAVE TO FIND ANOTHER SKATING PARTNER..
AH! THAT DARK-HAIRED LASS LOOKS LIKE SHE MIGHT BE INTERESTING... I'LL APPROACH HER IN THE TIME-HONORED CUSTOM
HOW ABOUT A SKATE, SWEETIE?
GET AWAY FROM ME, YOU STUPID BEAGLE!!
I APPROACHED HER IN THE TIME-HONORED CUSTOM, AND I WAS TURNED AWAY IN THE TIME-HONORED CUSTOM...
SCHULZ

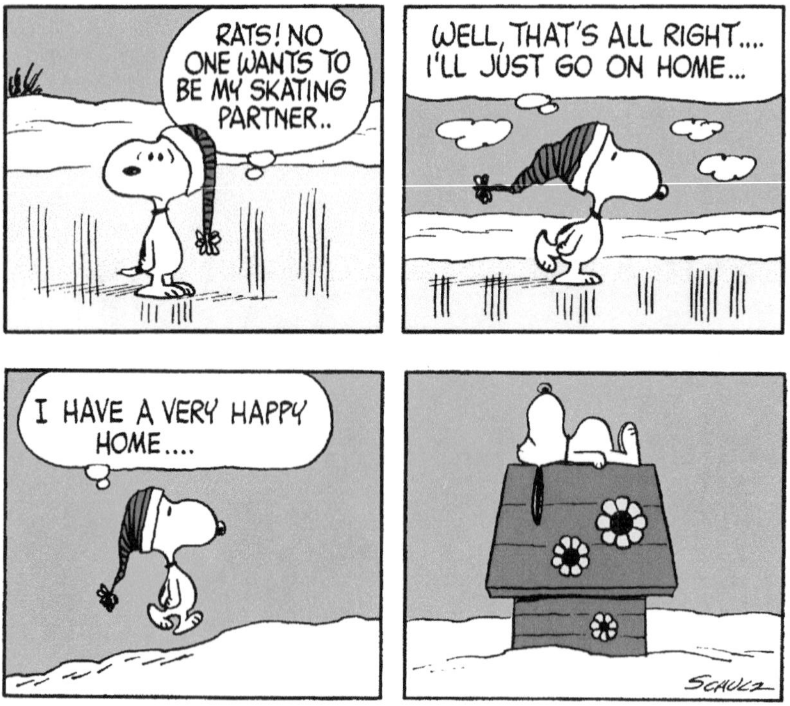
RATS! NO ONE WANTS TO BE MY SKATING PARTNER..
WELL, THAT'S ALL RIGHT.... I'LL JUST GO ON HOME...
I HAVE A VERY HAPPY HOME....
SCHULZ

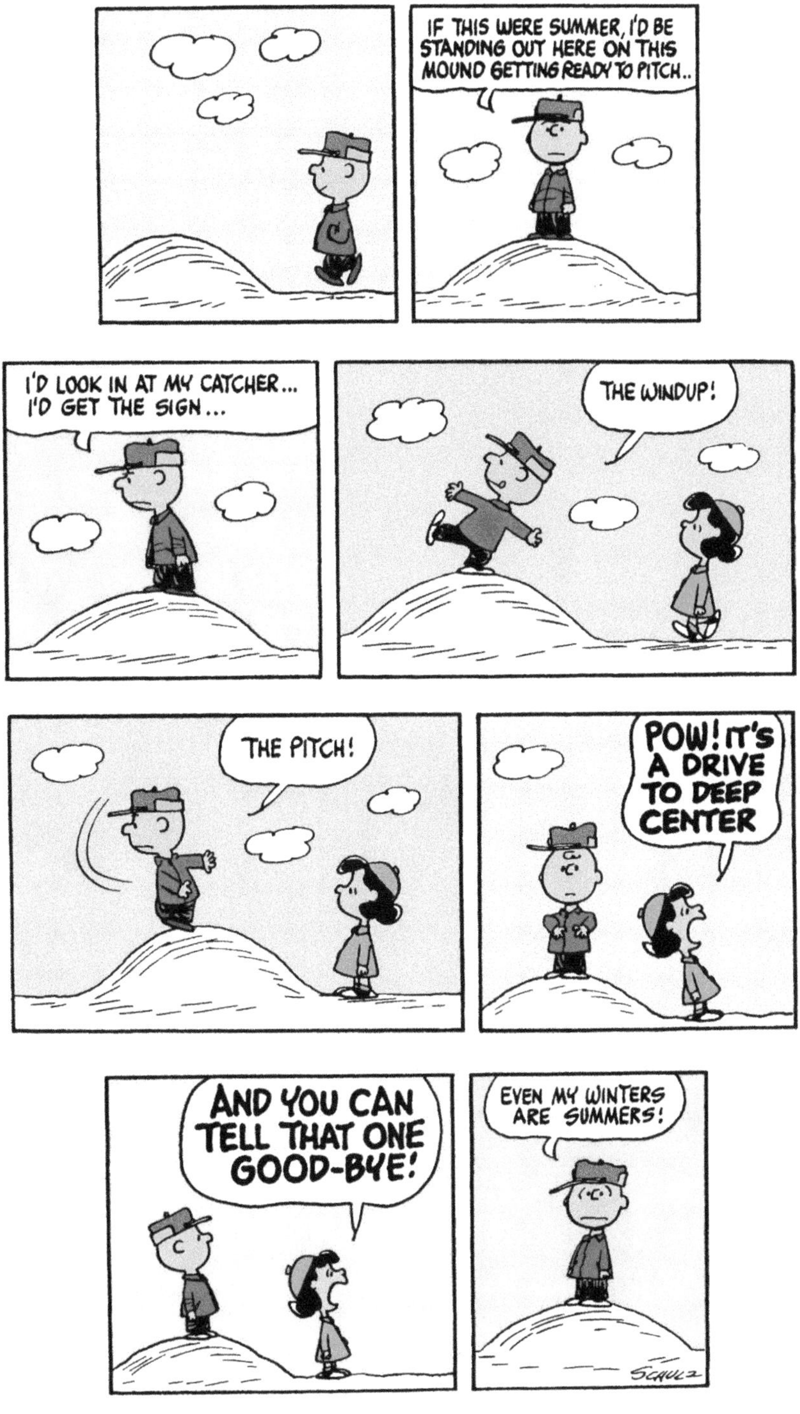
IF THIS WERE SUMMER, I'D BE STANDING OUT HERE ON THIS MOUND GETTING READY TO PITCH..
I'D LOOK IN AT MY CATCHER... I'D GET THE SIGN...
THE WINDUP!
THE PITCH!
POW! IT'S A DRIVE TO DEEP CENTER
AND YOU CAN TELL THAT ONE GOOD-BYE!
EVEN MY WINTERS ARE SUMMERS!
SCHULZ

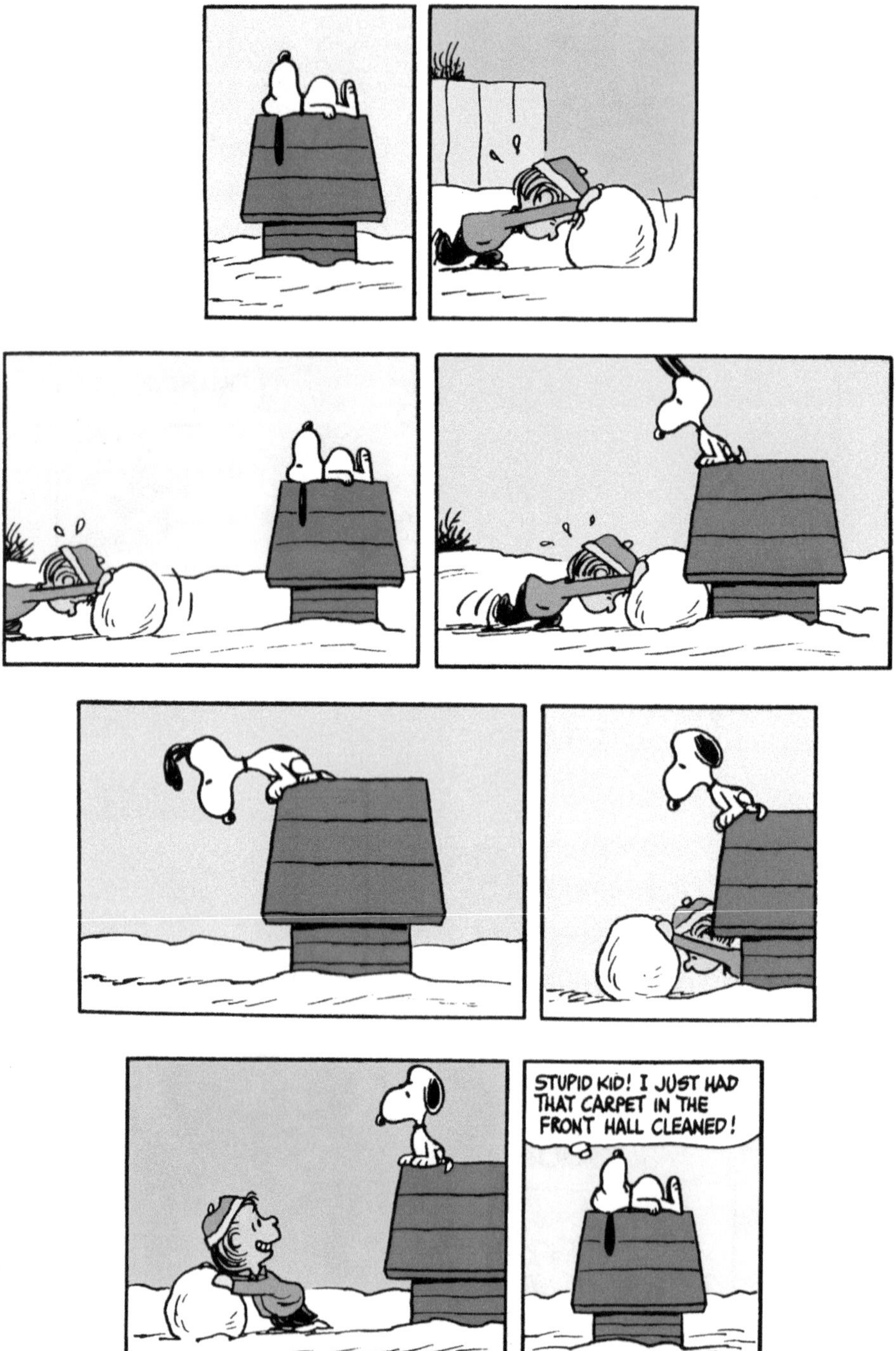
STUPID KID! I JUST HAD THAT CARPET IN THE FRONT HALL CLEANED!

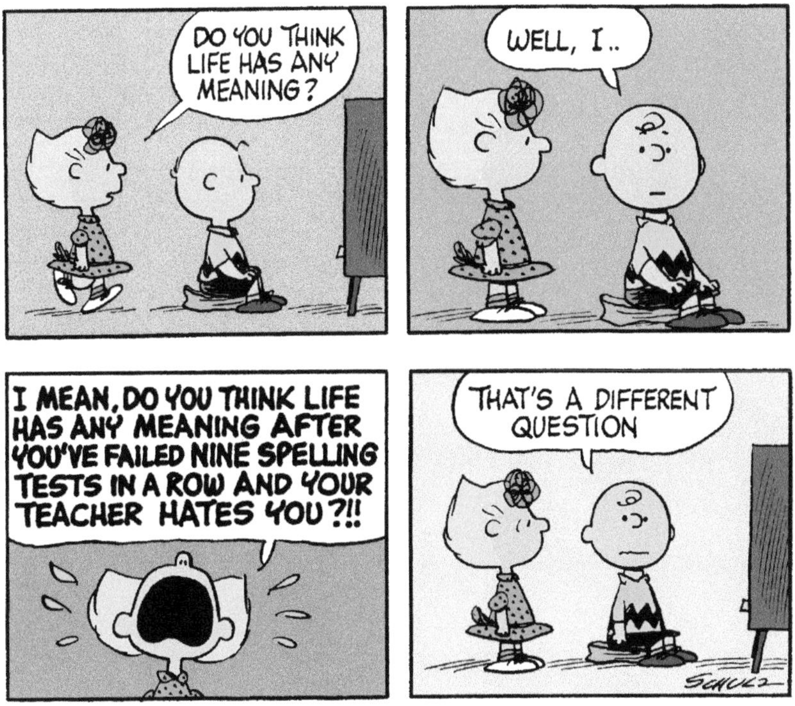
DO YOU THINK LIFE HAS ANY MEANING?
WELL, I..
I MEAN, DO YOU THINK LIFE HAS ANY MEANING AFTER YOU'VE FAILED NINE SPELLING TESTS IN A ROW AND YOUR TEACHER HATES YOU?!!
THAT'S A DIFFERENT QUESTION
SCHULZ

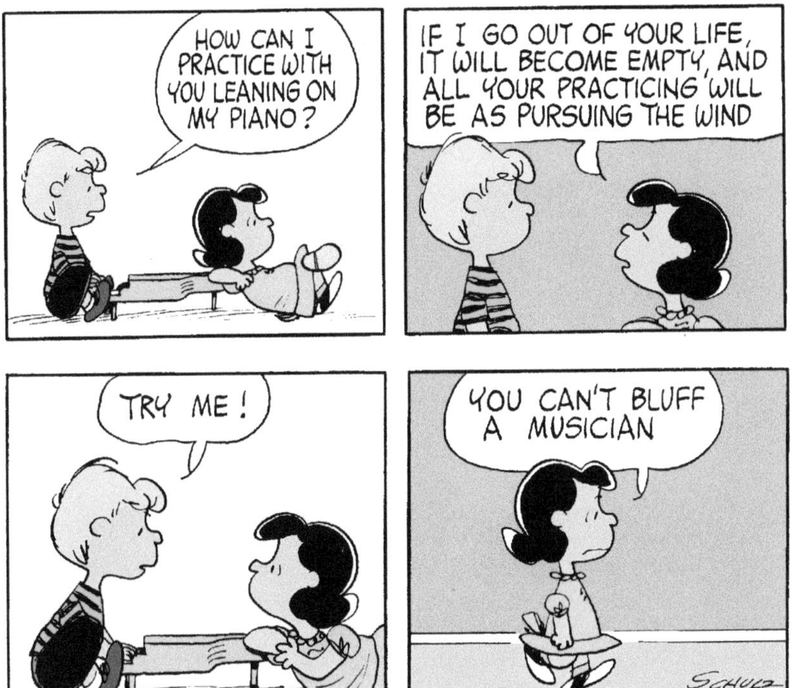
HOW CAN I PRACTICE WITH YOU LEANING ON MY PIANO?
IF I GO OUT OF YOUR LIFE, IT WILL BECOME EMPTY, AND ALL YOUR PRACTICING WILL BE AS PURSUING THE WIND
TRY ME!
YOU CAN'T BLUFF A MUSICIAN
SCHULZ

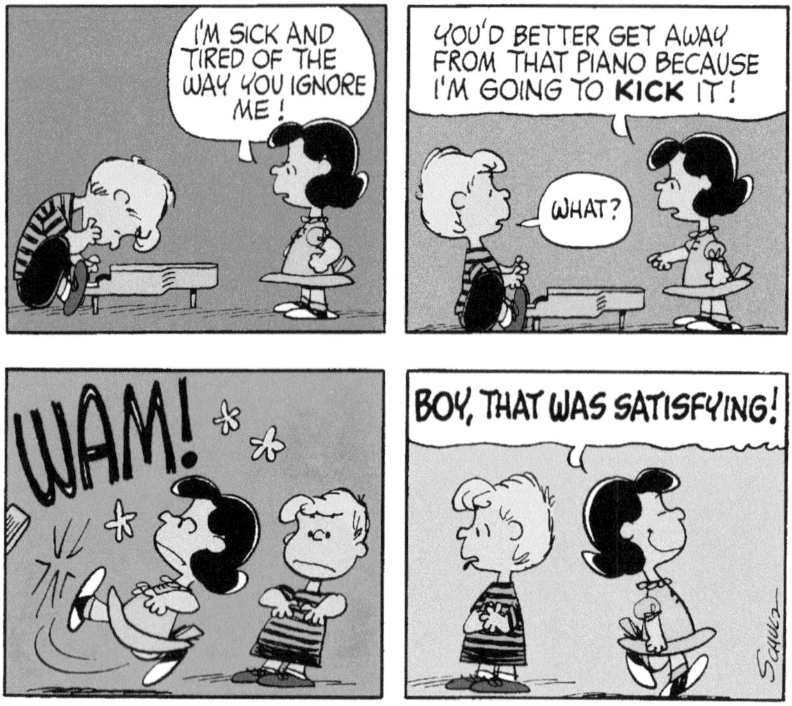
I'M SICK AND TIRED OF THE WAY YOU IGNORE ME!
YOU'D BETTER GET AWAY FROM THAT PIANO BECAUSE I'M GOING TO **KICK** IT!
WHAT?
WAM!
BOY, THAT WAS SATISFYING!
SCHULZ

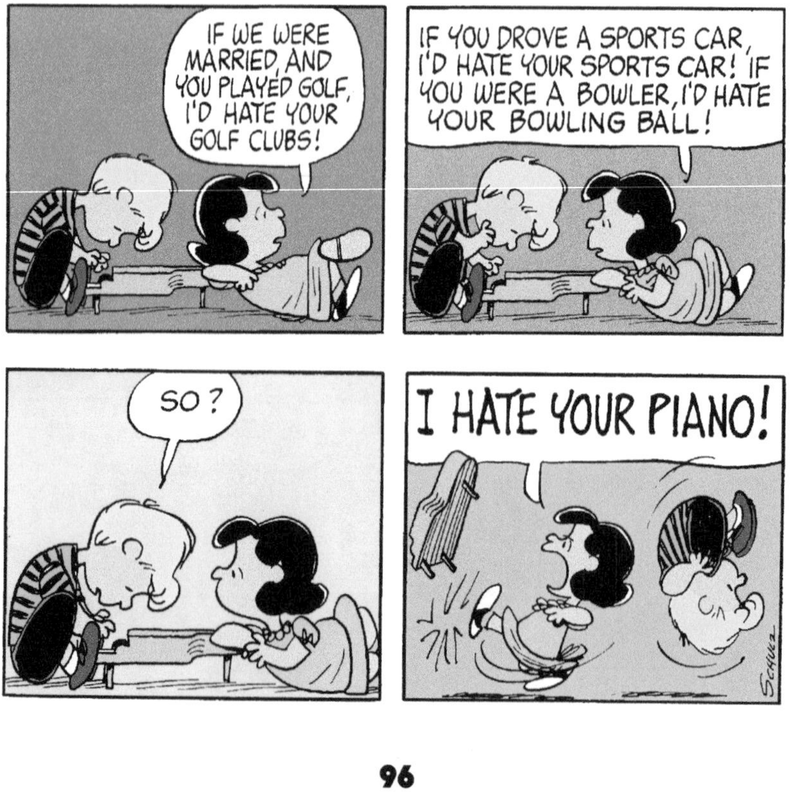
IF WE WERE MARRIED, AND YOU PLAYED GOLF, I'D HATE YOUR GOLF CLUBS!
IF YOU DROVE A SPORTS CAR, I'D HATE YOUR SPORTS CAR! IF YOU WERE A BOWLER, I'D HATE YOUR BOWLING BALL!
SO?
I HATE YOUR PIANO!
SCHULZ

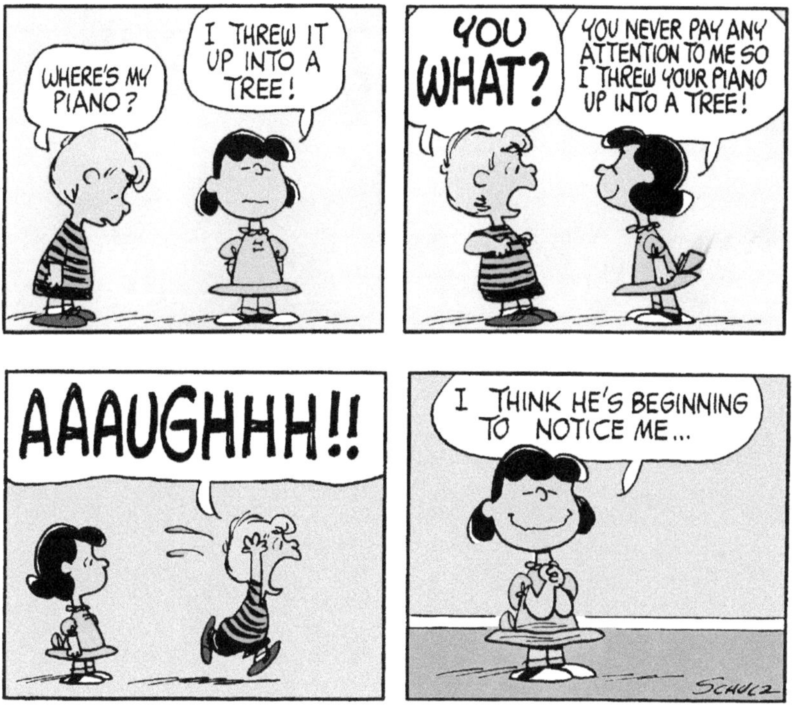
WHERE'S MY PIANO?
I THREW IT UP INTO A TREE!
YOU WHAT?
YOU NEVER PAY ANY ATTENTION TO ME SO I THREW YOUR PIANO UP INTO A TREE!
AAAUGHHH!!
I THINK HE'S BEGINNING TO NOTICE ME...
SCHULZ

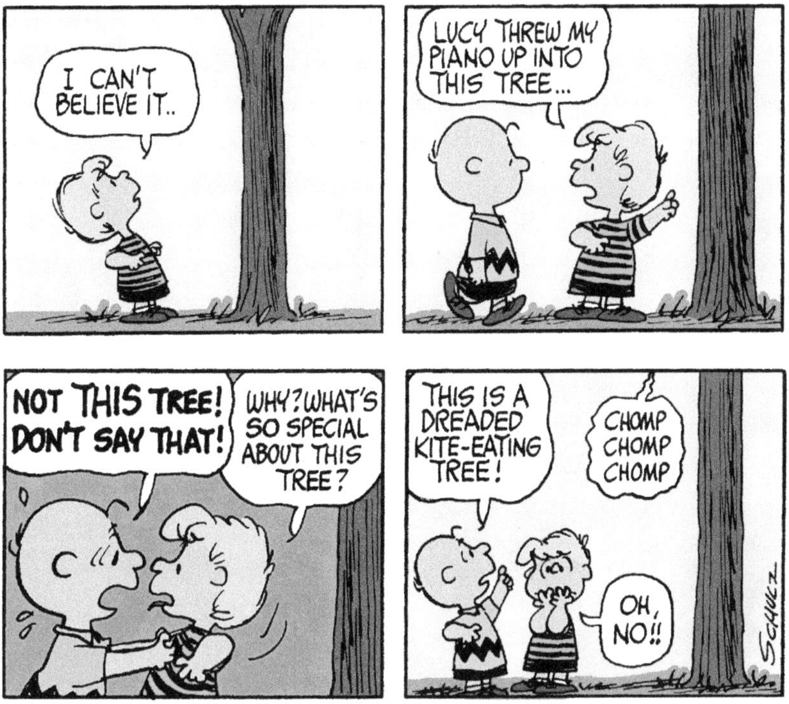
I CAN'T BELIEVE IT..
LUCY THREW MY PIANO UP INTO THIS TREE...
NOT THIS TREE! DON'T SAY THAT!
WHY? WHAT'S SO SPECIAL ABOUT THIS TREE?
THIS IS A DREADED KITE-EATING TREE!
CHOMP CHOMP CHOMP
OH, NO!!
SCHULZ

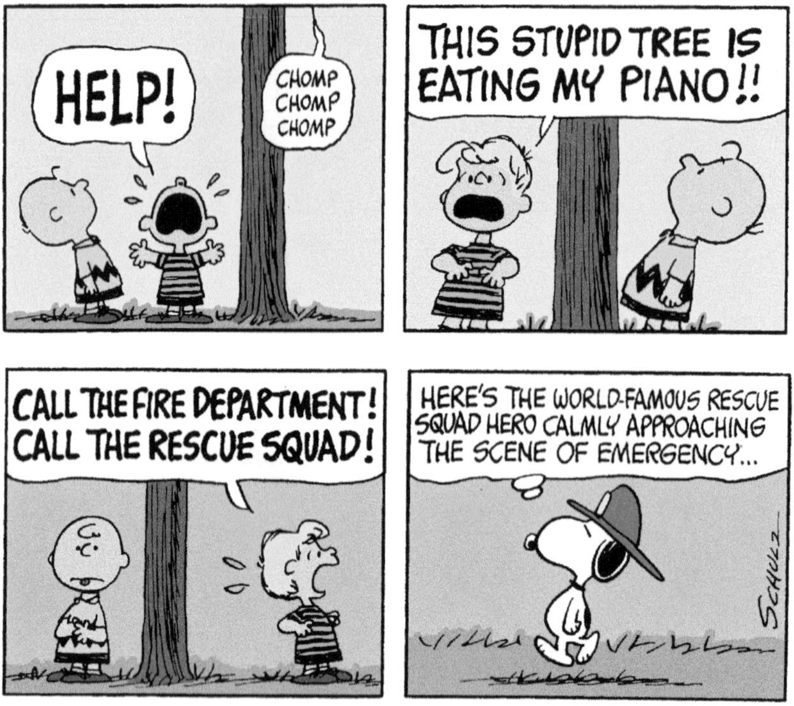
HELP!
CHOMP CHOMP CHOMP
THIS STUPID TREE IS EATING MY PIANO!!
CALL THE FIRE DEPARTMENT! CALL THE RESCUE SQUAD!
HERE'S THE WORLD-FAMOUS RESCUE SQUAD HERO CALMLY APPROACHING THE SCENE OF EMERGENCY...
SCHULZ

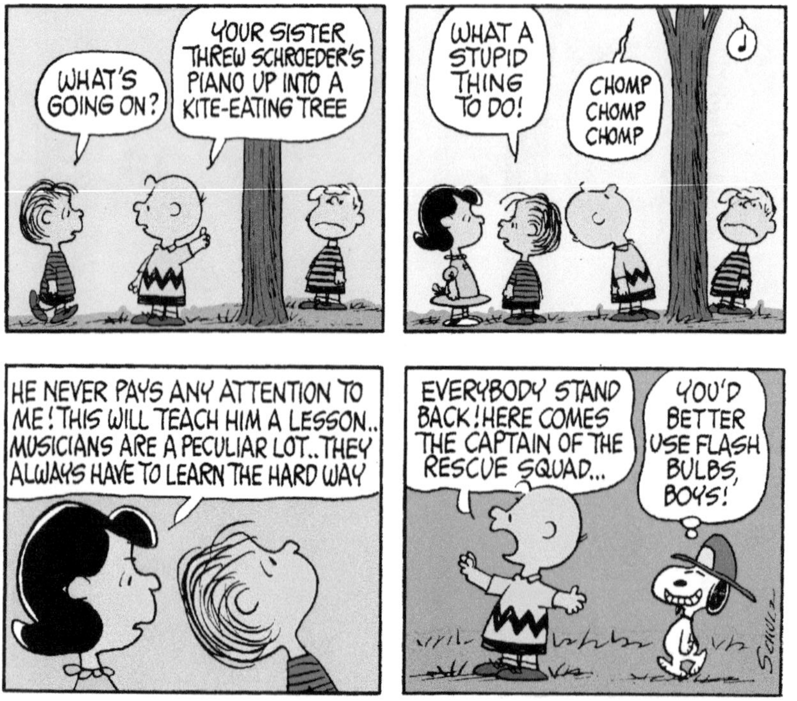
WHAT'S GOING ON?
YOUR SISTER THREW SCHROEDER'S PIANO UP INTO A KITE-EATING TREE
WHAT A STUPID THING TO DO!
CHOMP CHOMP CHOMP
HE NEVER PAYS ANY ATTENTION TO ME! THIS WILL TEACH HIM A LESSON.. MUSICIANS ARE A PECULIAR LOT.. THEY ALWAYS HAVE TO LEARN THE HARD WAY
EVERYBODY STAND BACK! HERE COMES THE CAPTAIN OF THE RESCUE SQUAD...
YOU'D BETTER USE FLASH BULBS, BOYS!
SCHULZ

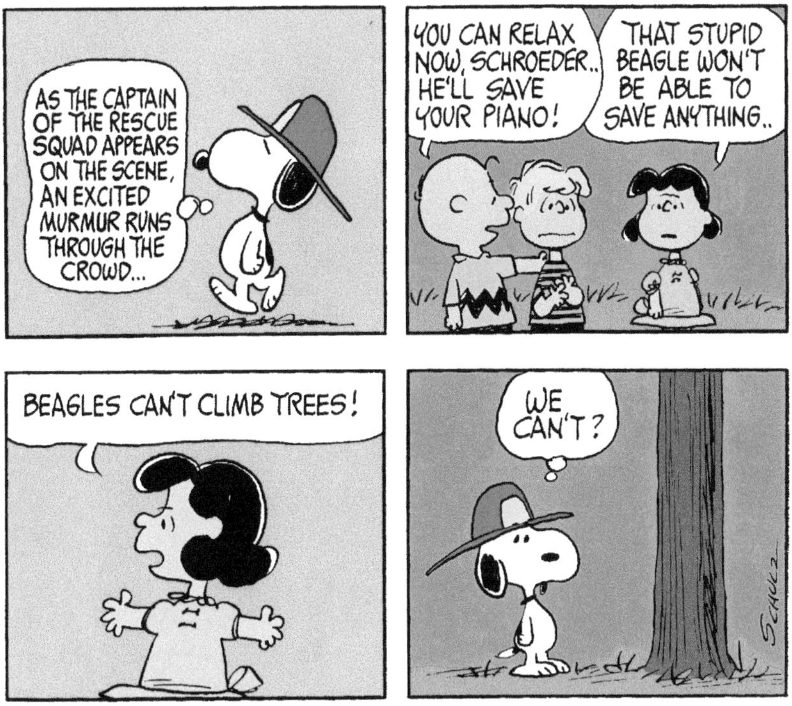
AS THE CAPTAIN OF THE RESCUE SQUAD APPEARS ON THE SCENE, AN EXCITED MURMUR RUNS THROUGH THE CROWD...
YOU CAN RELAX NOW, SCHROEDER.. HE'LL SAVE YOUR PIANO!
THAT STUPID BEAGLE WON'T BE ABLE TO SAVE ANYTHING..
BEAGLES CAN'T CLIMB TREES!
WE CAN'T?

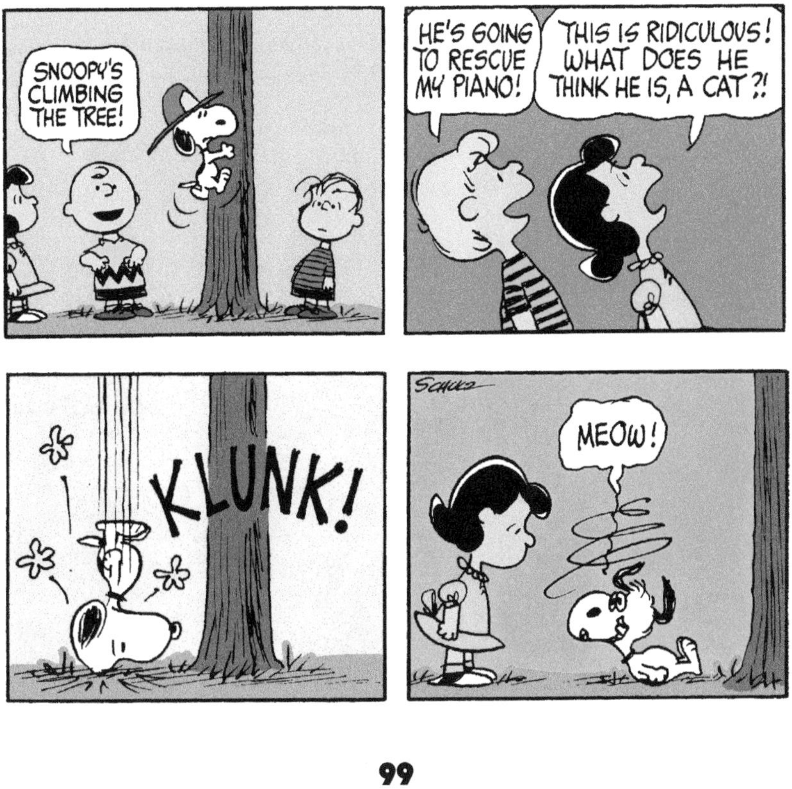
SNOOPY'S CLIMBING THE TREE!
HE'S GOING TO RESCUE MY PIANO!
THIS IS RIDICULOUS! WHAT DOES HE THINK HE IS, A CAT?!
KLUNK!
MEOW!

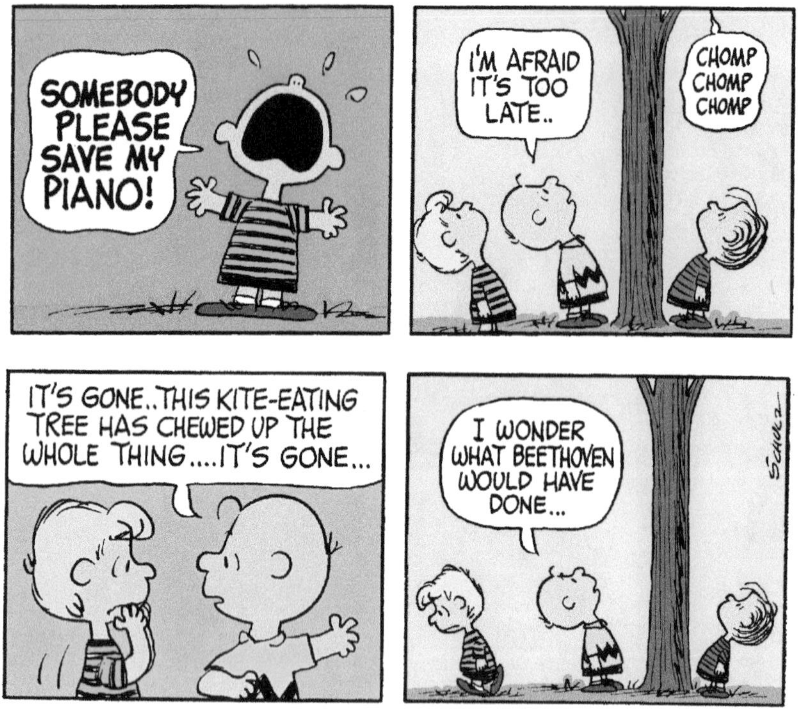
SOMEBODY PLEASE SAVE MY PIANO!
I'M AFRAID IT'S TOO LATE..
CHOMP CHOMP CHOMP
IT'S GONE..THIS KITE-EATING TREE HAS CHEWED UP THE WHOLE THING....IT'S GONE...
I WONDER WHAT BEETHOVEN WOULD HAVE DONE...
SCHULZ

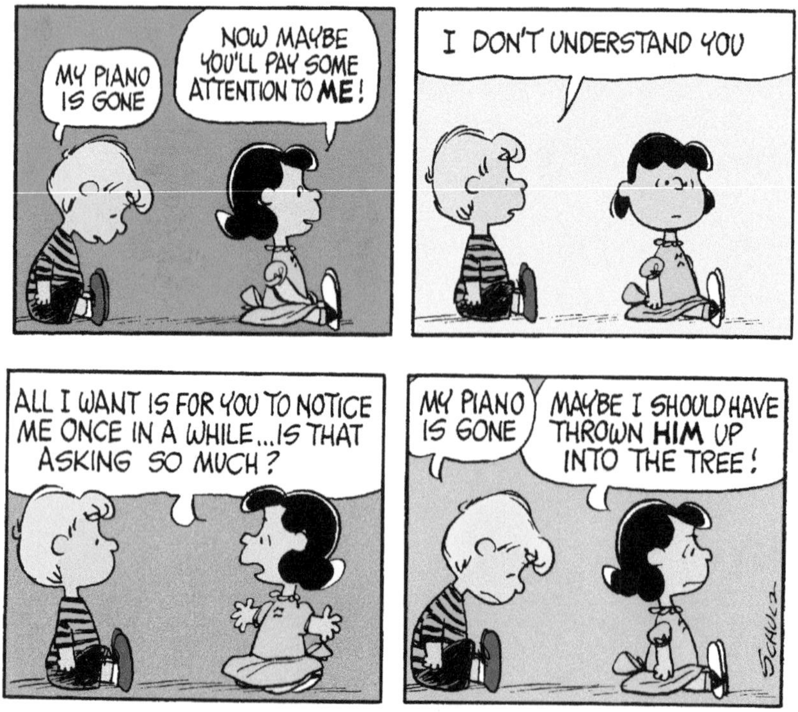
MY PIANO IS GONE
NOW MAYBE YOU'LL PAY SOME ATTENTION TO **ME**!
I DON'T UNDERSTAND YOU
ALL I WANT IS FOR YOU TO NOTICE ME ONCE IN A WHILE...IS THAT ASKING SO MUCH?
MY PIANO IS GONE
MAYBE I SHOULD HAVE THROWN **HIM** UP INTO THE TREE!
SCHULZ

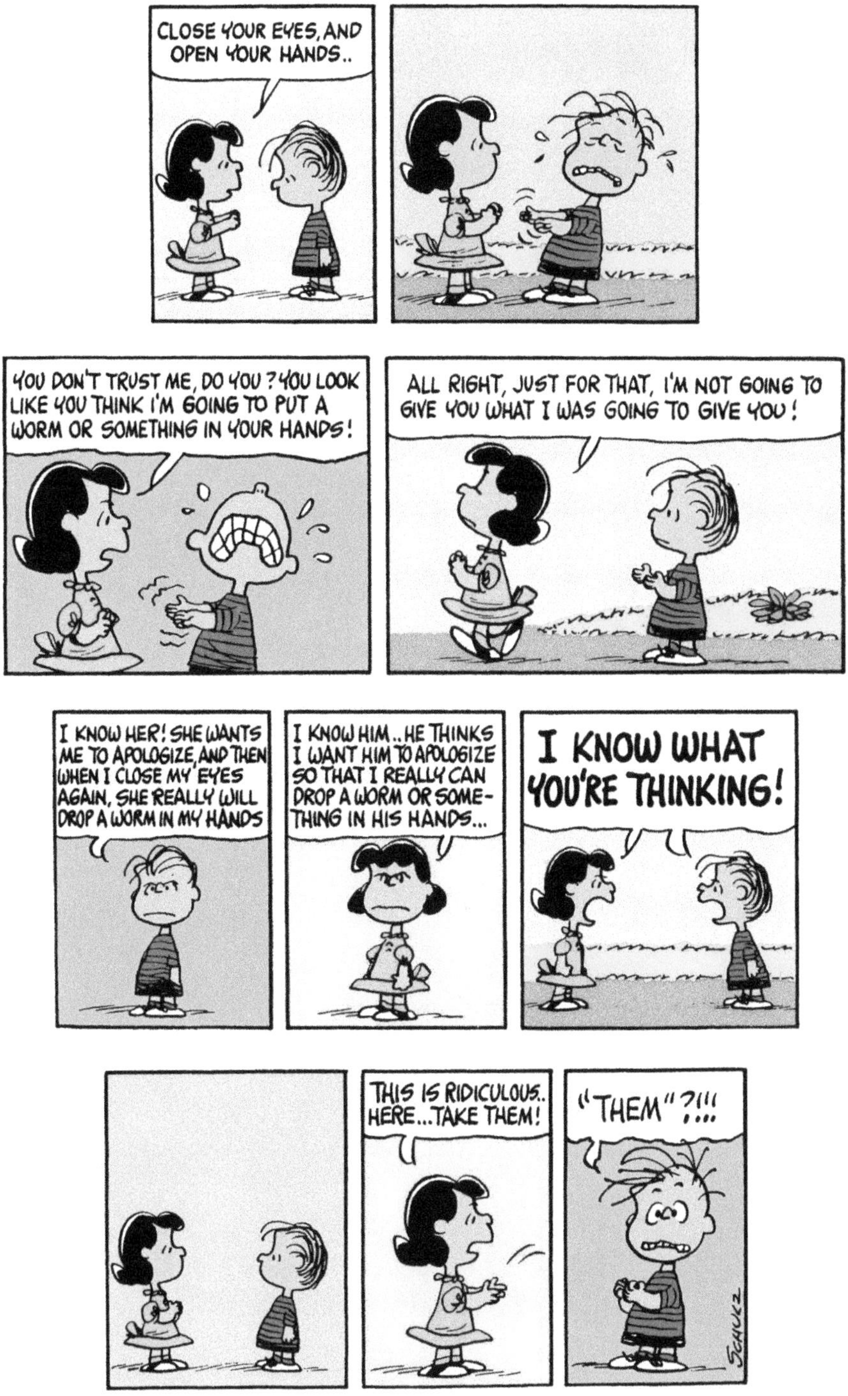
CLOSE YOUR EYES, AND OPEN YOUR HANDS..
YOU DON'T TRUST ME, DO YOU? YOU LOOK LIKE YOU THINK I'M GOING TO PUT A WORM OR SOMETHING IN YOUR HANDS!
ALL RIGHT, JUST FOR THAT, I'M NOT GOING TO GIVE YOU WHAT I WAS GOING TO GIVE YOU!
I KNOW HER! SHE WANTS ME TO APOLOGIZE, AND THEN WHEN I CLOSE MY EYES AGAIN, SHE REALLY WILL DROP A WORM IN MY HANDS
I KNOW HIM.. HE THINKS I WANT HIM TO APOLOGIZE SO THAT I REALLY CAN DROP A WORM OR SOMETHING IN HIS HANDS...
I KNOW WHAT YOU'RE THINKING!
THIS IS RIDICULOUS.. HERE...TAKE THEM!
"THEM"?!!!
SCHULZ

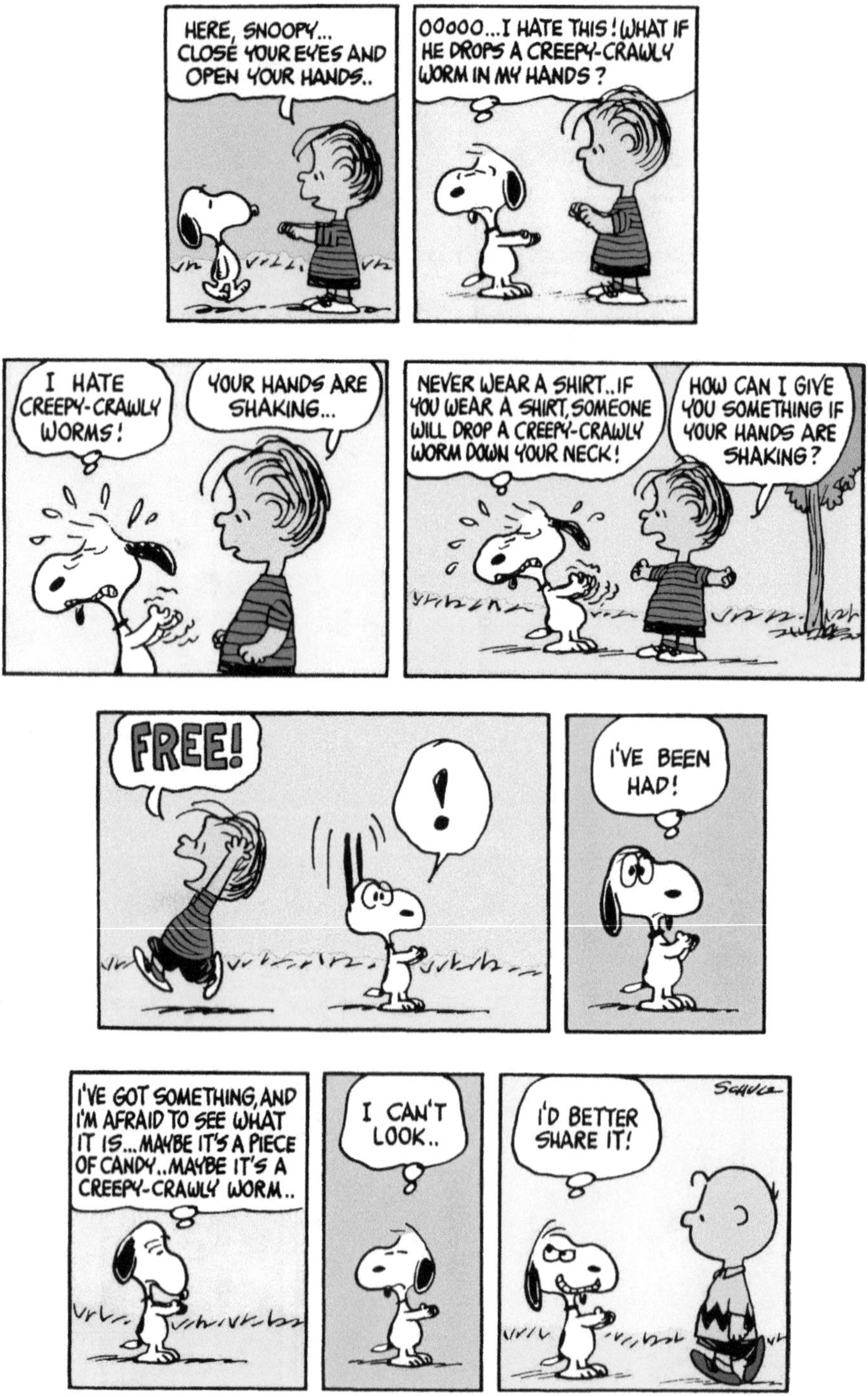
HERE, SNOOPY... CLOSE YOUR EYES AND OPEN YOUR HANDS..
OOOOO...I HATE THIS! WHAT IF HE DROPS A CREEPY-CRAWLY WORM IN MY HANDS?
I HATE CREEPY-CRAWLY WORMS!
YOUR HANDS ARE SHAKING...
NEVER WEAR A SHIRT..IF YOU WEAR A SHIRT, SOMEONE WILL DROP A CREEPY-CRAWLY WORM DOWN YOUR NECK!
HOW CAN I GIVE YOU SOMETHING IF YOUR HANDS ARE SHAKING?
FREE!
!
I'VE BEEN HAD!
I'VE GOT SOMETHING, AND I'M AFRAID TO SEE WHAT IT IS...MAYBE IT'S A PIECE OF CANDY..MAYBE IT'S A CREEPY-CRAWLY WORM..
I CAN'T LOOK..
I'D BETTER SHARE IT!
SCHULZ

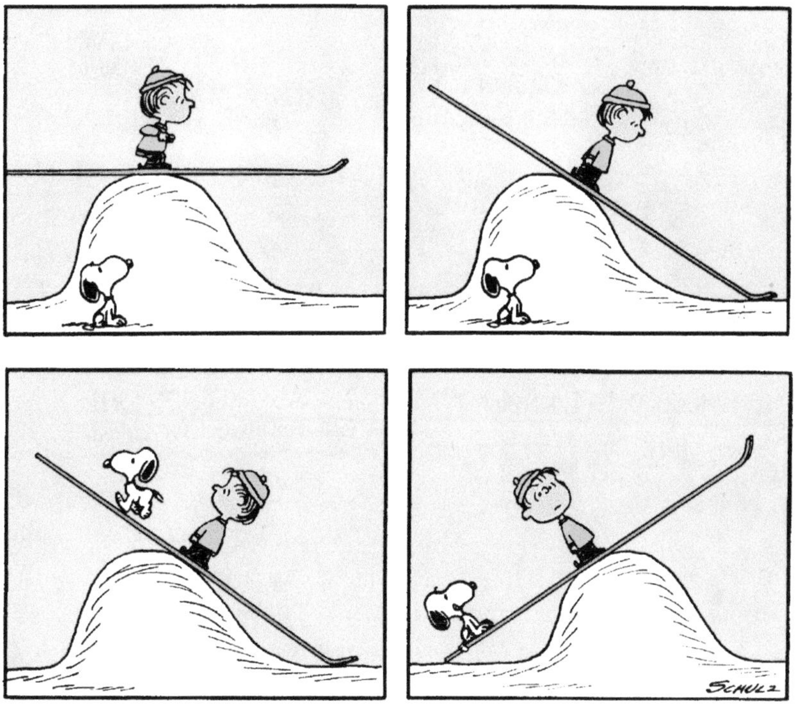
SCHULZ

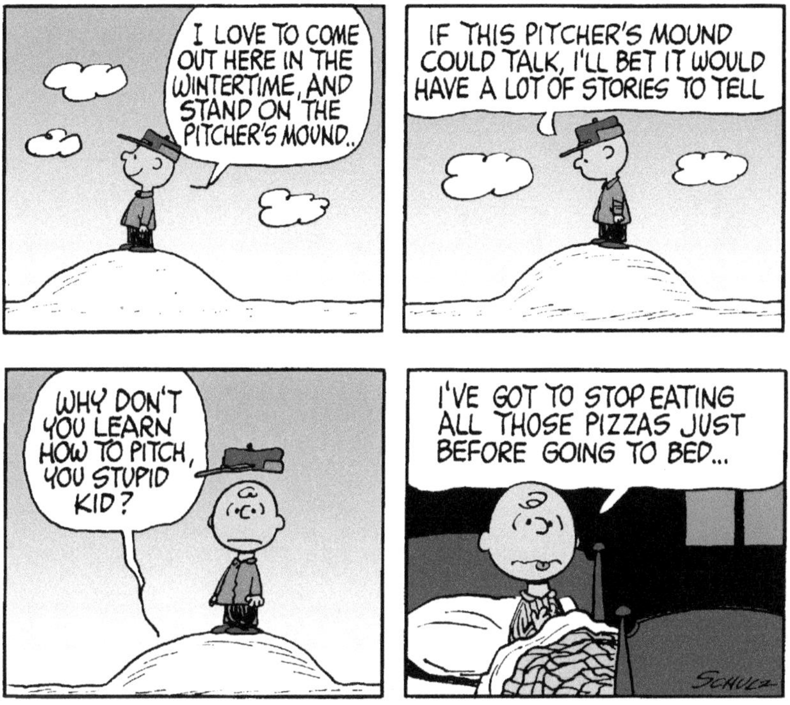
I LOVE TO COME OUT HERE IN THE WINTERTIME, AND STAND ON THE PITCHER'S MOUND..
IF THIS PITCHER'S MOUND COULD TALK, I'LL BET IT WOULD HAVE A LOT OF STORIES TO TELL
WHY DON'T YOU LEARN HOW TO PITCH, YOU STUPID KID?
I'VE GOT TO STOP EATING ALL THOSE PIZZAS JUST BEFORE GOING TO BED...
SCHULZ

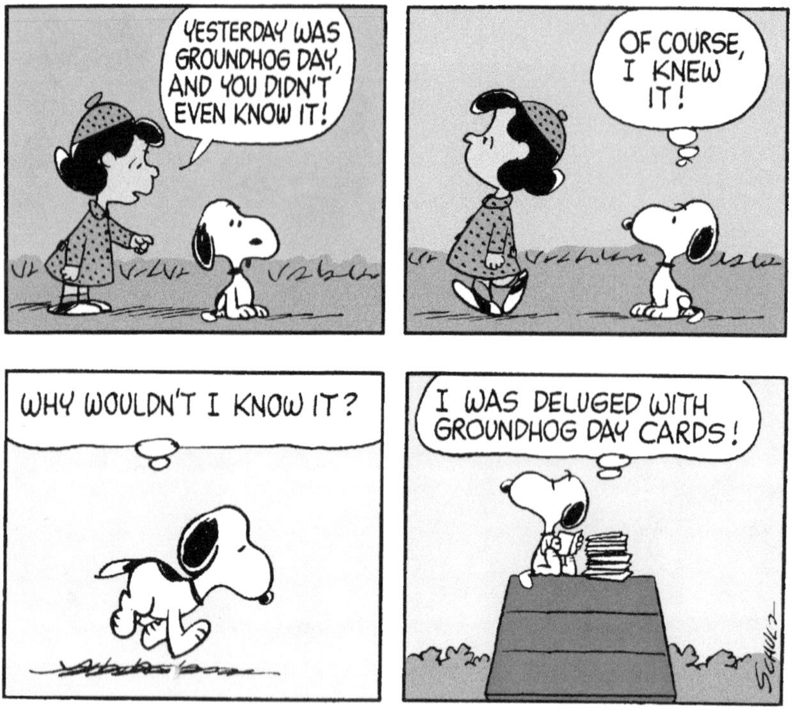
YESTERDAY WAS GROUNDHOG DAY, AND YOU DIDN'T EVEN KNOW IT!
OF COURSE, I KNEW IT!
WHY WOULDN'T I KNOW IT?
I WAS DELUGED WITH GROUNDHOG DAY CARDS!

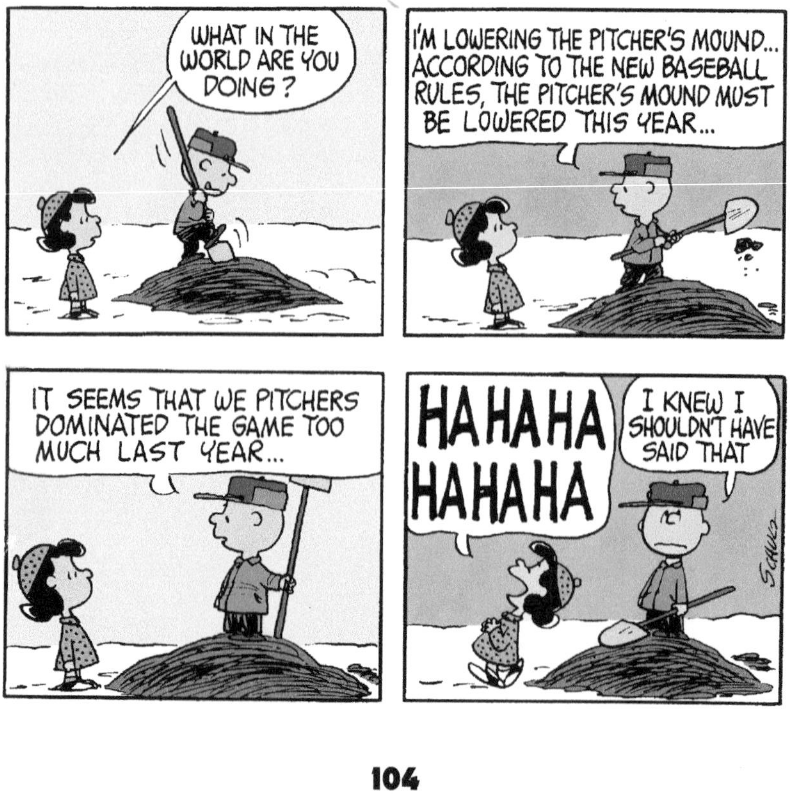
WHAT IN THE WORLD ARE YOU DOING?
I'M LOWERING THE PITCHER'S MOUND... ACCORDING TO THE NEW BASEBALL RULES, THE PITCHER'S MOUND MUST BE LOWERED THIS YEAR...
IT SEEMS THAT WE PITCHERS DOMINATED THE GAME TOO MUCH LAST YEAR...
HAHAHA HAHAHA
I KNEW I SHOULDN'T HAVE SAID THAT

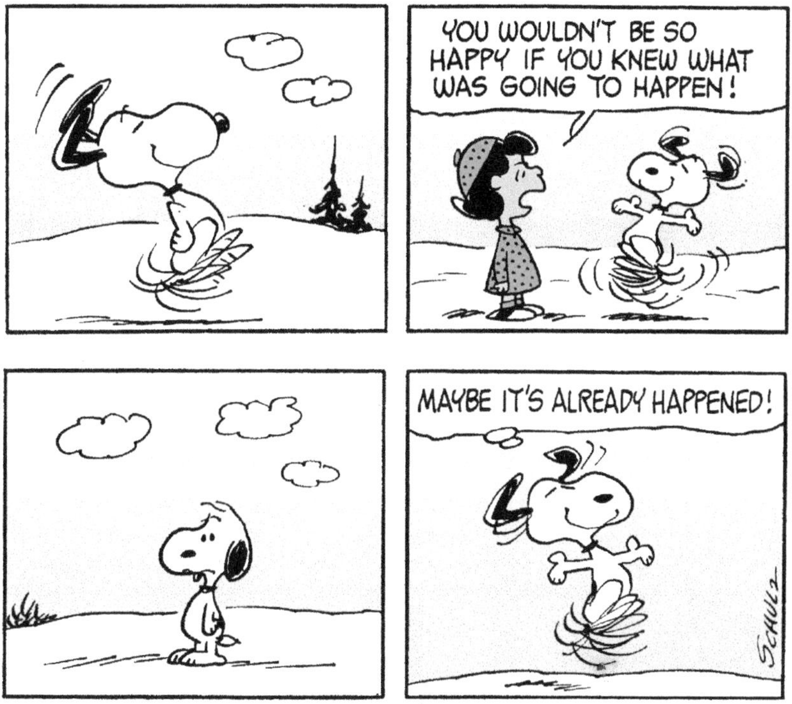
YOU WOULDN'T BE SO HAPPY IF YOU KNEW WHAT WAS GOING TO HAPPEN!
MAYBE IT'S ALREADY HAPPENED!
SCHULZ

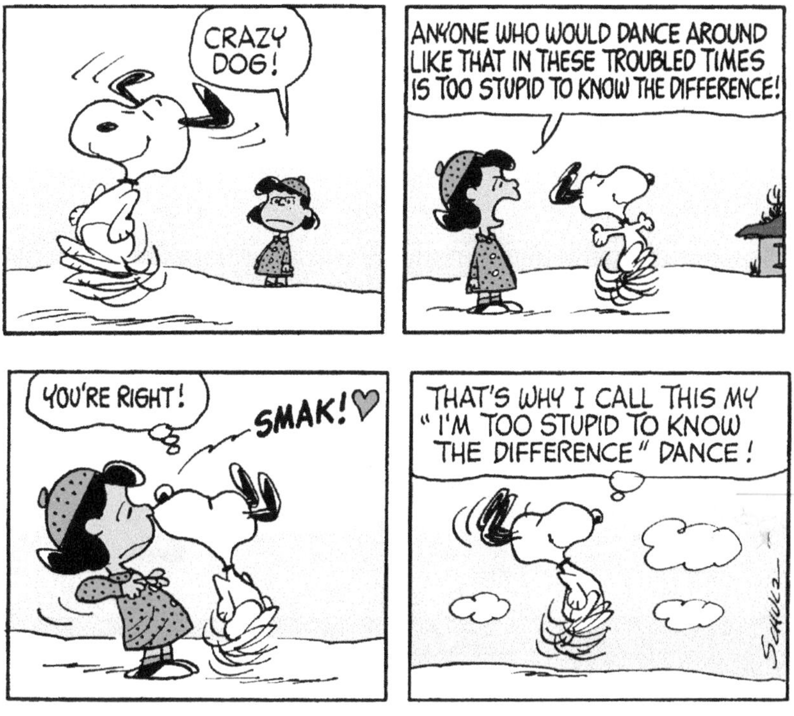
CRAZY DOG!
ANYONE WHO WOULD DANCE AROUND LIKE THAT IN THESE TROUBLED TIMES IS TOO STUPID TO KNOW THE DIFFERENCE!
YOU'RE RIGHT!
SMAK!
THAT'S WHY I CALL THIS MY "I'M TOO STUPID TO KNOW THE DIFFERENCE" DANCE!
SCHULZ

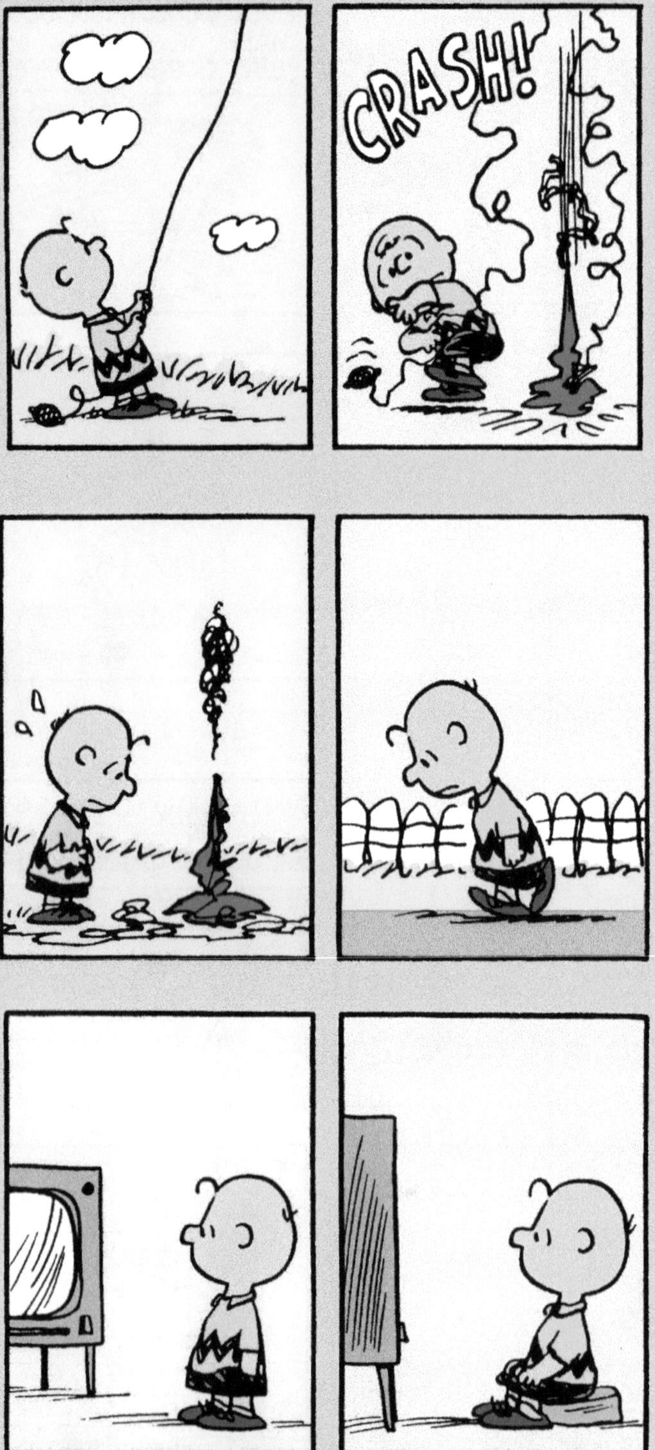
CRASH!

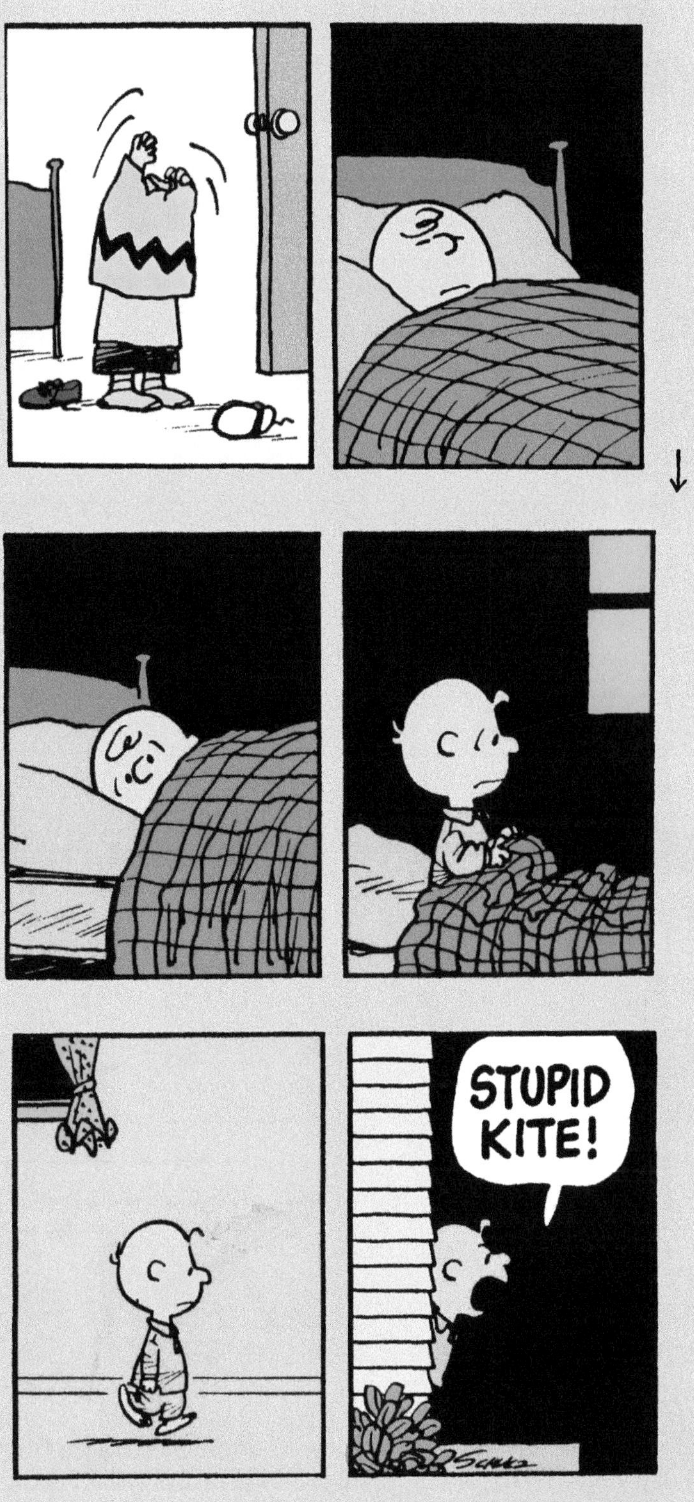
STUPID KITE!

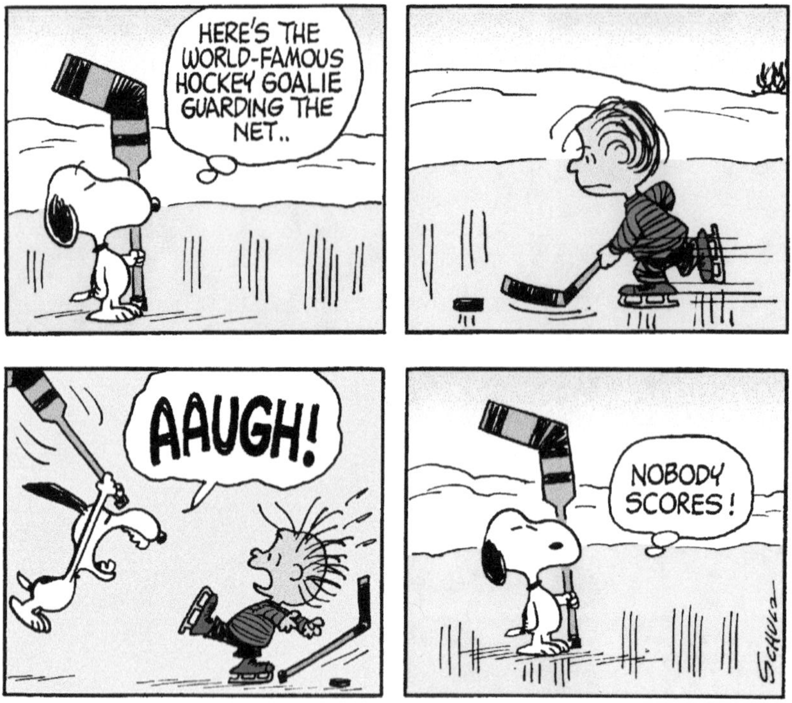
HERE'S THE WORLD-FAMOUS HOCKEY GOALIE GUARDING THE NET..
AAUGH!
NOBODY SCORES!
SCHULZ

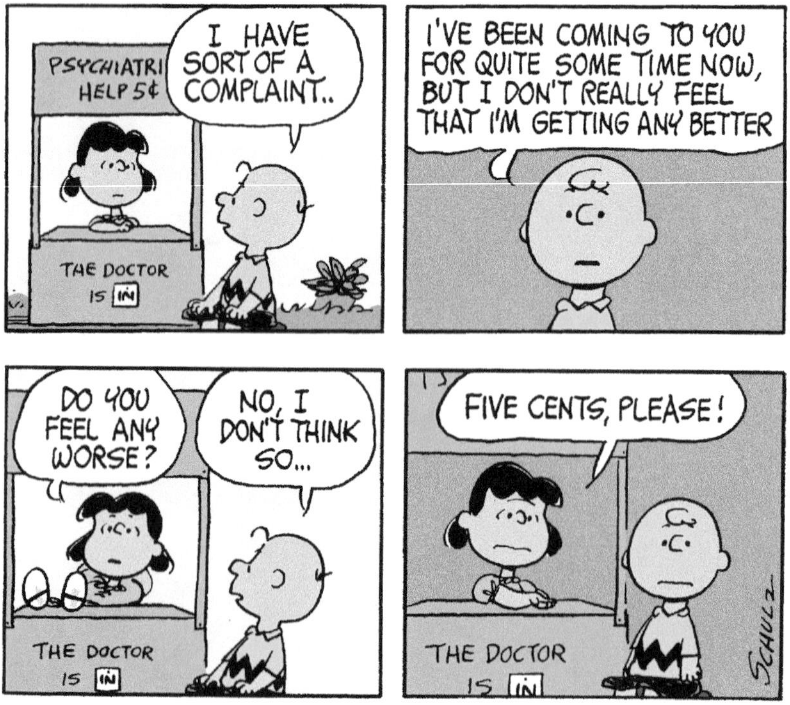
PSYCHIATRI HELP 5¢
THE DOCTOR IS IN
I HAVE SORT OF A COMPLAINT..
I'VE BEEN COMING TO YOU FOR QUITE SOME TIME NOW, BUT I DON'T REALLY FEEL THAT I'M GETTING ANY BETTER
DO YOU FEEL ANY WORSE?
NO, I DON'T THINK SO...
FIVE CENTS, PLEASE!
SCHULZ

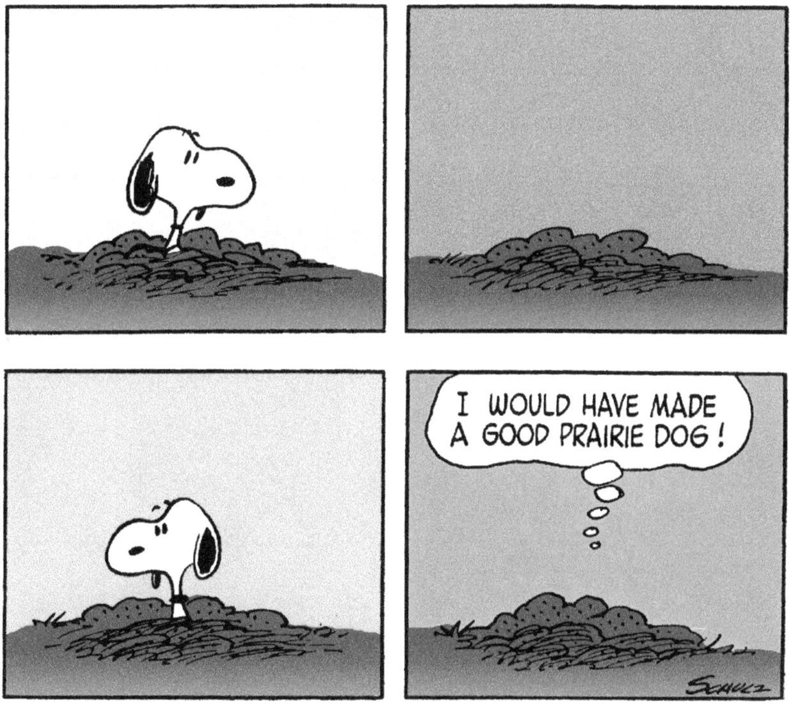
I WOULD HAVE MADE A GOOD PRAIRIE DOG!

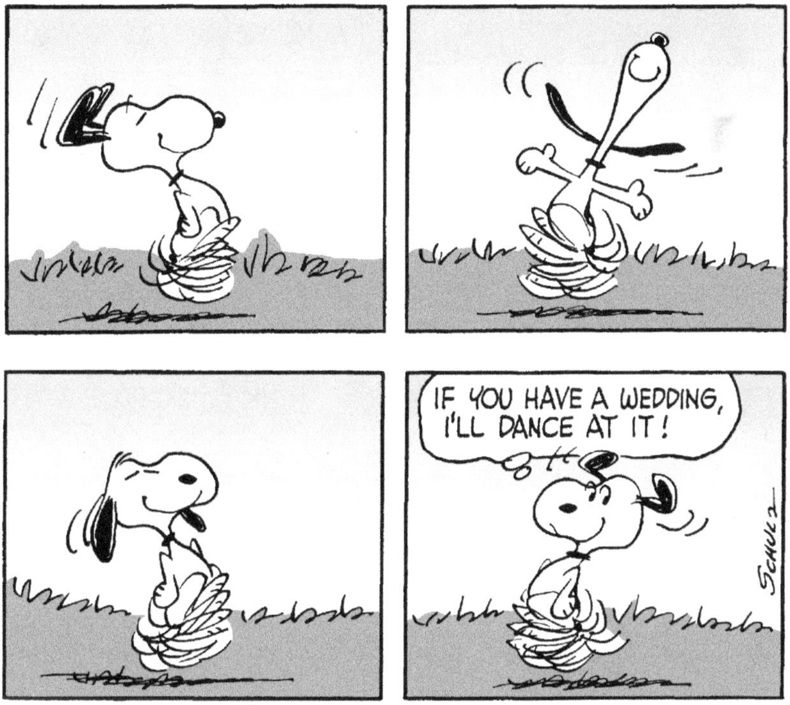
IF YOU HAVE A WEDDING, I'LL DANCE AT IT!

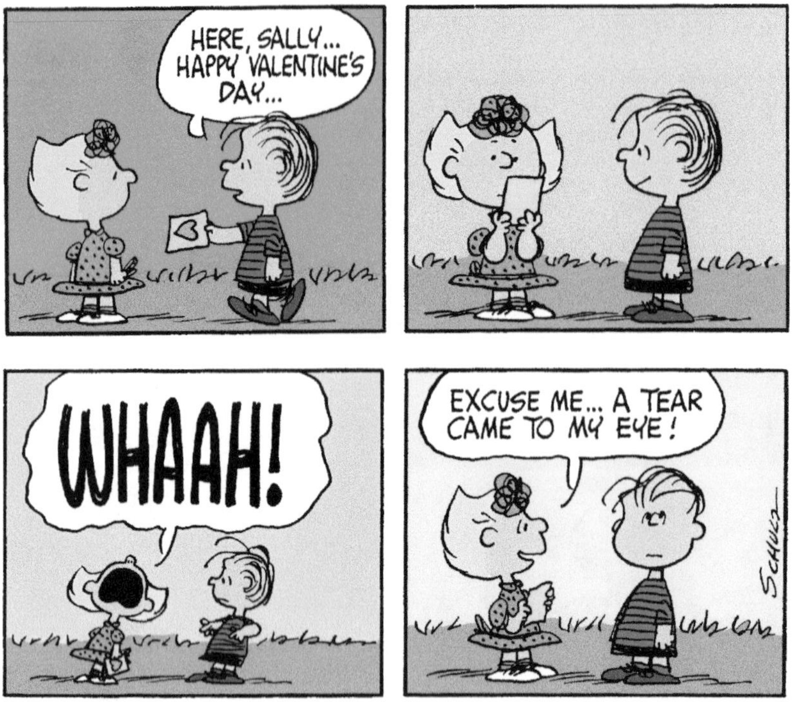
HERE, SALLY... HAPPY VALENTINE'S DAY...
WHAAH!
EXCUSE ME... A TEAR CAME TO MY EYE!

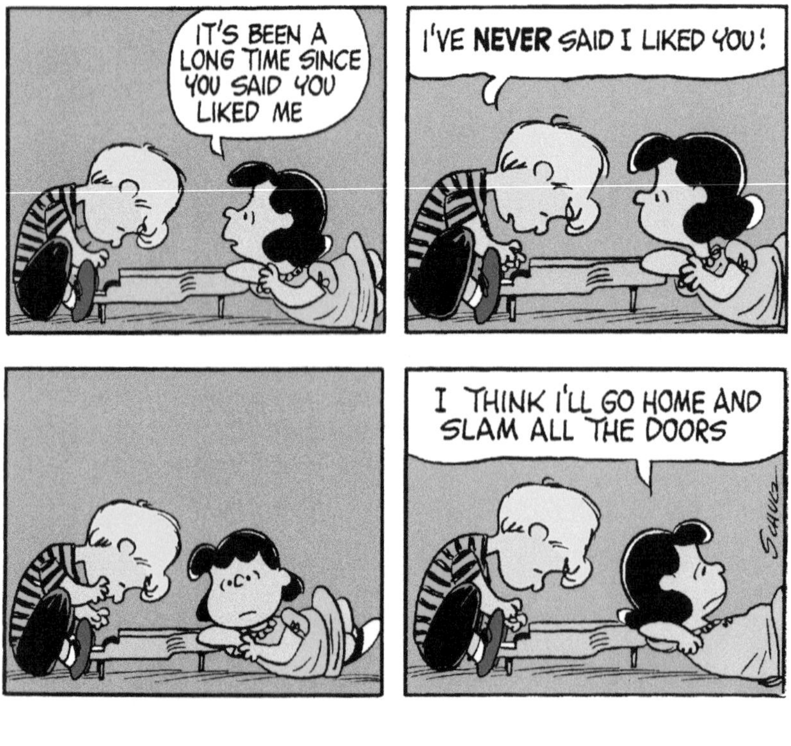
IT'S BEEN A LONG TIME SINCE YOU SAID YOU LIKED ME
I'VE NEVER SAID I LIKED YOU!
I THINK I'LL GO HOME AND SLAM ALL THE DOORS

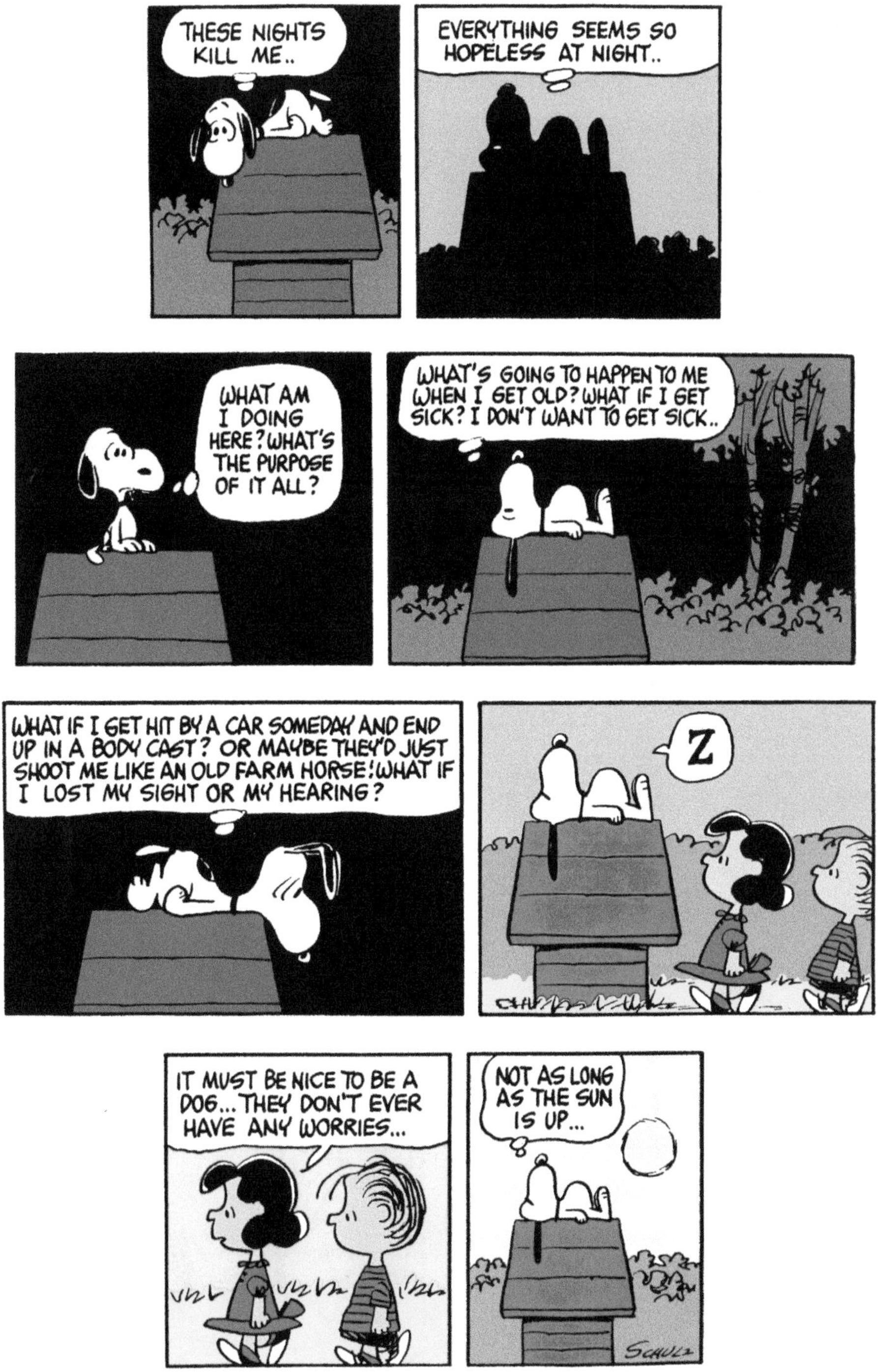
THESE NIGHTS KILL ME..
EVERYTHING SEEMS SO HOPELESS AT NIGHT..
WHAT AM I DOING HERE? WHAT'S THE PURPOSE OF IT ALL?
WHAT'S GOING TO HAPPEN TO ME WHEN I GET OLD? WHAT IF I GET SICK? I DON'T WANT TO GET SICK..
WHAT IF I GET HIT BY A CAR SOMEDAY AND END UP IN A BODY CAST? OR MAYBE THEY'D JUST SHOOT ME LIKE AN OLD FARM HORSE! WHAT IF I LOST MY SIGHT OR MY HEARING?
Z
IT MUST BE NICE TO BE A DOG... THEY DON'T EVER HAVE ANY WORRIES...
NOT AS LONG AS THE SUN IS UP...
SCHULZ

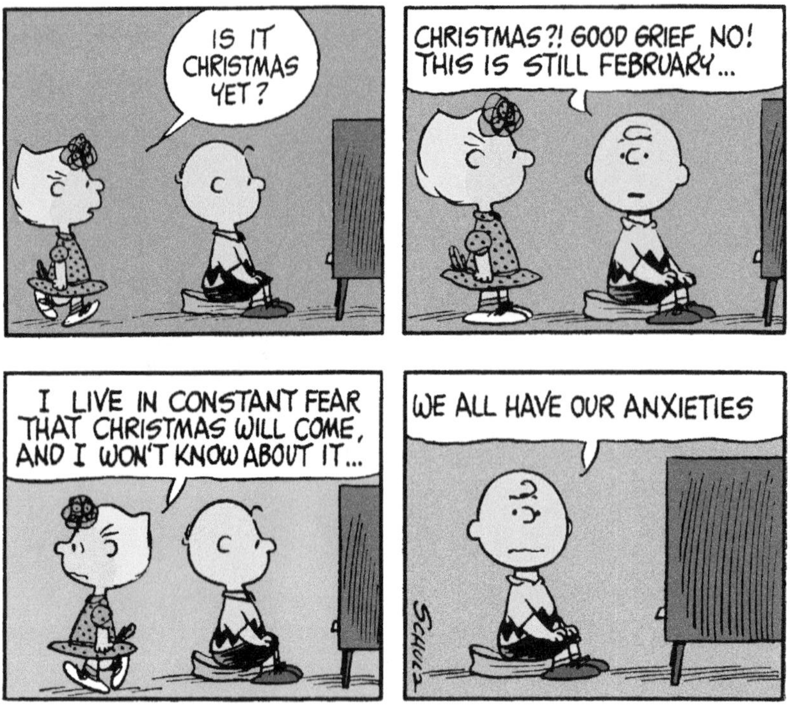
IS IT CHRISTMAS YET?
CHRISTMAS?! GOOD GRIEF, NO! THIS IS STILL FEBRUARY...
I LIVE IN CONSTANT FEAR THAT CHRISTMAS WILL COME, AND I WON'T KNOW ABOUT IT...
WE ALL HAVE OUR ANXIETIES
SCHULZ

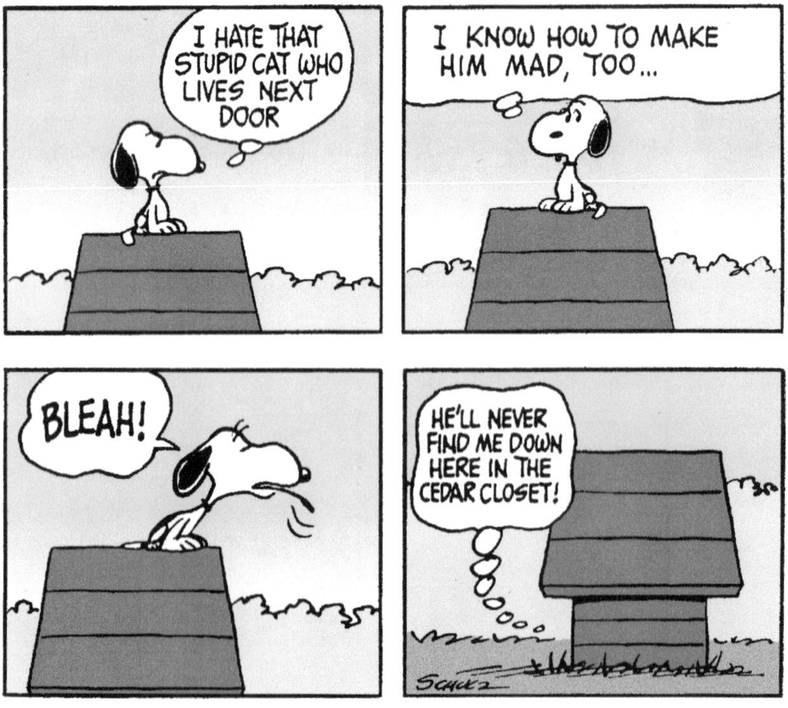
I HATE THAT STUPID CAT WHO LIVES NEXT DOOR
I KNOW HOW TO MAKE HIM MAD, TOO...
BLEAH!
HE'LL NEVER FIND ME DOWN HERE IN THE CEDAR CLOSET!
SCHULZ

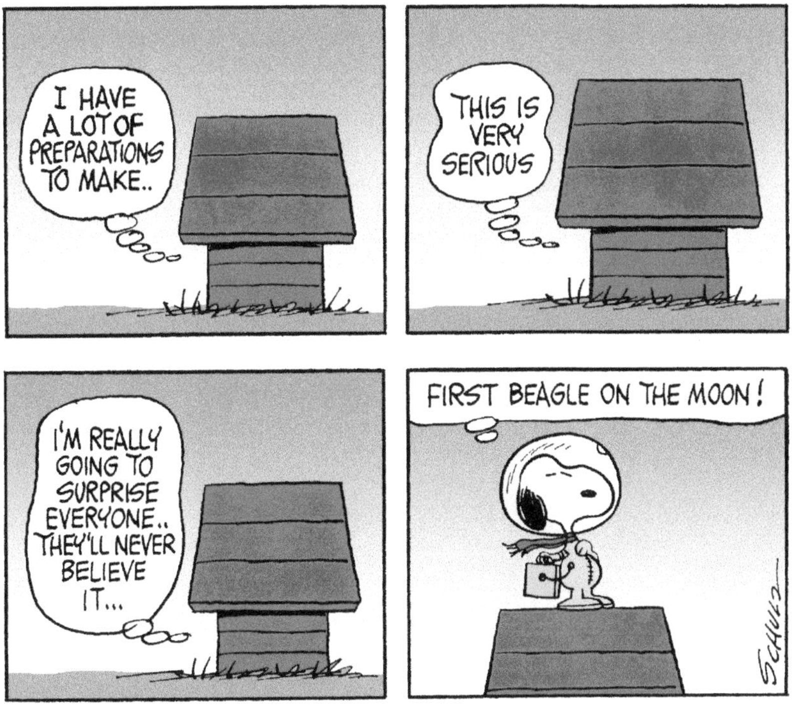
I HAVE A LOT OF PREPARATIONS TO MAKE..
THIS IS VERY SERIOUS
I'M REALLY GOING TO SURPRISE EVERYONE.. THEY'LL NEVER BELIEVE IT...
FIRST BEAGLE ON THE MOON!
SCHULZ

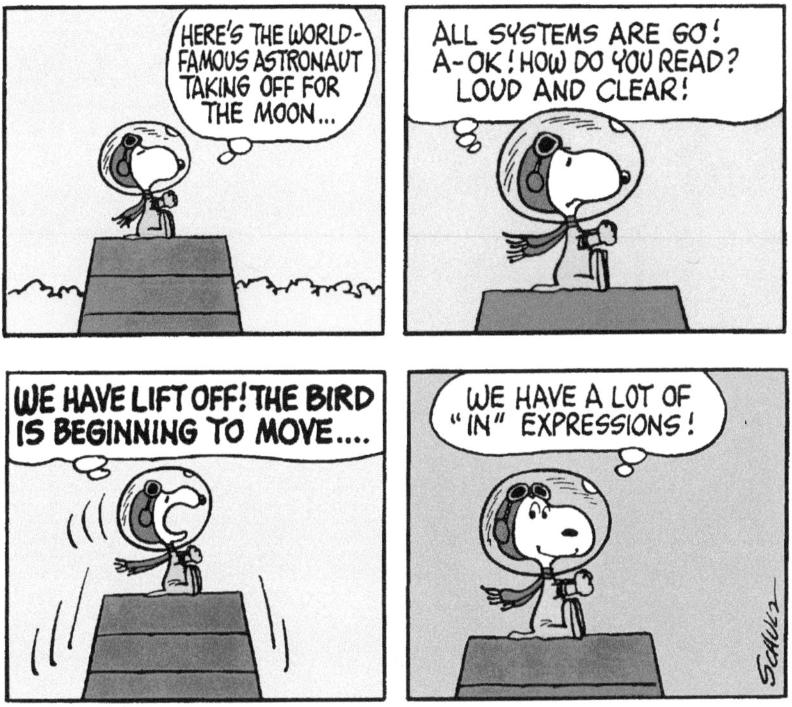
HERE'S THE WORLD-FAMOUS ASTRONAUT TAKING OFF FOR THE MOON...
ALL SYSTEMS ARE GO! A-OK! HOW DO YOU READ? LOUD AND CLEAR!
WE HAVE LIFT OFF! THE BIRD IS BEGINNING TO MOVE....
WE HAVE A LOT OF "IN" EXPRESSIONS!
SCHULZ

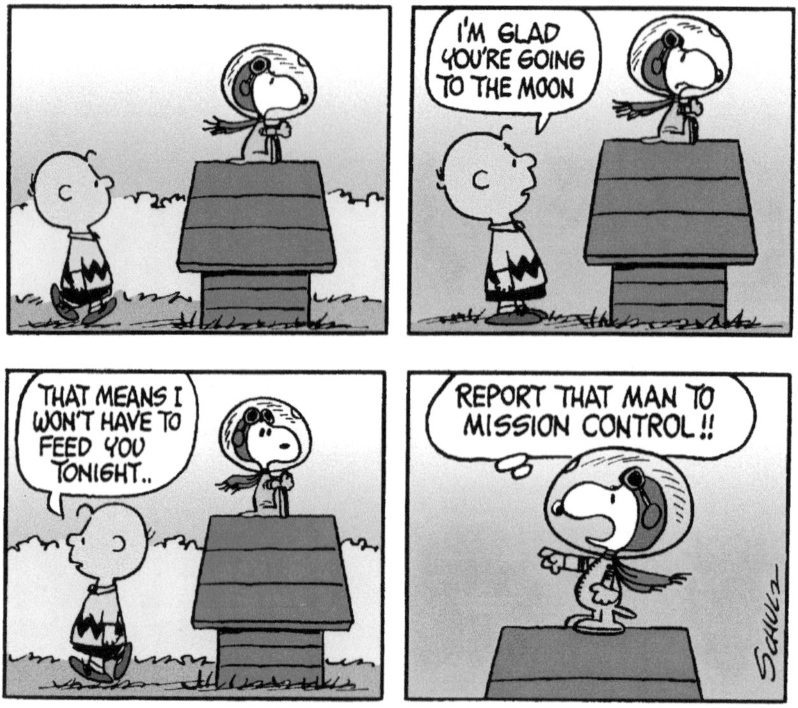
I'M GLAD YOU'RE GOING TO THE MOON
THAT MEANS I WON'T HAVE TO FEED YOU TONIGHT..
REPORT THAT MAN TO MISSION CONTROL!!
SCHULZ

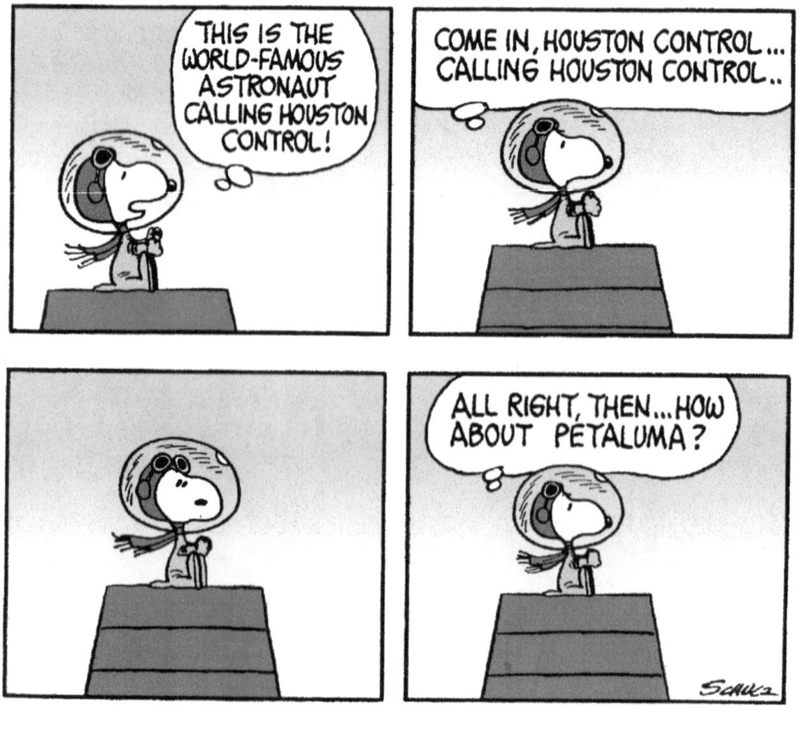
THIS IS THE WORLD-FAMOUS ASTRONAUT CALLING HOUSTON CONTROL!
COME IN, HOUSTON CONTROL... CALLING HOUSTON CONTROL..
ALL RIGHT, THEN...HOW ABOUT PETALUMA?
SCHULZ

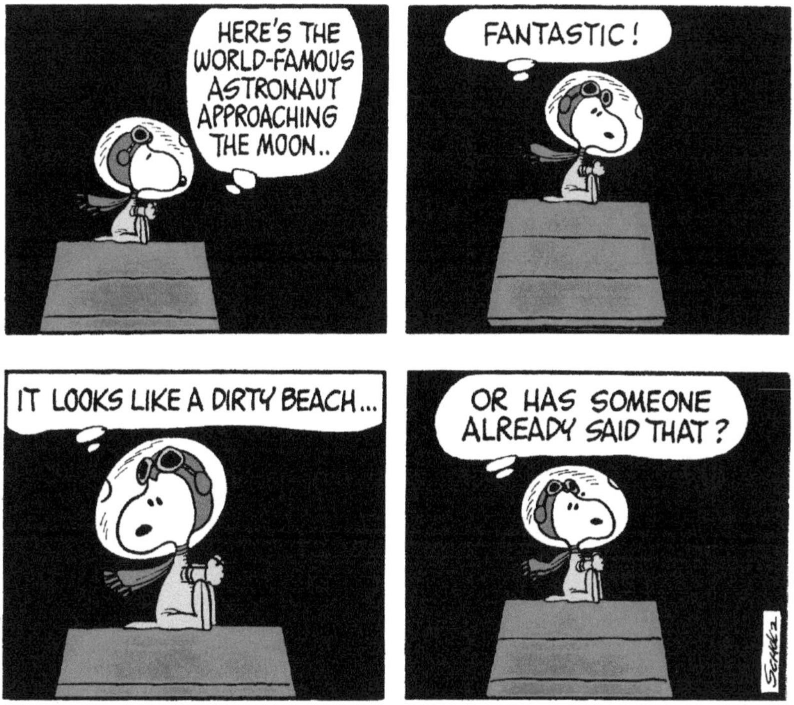
HERE'S THE WORLD-FAMOUS ASTRONAUT APPROACHING THE MOON..
FANTASTIC!
IT LOOKS LIKE A DIRTY BEACH...
OR HAS SOMEONE ALREADY SAID THAT?

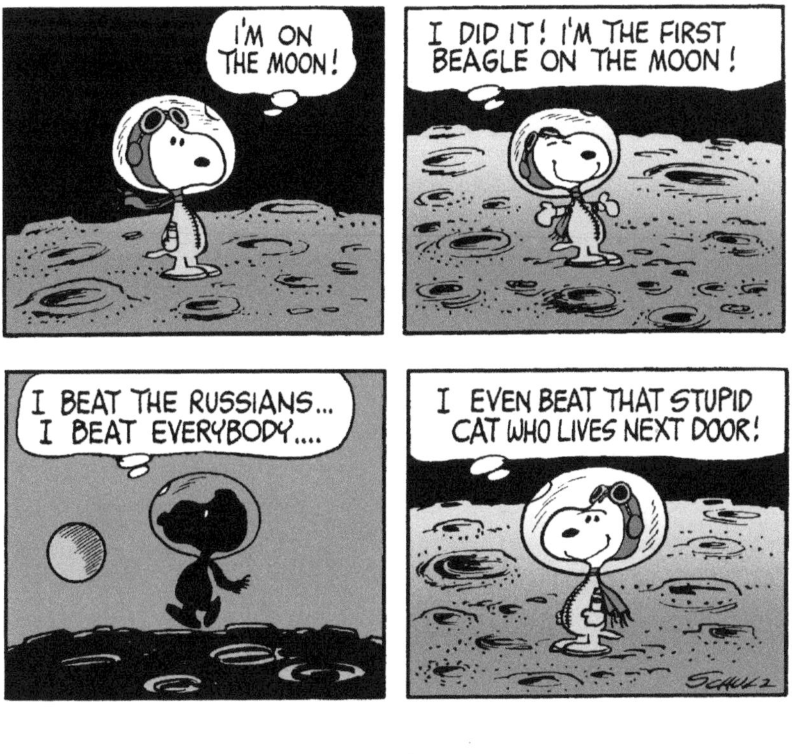
I'M ON THE MOON!
I DID IT! I'M THE FIRST BEAGLE ON THE MOON!
I BEAT THE RUSSIANS... I BEAT EVERYBODY....
I EVEN BEAT THAT STUPID CAT WHO LIVES NEXT DOOR!

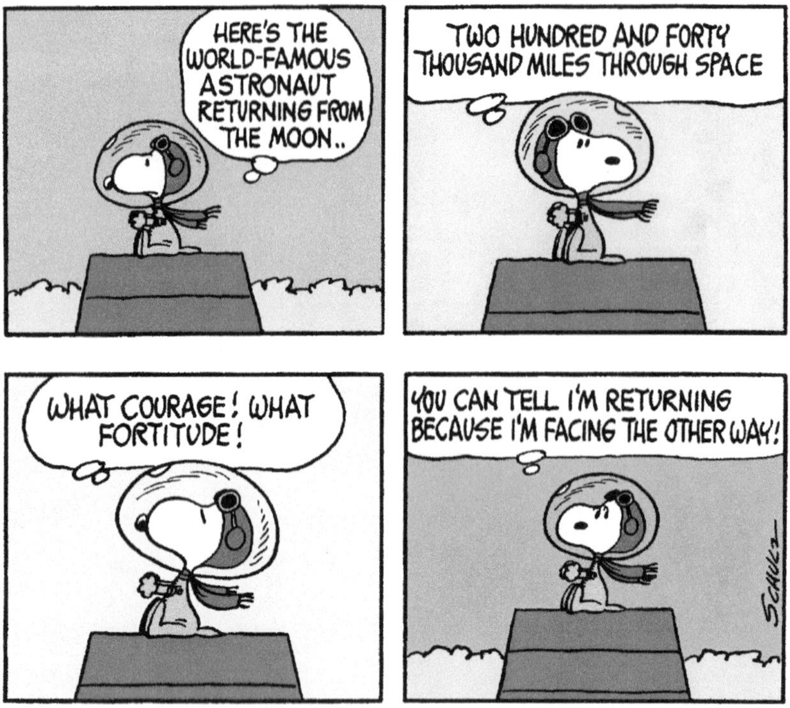
HERE'S THE WORLD-FAMOUS ASTRONAUT RETURNING FROM THE MOON..
TWO HUNDRED AND FORTY THOUSAND MILES THROUGH SPACE
WHAT COURAGE! WHAT FORTITUDE!
YOU CAN TELL I'M RETURNING BECAUSE I'M FACING THE OTHER WAY!

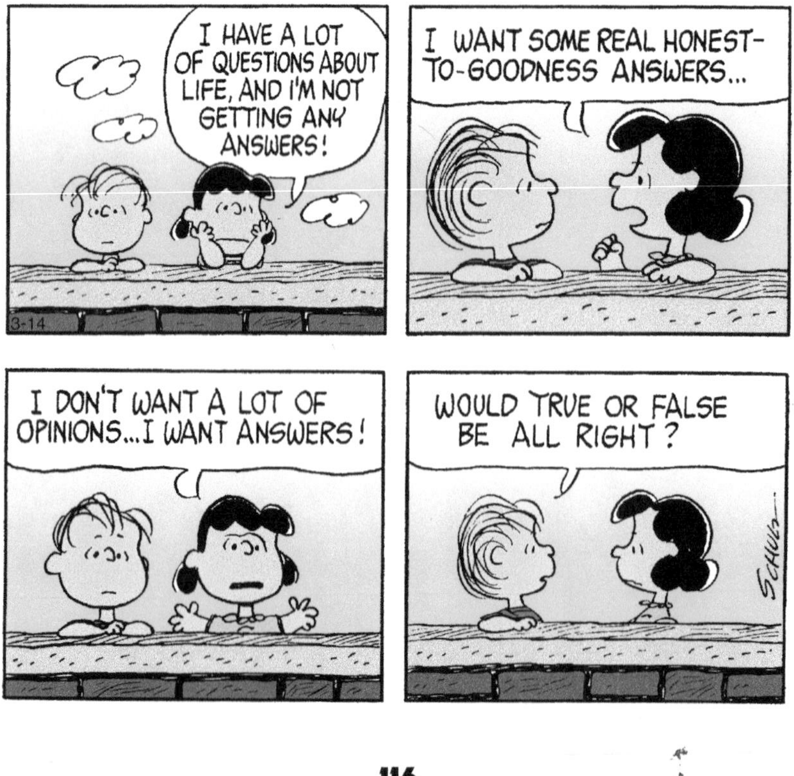
I HAVE A LOT OF QUESTIONS ABOUT LIFE, AND I'M NOT GETTING ANY ANSWERS!
I WANT SOME REAL HONEST-TO-GOODNESS ANSWERS...
I DON'T WANT A LOT OF OPINIONS...I WANT ANSWERS!
WOULD TRUE OR FALSE BE ALL RIGHT?

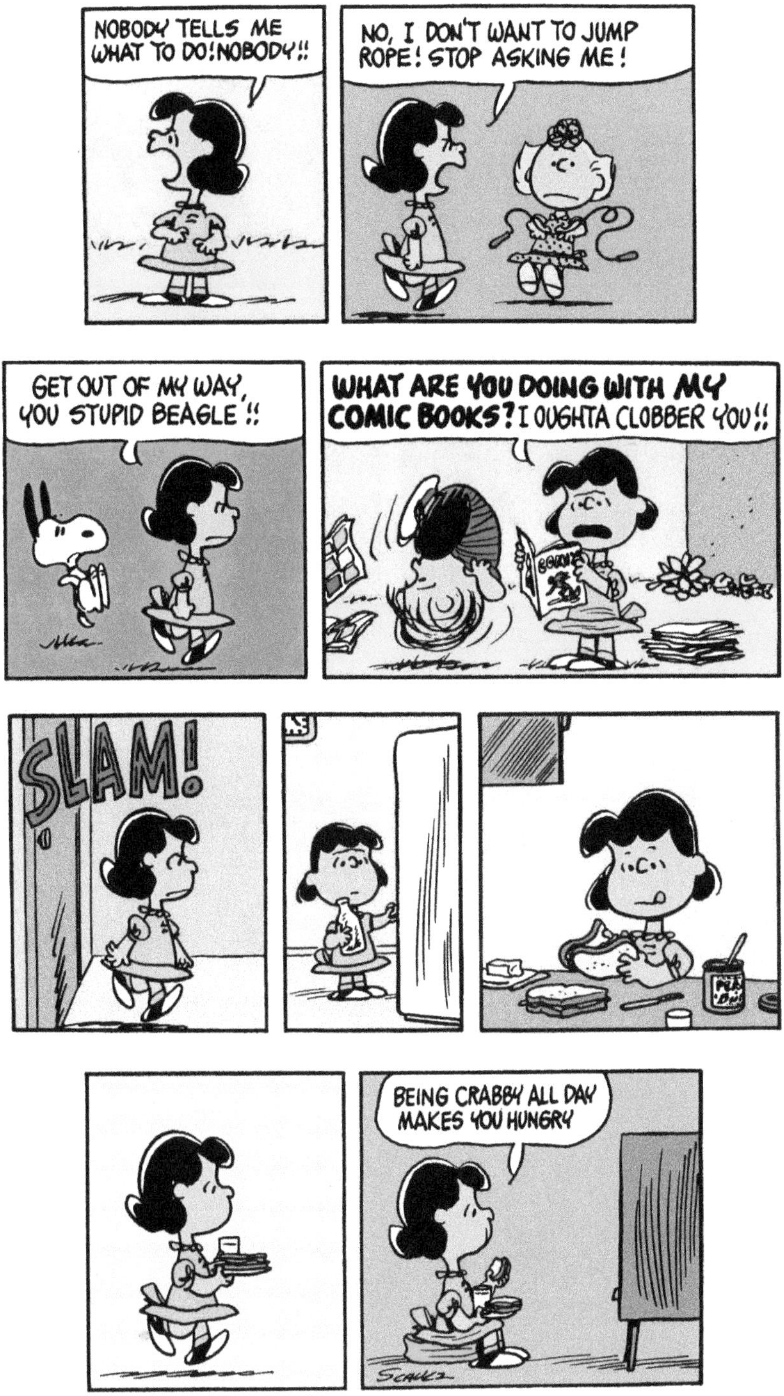
NOBODY TELLS ME WHAT TO DO! NOBODY!!
NO, I DON'T WANT TO JUMP ROPE! STOP ASKING ME!
GET OUT OF MY WAY, YOU STUPID BEAGLE!!
WHAT ARE YOU DOING WITH MY COMIC BOOKS? I OUGHTA CLOBBER YOU!!
SLAM!
BEING CRABBY ALL DAY MAKES YOU HUNGRY
SCHULZ

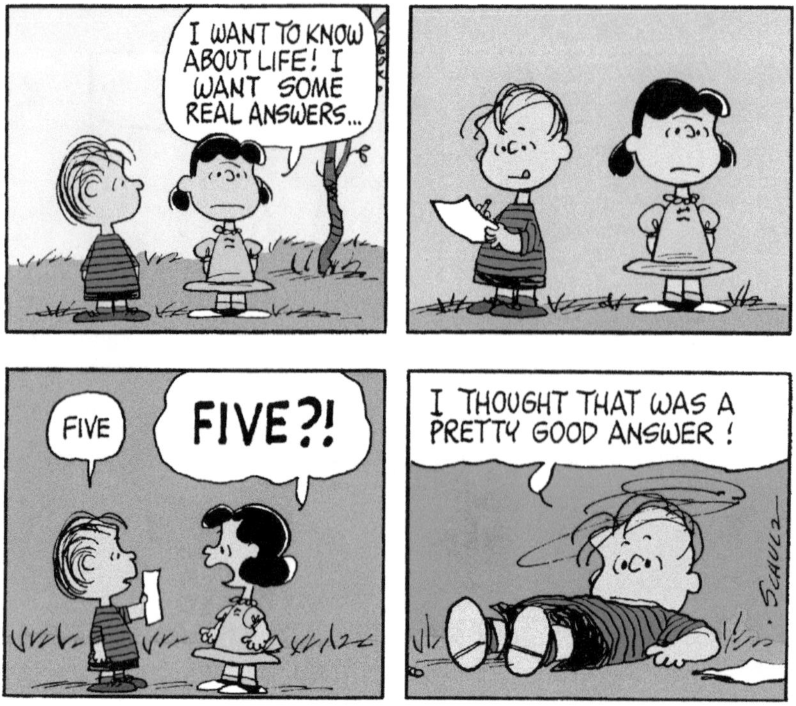
I WANT TO KNOW ABOUT LIFE! I WANT SOME REAL ANSWERS...
FIVE
FIVE?!
I THOUGHT THAT WAS A PRETTY GOOD ANSWER!

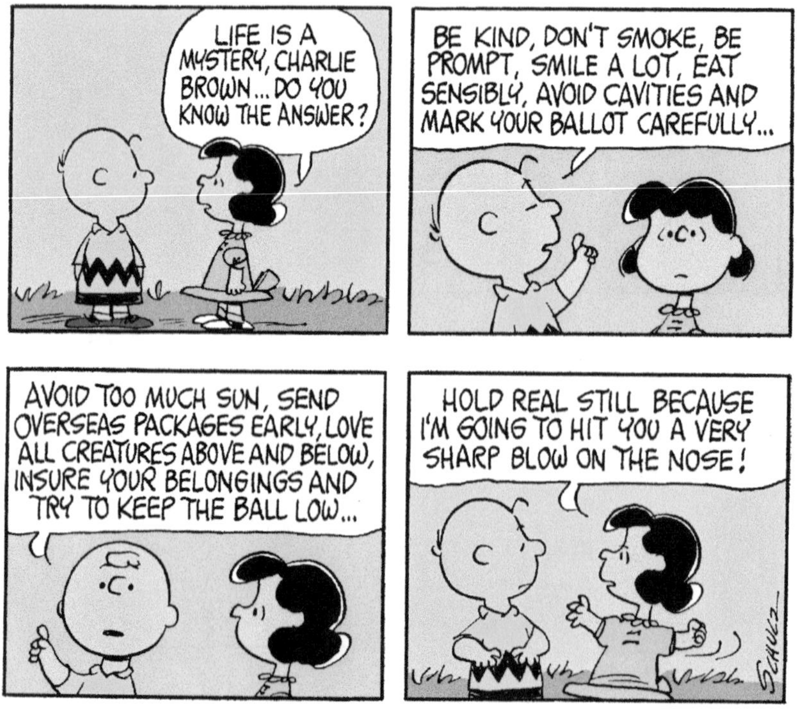
LIFE IS A MYSTERY, CHARLIE BROWN... DO YOU KNOW THE ANSWER?
BE KIND, DON'T SMOKE, BE PROMPT, SMILE A LOT, EAT SENSIBLY, AVOID CAVITIES AND MARK YOUR BALLOT CAREFULLY...
AVOID TOO MUCH SUN, SEND OVERSEAS PACKAGES EARLY, LOVE ALL CREATURES ABOVE AND BELOW, INSURE YOUR BELONGINGS AND TRY TO KEEP THE BALL LOW...
HOLD REAL STILL BECAUSE I'M GOING TO HIT YOU A VERY SHARP BLOW ON THE NOSE!

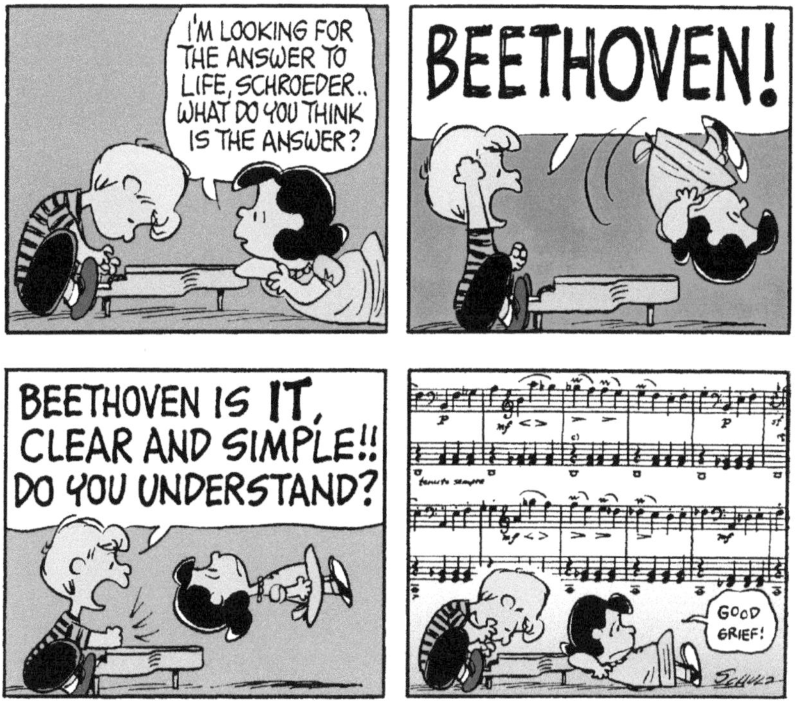
I'M LOOKING FOR THE ANSWER TO LIFE, SCHROEDER.. WHAT DO YOU THINK IS THE ANSWER?
BEETHOVEN!
BEETHOVEN IS IT, CLEAR AND SIMPLE!! DO YOU UNDERSTAND?
GOOD GRIEF!

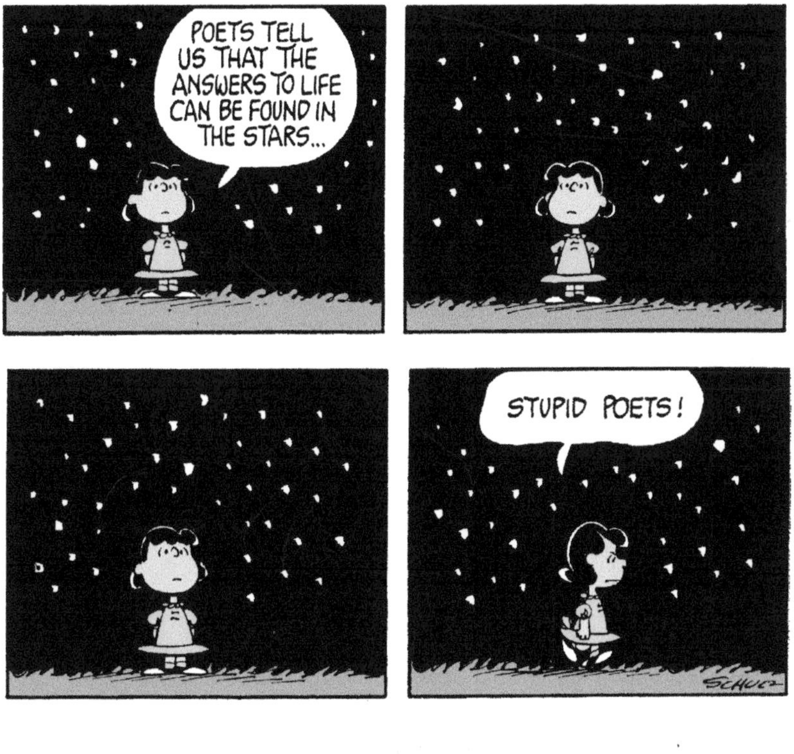
POETS TELL US THAT THE ANSWERS TO LIFE CAN BE FOUND IN THE STARS...
STUPID POETS!

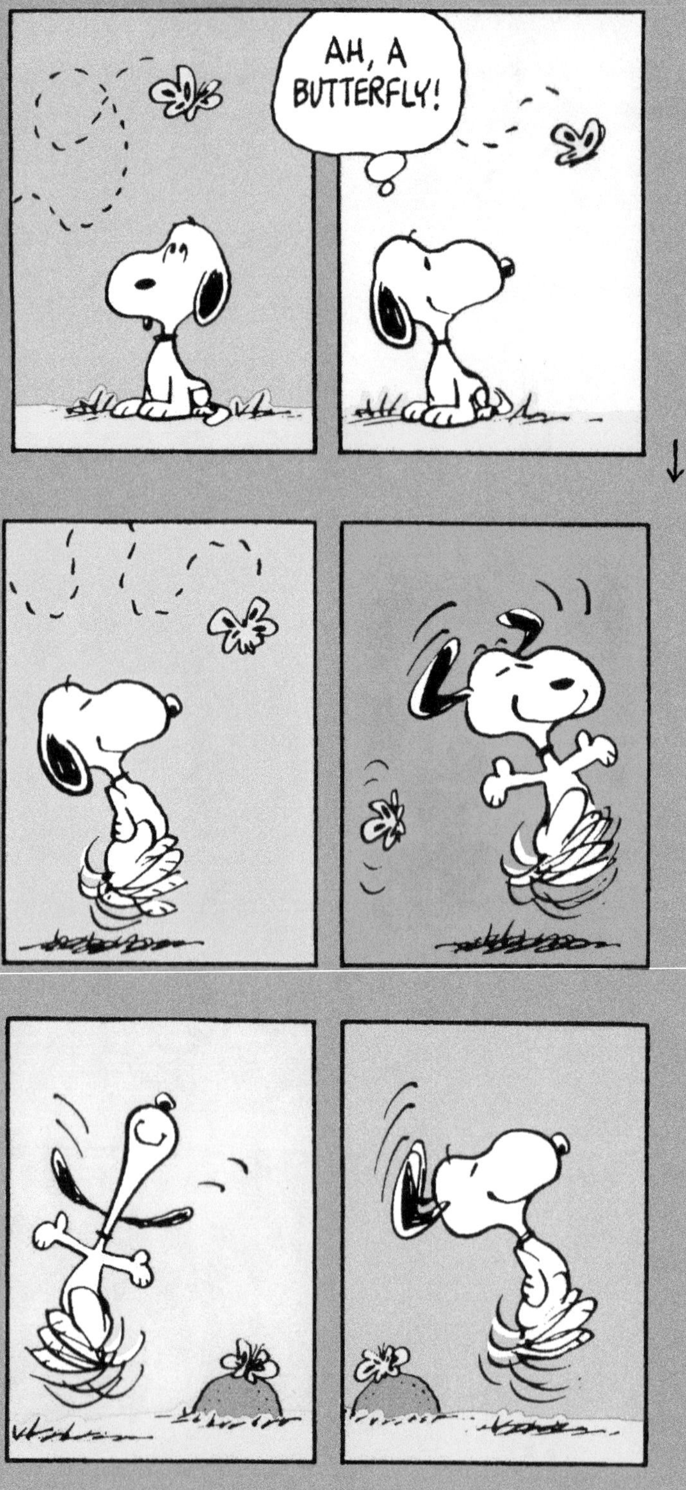
AH, A BUTTERFLY!

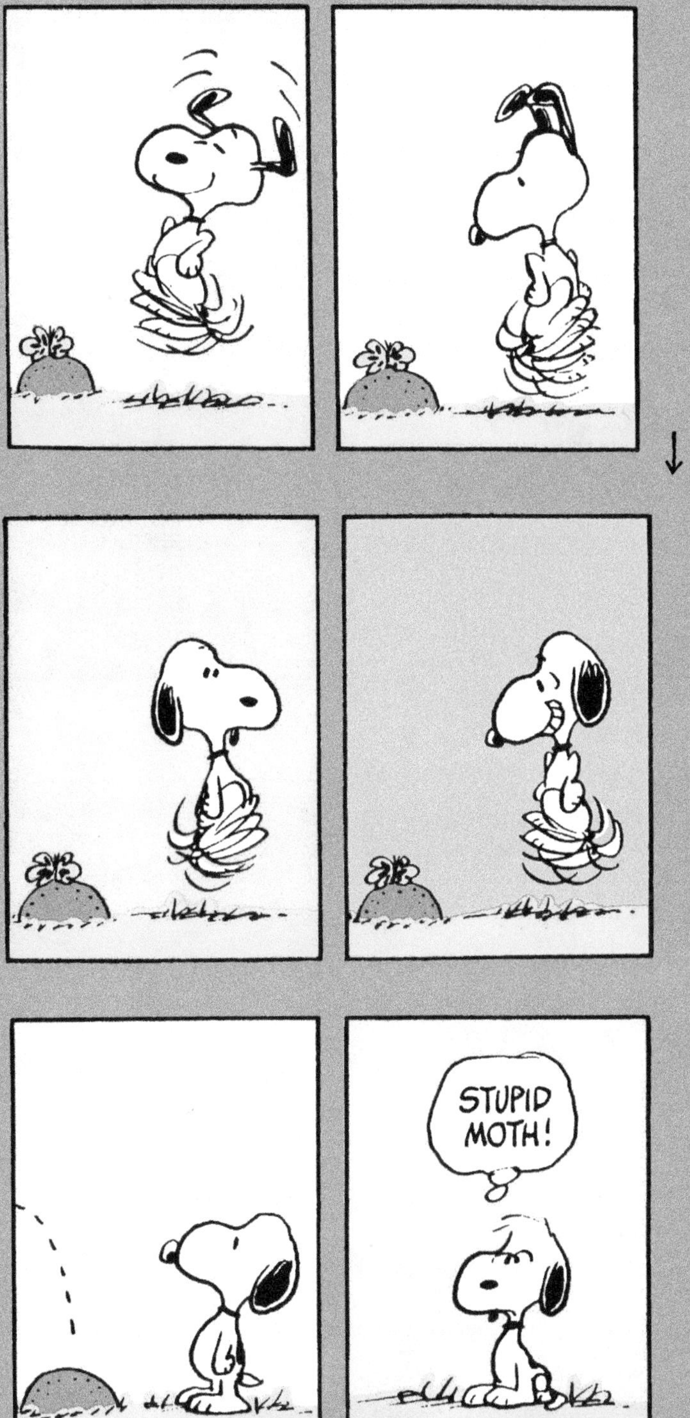
STUPID MOTH!
SCHULZ

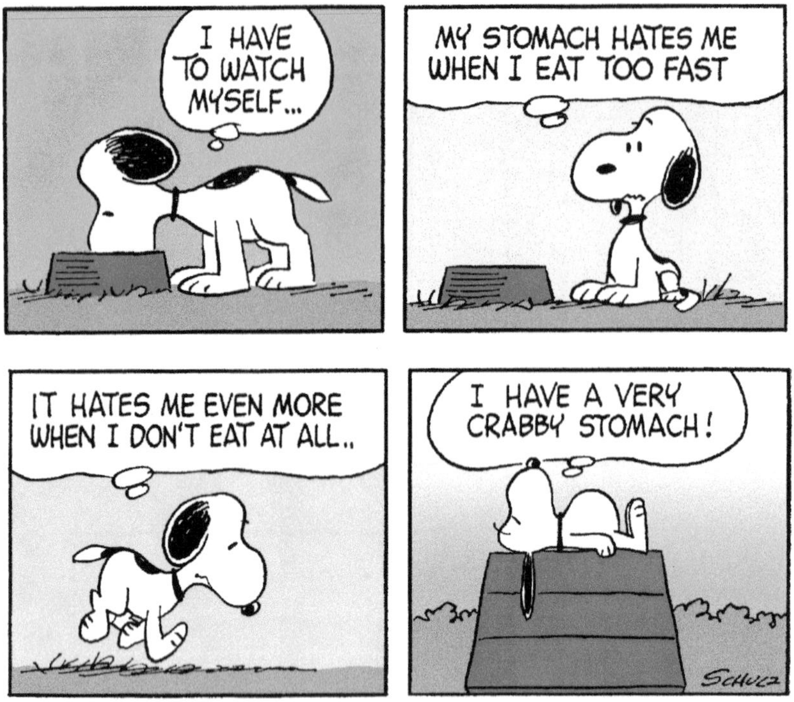
I HAVE TO WATCH MYSELF...
MY STOMACH HATES ME WHEN I EAT TOO FAST
IT HATES ME EVEN MORE WHEN I DON'T EAT AT ALL..
I HAVE A VERY CRABBY STOMACH!
SCHULZ

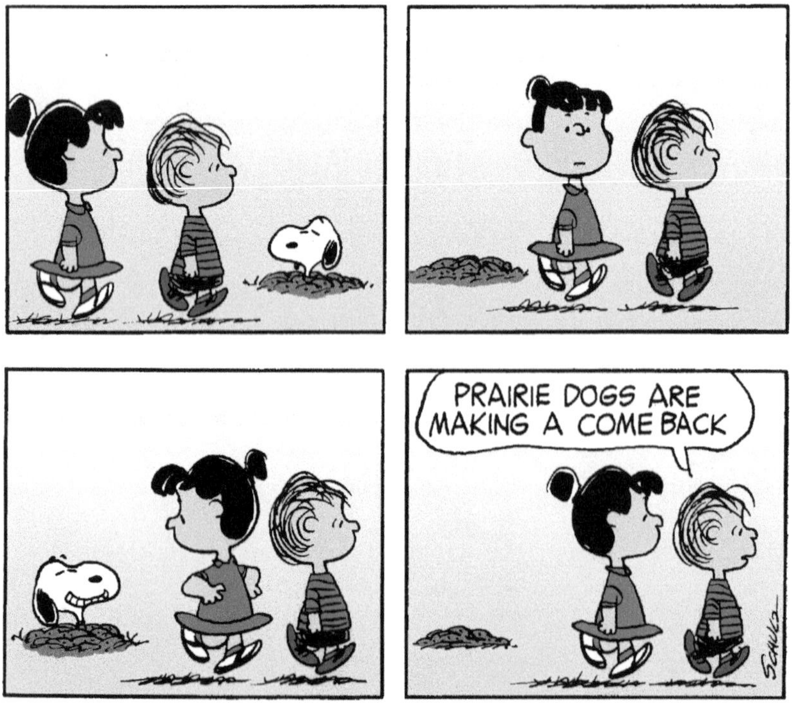
PRAIRIE DOGS ARE MAKING A COME BACK
SCHULZ

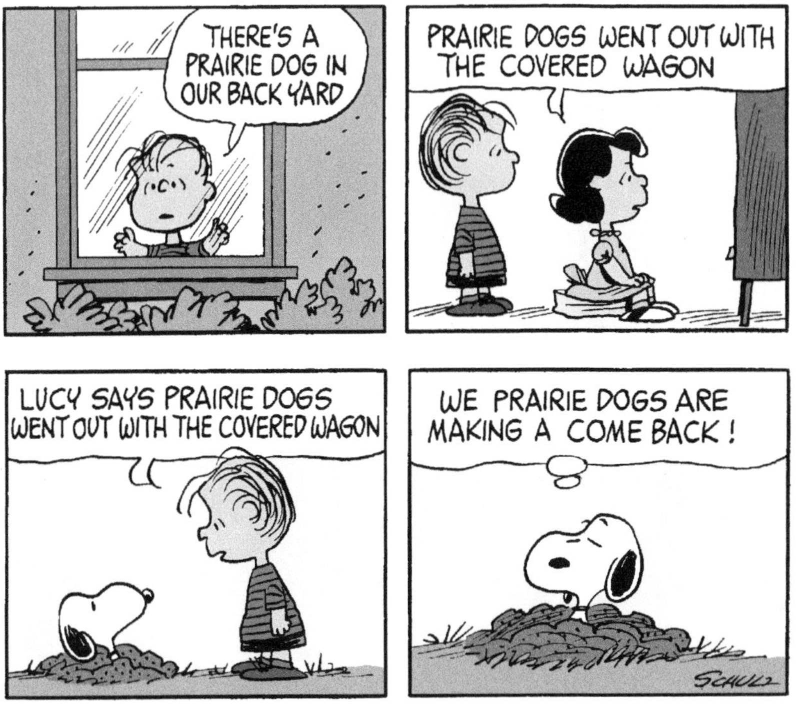
THERE'S A PRAIRIE DOG IN OUR BACK YARD
PRAIRIE DOGS WENT OUT WITH THE COVERED WAGON
LUCY SAYS PRAIRIE DOGS WENT OUT WITH THE COVERED WAGON
WE PRAIRIE DOGS ARE MAKING A COME BACK!
SCHULZ

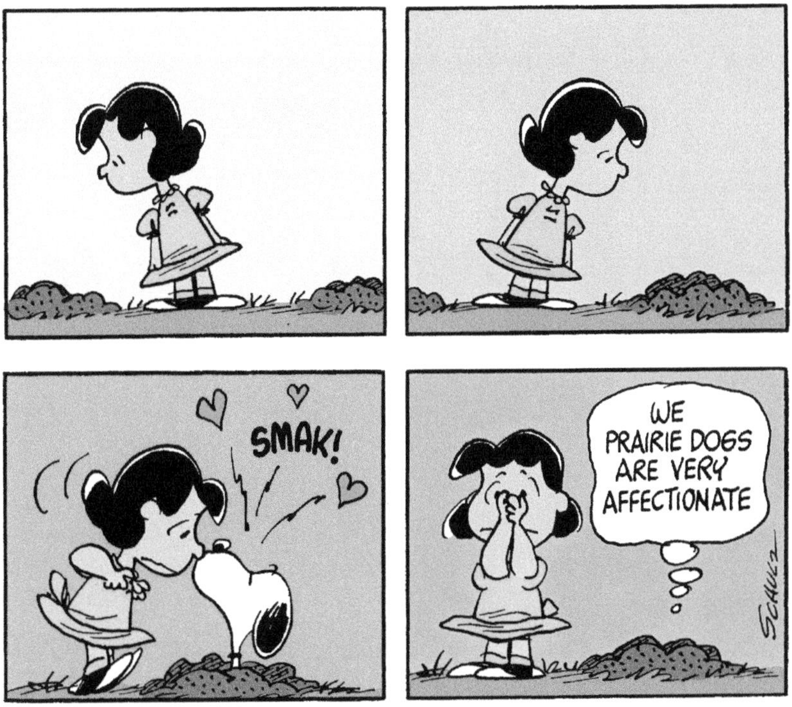
SMAK!
WE PRAIRIE DOGS ARE VERY AFFECTIONATE
SCHULZ

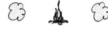

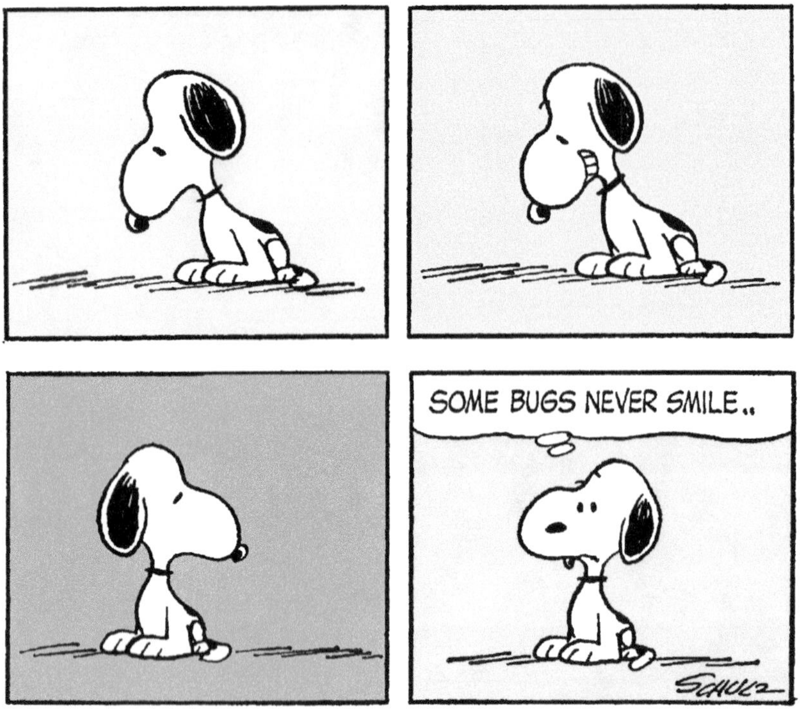
SOME BUGS NEVER SMILE..

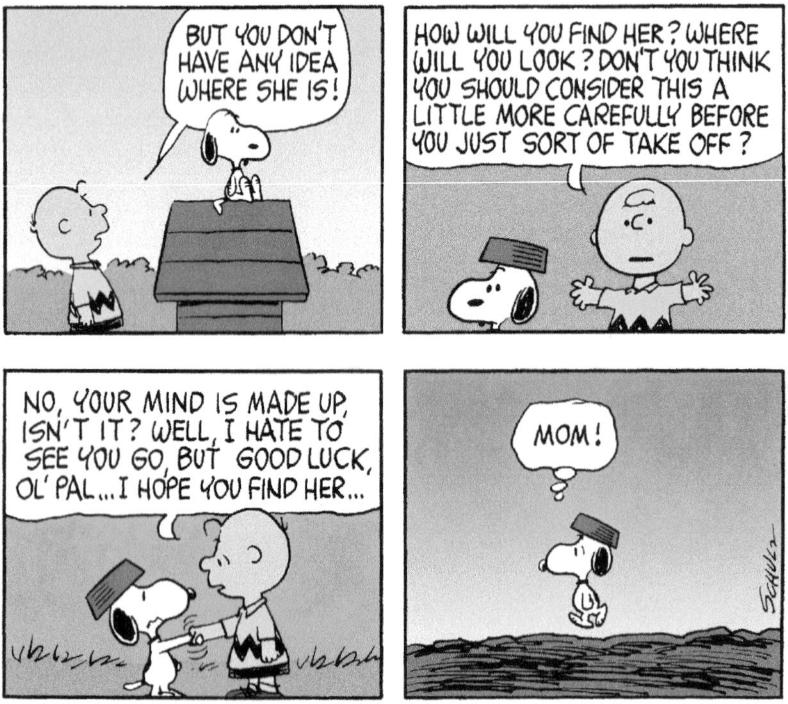
BUT YOU DON'T HAVE ANY IDEA WHERE SHE IS!
HOW WILL YOU FIND HER? WHERE WILL YOU LOOK? DON'T YOU THINK YOU SHOULD CONSIDER THIS A LITTLE MORE CAREFULLY BEFORE YOU JUST SORT OF TAKE OFF?
NO, YOUR MIND IS MADE UP, ISN'T IT? WELL, I HATE TO SEE YOU GO, BUT GOOD LUCK, OL' PAL...I HOPE YOU FIND HER...
MOM!

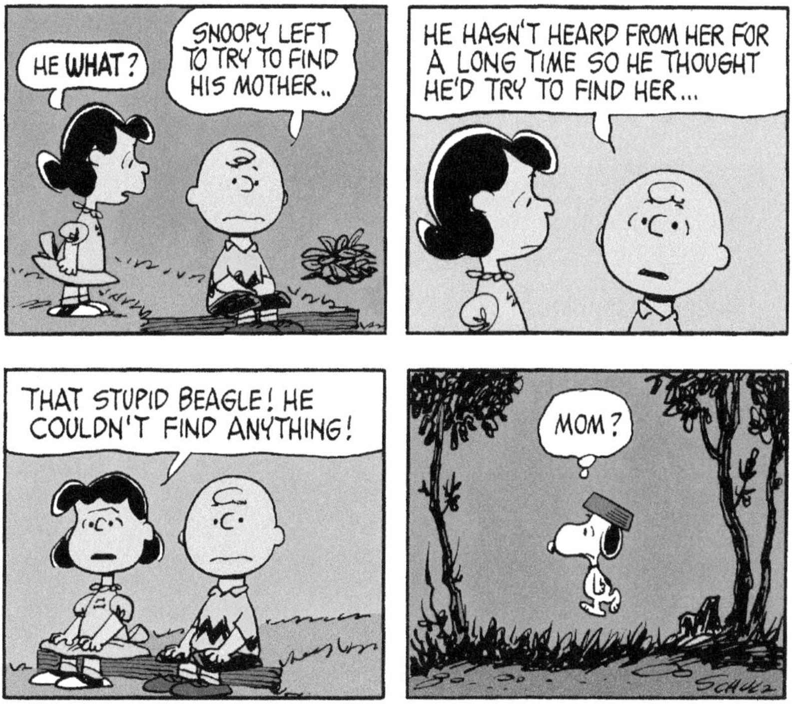
HE WHAT?
SNOOPY LEFT TO TRY TO FIND HIS MOTHER..
HE HASN'T HEARD FROM HER FOR A LONG TIME SO HE THOUGHT HE'D TRY TO FIND HER...
THAT STUPID BEAGLE! HE COULDN'T FIND ANYTHING!
MOM?

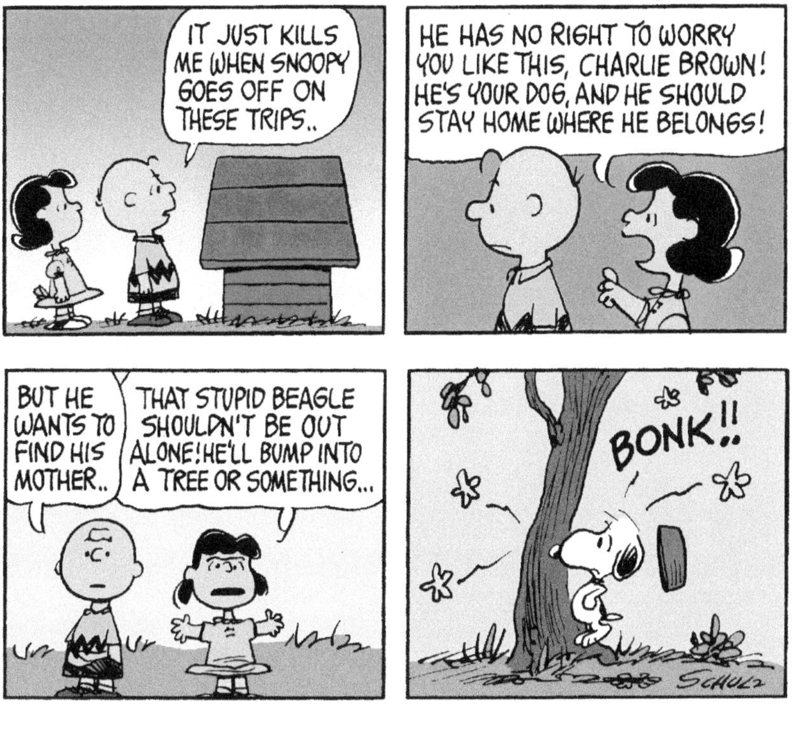
IT JUST KILLS ME WHEN SNOOPY GOES OFF ON THESE TRIPS..
HE HAS NO RIGHT TO WORRY YOU LIKE THIS, CHARLIE BROWN! HE'S YOUR DOG, AND HE SHOULD STAY HOME WHERE HE BELONGS!
BUT HE WANTS TO FIND HIS MOTHER..
THAT STUPID BEAGLE SHOULDN'T BE OUT ALONE! HE'LL BUMP INTO A TREE OR SOMETHING...
BONK!!

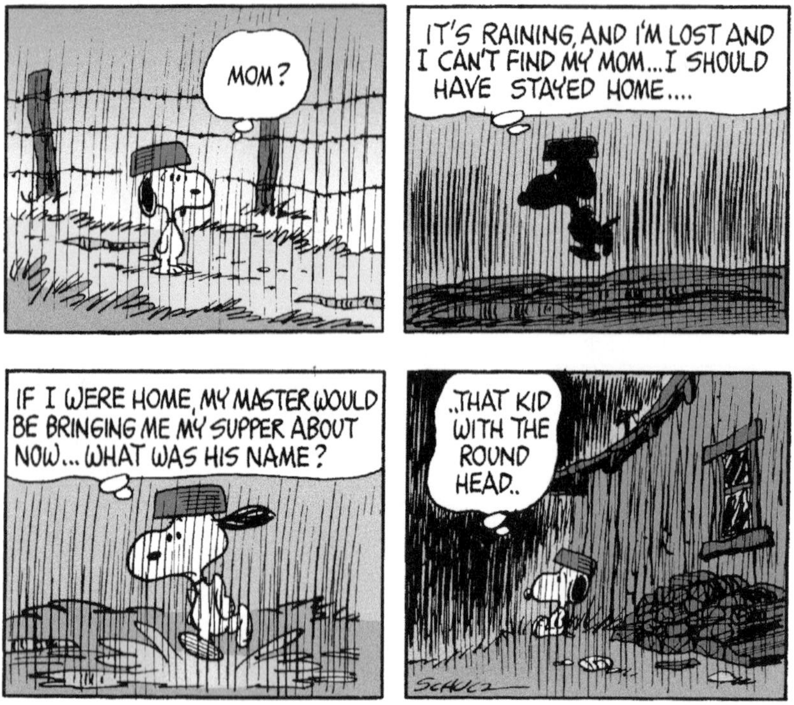
MOM?
IT'S RAINING, AND I'M LOST AND I CAN'T FIND MY MOM... I SHOULD HAVE STAYED HOME....
IF I WERE HOME, MY MASTER WOULD BE BRINGING ME MY SUPPER ABOUT NOW... WHAT WAS HIS NAME?
..THAT KID WITH THE ROUND HEAD..
SCHULZ

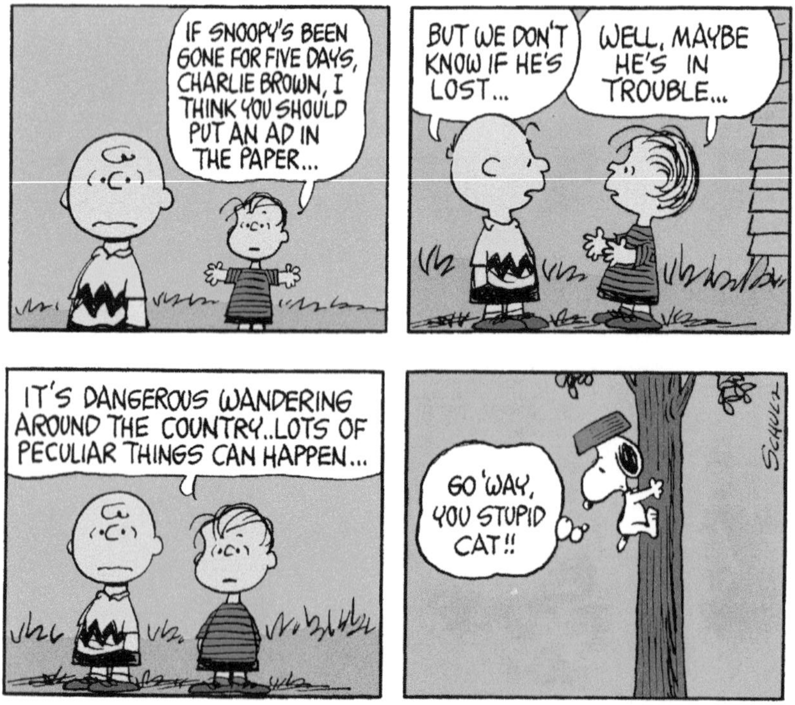
IF SNOOPY'S BEEN GONE FOR FIVE DAYS, CHARLIE BROWN, I THINK YOU SHOULD PUT AN AD IN THE PAPER...
BUT WE DON'T KNOW IF HE'S LOST...
WELL, MAYBE HE'S IN TROUBLE...
IT'S DANGEROUS WANDERING AROUND THE COUNTRY..LOTS OF PECULIAR THINGS CAN HAPPEN...
GO 'WAY, YOU STUPID CAT!!
SCHULZ

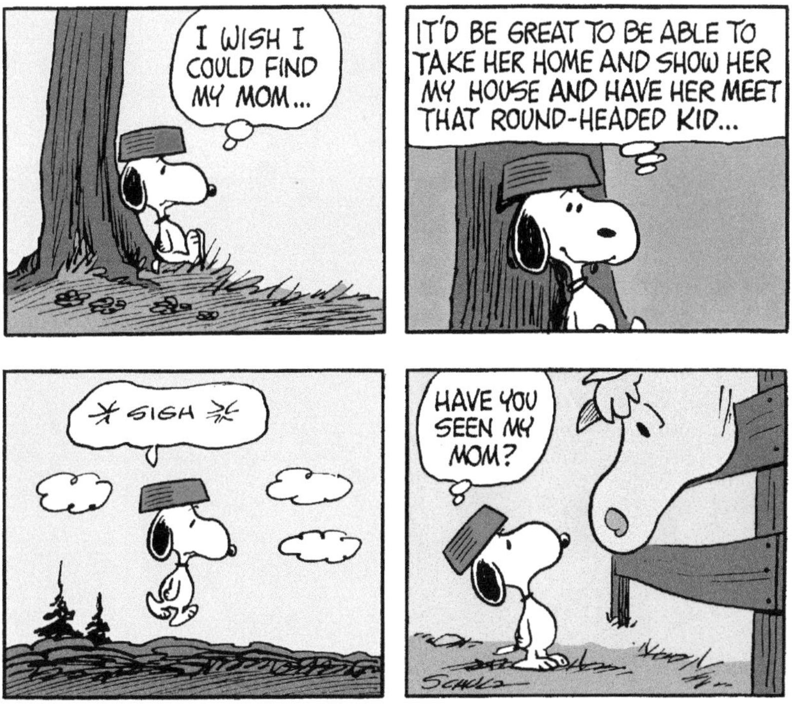
I WISH I COULD FIND MY MOM...
IT'D BE GREAT TO BE ABLE TO TAKE HER HOME AND SHOW HER MY HOUSE AND HAVE HER MEET THAT ROUND-HEADED KID...
SIGH
HAVE YOU SEEN MY MOM?
SCHULZ

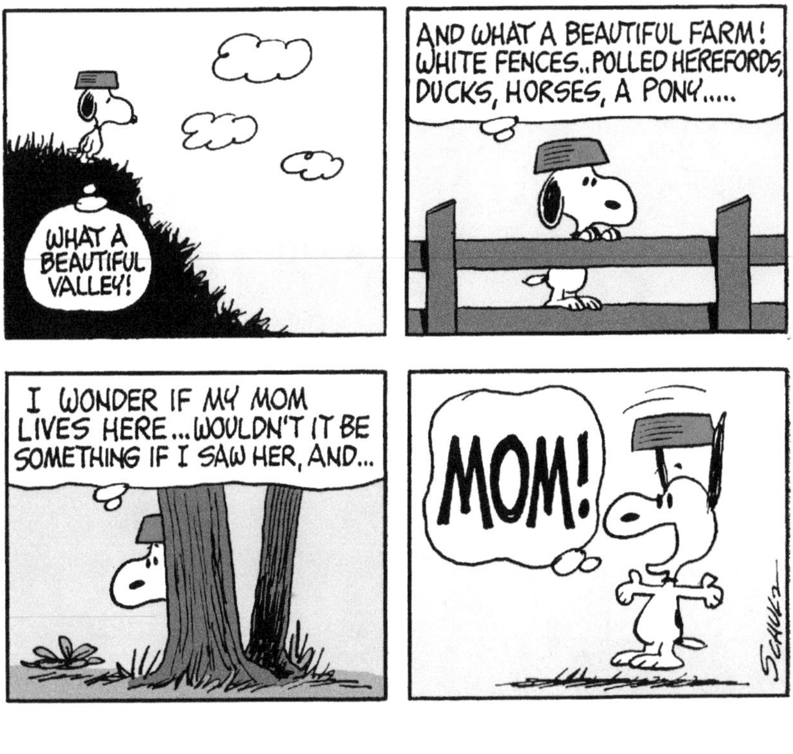
WHAT A BEAUTIFUL VALLEY!
AND WHAT A BEAUTIFUL FARM! WHITE FENCES..POLLED HEREFORDS, DUCKS, HORSES, A PONY.....
I WONDER IF MY MOM LIVES HERE...WOULDN'T IT BE SOMETHING IF I SAW HER, AND...
MOM!
SCHULZ

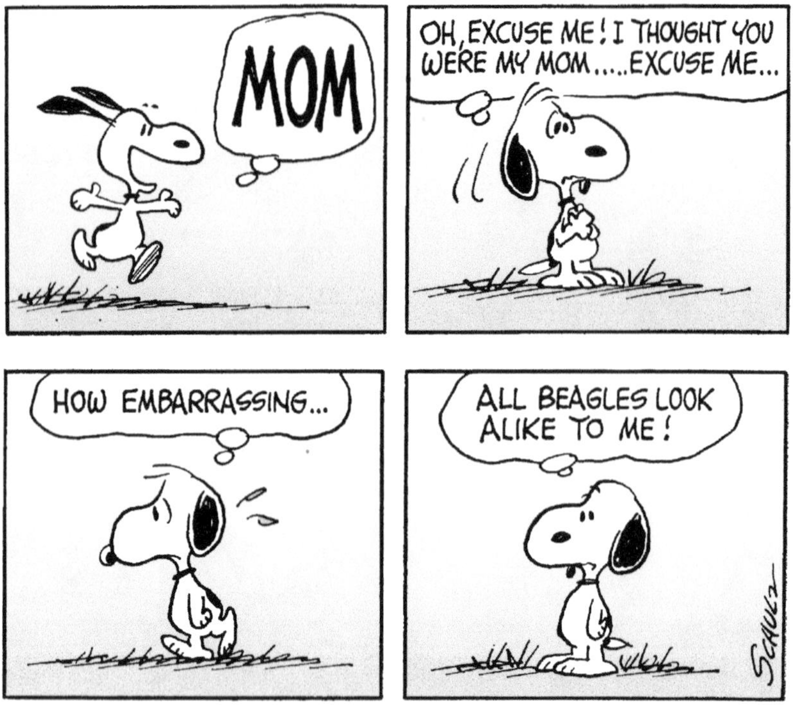
MOM
OH, EXCUSE ME! I THOUGHT YOU WERE MY MOM.....EXCUSE ME...
HOW EMBARRASSING...
ALL BEAGLES LOOK ALIKE TO ME!
SCHULZ

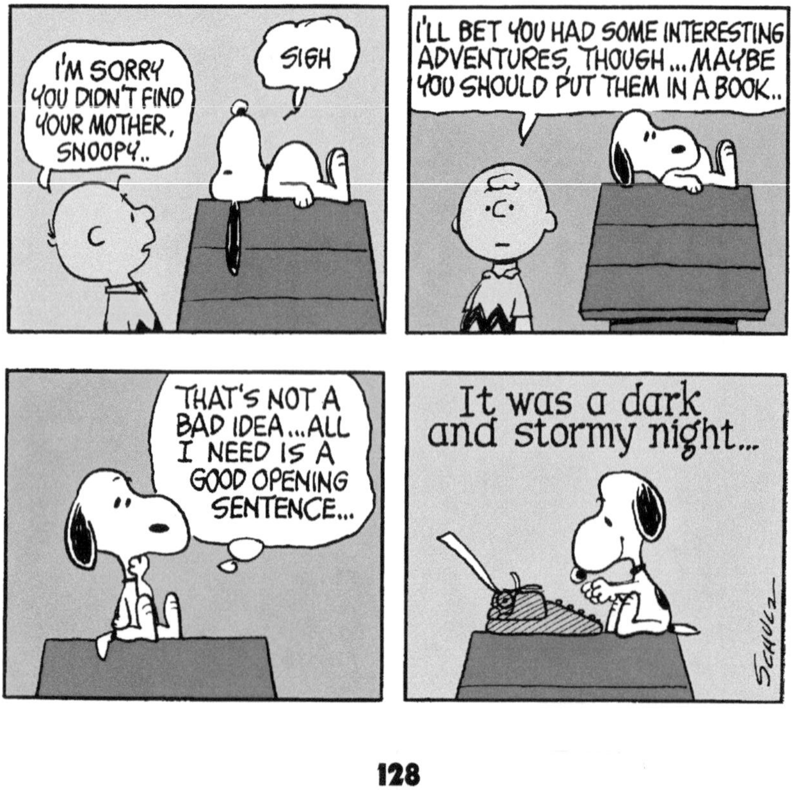
I'M SORRY YOU DIDN'T FIND YOUR MOTHER, SNOOPY..
SIGH
I'LL BET YOU HAD SOME INTERESTING ADVENTURES, THOUGH...MAYBE YOU SHOULD PUT THEM IN A BOOK..
THAT'S NOT A BAD IDEA...ALL I NEED IS A GOOD OPENING SENTENCE...
It was a dark and stormy night...
SCHULZ

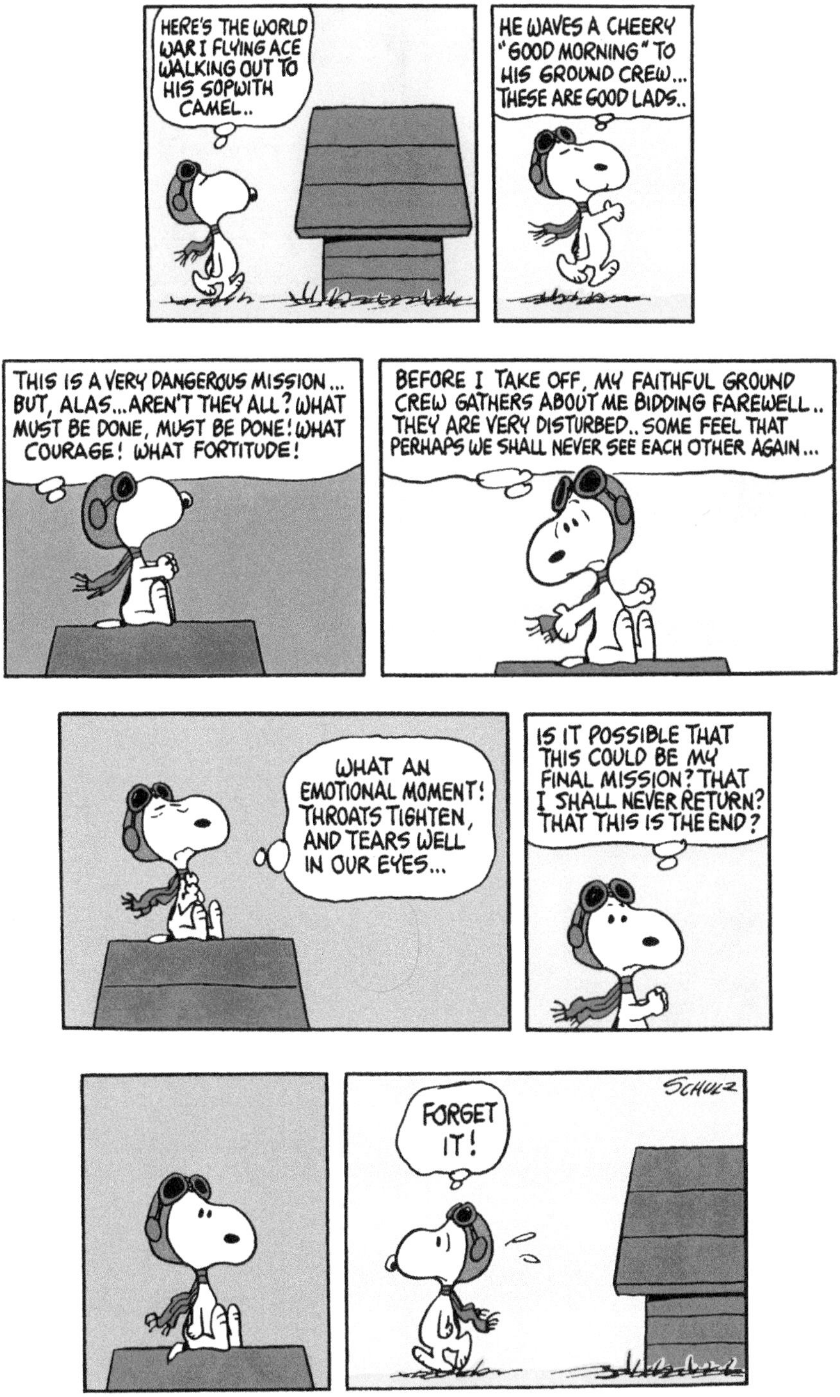
HERE'S THE WORLD WAR I FLYING ACE WALKING OUT TO HIS SOPWITH CAMEL..
HE WAVES A CHEERY "GOOD MORNING" TO HIS GROUND CREW... THESE ARE GOOD LADS..
THIS IS A VERY DANGEROUS MISSION... BUT, ALAS...AREN'T THEY ALL? WHAT MUST BE DONE, MUST BE DONE! WHAT COURAGE! WHAT FORTITUDE!
BEFORE I TAKE OFF, MY FAITHFUL GROUND CREW GATHERS ABOUT ME BIDDING FAREWELL.. THEY ARE VERY DISTURBED.. SOME FEEL THAT PERHAPS WE SHALL NEVER SEE EACH OTHER AGAIN...
WHAT AN EMOTIONAL MOMENT! THROATS TIGHTEN, AND TEARS WELL IN OUR EYES...
IS IT POSSIBLE THAT THIS COULD BE MY FINAL MISSION? THAT I SHALL NEVER RETURN? THAT THIS IS THE END?
FORGET IT!
SCHULZ

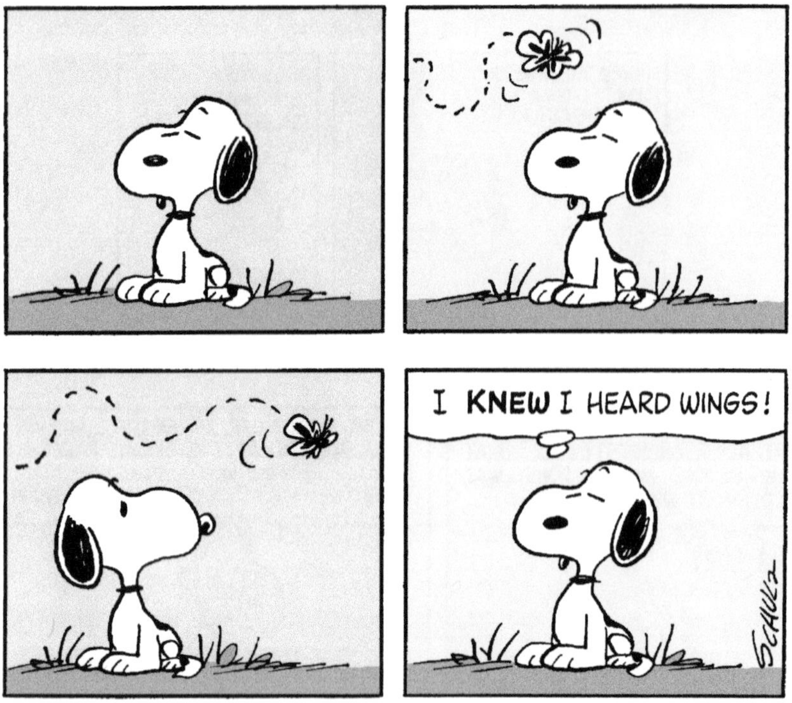
I KNEW I HEARD WINGS!

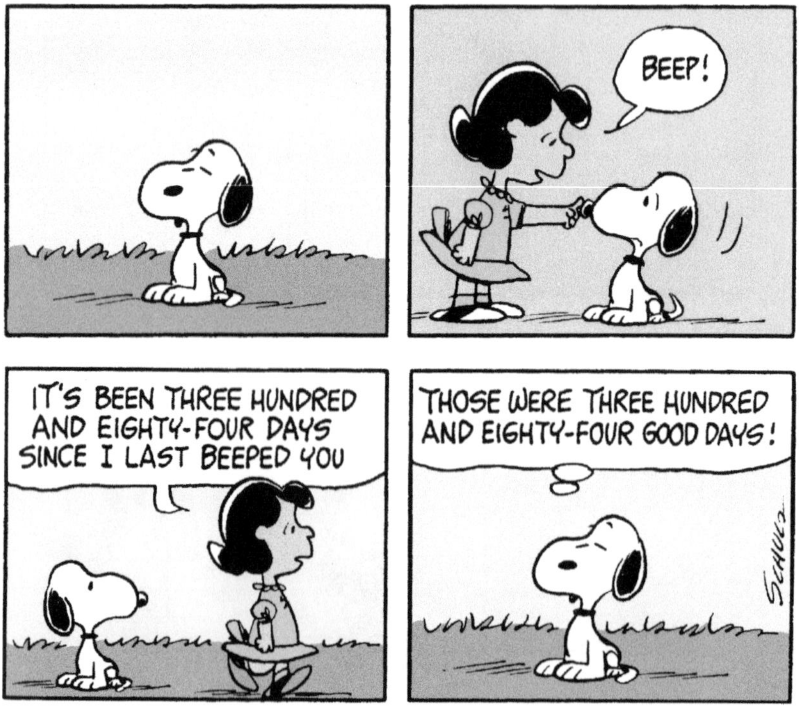
BEEP!
IT'S BEEN THREE HUNDRED AND EIGHTY-FOUR DAYS SINCE I LAST BEEPED YOU
THOSE WERE THREE HUNDRED AND EIGHTY-FOUR GOOD DAYS!

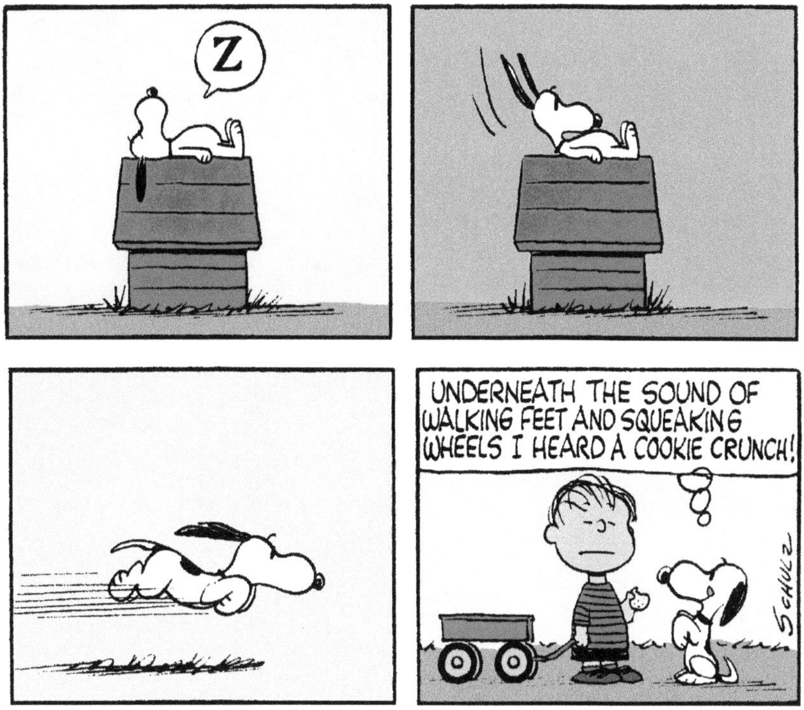
Z
UNDERNEATH THE SOUND OF WALKING FEET AND SQUEAKING WHEELS I HEARD A COOKIE CRUNCH!
SCHULZ

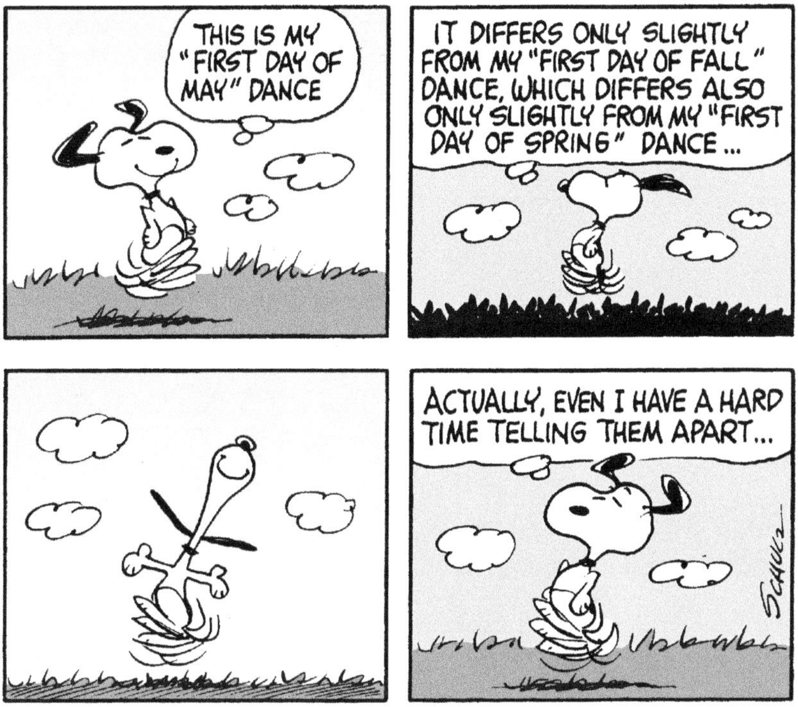
THIS IS MY "FIRST DAY OF MAY" DANCE
IT DIFFERS ONLY SLIGHTLY FROM MY "FIRST DAY OF FALL" DANCE, WHICH DIFFERS ALSO ONLY SLIGHTLY FROM MY "FIRST DAY OF SPRING" DANCE...
ACTUALLY, EVEN I HAVE A HARD TIME TELLING THEM APART...
SCHULZ

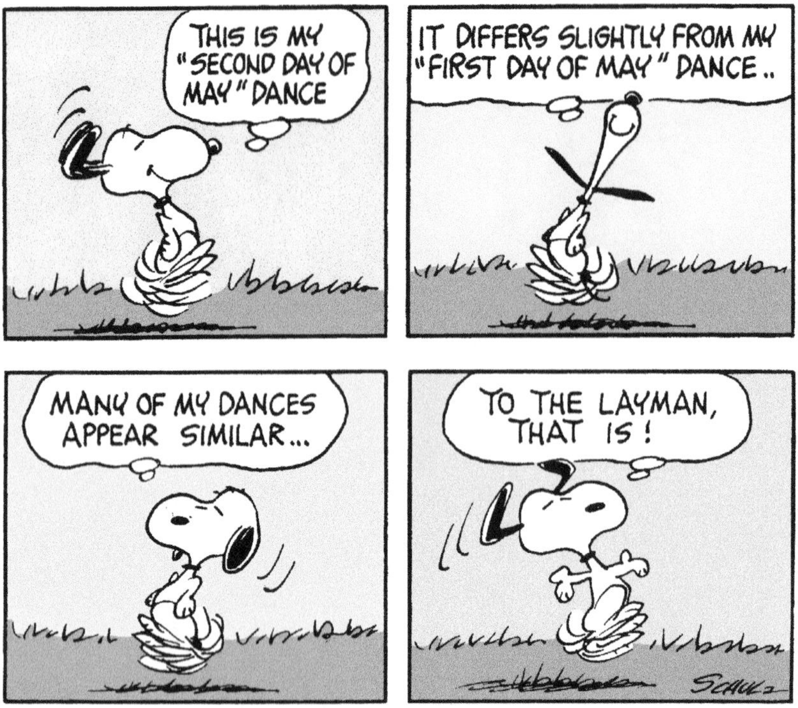
THIS IS MY "SECOND DAY OF MAY" DANCE
IT DIFFERS SLIGHTLY FROM MY "FIRST DAY OF MAY" DANCE..
MANY OF MY DANCES APPEAR SIMILAR...
TO THE LAYMAN, THAT IS!
SCHULZ

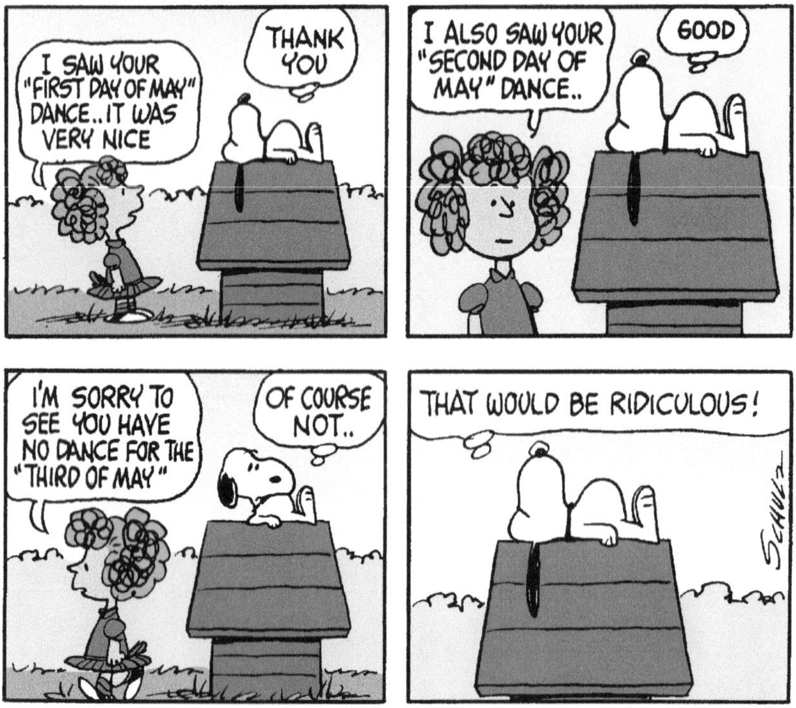
I SAW YOUR "FIRST DAY OF MAY" DANCE..IT WAS VERY NICE
THANK YOU
I ALSO SAW YOUR "SECOND DAY OF MAY" DANCE..
GOOD
I'M SORRY TO SEE YOU HAVE NO DANCE FOR THE "THIRD OF MAY"
OF COURSE NOT..
THAT WOULD BE RIDICULOUS!
SCHULZ

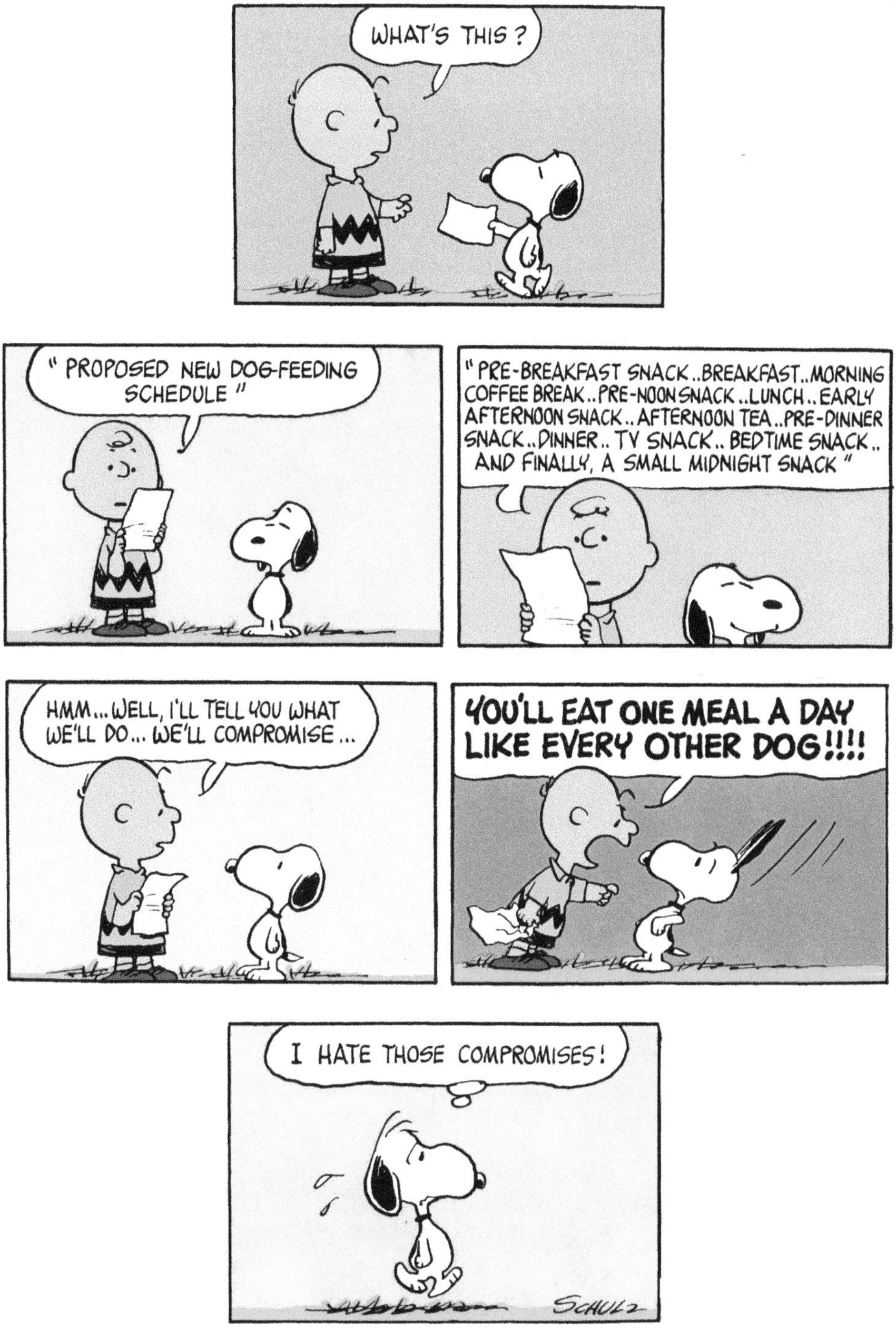
WHAT'S THIS ?
" PROPOSED NEW DOG-FEEDING SCHEDULE "
" PRE-BREAKFAST SNACK..BREAKFAST..MORNING COFFEE BREAK..PRE-NOON SNACK..LUNCH..EARLY AFTERNOON SNACK..AFTERNOON TEA..PRE-DINNER SNACK..DINNER.. TV SNACK.. BEDTIME SNACK.. AND FINALLY, A SMALL MIDNIGHT SNACK "
HMM...WELL, I'LL TELL YOU WHAT WE'LL DO... WE'LL COMPROMISE...
YOU'LL EAT ONE MEAL A DAY LIKE EVERY OTHER DOG!!!!
I HATE THOSE COMPROMISES!
SCHULZ

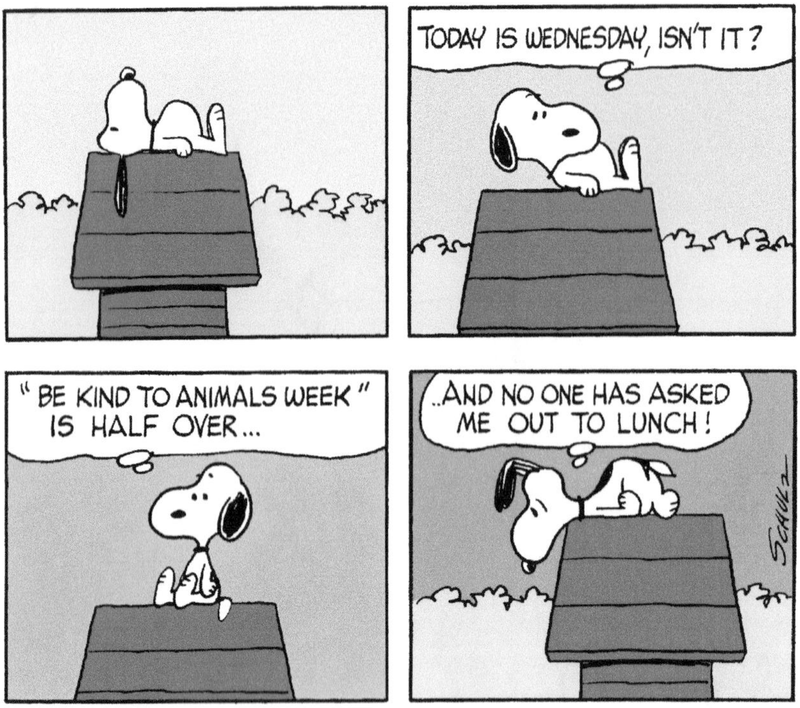
TODAY IS WEDNESDAY, ISN'T IT?
" BE KIND TO ANIMALS WEEK " IS HALF OVER...
..AND NO ONE HAS ASKED ME OUT TO LUNCH!
SCHULZ

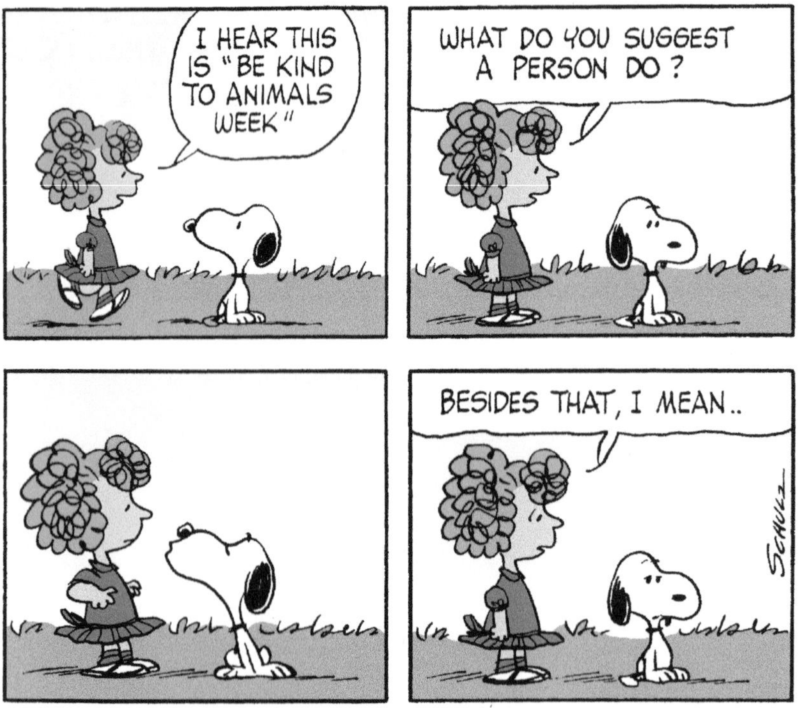
I HEAR THIS IS "BE KIND TO ANIMALS WEEK"
WHAT DO YOU SUGGEST A PERSON DO?
BESIDES THAT, I MEAN..
SCHULZ

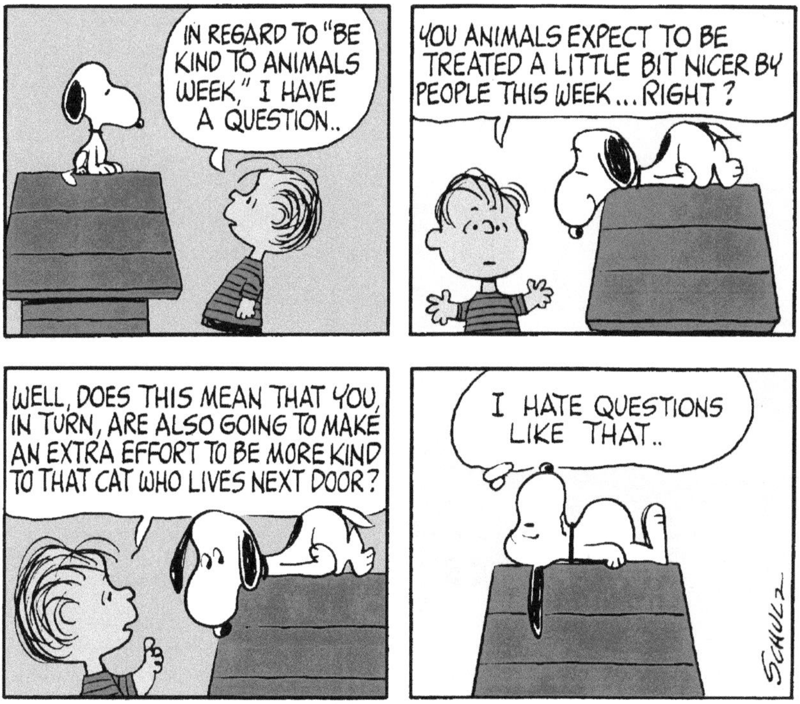
IN REGARD TO "BE KIND TO ANIMALS WEEK," I HAVE A QUESTION..
YOU ANIMALS EXPECT TO BE TREATED A LITTLE BIT NICER BY PEOPLE THIS WEEK... RIGHT ?
WELL, DOES THIS MEAN THAT YOU, IN TURN, ARE ALSO GOING TO MAKE AN EXTRA EFFORT TO BE MORE KIND TO THAT CAT WHO LIVES NEXT DOOR ?
I HATE QUESTIONS LIKE THAT..
SCHULZ

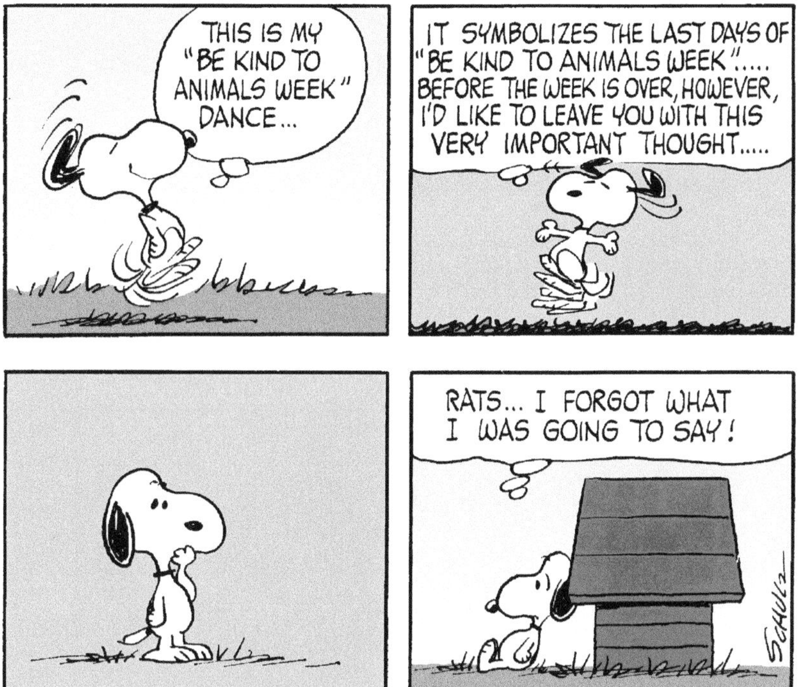
THIS IS MY "BE KIND TO ANIMALS WEEK" DANCE...
IT SYMBOLIZES THE LAST DAYS OF "BE KIND TO ANIMALS WEEK"..... BEFORE THE WEEK IS OVER, HOWEVER, I'D LIKE TO LEAVE YOU WITH THIS VERY IMPORTANT THOUGHT.....
RATS... I FORGOT WHAT I WAS GOING TO SAY !
SCHULZ

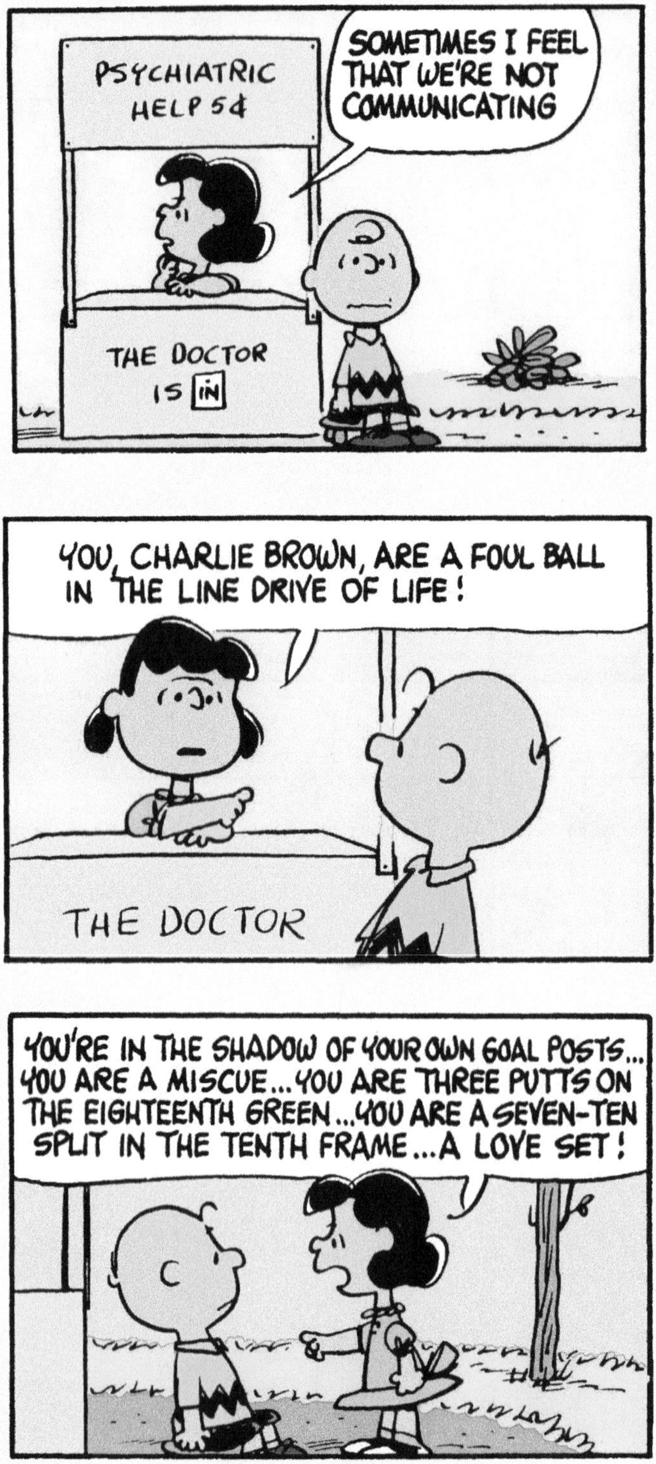
PSYCHIATRIC HELP 5¢
SOMETIMES I FEEL THAT WE'RE NOT COMMUNICATING
THE DOCTOR IS IN
YOU, CHARLIE BROWN, ARE A FOUL BALL IN THE LINE DRIVE OF LIFE!
THE DOCTOR
YOU'RE IN THE SHADOW OF YOUR OWN GOAL POSTS... YOU ARE A MISCUE... YOU ARE THREE PUTTS ON THE EIGHTEENTH GREEN... YOU ARE A SEVEN-TEN SPLIT IN THE TENTH FRAME... A LOVE SET!

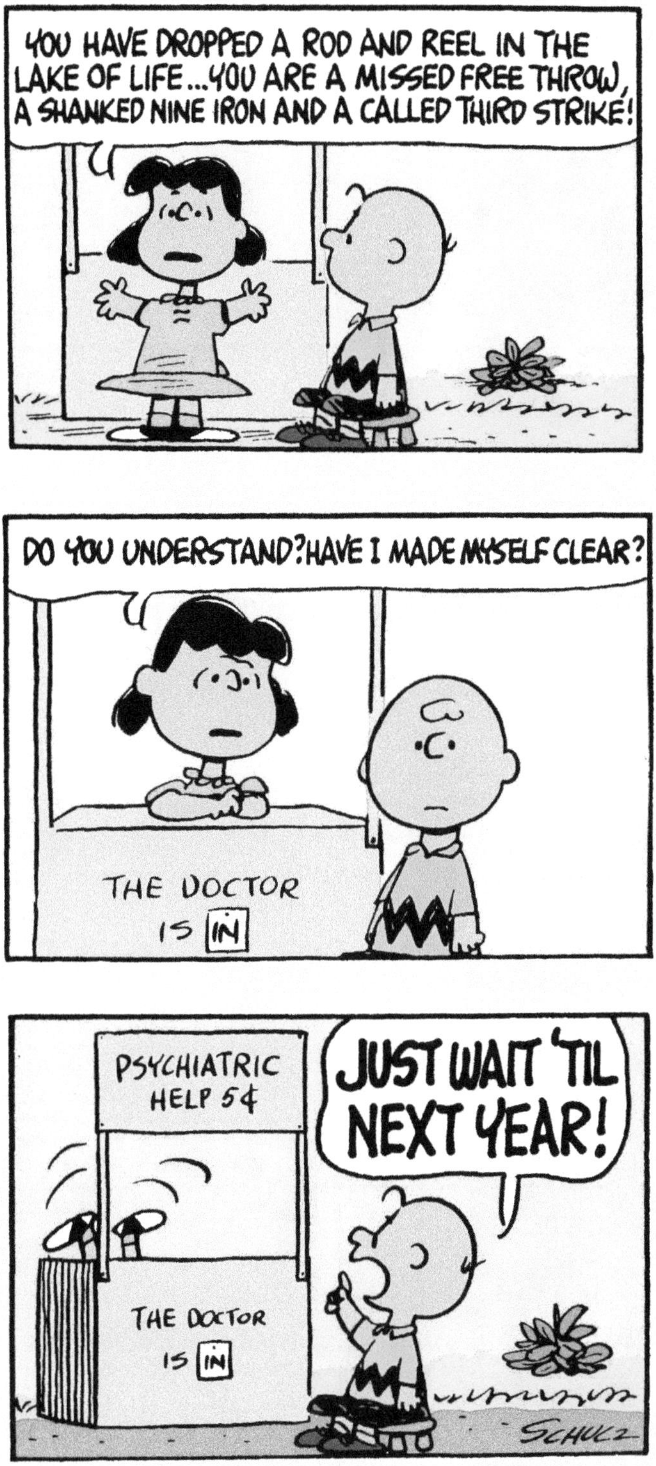
YOU HAVE DROPPED A ROD AND REEL IN THE LAKE OF LIFE...YOU ARE A MISSED FREE THROW, A SHANKED NINE IRON AND A CALLED THIRD STRIKE!
DO YOU UNDERSTAND? HAVE I MADE MYSELF CLEAR?
THE DOCTOR IS IN
PSYCHIATRIC HELP 5¢
THE DOCTOR IS IN
JUST WAIT 'TIL NEXT YEAR!
SCHULZ

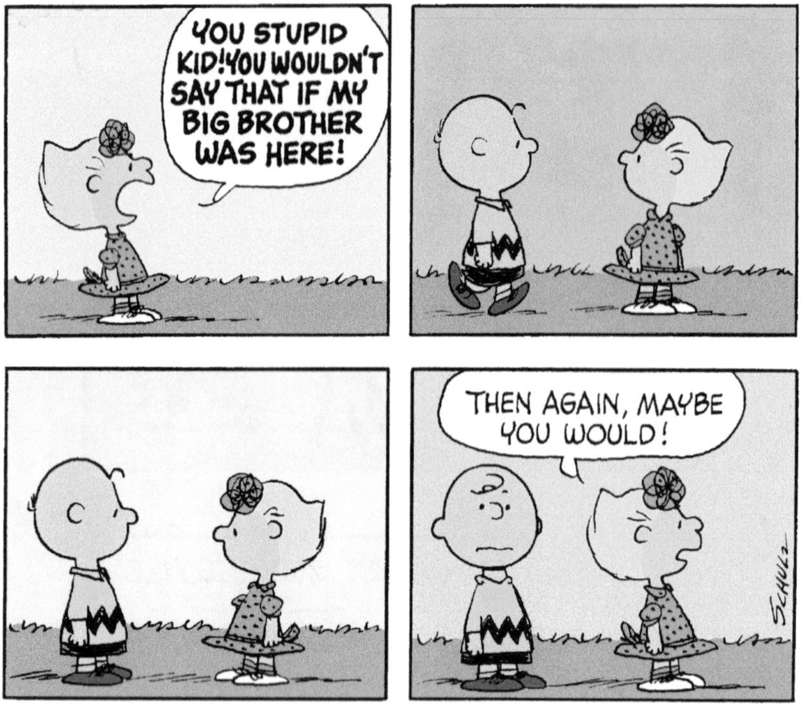
YOU STUPID KID! YOU WOULDN'T SAY THAT IF MY BIG BROTHER WAS HERE!
THEN AGAIN, MAYBE YOU WOULD!
SCHULZ

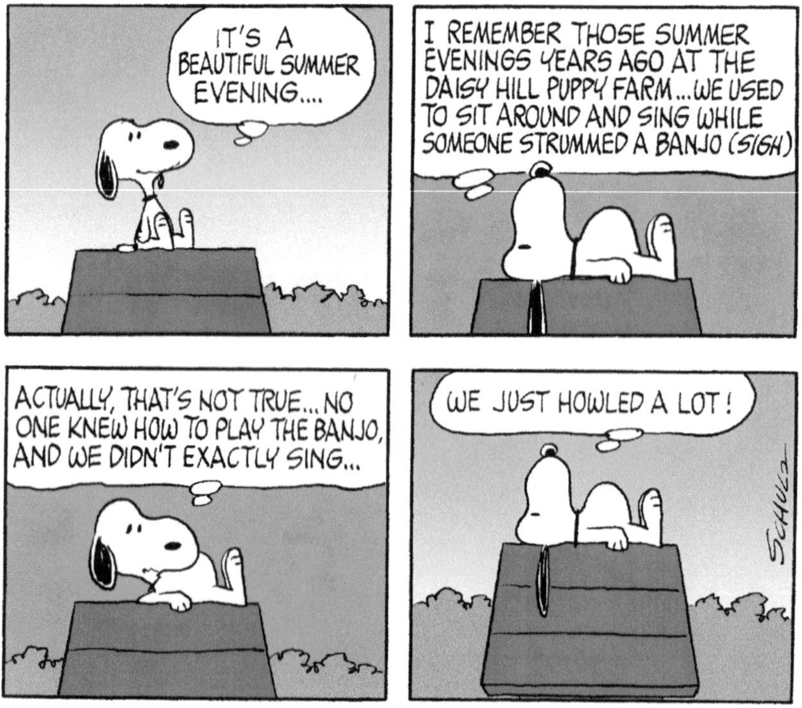
IT'S A BEAUTIFUL SUMMER EVENING....
I REMEMBER THOSE SUMMER EVENINGS YEARS AGO AT THE DAISY HILL PUPPY FARM...WE USED TO SIT AROUND AND SING WHILE SOMEONE STRUMMED A BANJO (SIGH)
ACTUALLY, THAT'S NOT TRUE... NO ONE KNEW HOW TO PLAY THE BANJO, AND WE DIDN'T EXACTLY SING...
WE JUST HOWLED A LOT!
SCHULZ

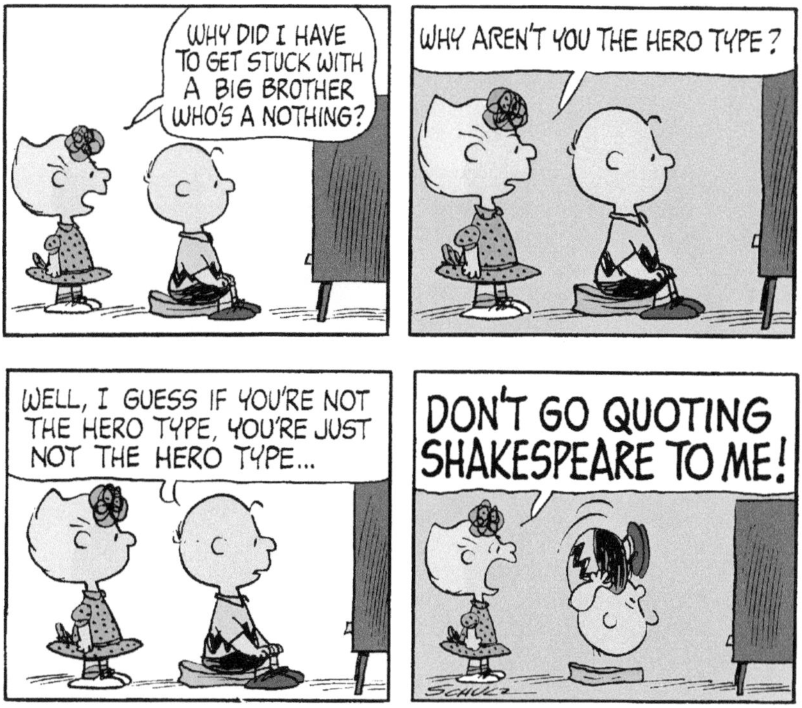
WHY DID I HAVE TO GET STUCK WITH A BIG BROTHER WHO'S A NOTHING?
WHY AREN'T YOU THE HERO TYPE?
WELL, I GUESS IF YOU'RE NOT THE HERO TYPE, YOU'RE JUST NOT THE HERO TYPE...
DON'T GO QUOTING SHAKESPEARE TO ME!

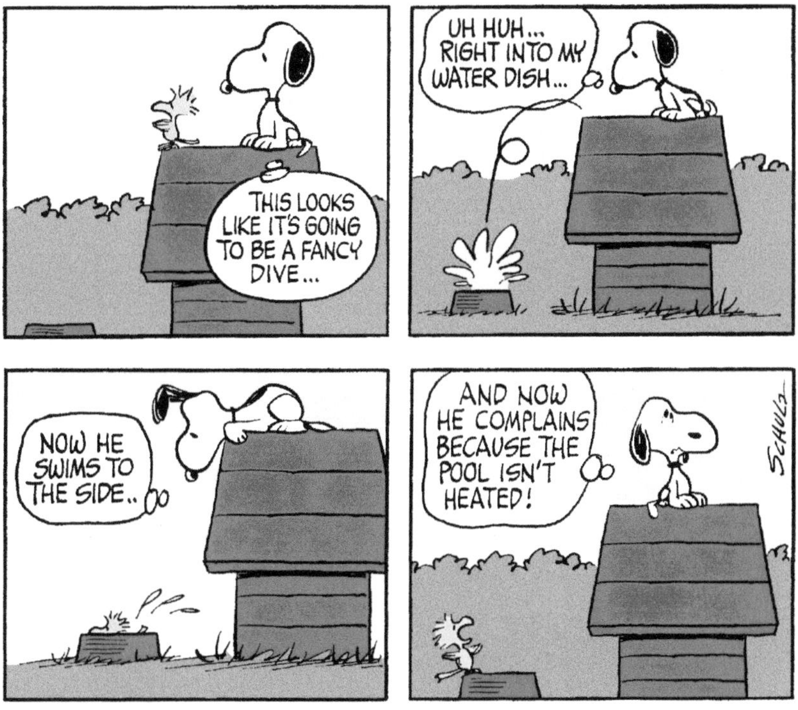
THIS LOOKS LIKE IT'S GOING TO BE A FANCY DIVE...
UH HUH... RIGHT INTO MY WATER DISH...
NOW HE SWIMS TO THE SIDE..
AND NOW HE COMPLAINS BECAUSE THE POOL ISN'T HEATED!

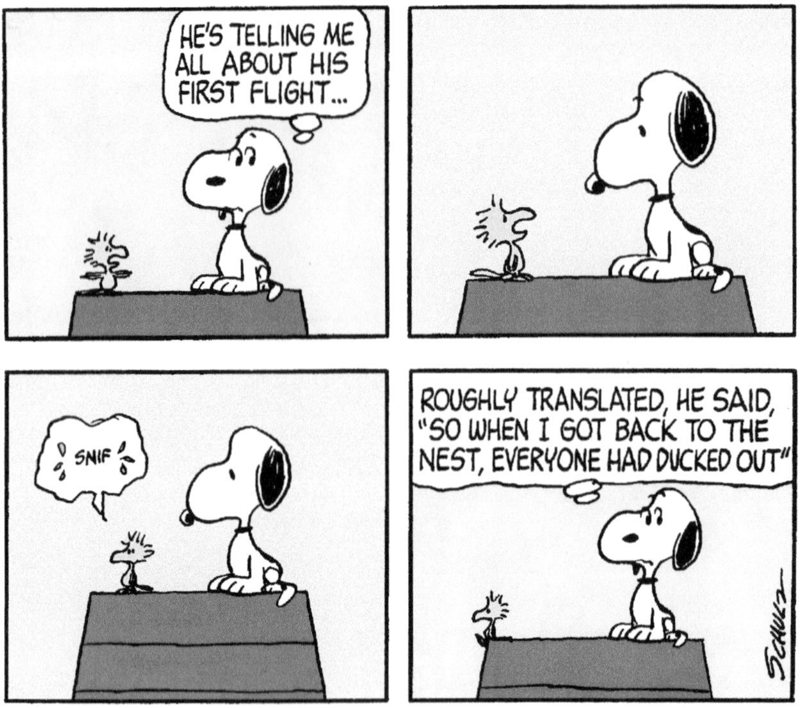
HE'S TELLING ME ALL ABOUT HIS FIRST FLIGHT...
SNIF
ROUGHLY TRANSLATED, HE SAID, "SO WHEN I GOT BACK TO THE NEST, EVERYONE HAD DUCKED OUT"
SCHULZ

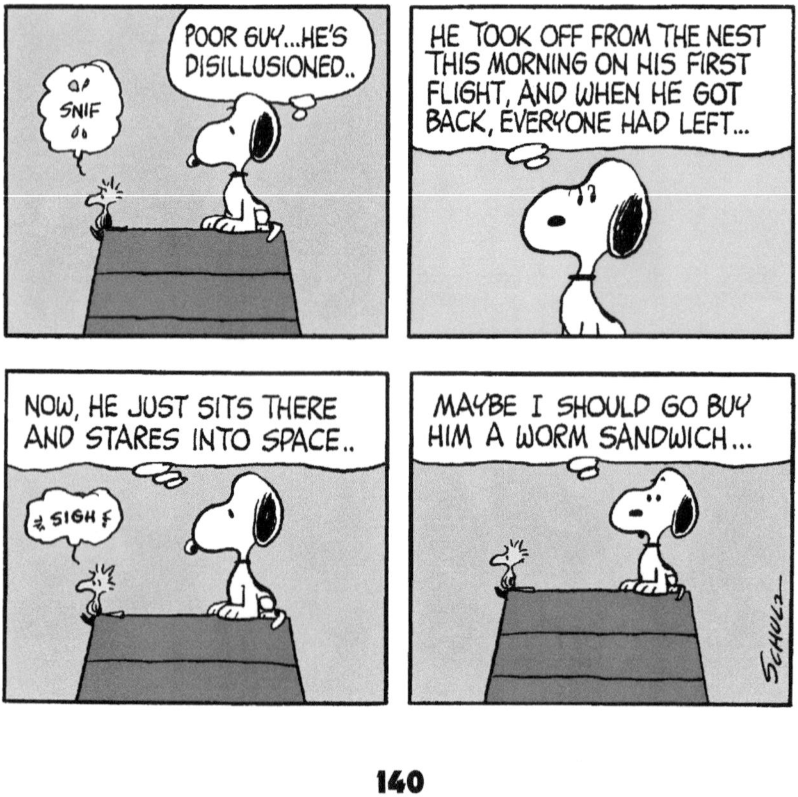
POOR GUY...HE'S DISILLUSIONED..
SNIF
HE TOOK OFF FROM THE NEST THIS MORNING ON HIS FIRST FLIGHT, AND WHEN HE GOT BACK, EVERYONE HAD LEFT...
NOW, HE JUST SITS THERE AND STARES INTO SPACE..
SIGH
MAYBE I SHOULD GO BUY HIM A WORM SANDWICH...
SCHULZ

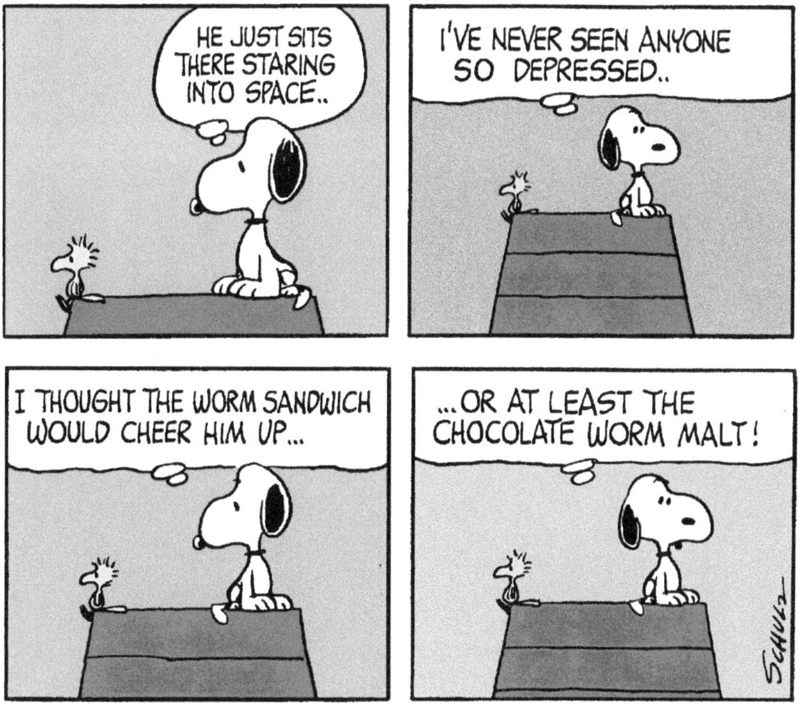
HE JUST SITS THERE STARING INTO SPACE..
I'VE NEVER SEEN ANYONE SO DEPRESSED..
I THOUGHT THE WORM SANDWICH WOULD CHEER HIM UP...
...OR AT LEAST THE CHOCOLATE WORM MALT!
SCHULZ

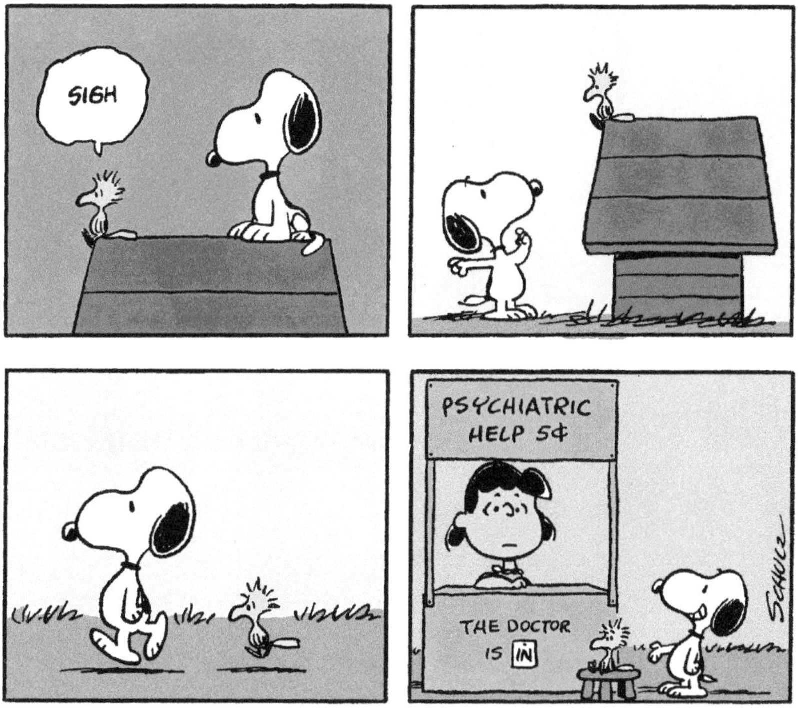
SIGH
PSYCHIATRIC HELP 5¢
THE DOCTOR IS IN
SCHULZ

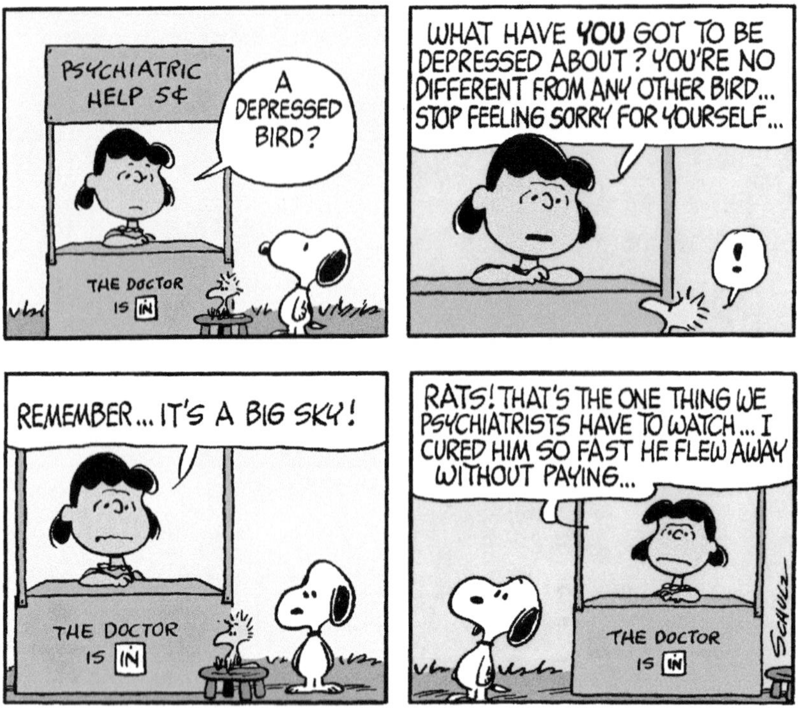
PSYCHIATRIC HELP 5¢
THE DOCTOR IS IN
A DEPRESSED BIRD?
WHAT HAVE **YOU** GOT TO BE DEPRESSED ABOUT? YOU'RE NO DIFFERENT FROM ANY OTHER BIRD... STOP FEELING SORRY FOR YOURSELF...
!
REMEMBER... IT'S A BIG SKY!
THE DOCTOR IS IN
RATS! THAT'S THE ONE THING WE PSYCHIATRISTS HAVE TO WATCH... I CURED HIM SO FAST HE FLEW AWAY WITHOUT PAYING...
THE DOCTOR IS IN
SCHULZ

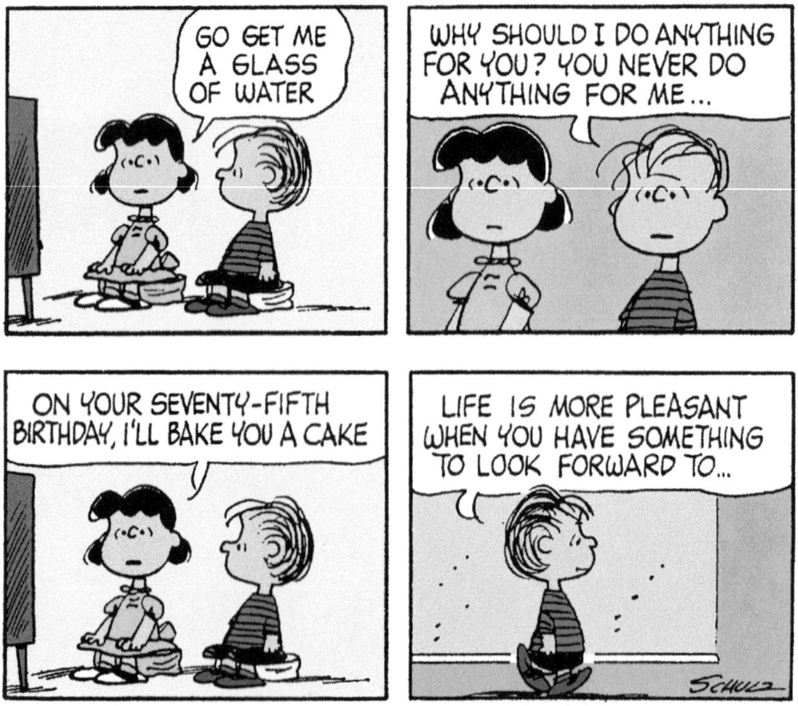
GO GET ME A GLASS OF WATER
WHY SHOULD I DO ANYTHING FOR YOU? YOU NEVER DO ANYTHING FOR ME...
ON YOUR SEVENTY-FIFTH BIRTHDAY, I'LL BAKE YOU A CAKE
LIFE IS MORE PLEASANT WHEN YOU HAVE SOMETHING TO LOOK FORWARD TO...
SCHULZ

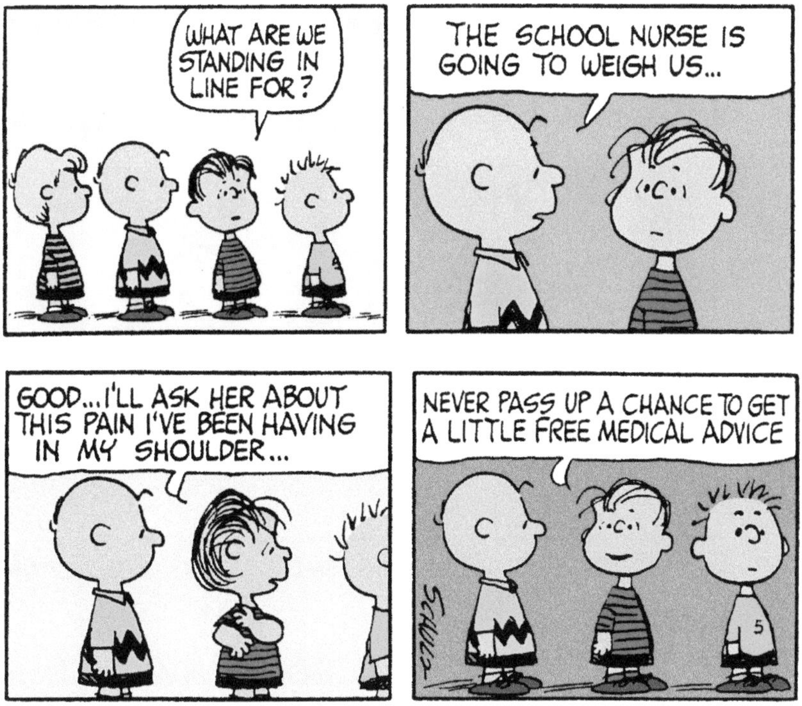
WHAT ARE WE STANDING IN LINE FOR?
THE SCHOOL NURSE IS GOING TO WEIGH US...
GOOD...I'LL ASK HER ABOUT THIS PAIN I'VE BEEN HAVING IN MY SHOULDER...
NEVER PASS UP A CHANCE TO GET A LITTLE FREE MEDICAL ADVICE
5
SCHULZ

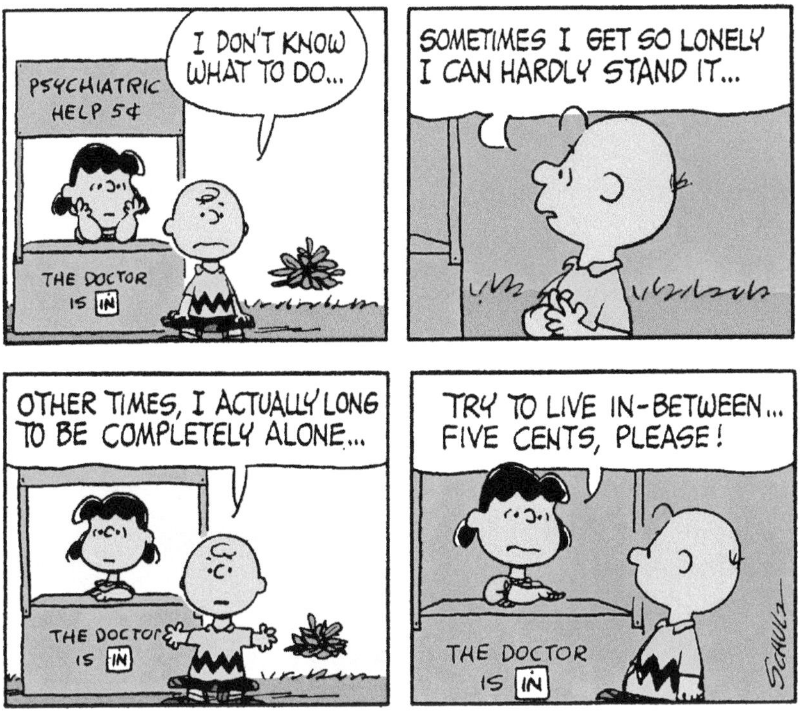
PSYCHIATRIC HELP 5¢
THE DOCTOR IS IN
I DON'T KNOW WHAT TO DO...
SOMETIMES I GET SO LONELY I CAN HARDLY STAND IT...
OTHER TIMES, I ACTUALLY LONG TO BE COMPLETELY ALONE...
TRY TO LIVE IN-BETWEEN... FIVE CENTS, PLEASE!
SCHULZ

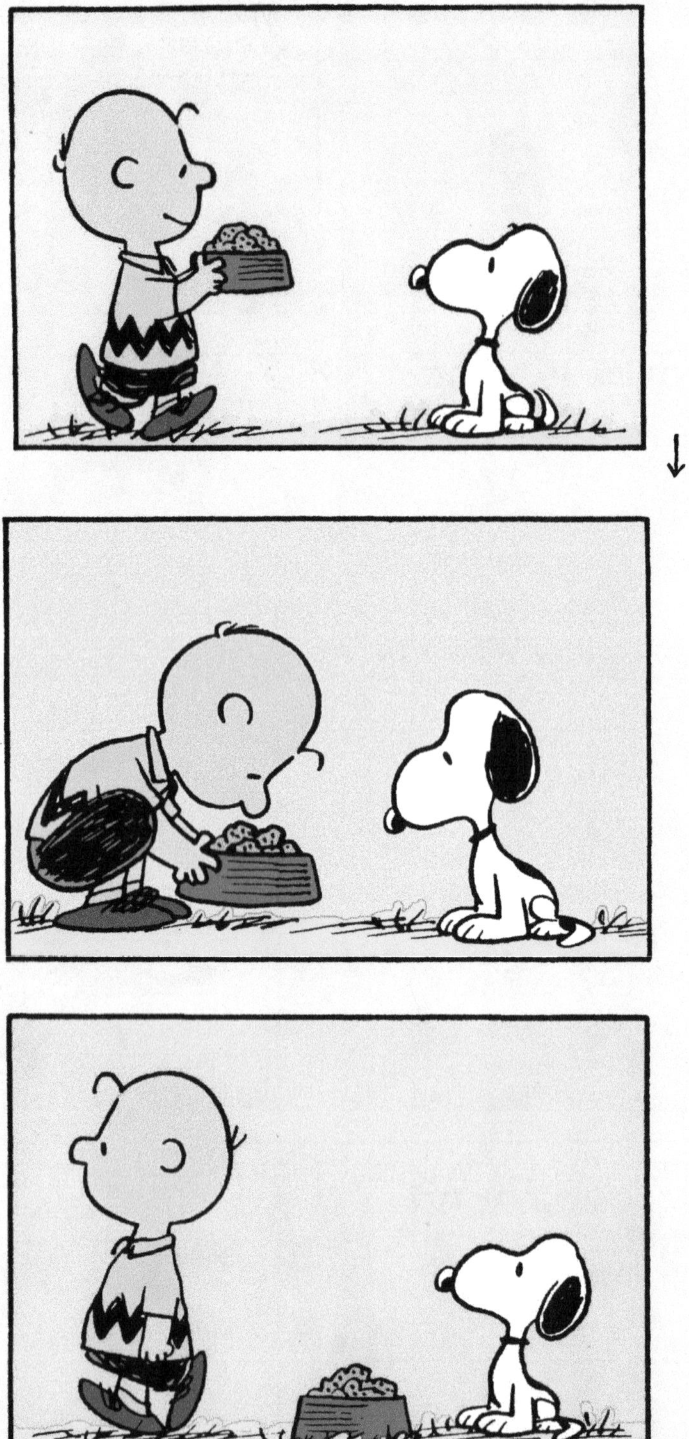

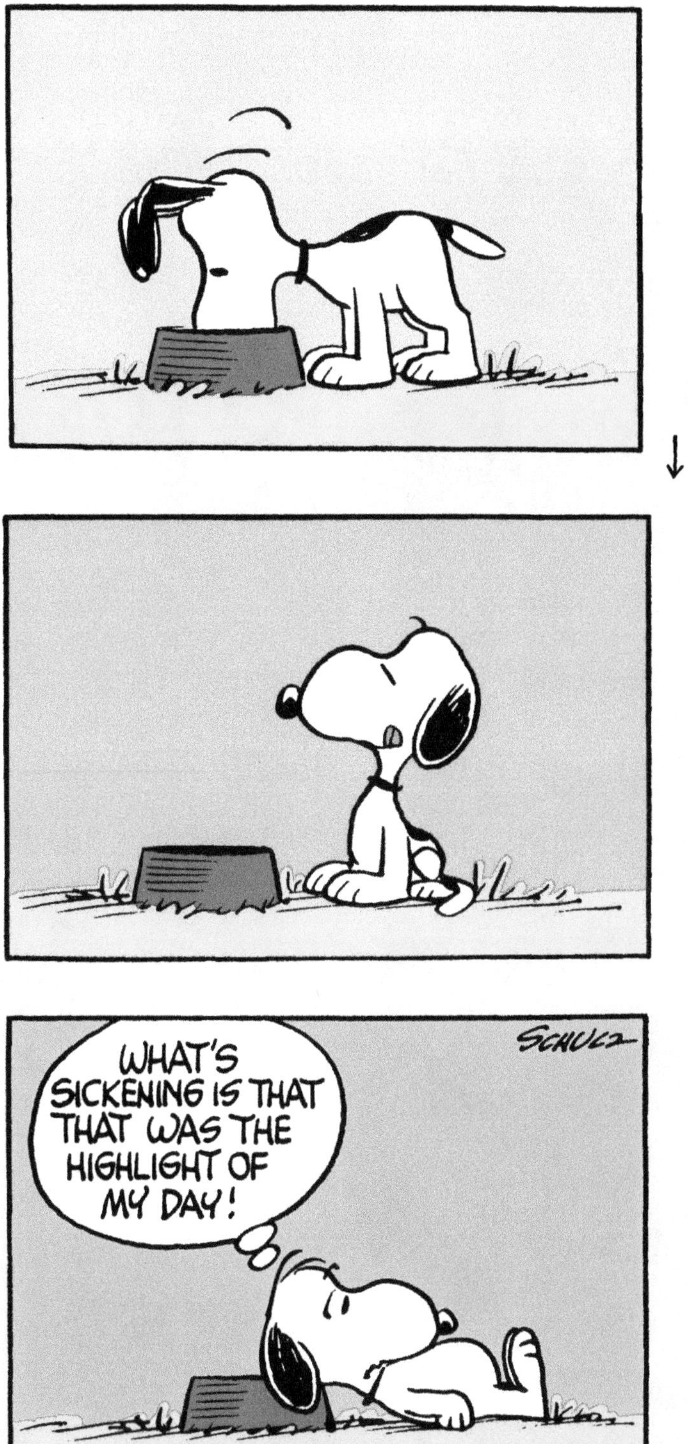
WHAT'S SICKENING IS THAT THAT WAS THE HIGHLIGHT OF MY DAY!
SCHULZ

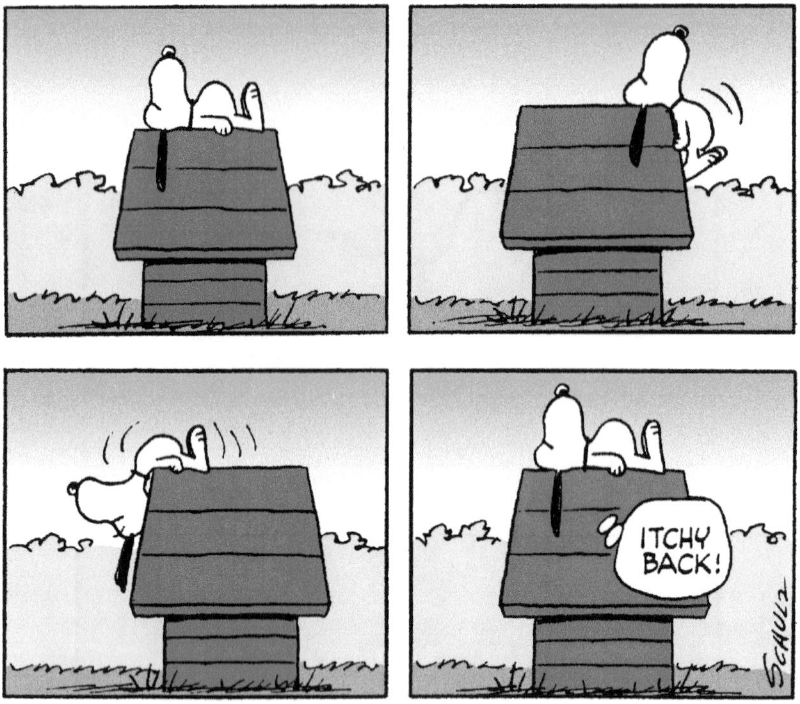
ITCHY BACK!

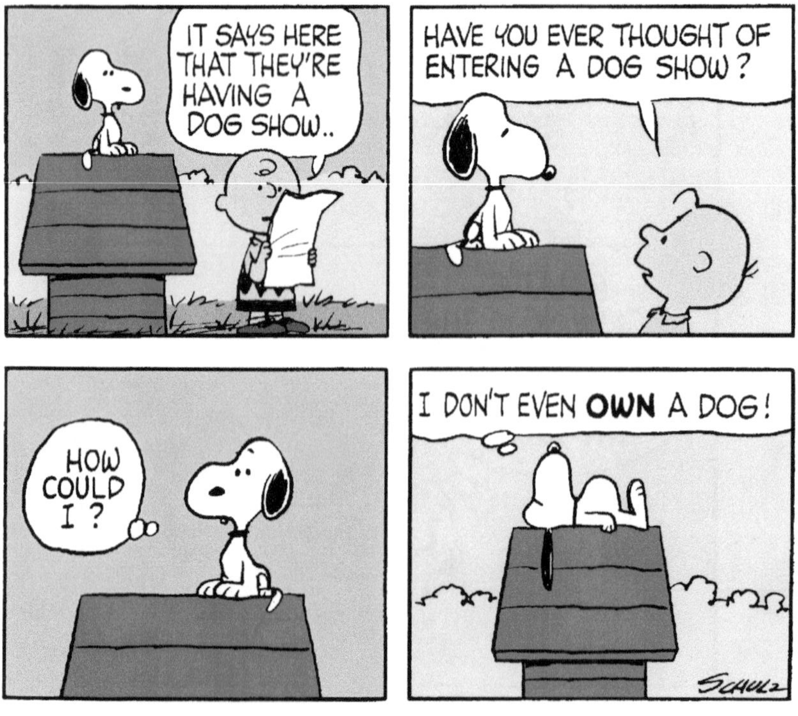
IT SAYS HERE THAT THEY'RE HAVING A DOG SHOW..
HAVE YOU EVER THOUGHT OF ENTERING A DOG SHOW?
HOW COULD I?
I DON'T EVEN **OWN** A DOG!

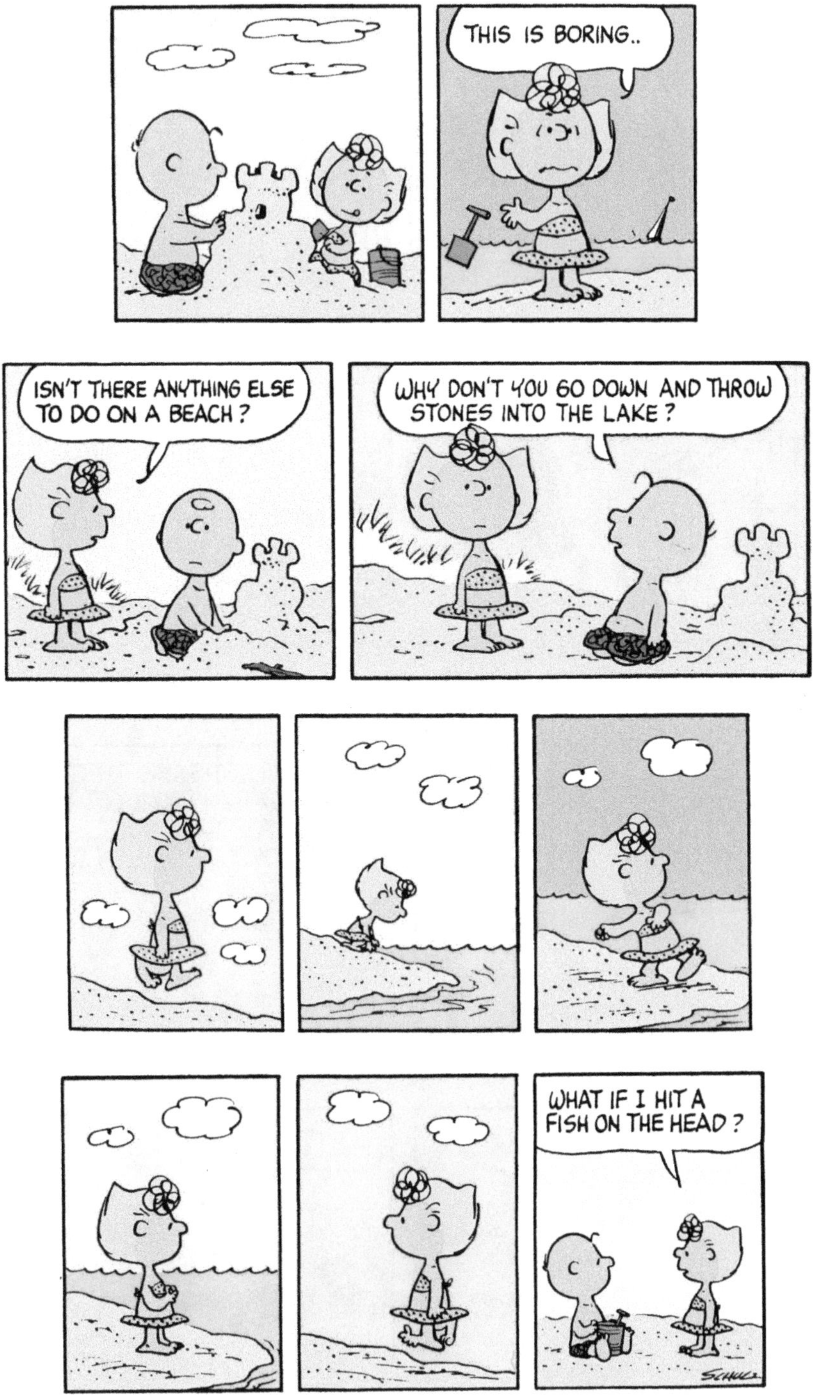
THIS IS BORING..
ISN'T THERE ANYTHING ELSE TO DO ON A BEACH?
WHY DON'T YOU GO DOWN AND THROW STONES INTO THE LAKE?
WHAT IF I HIT A FISH ON THE HEAD?

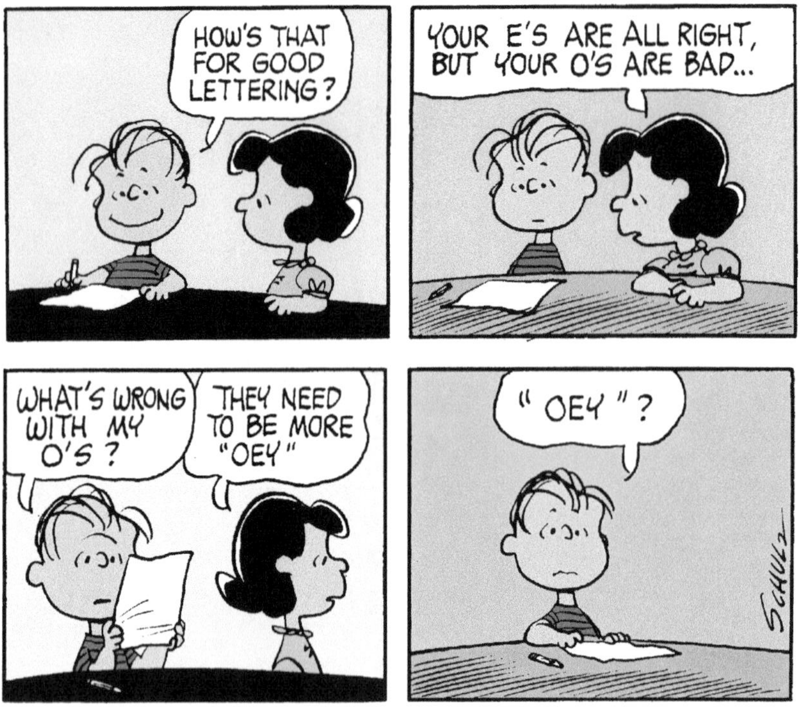
HOW'S THAT FOR GOOD LETTERING?
YOUR E'S ARE ALL RIGHT, BUT YOUR O'S ARE BAD...
WHAT'S WRONG WITH MY O'S?
THEY NEED TO BE MORE "OEY"
"OEY"?
SCHULZ

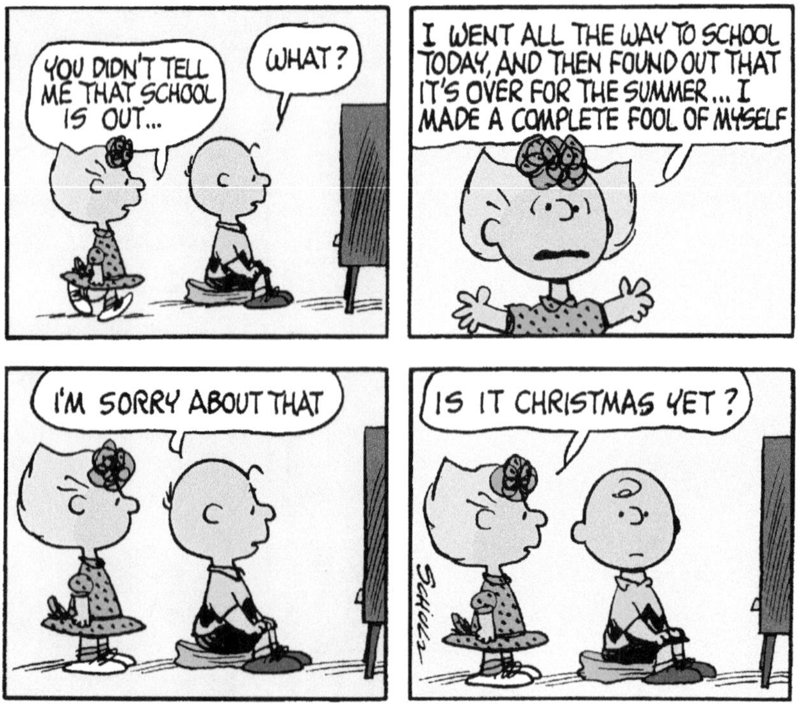
YOU DIDN'T TELL ME THAT SCHOOL IS OUT...
WHAT?
I WENT ALL THE WAY TO SCHOOL TODAY, AND THEN FOUND OUT THAT IT'S OVER FOR THE SUMMER... I MADE A COMPLETE FOOL OF MYSELF
I'M SORRY ABOUT THAT
IS IT CHRISTMAS YET?
SCHULZ

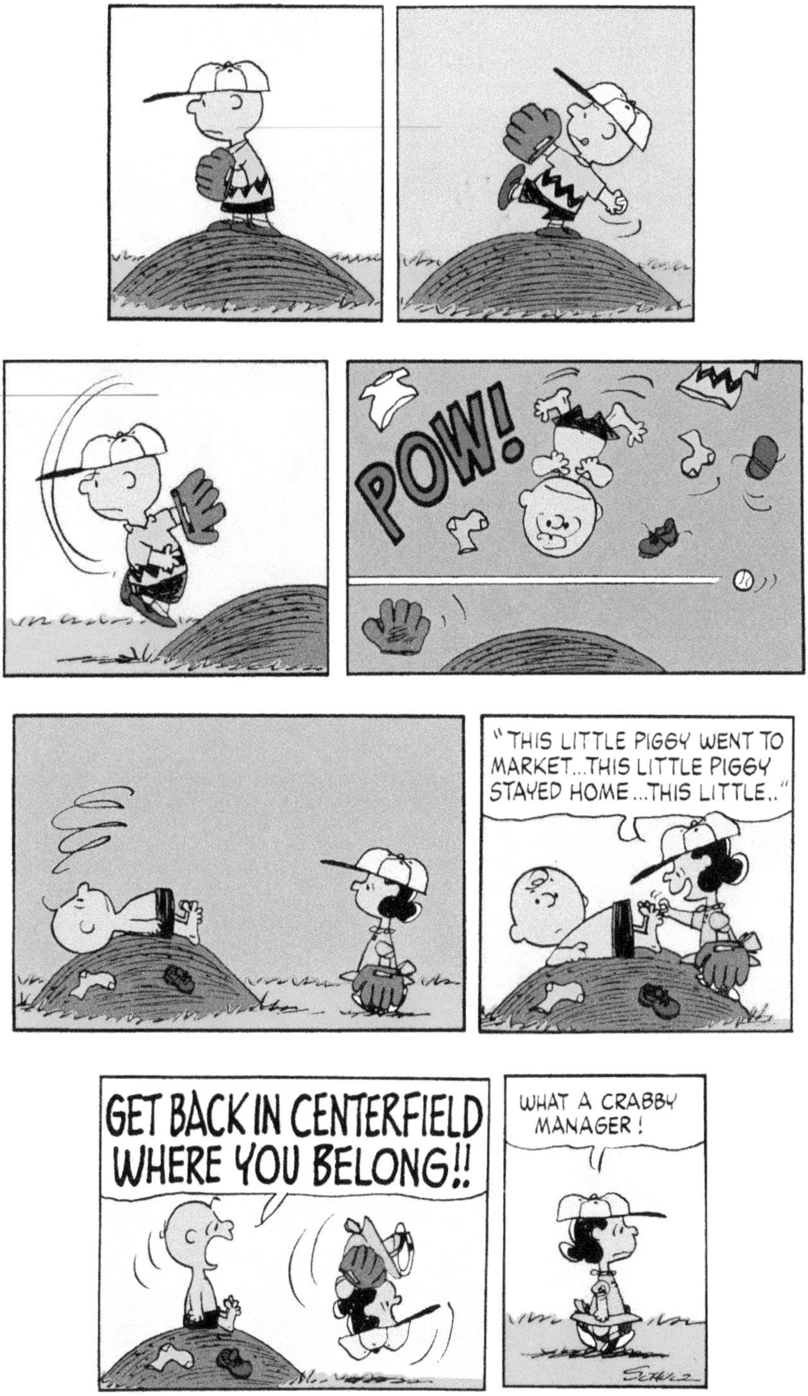
POW!
"THIS LITTLE PIGGY WENT TO MARKET...THIS LITTLE PIGGY STAYED HOME...THIS LITTLE.."
GET BACK IN CENTERFIELD WHERE YOU BELONG!!
WHAT A CRABBY MANAGER!

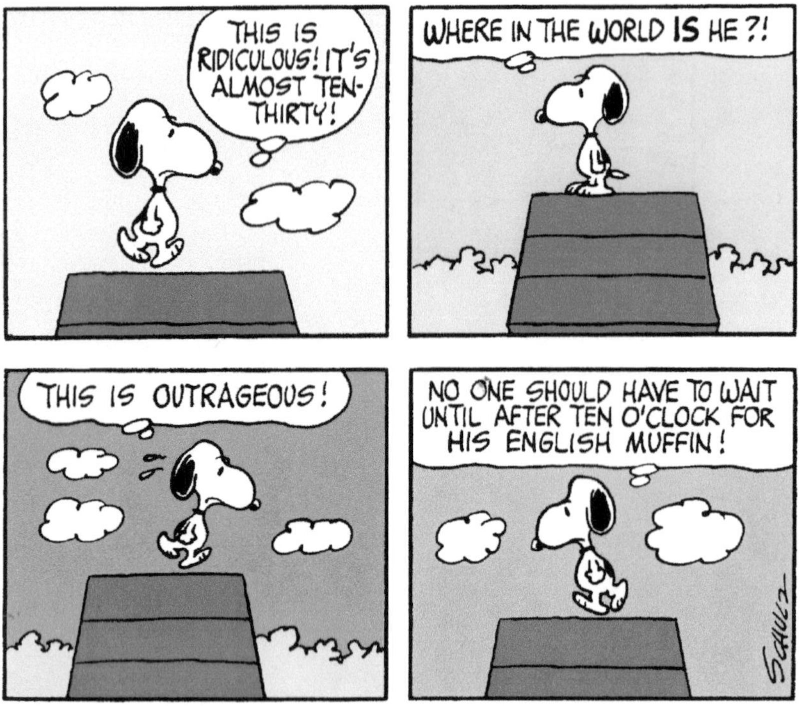
THIS IS RIDICULOUS! IT'S ALMOST TEN-THIRTY!
WHERE IN THE WORLD IS HE?!
THIS IS OUTRAGEOUS!
NO ONE SHOULD HAVE TO WAIT UNTIL AFTER TEN O'CLOCK FOR HIS ENGLISH MUFFIN!

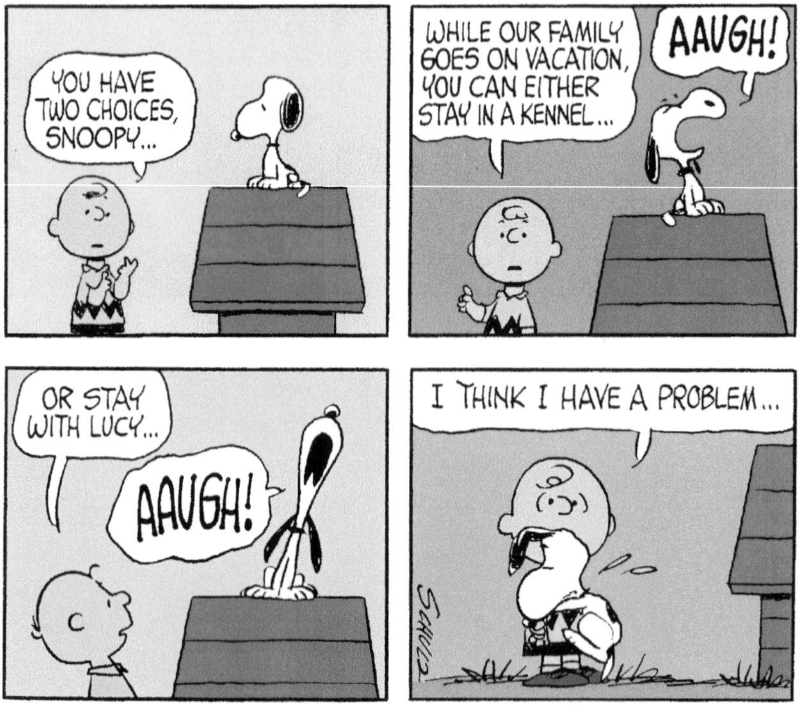
YOU HAVE TWO CHOICES, SNOOPY...
WHILE OUR FAMILY GOES ON VACATION, YOU CAN EITHER STAY IN A KENNEL...
AAUGH!
OR STAY WITH LUCY...
AAUGH!
I THINK I HAVE A PROBLEM...

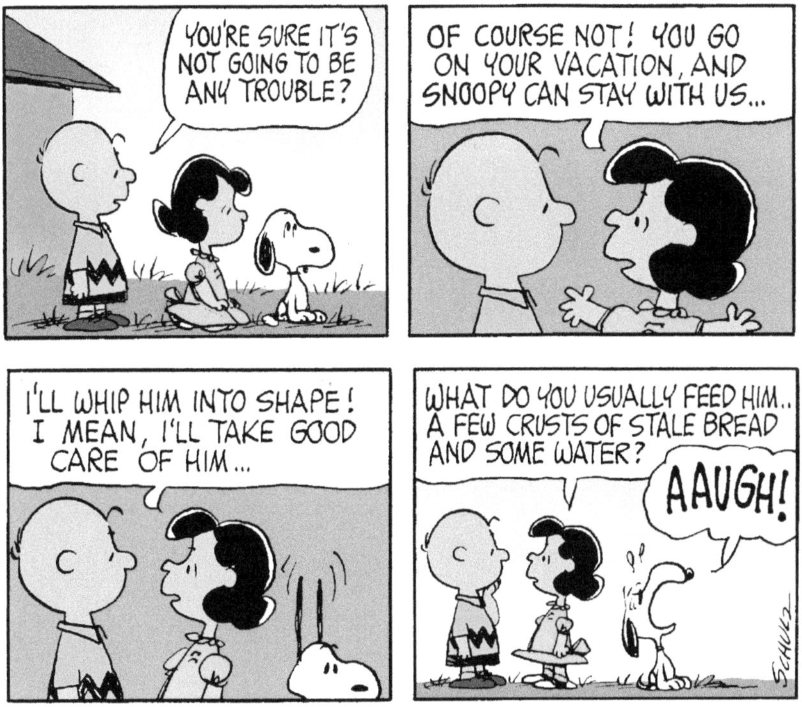
YOU'RE SURE IT'S NOT GOING TO BE ANY TROUBLE?
OF COURSE NOT! YOU GO ON YOUR VACATION, AND SNOOPY CAN STAY WITH US...
I'LL WHIP HIM INTO SHAPE! I MEAN, I'LL TAKE GOOD CARE OF HIM...
WHAT DO YOU USUALLY FEED HIM.. A FEW CRUSTS OF STALE BREAD AND SOME WATER?
AAUGH!
SCHULZ

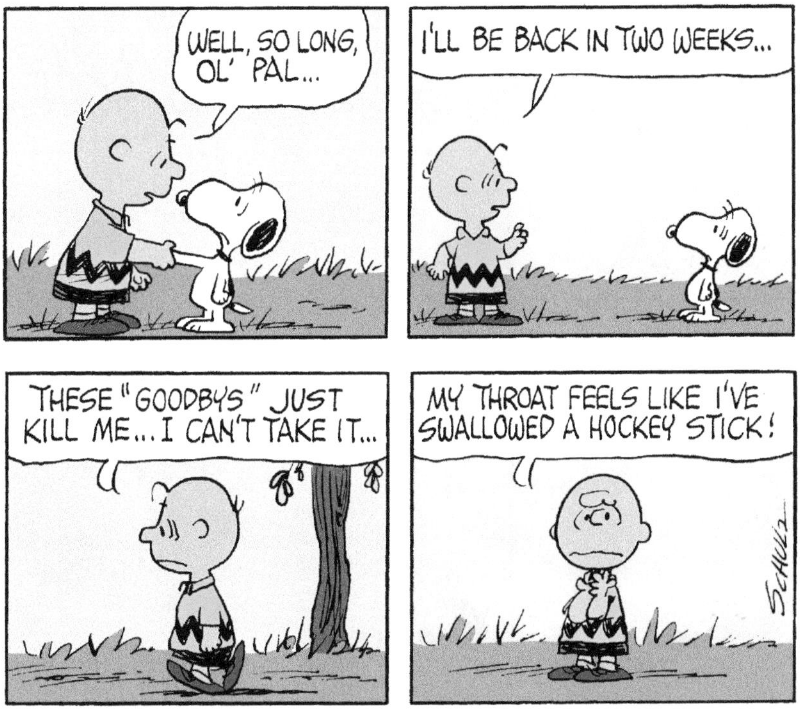
WELL, SO LONG, OL' PAL...
I'LL BE BACK IN TWO WEEKS...
THESE "GOODBYS" JUST KILL ME... I CAN'T TAKE IT...
MY THROAT FEELS LIKE I'VE SWALLOWED A HOCKEY STICK!
SCHULZ

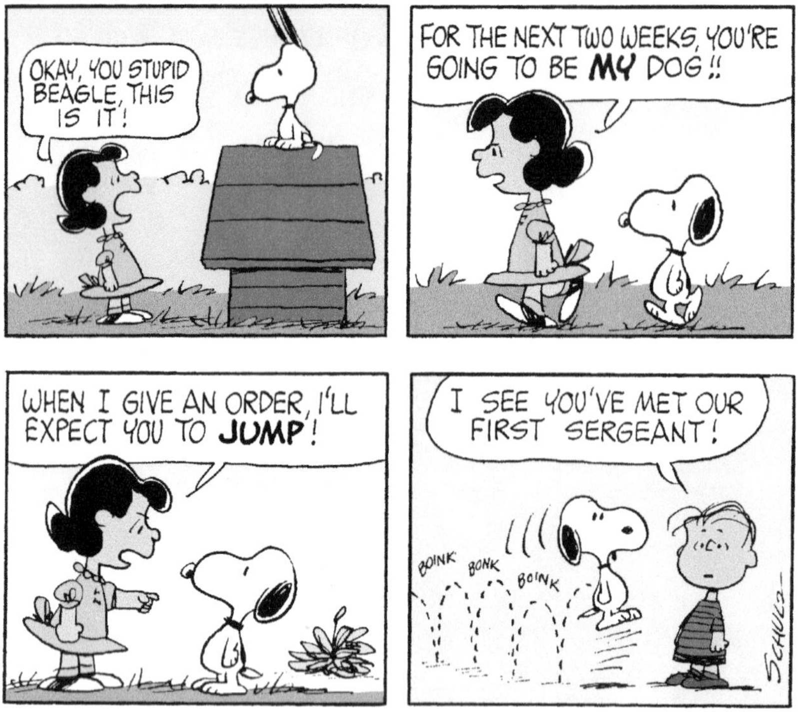
OKAY, YOU STUPID BEAGLE, THIS IS IT!
FOR THE NEXT TWO WEEKS, YOU'RE GOING TO BE **MY** DOG!!
WHEN I GIVE AN ORDER, I'LL EXPECT YOU TO **JUMP**!
I SEE YOU'VE MET OUR FIRST SERGEANT!
BOINK
BONK
BOINK

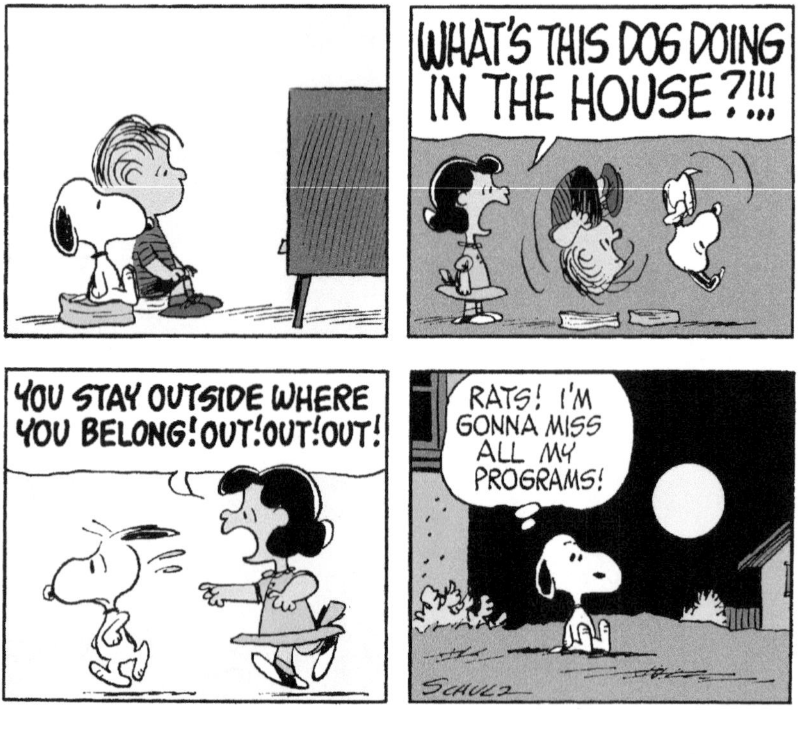
WHAT'S THIS DOG DOING IN THE HOUSE?!!!
YOU STAY OUTSIDE WHERE YOU BELONG! OUT! OUT! OUT!
RATS! I'M GONNA MISS ALL MY PROGRAMS!

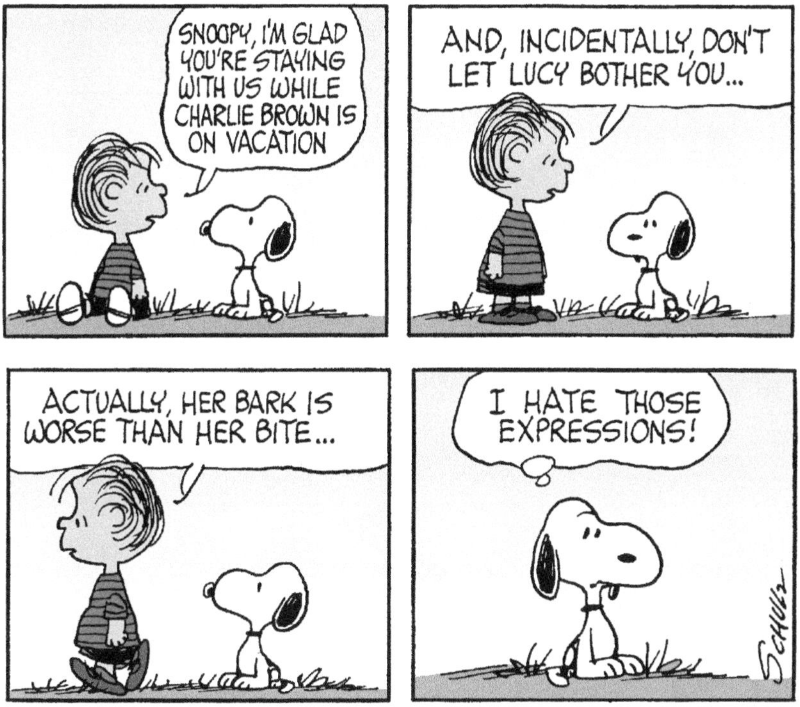
SNOOPY, I'M GLAD YOU'RE STAYING WITH US WHILE CHARLIE BROWN IS ON VACATION
AND, INCIDENTALLY, DON'T LET LUCY BOTHER YOU...
ACTUALLY, HER BARK IS WORSE THAN HER BITE...
I HATE THOSE EXPRESSIONS!
SCHULZ

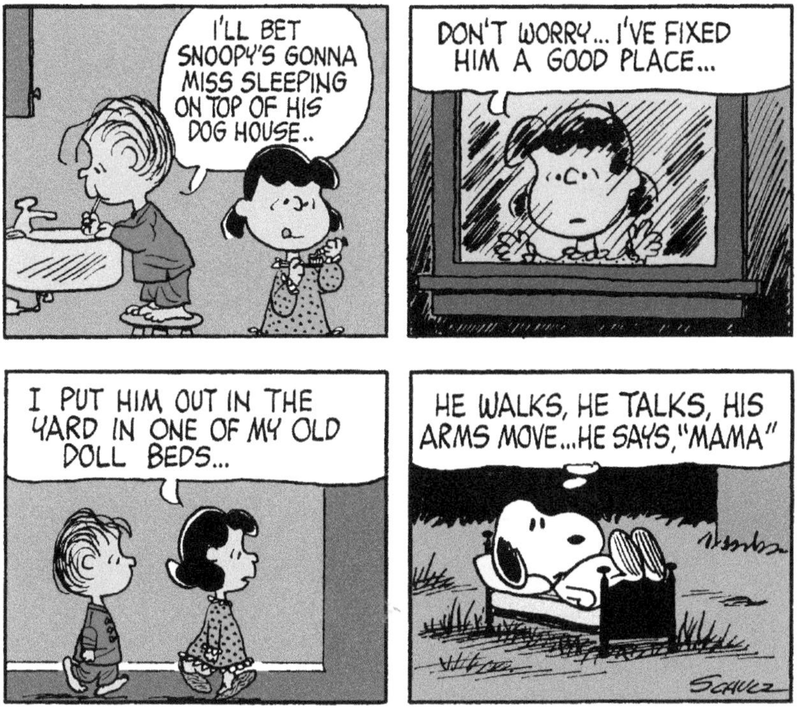
I'LL BET SNOOPY'S GONNA MISS SLEEPING ON TOP OF HIS DOG HOUSE..
DON'T WORRY... I'VE FIXED HIM A GOOD PLACE...
I PUT HIM OUT IN THE YARD IN ONE OF MY OLD DOLL BEDS...
HE WALKS, HE TALKS, HIS ARMS MOVE...HE SAYS, "MAMA"
SCHULZ

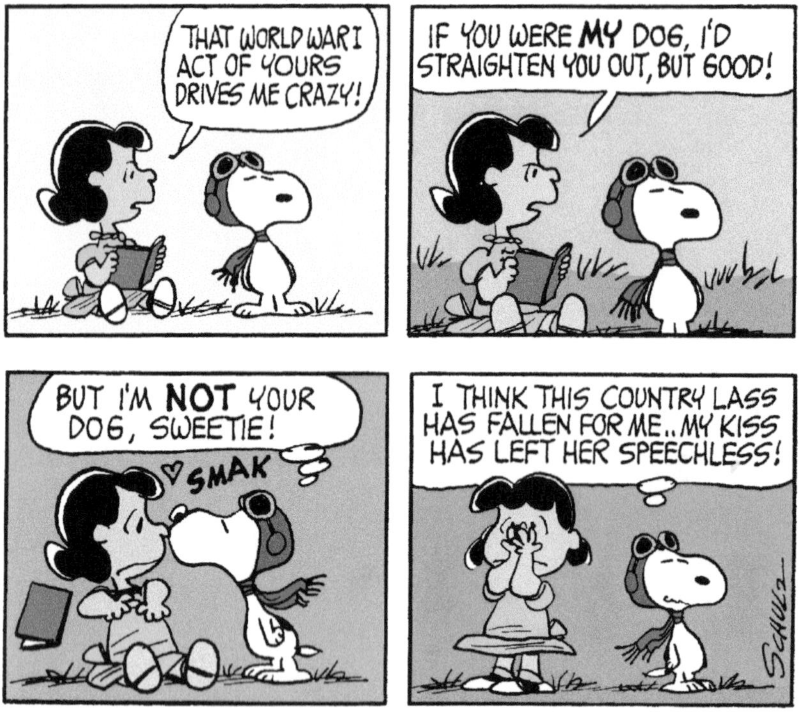
THAT WORLD WAR I ACT OF YOURS DRIVES ME CRAZY!
IF YOU WERE MY DOG, I'D STRAIGHTEN YOU OUT, BUT GOOD!
BUT I'M NOT YOUR DOG, SWEETIE!
SMAK
I THINK THIS COUNTRY LASS HAS FALLEN FOR ME.. MY KISS HAS LEFT HER SPEECHLESS!
SCHULZ

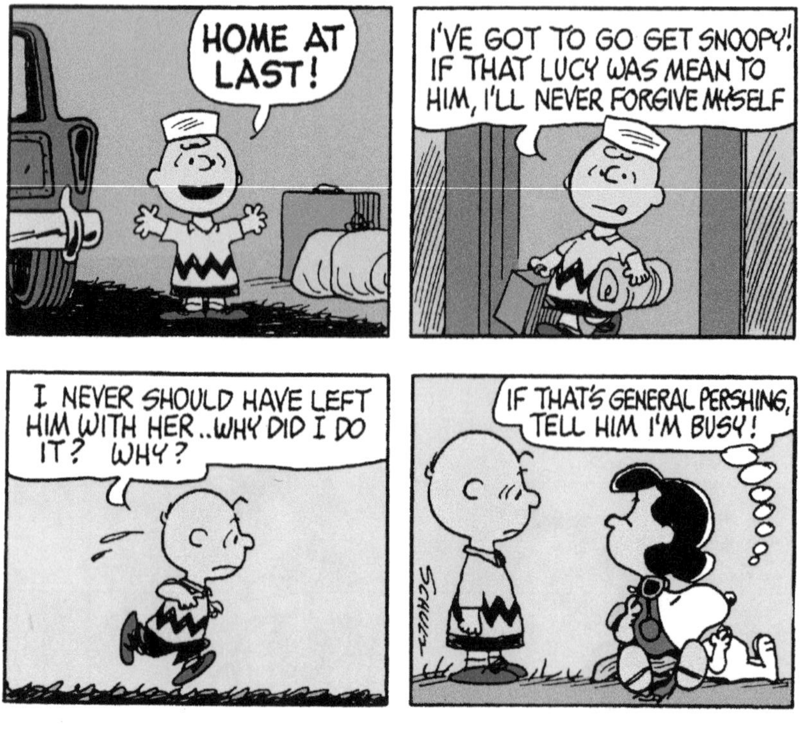
HOME AT LAST!
I'VE GOT TO GO GET SNOOPY! IF THAT LUCY WAS MEAN TO HIM, I'LL NEVER FORGIVE MYSELF
I NEVER SHOULD HAVE LEFT HIM WITH HER..WHY DID I DO IT? WHY?
IF THAT'S GENERAL PERSHING, TELL HIM I'M BUSY!
SCHULZ

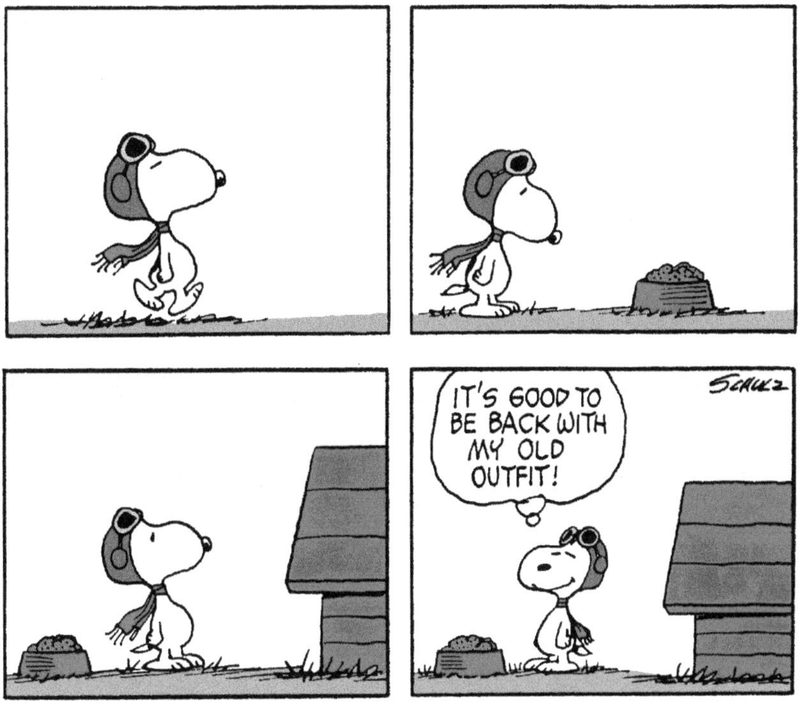
IT'S GOOD TO BE BACK WITH MY OLD OUTFIT!

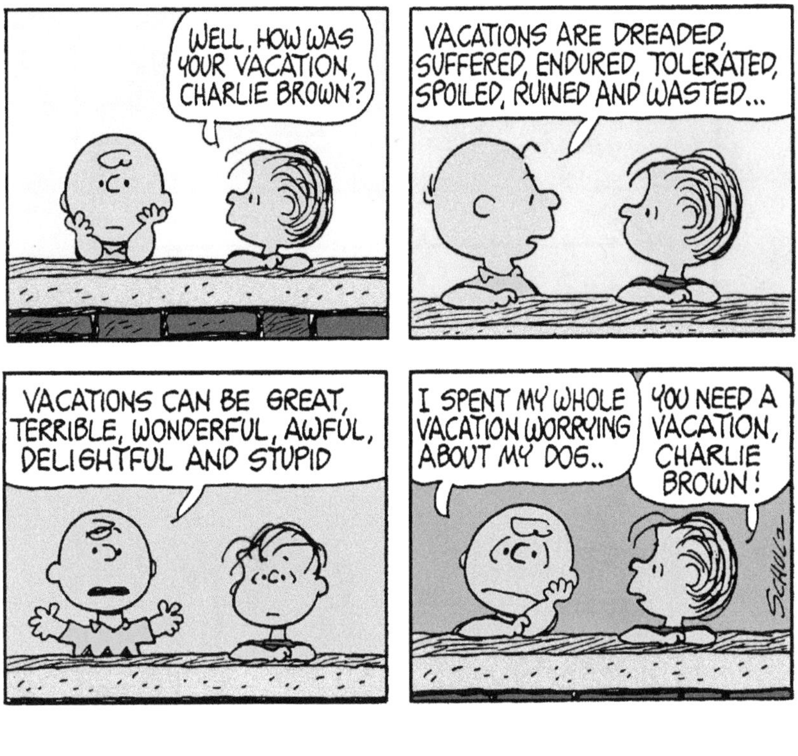
WELL, HOW WAS YOUR VACATION, CHARLIE BROWN?
VACATIONS ARE DREADED, SUFFERED, ENDURED, TOLERATED, SPOILED, RUINED AND WASTED...
VACATIONS CAN BE GREAT, TERRIBLE, WONDERFUL, AWFUL, DELIGHTFUL AND STUPID
I SPENT MY WHOLE VACATION WORRYING ABOUT MY DOG..
YOU NEED A VACATION, CHARLIE BROWN!

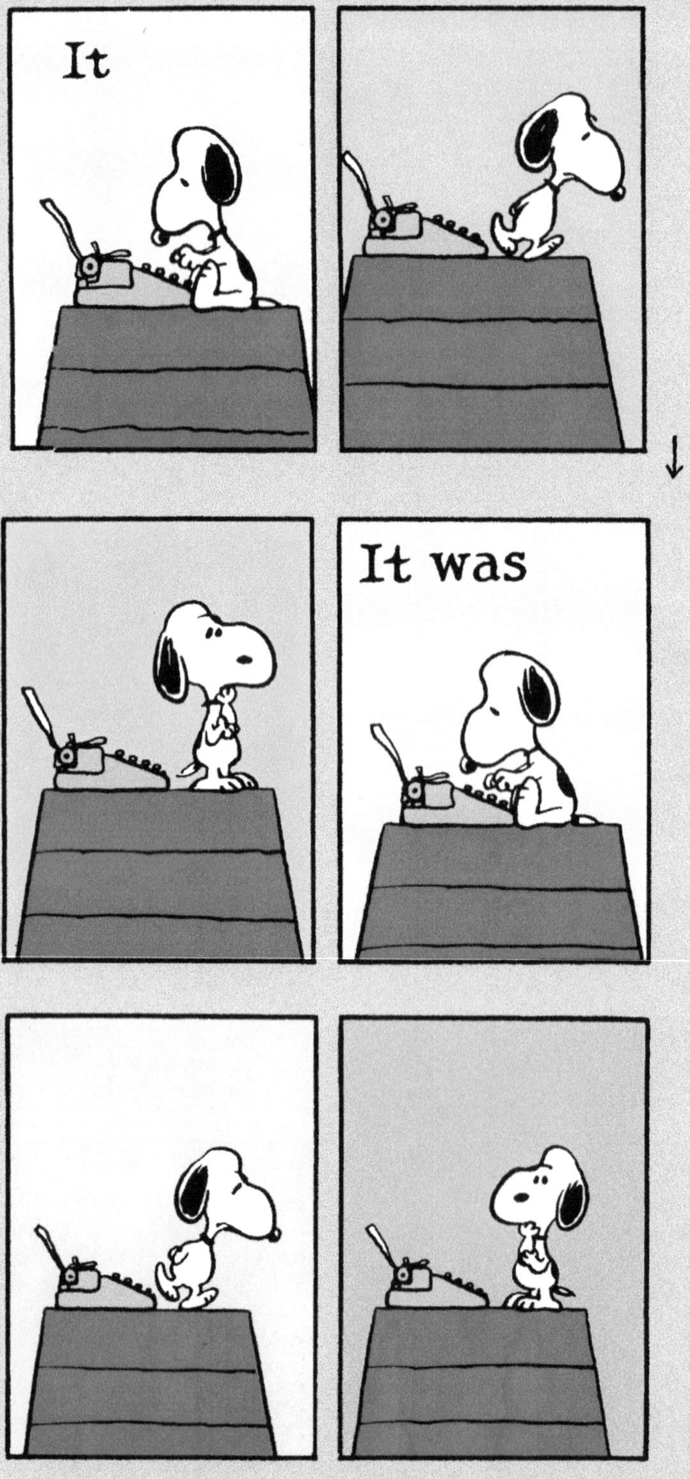
It
It was

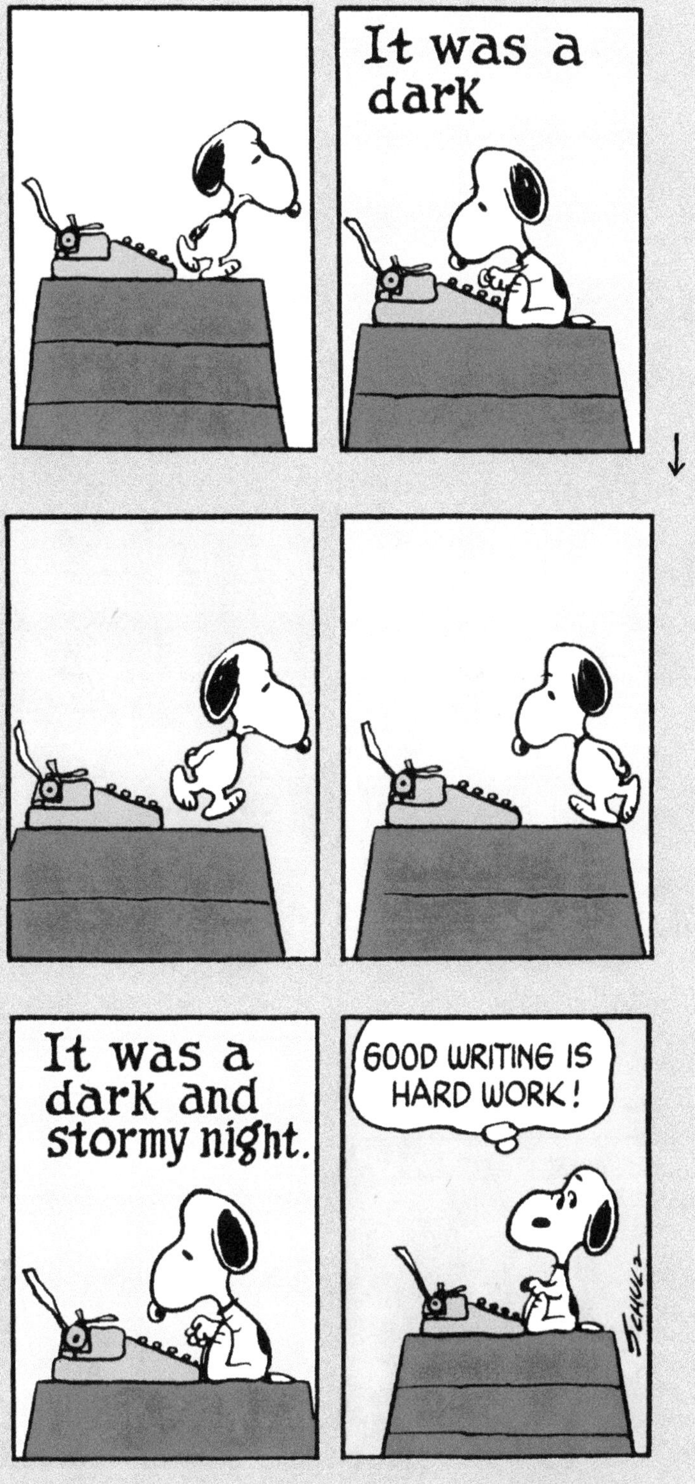
It was a dark
It was a dark and stormy night.
GOOD WRITING IS HARD WORK!
SCHULZ

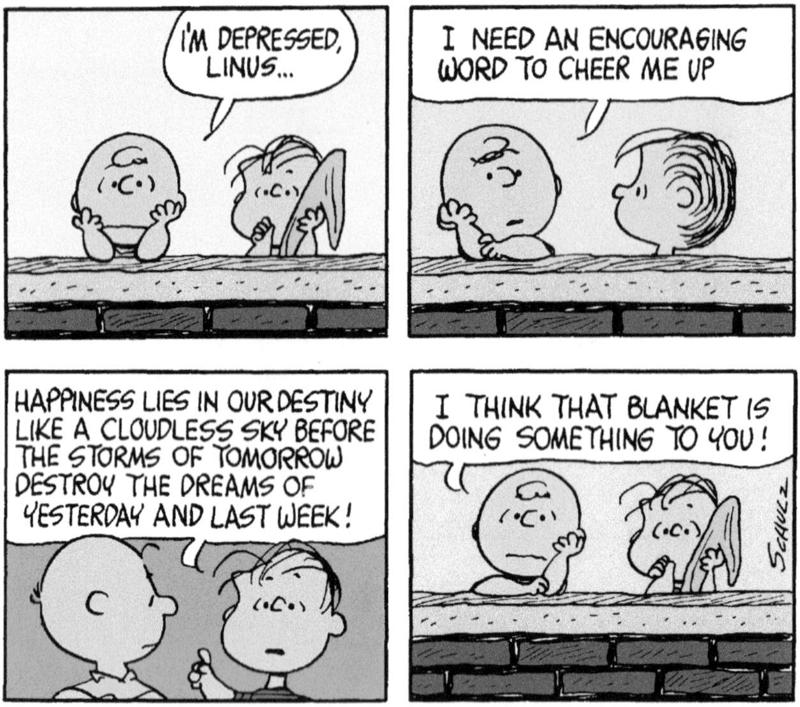
I'M DEPRESSED, LINUS...
I NEED AN ENCOURAGING WORD TO CHEER ME UP
HAPPINESS LIES IN OUR DESTINY LIKE A CLOUDLESS SKY BEFORE THE STORMS OF TOMORROW DESTROY THE DREAMS OF YESTERDAY AND LAST WEEK!
I THINK THAT BLANKET IS DOING SOMETHING TO YOU!
SCHULZ

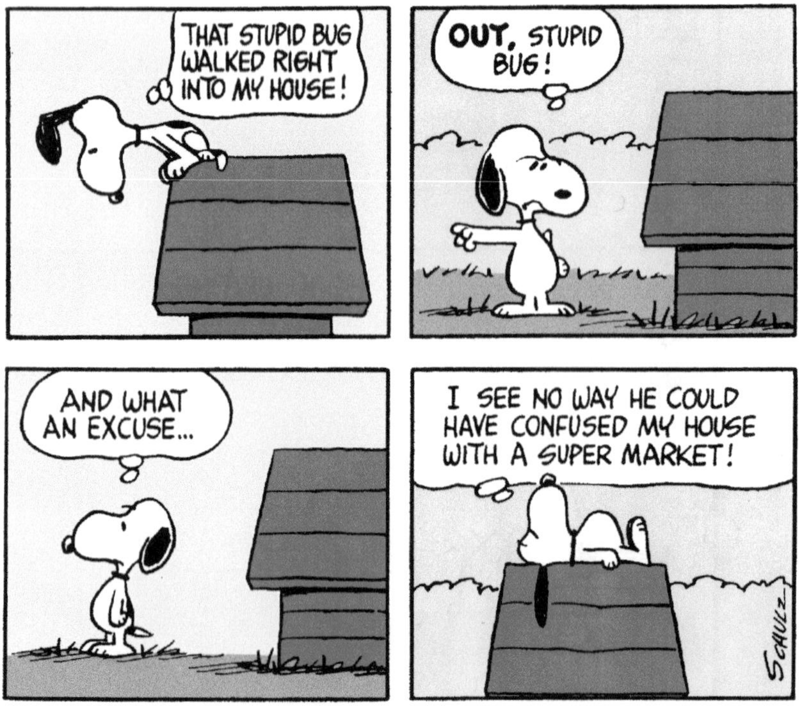
THAT STUPID BUG WALKED RIGHT INTO MY HOUSE!
OUT, STUPID BUG!
AND WHAT AN EXCUSE...
I SEE NO WAY HE COULD HAVE CONFUSED MY HOUSE WITH A SUPER MARKET!
SCHULZ

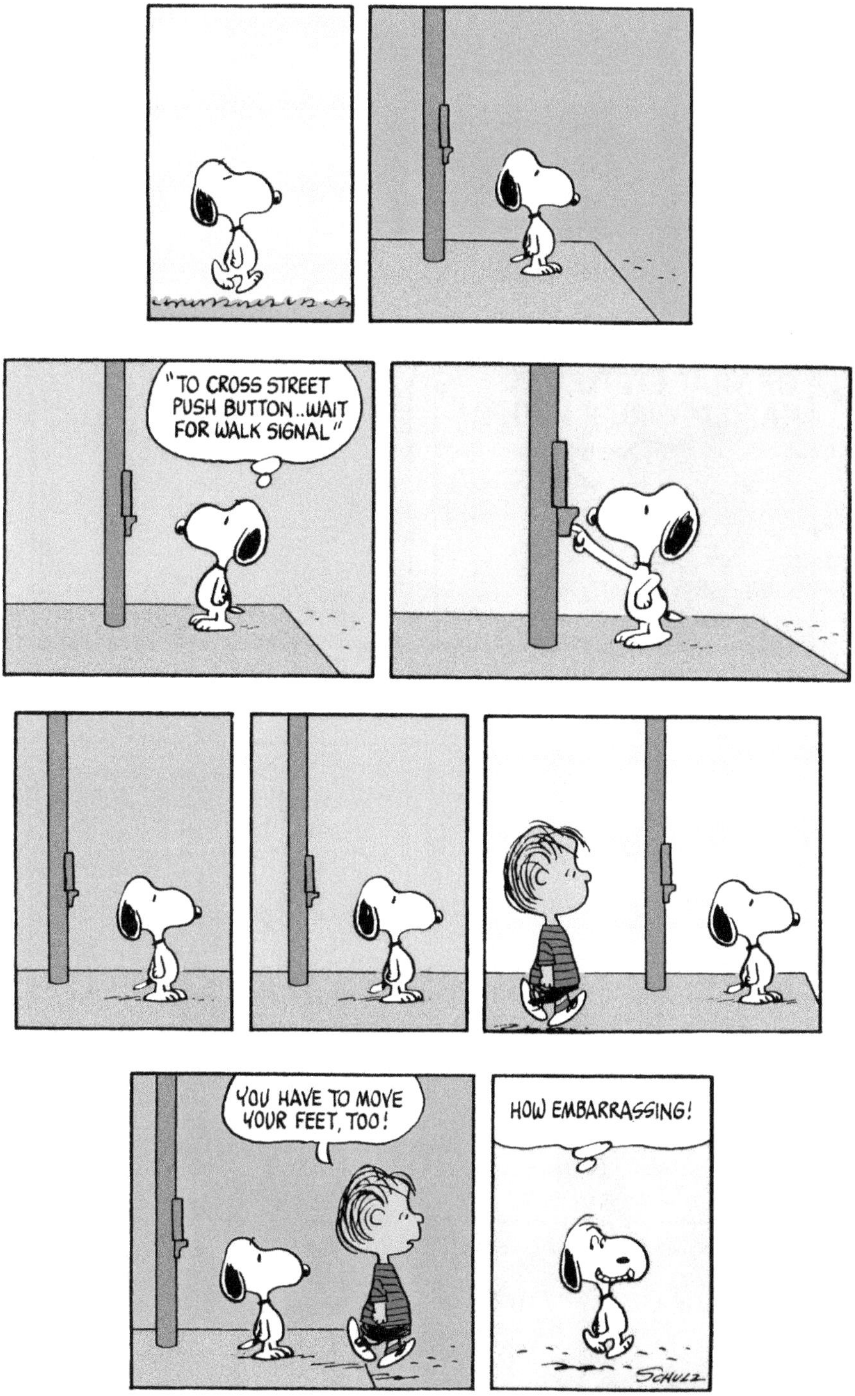
"TO CROSS STREET PUSH BUTTON..WAIT FOR WALK SIGNAL"
YOU HAVE TO MOVE YOUR FEET, TOO!
HOW EMBARRASSING!
SCHULZ

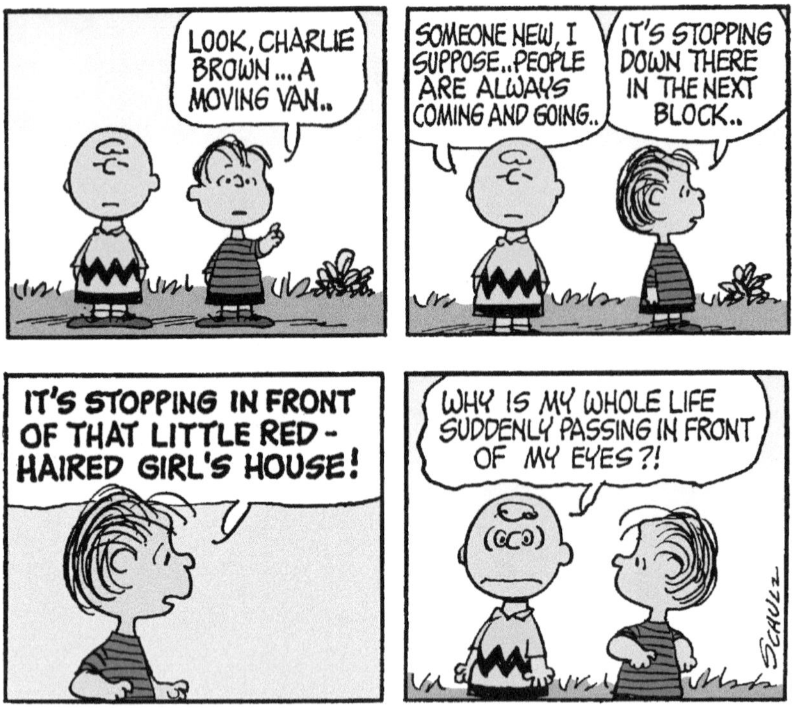
LOOK, CHARLIE BROWN ... A MOVING VAN..
SOMEONE NEW, I SUPPOSE..PEOPLE ARE ALWAYS COMING AND GOING..
IT'S STOPPING DOWN THERE IN THE NEXT BLOCK..
IT'S STOPPING IN FRONT OF THAT LITTLE RED-HAIRED GIRL'S HOUSE!
WHY IS MY WHOLE LIFE SUDDENLY PASSING IN FRONT OF MY EYES?!
SCHULZ

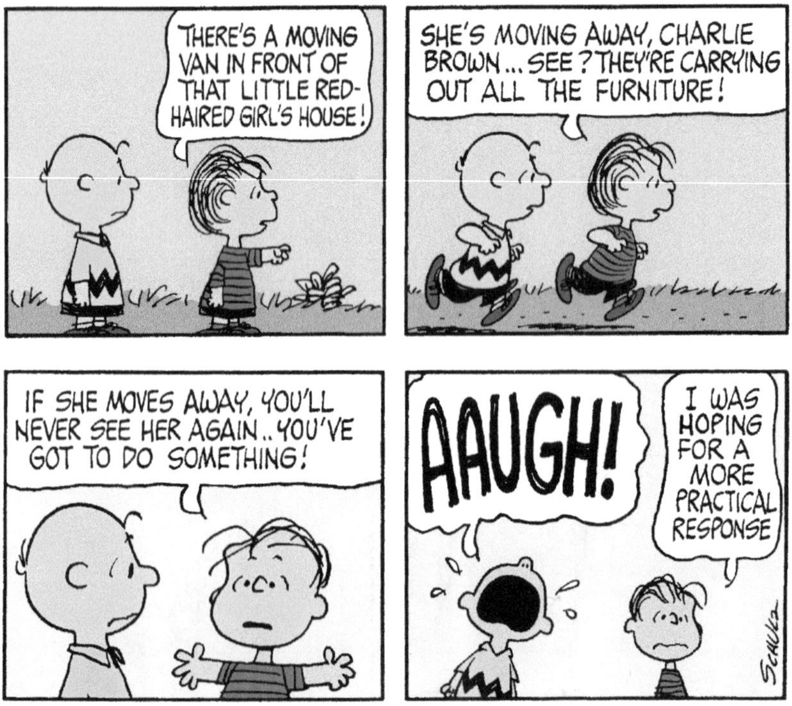
THERE'S A MOVING VAN IN FRONT OF THAT LITTLE RED-HAIRED GIRL'S HOUSE!
SHE'S MOVING AWAY, CHARLIE BROWN ... SEE? THEY'RE CARRYING OUT ALL THE FURNITURE!
IF SHE MOVES AWAY, YOU'LL NEVER SEE HER AGAIN..YOU'VE GOT TO DO SOMETHING!
AAUGH!
I WAS HOPING FOR A MORE PRACTICAL RESPONSE
SCHULZ

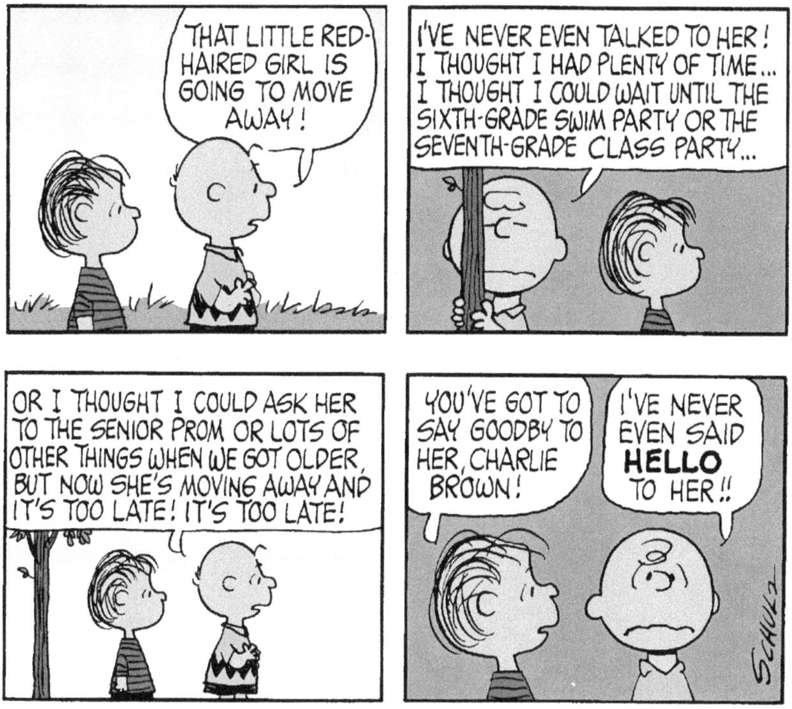
THAT LITTLE RED-HAIRED GIRL IS GOING TO MOVE AWAY!
I'VE NEVER EVEN TALKED TO HER! I THOUGHT I HAD PLENTY OF TIME... I THOUGHT I COULD WAIT UNTIL THE SIXTH-GRADE SWIM PARTY OR THE SEVENTH-GRADE CLASS PARTY...
OR I THOUGHT I COULD ASK HER TO THE SENIOR PROM OR LOTS OF OTHER THINGS WHEN WE GOT OLDER, BUT NOW SHE'S MOVING AWAY AND IT'S TOO LATE! IT'S TOO LATE!
YOU'VE GOT TO SAY GOODBY TO HER, CHARLIE BROWN!
I'VE NEVER EVEN SAID **HELLO** TO HER!!
SCHULZ

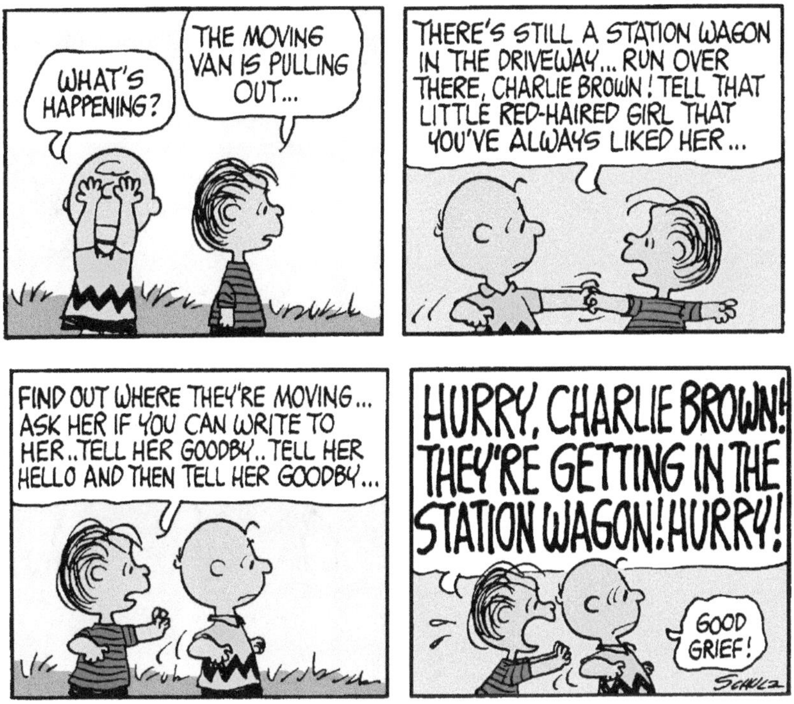
WHAT'S HAPPENING?
THE MOVING VAN IS PULLING OUT...
THERE'S STILL A STATION WAGON IN THE DRIVEWAY... RUN OVER THERE, CHARLIE BROWN! TELL THAT LITTLE RED-HAIRED GIRL THAT YOU'VE ALWAYS LIKED HER...
FIND OUT WHERE THEY'RE MOVING... ASK HER IF YOU CAN WRITE TO HER..TELL HER GOODBY..TELL HER HELLO AND THEN TELL HER GOODBY...
HURRY, CHARLIE BROWN! THEY'RE GETTING IN THE STATION WAGON! HURRY!
GOOD GRIEF!
SCHULZ

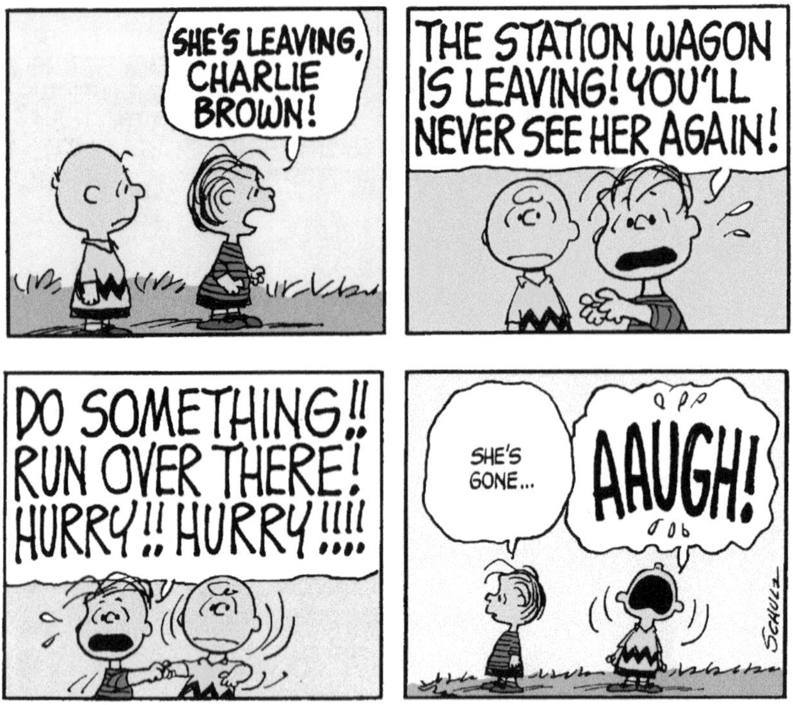
SHE'S LEAVING, CHARLIE BROWN!
THE STATION WAGON IS LEAVING! YOU'LL NEVER SEE HER AGAIN!
DO SOMETHING!! RUN OVER THERE! HURRY!! HURRY!!!!
SHE'S GONE...
AAUGH!
SCHULZ

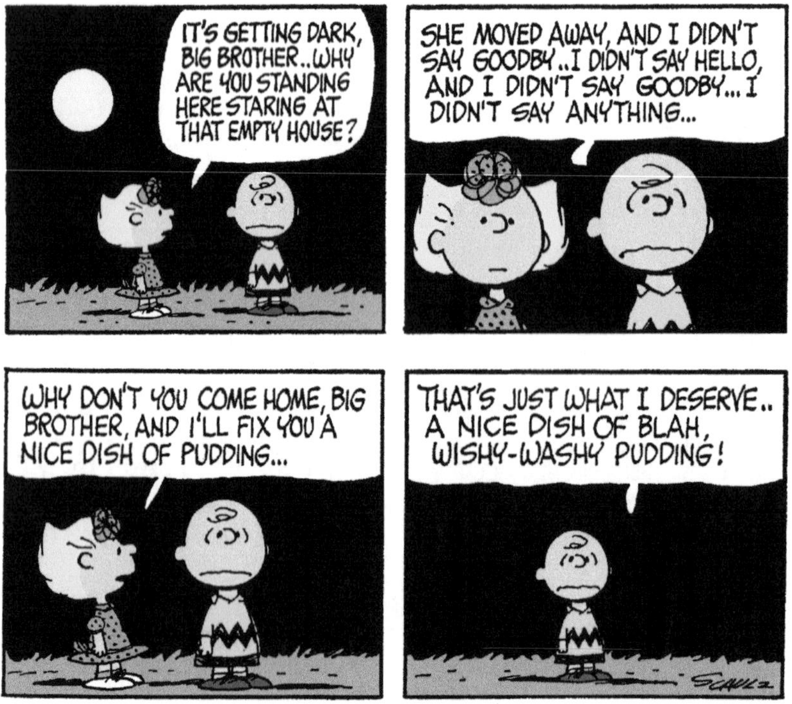
IT'S GETTING DARK, BIG BROTHER..WHY ARE YOU STANDING HERE STARING AT THAT EMPTY HOUSE?
SHE MOVED AWAY, AND I DIDN'T SAY GOODBY..I DIDN'T SAY HELLO, AND I DIDN'T SAY GOODBY... I DIDN'T SAY ANYTHING...
WHY DON'T YOU COME HOME, BIG BROTHER, AND I'LL FIX YOU A NICE DISH OF PUDDING...
THAT'S JUST WHAT I DESERVE.. A NICE DISH OF BLAH, WISHY-WASHY PUDDING!
SCHULZ

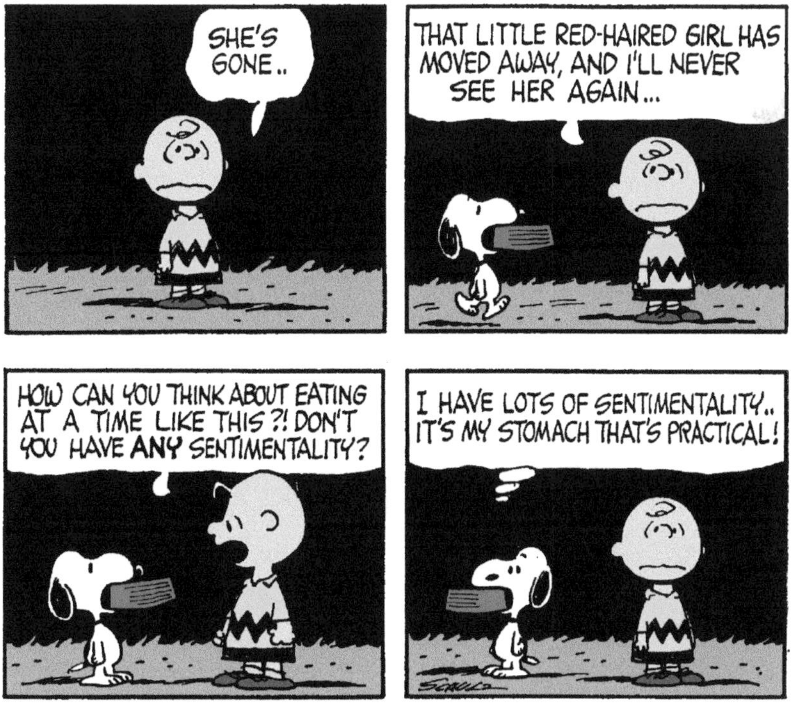
SHE'S GONE..
THAT LITTLE RED-HAIRED GIRL HAS MOVED AWAY, AND I'LL NEVER SEE HER AGAIN...
HOW CAN YOU THINK ABOUT EATING AT A TIME LIKE THIS?! DON'T YOU HAVE **ANY** SENTIMENTALITY?
I HAVE LOTS OF SENTIMENTALITY.. IT'S MY STOMACH THAT'S PRACTICAL!

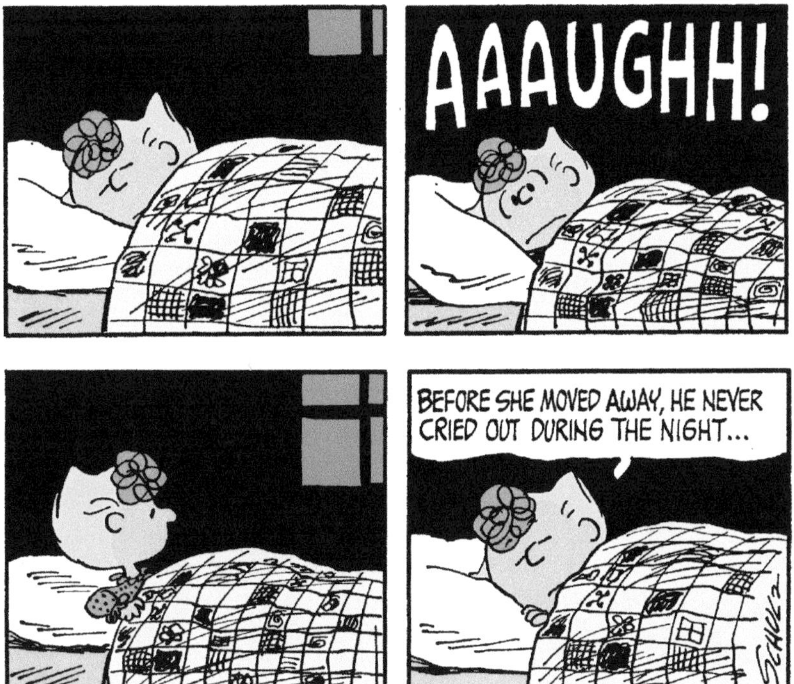
AAAUGHH!
BEFORE SHE MOVED AWAY, HE NEVER CRIED OUT DURING THE NIGHT...

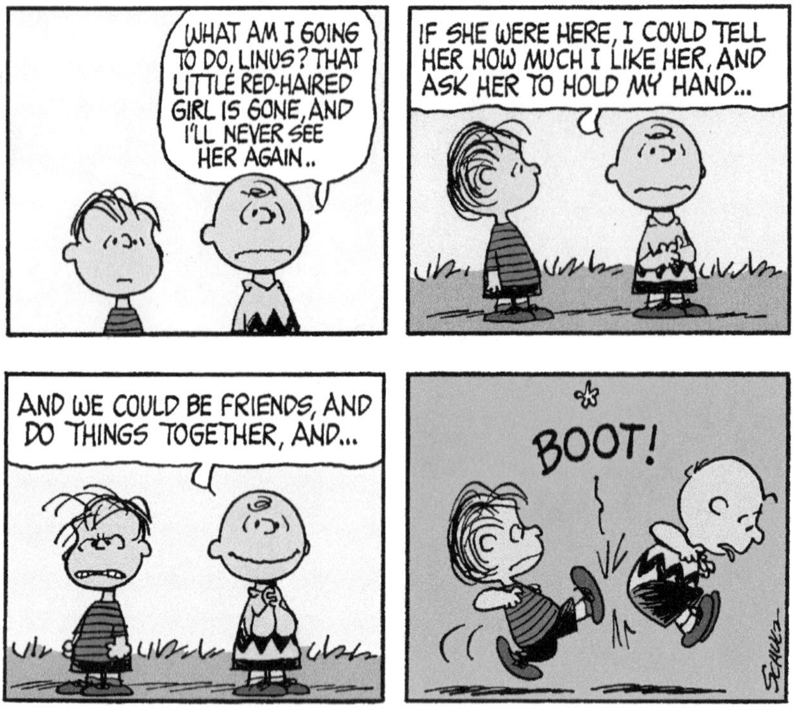
WHAT AM I GOING TO DO, LINUS? THAT LITTLE RED-HAIRED GIRL IS GONE, AND I'LL NEVER SEE HER AGAIN..
IF SHE WERE HERE, I COULD TELL HER HOW MUCH I LIKE HER, AND ASK HER TO HOLD MY HAND...
AND WE COULD BE FRIENDS, AND DO THINGS TOGETHER, AND...
BOOT!

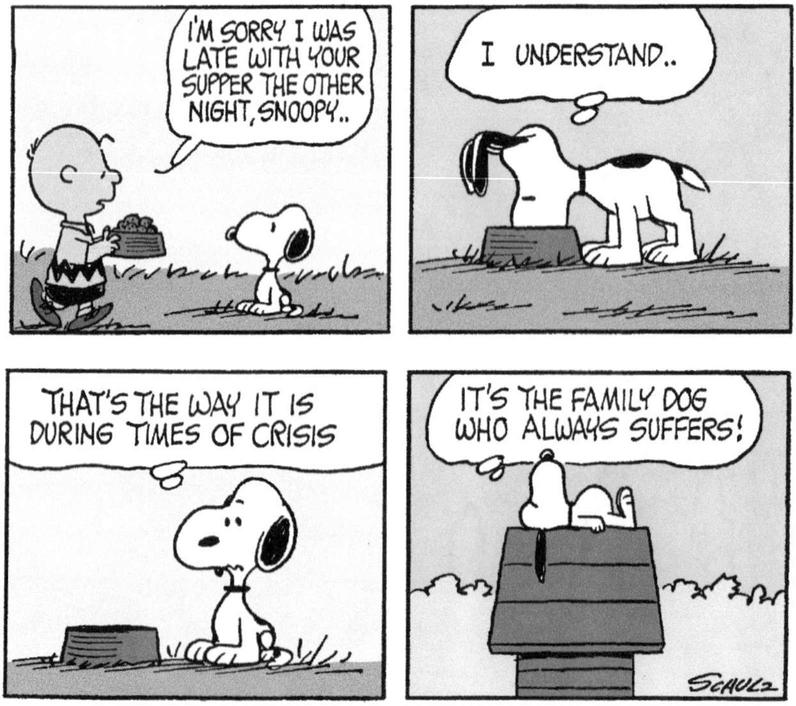
I'M SORRY I WAS LATE WITH YOUR SUPPER THE OTHER NIGHT, SNOOPY..
I UNDERSTAND..
THAT'S THE WAY IT IS DURING TIMES OF CRISIS
IT'S THE FAMILY DOG WHO ALWAYS SUFFERS!

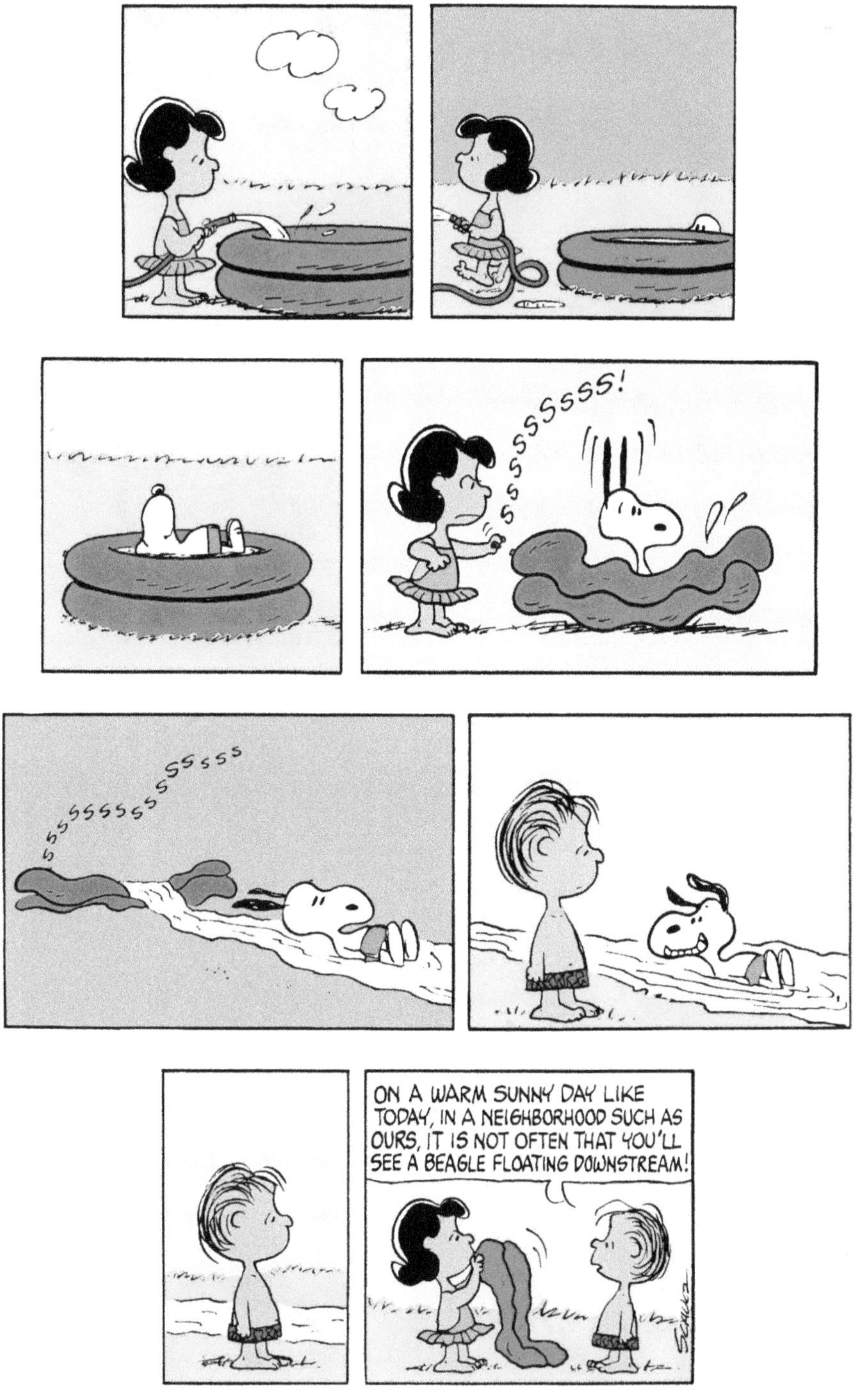
SSSSSSS!
SSSSSSSSSSSSSS
ON A WARM SUNNY DAY LIKE TODAY, IN A NEIGHBORHOOD SUCH AS OURS, IT IS NOT OFTEN THAT YOU'LL SEE A BEAGLE FLOATING DOWNSTREAM!
SCHULZ

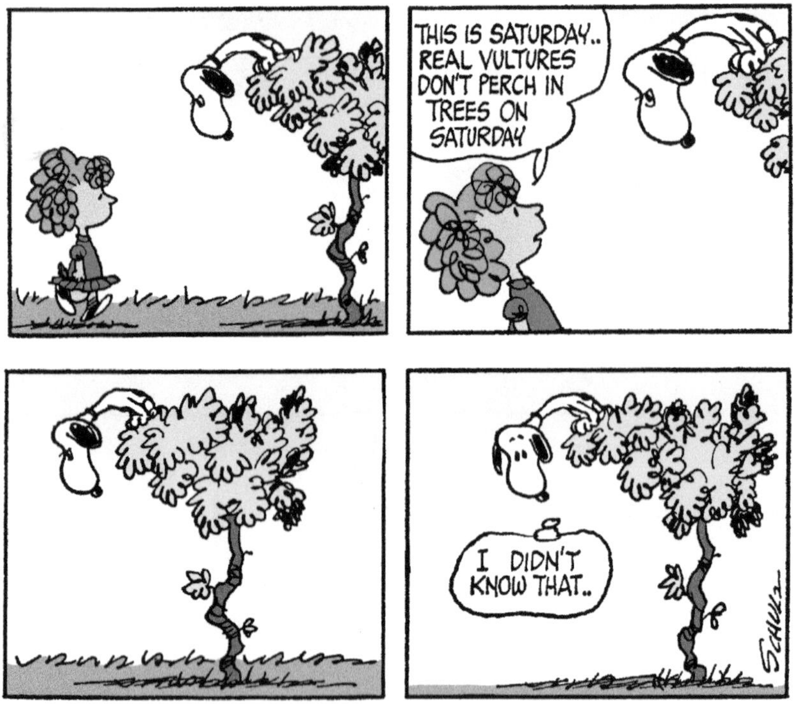
THIS IS SATURDAY.. REAL VULTURES DON'T PERCH IN TREES ON SATURDAY
I DIDN'T KNOW THAT..

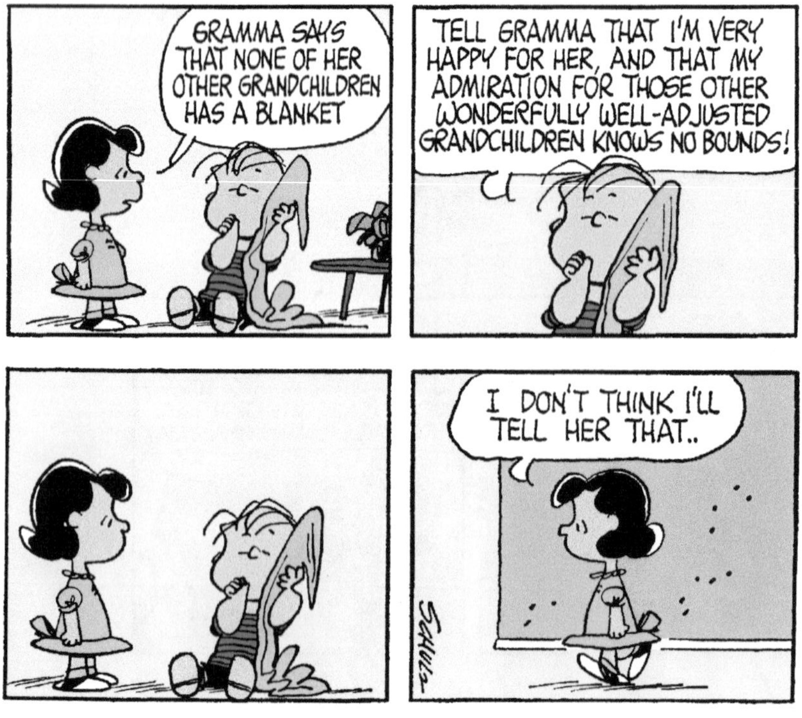
GRAMMA SAYS THAT NONE OF HER OTHER GRANDCHILDREN HAS A BLANKET
TELL GRAMMA THAT I'M VERY HAPPY FOR HER, AND THAT MY ADMIRATION FOR THOSE OTHER WONDERFULLY WELL-ADJUSTED GRANDCHILDREN KNOWS NO BOUNDS!
I DON'T THINK I'LL TELL HER THAT..

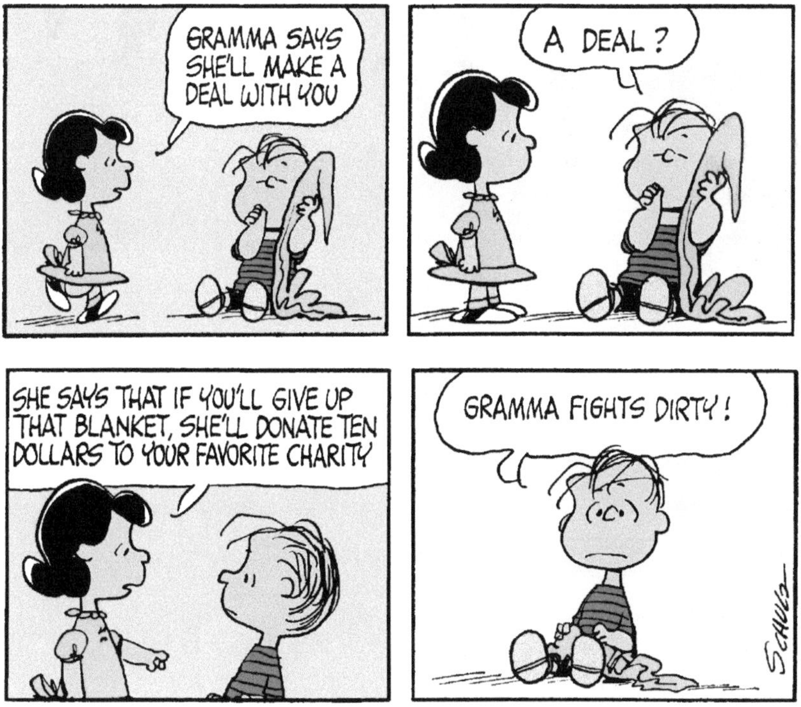
GRAMMA SAYS SHE'LL MAKE A DEAL WITH YOU
A DEAL ?
SHE SAYS THAT IF YOU'LL GIVE UP THAT BLANKET, SHE'LL DONATE TEN DOLLARS TO YOUR FAVORITE CHARITY
GRAMMA FIGHTS DIRTY !

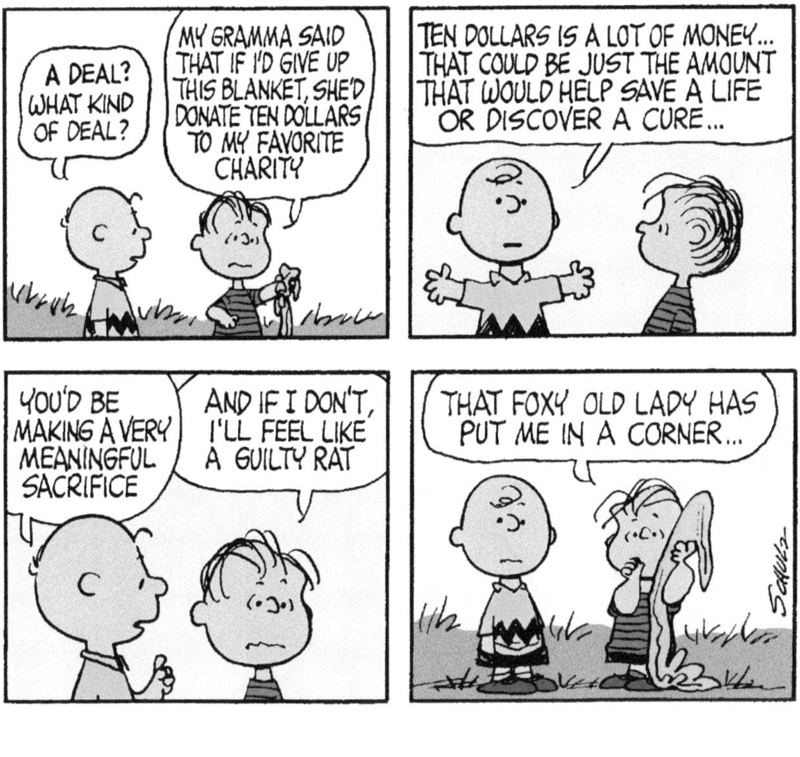
A DEAL? WHAT KIND OF DEAL?
MY GRAMMA SAID THAT IF I'D GIVE UP THIS BLANKET, SHE'D DONATE TEN DOLLARS TO MY FAVORITE CHARITY
TEN DOLLARS IS A LOT OF MONEY... THAT COULD BE JUST THE AMOUNT THAT WOULD HELP SAVE A LIFE OR DISCOVER A CURE...
YOU'D BE MAKING A VERY MEANINGFUL SACRIFICE
AND IF I DON'T, I'LL FEEL LIKE A GUILTY RAT
THAT FOXY OLD LADY HAS PUT ME IN A CORNER...

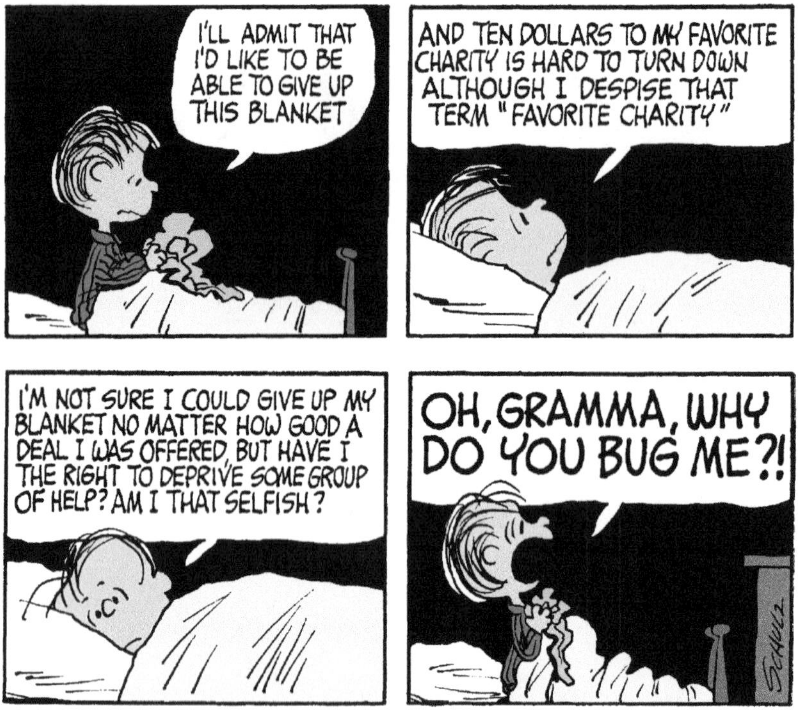
I'LL ADMIT THAT I'D LIKE TO BE ABLE TO GIVE UP THIS BLANKET
AND TEN DOLLARS TO MY FAVORITE CHARITY IS HARD TO TURN DOWN ALTHOUGH I DESPISE THAT TERM "FAVORITE CHARITY"
I'M NOT SURE I COULD GIVE UP MY BLANKET NO MATTER HOW GOOD A DEAL I WAS OFFERED, BUT HAVE I THE RIGHT TO DEPRIVE SOME GROUP OF HELP? AM I THAT SELFISH?
OH, GRAMMA, WHY DO YOU BUG ME?!
SCHULZ

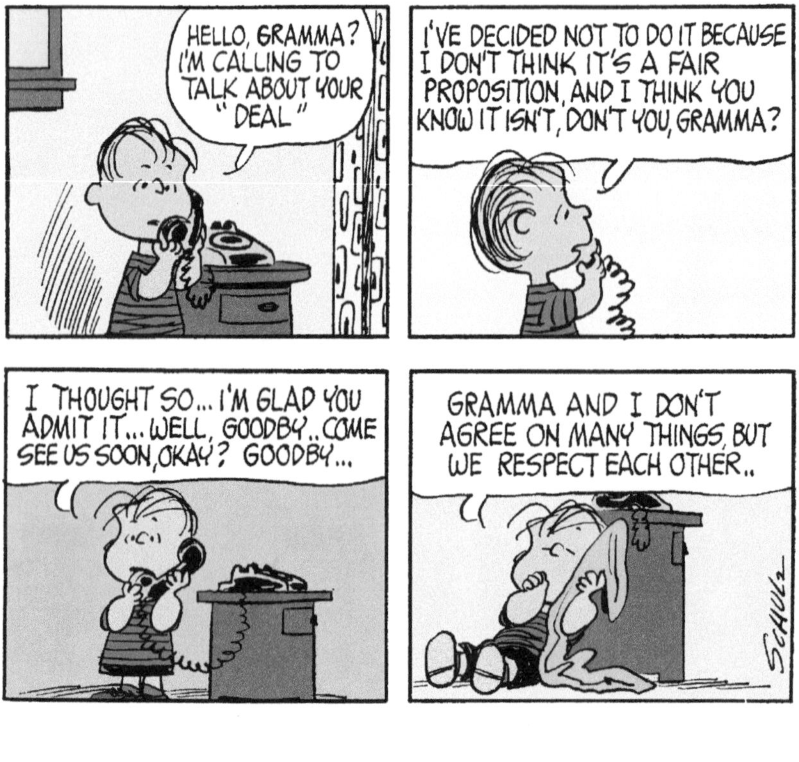
HELLO, GRAMMA? I'M CALLING TO TALK ABOUT YOUR "DEAL"
I'VE DECIDED NOT TO DO IT BECAUSE I DON'T THINK IT'S A FAIR PROPOSITION, AND I THINK YOU KNOW IT ISN'T, DON'T YOU, GRAMMA?
I THOUGHT SO... I'M GLAD YOU ADMIT IT... WELL, GOODBY.. COME SEE US SOON, OKAY? GOODBY...
GRAMMA AND I DON'T AGREE ON MANY THINGS, BUT WE RESPECT EACH OTHER..
SCHULZ

MORE TO EXPLORE!

Featuring cool activities and fun facts!

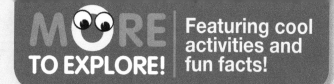

SNOOPY GOES ON THE ROAD AND FLIES TO THE MOON!

Snoopy is always up for fun times and great adventures. Discover the behind-the-scenes facts about the exciting journeys Snoopy had in this collection.

Thanks to our friends at the Charles M. Schulz Museum and Research Center in Santa Rosa, California, for letting us share their fascinating NASA information and photos.

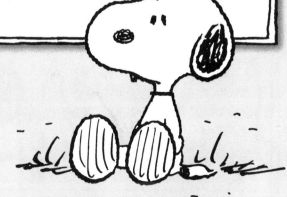

To the Moon: Snoopy Soars in the Comics and with NASA

Snoopy was "the first beagle on the moon" earlier in this book, actually touching down on the lunar surface in March 1969, besting NASA's record by several months! In addition, Snoopy has a strong connection to the space program.

Snoopy, who had already taken on an important role as NASA's safety mascot in 1968, was further honored in 1969 when the astronauts of Apollo 10 nicknamed their lunar module *Snoopy* and their command module *Charlie Brown*. *Snoopy* (and *Charlie Brown*!) soared out of Earth's gravity on May 18, 1969, on their way to perform a "dress rehearsal" for the moon landing that was slated for July 1969. The astronauts of Apollo 10—Commander Thomas Stafford, Command Module Pilot John Young, and Lunar Module Pilot Eugene Cernan—carried paintings of Snoopy and Charlie Brown aboard their spacecraft and were also surprised to find original Schulz drawings of Snoopy, hidden by backup crew members, in their onboard checklists! Stafford and Cernan piloted *Snoopy* within fifty thousand feet of the lunar surface as they scouted the landing area for the Apollo 11 mission. After the linkup, *Snoopy* was jettisoned (and entered the sun's orbit where it remains to this day) and the crew started their long journey home. On May 26, 1969, command module *Charlie Brown* returned all three astronauts safely back to the Earth, concluding a very successful mission.

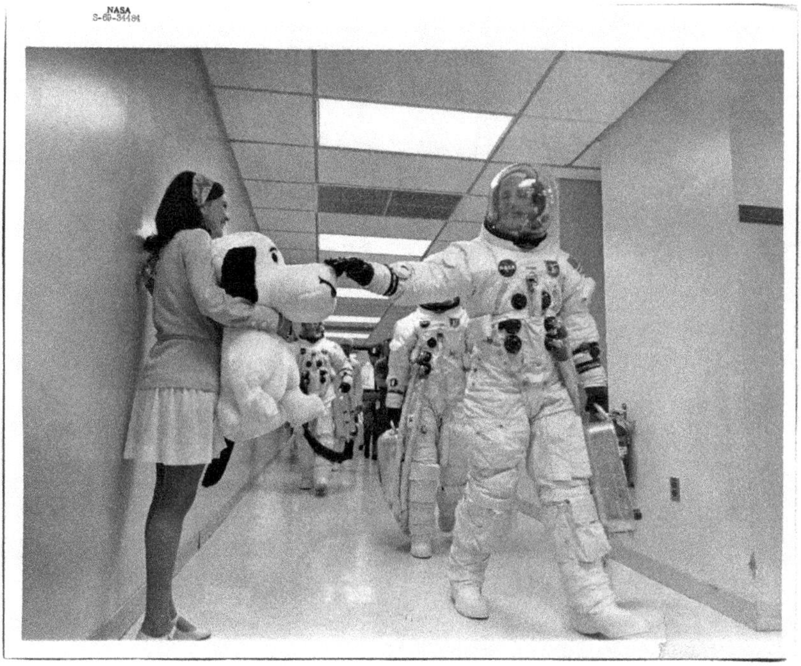
NASA
S-69-34484

In the first of these photographs, Jamye Flowers (Coplin) waits in the hallway to spring a prank on Eugene Cernan, as Tom Stafford walks by and gives Snoopy a pat on the nose.

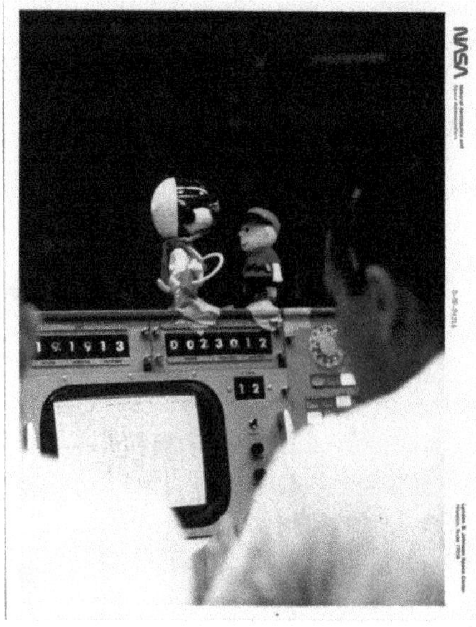
NASA

A close-up view of Charlie Brown and Snoopy riding the Mission Operations Control Room console at Mission Control Center in Houston, Texas, on the first day of the Apollo 10 mission, May 18, 1969.

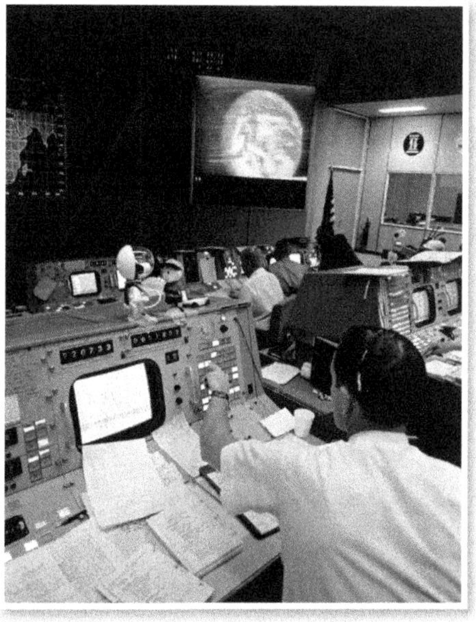

NASA's Director of Flight Crew Operations Donald "Deke" Slayton and astronaut Charles Duke, Apollo 10's "CAPCOM" or capsule communicator, with Snoopy and Charlie Brown in the foreground at the Mission Control Center in Houston, Texas. The CAPCOM was generally another astronaut and the only person who communicated directly with the astronauts in space. It was believed that another astronaut, the CAPCOM, would be most able to understand the situation in the spacecraft and pass information along in the clearest and most efficient way.

Space and Space Travel

WHAT IS SPACE?

Space is the huge area beyond the Earth's atmosphere (the air that surrounds the Earth). You can't breathe in space because there is no air; astronauts have to take a supply of air with them. Space is very cold—nearly 460 degrees below zero Fahrenheit. BRRRR!

WHY DO WE NEED ROCKETS?

A rocket is a kind of motor or engine that is needed to lift a very heavy spacecraft off the Earth, break free from Earth's gravity, and fly through space. To pull away from Earth's gravity, a rocket must be traveling twenty-five thousand miles per hour!

WHO ARE THE ASTRONAUTS?

When the space program was first getting started, all of the astronauts were men. Many were engineers and pilots before they became astronauts. The first American woman astronaut was Dr. Sally Ride, a scientist and an athlete. She flew into space in 1983. Nowadays both men and women are astronauts. Maybe you will be an astronaut one day!

A funny fact: Astronauts on long space missions can grow an inch or two taller because there is no gravity in space and the bones in their spines move apart slightly. Once an astronaut returns to Earth—and to gravity—they shrink back to their normal size!

WHEN DO ASTRONAUTS NEED SPACE SUITS ?

Space suits keep the astronauts safe and healthy whenever the astronaut leaves the spacecraft to take a space walk or walk on the moon as the Apollo astronauts did nearly fifty years ago. Some people think of space suits as a separate little spacecraft because they protect the astronauts from the extreme heat and cold of space and provide them with air to breathe.

Launch a Balloon Rocket

MATERIALS: balloon, paper clip, tape, straw, paper cup, string

INSTRUCTIONS:

1. Blow up a balloon and use a paper clip to hold the end closed.
2. Tape a straw to the balloon.
3. Add a paper cup to the end of the balloon as a nose.
4. Thread the string through the straw and stretch it tight.
5. Remove the paper clip and watch your rocket go.

The air rushing out of the balloon pushes against the air in the room. This is called *thrust*. Real rockets create thrust by burning fuel. Can you get your rocket to fly any faster or farther? Experiment to find out which type of balloon goes the farthest (round, long, etc.). Does the size of the straw affect how far the rocket travels? Does the nose help or hurt your flight? What else can you change to make your rocket fly farther?

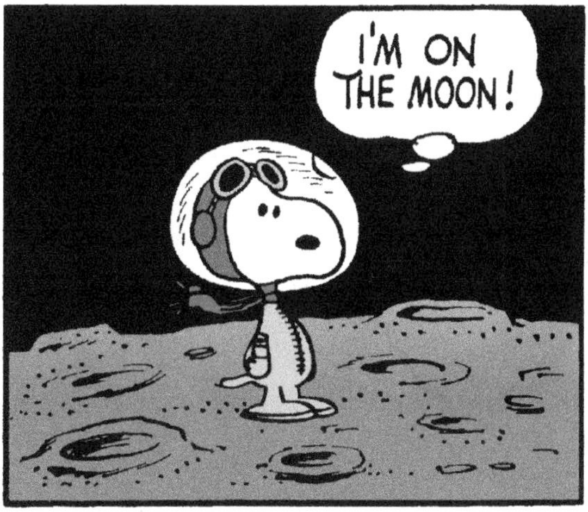
I'M ON THE MOON!

Petaluma?

In this book, Charlie Brown encourages Snoopy to go to Petaluma, California, to compete in the annual World's Wrist Wrestling Championship. Snoopy sets off on his trek, using a globe as his map, eager to compete.

Believe it or not, this championship was real!

SKIP SOMMER
FOR THE *ARGUS-COURIER* |
August 28, 2016, 12:01 A.M.

In 1952, in a small saloon in Petaluma, *Argus-Courier* columnist Bill Soberanes witnessed a couple of guys wrist wrestling and thought it would be a pretty good draw for the community to sponsor a contest.

Soberanes never dreamed, however, what a big deal this would be and how "wrist wrestling" would become as synonymous with the name of Petaluma as chickens, when he saw Oliver Kolberg defeat Jack Homell at "Diamond Mike" Gilardi's corner saloon that day.

The contest was first called The Petaluma Wrist Wrestling Championship. But it shortly became the Northern California Championship, then went statewide and, in 1962, Bill teamed up with promoter Dave Devoto and formed The World Wrist Wrestling Championship.

Contestants came from all over the world, too. It was not unusual to have more than 300 guys (and gals) competing in 35 different divisions. The first World Unlimited Champion was Earl Hagerman.

By 1968, cartoonist Charles M. Schulz penned a series of 11 comic strips that sent Snoopy to Petaluma to compete in the WWC. Unfortunately, Schulz had the famous pup eliminated early on in his wrist-wrestling career, because it was noticed that he didn't have a thumb.

The *Peanuts* strips were distributed throughout the world and gave the WWC an even larger audience.

Andrews McMeel Publishing
a division of Andrews McMeel Universal
1130 Walnut Street, Kansas City, Missouri 64106

www.andrewsmcmeel.com

www.peanuts.com

ISBN: 978-1-4494-8612-9

Library of Congress Control Number: 2016950041

ATTENTION: SCHOOLS AND BUSINESSES

Andrews McMeel books are available at quantity discounts with bulk purchase for educational, business, or sales promotional use. For information, please e-mail the Andrews McMeel Publishing Special Sales Department: specialsales@amuniversal.com.

Check out these and other books at ampkids.com

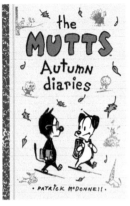

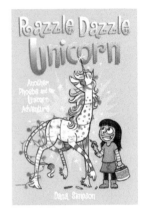

Also available:
Teaching and activity guides for each title.
AMP! Comics for Kids books make reading FUN!

CPSIA information can be obtained
at www.ICGtesting.com
Printed in the USA
LVHW071502200220
647641LV00019B/583

9 781449 486129